# VAMPIRE WEEKEND

**Also by Mike Chen**

*HERE AND NOW AND THEN*
*A BEGINNING AT THE END*
*WE COULD BE HEROES*
*LIGHT YEARS FROM HOME*

# MIKE CHEN

# VAMPIRE WEEKEND

mira

ISBN-13: 978-0-7783-3431-6

Vampire Weekend

Mira
22 Adelaide St. West, 41st Floor
Toronto, Ontario M5H 4E3, Canada
BookClubbish.com

**Printed in U.S.A.**

For the musicians in my life

**CHAPTER 1**

THERE'S ONE RULE WE vampires live by: Never reveal your true nature to a human.

Which made sneezing blood during band practice kind of a problem.

Nose tickles are rare for vampires, but something triggered it here, at a *really* inopportune moment. My face squinched, a full-body tension to successfully hold it in, and I continued without missing a beat. My left hand pressed guitar strings taut against frets, my right hand strummed at a steady rhythm, switching to single plucks as notes rang out until going back to chords for the song's outro.

For the moment, I abided by the cardinal rule for vampires. Because as scattered as we were, exposure was *really* frowned upon, enough that rumors of so-called "fixers" swirled—vampires that put others back in line if they got a little too flippant with community secrets. So it probably wasn't great that I'd revealed the truth twice already, first to my late aunt Laura, and second by being honest with my best friend/bandmate, Marshall.

And though that last time ended in all sorts of heartache and misery, I vowed *this* time would be different. I'd get close enough to humans to play in a band while being a good vampire citizen.

Because for a vampire like me, music was nearly as important as blood. And I'd starved myself of it for too long. That's why I was here, trying out for Copper Beach—the third band I'd auditioned for in two months.

We sped through the audition set, every beat and note building dreams of jam sessions, set lists, earsplitting drums, and crashing guitars in a shitty empty bar. With each passing second, my whole body felt more in sync, the vitality of band life becoming part of me once again. In movies, vampires were desiccated husks until they drank gallons of blood; I'd starved myself of other musicians for so long that I felt that way, and every chord strummed restored me to full strength.

A cymbal crashed to end the set's final song and our collective noise faded, leaving only the muffled rumbles from adjacent rooms. The run-down Oakland warehouse was filled with bands stuffed into similarly tiny practice rooms, sound-insulated spaces where magic happened despite bad ventilation and faulty electrical outlets. Glances exchanged, an unspoken vibe that seemed to acknowledge that my guitar work fit them well.

The drummer, a scientist-looking guy named Josh, nodded at me while adjusting a snare bolt, and I offered a smile so pleasant my fangs likely showed.

"I think that sounded pretty—" I started before the worst possible thing happened:

Another sneeze came. A full explosion, a clear allergic reaction to something in the air too powerful to stifle.

Suddenly, blood sprayed all over David—David, as in my white Epiphone guitar. I named all my guitars, and in this case, the Epiphone's bright crunchy tone matched the glam sound of David Bowie's Ziggy Stardust/Aladdin Sane period to earn the name. And, in that moment, covered in blood: a light splatter over David's smooth body and the black pickguard.

But what triggered it? Not many odors affected me these days, at least not in the allergic way that plagued my human youth. Vampire life meant that our bodies traded things like functioning digestive and sex organs for a diet of blood, which then increased our immune responses and metabolism to the level of "fairly freaking awesome." *Immortal* wasn't *indestructible*, though; crossing the street or swimming still required precautions. Perhaps more so—at least humans in car wrecks could go to any old hospital rather than a community's secret vampire doctors.

I turned my back to the band, and as I pulled David's cord from the extra amp they let me use for the audition, I caught a distinct smell.

Garlic. One of the few things that triggered a universal allergic response in our bodies.

Goddamn it.

Behind me, lead singer, Aidan, and bassist, Sally, talked about how to minimize microphone feedback while Josh carefully tore down each piece of his kit. "Bless you," Josh said without a glance. I looked up to find a vent in the corner of the small practice space, the clear origin of the smell. Though sound-proof insulation lined the walls, I heard the distinctive *thunk-thunk* of a microwave, and I remembered that when I loaded in, Copper Beach's practice space sat right next to the break room.

Someone microwaved garlic fries or something similar, a dish so strong it would make humans sweat out the odor.

Another nose tickle arrived, causing my eyes to twitch. My hands clenched as I forced it away, a burst going mute before it could escape. I squeezed my eyes tight, and after several moments, everything relaxed. No one even noticed me wiping the front of David with the bottom of my black shirt, a quick, awkward tug-and-scrub—it didn't restore my gear's usual pristine condition, but that could wait until after work tonight. Some of the blood-snot absorbed into my T-shirt, enough to hide what happened and focus on the much bigger deal:

This audition went really, really well. It might actually work, as long as I left without anyone noticing the blood smears on my guitar.

David's strings pressed against my body as I carried him over to the case in the corner. A few clicks later and he sat nestled in its fuzzy lining.

Audition done. Mission accomplished. I took a breath and hoisted my backpack of pedals and cables. Though an hour remained before my work shift started, it seemed best to escape any lingering smell.

Except a pocket of garlic hit me again after two steps, the ventilation clearly not upgraded to post-COVID standards. That devastating pandemic didn't affect vampires; our immune response proved to be too strong. Garlic, on the other hand, would easily give me fits of bloody sneezes for hours with one good inhale. I fought the oncoming nose tickles before picking up David's case. "Well, I thought that we sounded good together—"

"What the fuck?" Sally asked. Then Aidan glanced over his keyboard rig. Then Josh looked.

"Oh," I said, mind seeking excuses. I'd wiped up David with my shirt, maybe the bloodstains were more obvious than I thought. "You know what? I'd spilled some cranberry sauce on this shirt earlier today, I think—"

"Louise, your eyes are *bleeding*."

My eyes. I'd been so concerned with David I'd totally forgotten my eyes.

"Shit, shit, shit," Sally said. She walked with purpose, keeping a wide perimeter before throwing the door open.

"Oh, you know what, it's, um, allergies. I have a garlic allergy." Which was technically true. The garlic attack must have produced some tears during my sneezing fit; like snot and saliva, tears mixed with blood for us, and against my paler-than-usual skin, the contrast certainly stood out. "You smell that? I must have, um, burst a blood vessel when I sneezed. It happens," I said, riffing on the fly. "I've got very sensitive blood vessels—"

"I don't care what it is. I'm not dealing with any weird health stuff again." She reached down and put on a mask, then pointed at me. "I'm not taking any risks—get the fuck out. I can't believe you didn't tell us about this."

I blinked, and as I did, I felt the slightest of tears trickle from my left eye, no doubt streaking blood down the side of my face. My knuckles rubbed against it, a poor stab at appearing casual, though the repeated swipes probably didn't help. "I'm serious, it's allergies—"

Not only was I blowing my shot with Copper Beach, if this got out to the vampire community, I could be in serious trouble. I might even find out if the whole fixer thing was real. I turned to hide my blood tears, just in case anyone got the urge to snap a photo of it.

"Get your shit and go," Sally said.

"Wait, I think we sounded great and—"

"Go. Leave now."

Given the state of blood on my face, I tried *not* to face the band, and instead walked in a slow, awkward gait, holding my guitar case. "Hey, um, look, I understand where you're coming from, but can you do me a favor and *not* say anything about my allergy...like, anywhere?"

*"Get out."*

And just like that, I was forced out, blood smeared across my face. From behind, an argument between Copper Beach broke out, Sally yelling about how she refused to take any health chances while Aidan lobbied that they should give it a try and Josh read off things he'd googled about bloody tears and whether they were contagious or a sign of any infection.

Vampirism wasn't infectious, of course. I couldn't even turn people if I wanted to.

In the end, though, it didn't matter. Yet another chance with human musicians failed, a pattern that was becoming so consistent that I wondered if the universe was telling me something, like I was destined to record at home, the only other living creature in the studio with me being my dog. But, as adorable as Lola the corgi was, she didn't exactly excel at drums.

I blew out a sigh and headed through a thankfully empty hallway out to my car, the hatchback of my white Prius popping open with a beep. The case slid in the back, then I tossed a blanket and several empty reusable bags on top of it. I wouldn't normally leave my gear hidden in my car, but the audition and my work schedule didn't provide a lot of breathing room.

Especially on the second Friday of the month. Also known as blood bag day. I couldn't miss one of those.

As I settled into the driver's seat, I pulled a metal thermos from a small ice-filled cooler on the passenger seat and unscrewed the top, picking off the loose corgi fur that was wrapped around the lid. Those stumpy legs were adorable, and the unwavering loyalty was nice, but no one warned me about how much fur corgis shed.

That was the life of Louise Chao, Very Ordinary Vampire: blood and dog hair. In some parallel universe, vampires actually existed like those in movies or Anne Rice's books: cool powers and ornate living while prancing around with luscious hair and Victorian clothes. Here, I dressed like Joan Jett circa the late 1970s, except with Lola's fur clinging to my pants. The closest thing about me to Louis from *Interview with the Vampire* was my name and maybe that one time I traveled in search of kindred spirits. Except, unlike Louis's global search for vampires, I'd followed the Ramones on a few dates of their 1996 farewell tour—until I ran out of money and had to drive for two days to get back to San Francisco.

Not quite as glamorous. But way more punk rock.

The viscous flow hit my lips, a blend of nutrition and hydration that would get me through most of the night. I drank a little slower than normal—blood wasn't particularly tasty, so savoring it mostly wasted time. Here, the mere act of drinking gave space to ruminate, along with the simple rhythm of inhale/exhale to calm my nerves. I watched the building's entrance, hoping a member of Copper Beach would sprint out and breathlessly say it was all a misunderstanding.

I took another sip, watching the small circle of people smoking outside of the building's entrance. Seconds counted by, eventually leading to me finding *anything* on my phone as a distraction. Except the first news headline caused me to pause in a completely different way.

12 Vampire Powers We Wish We Had.

Did my phone know I was a vampire? Why else would it pop up? Another semiofficial vampire rule forbade any online mentions of what we were, not even dumb blood puns. I nearly went scorched earth with a factory reset to protect my privacy when the truth hit me.

Of course tech companies didn't know about vampires. Because vampires were superboring. Most of us worried about balancing night jobs (they're not that easy to find) and getting weekly blood needs met without biting people (really not as common as pop culture would have you believe) rather than wielding uncanny powers.

I clicked the link, and it became clear that this had nothing to do with real vampires. Everything people assumed about vampires was wrong.

Case in point, the first vampire power myth from this article: superspeed.

Which I obviously didn't have, otherwise I might have been able to wipe the blood tears so fast they would have appeared a trick of the light.

I skimmed the list, then purged it from my thoughts once I confirmed an algorithm hadn't identified my biology, though it did pull up the related headline of Victim Hospitalized in Bay Area's Third "Vampire" Attack.

I pondered the headline when my phone interrupted with a buzz, a notification appearing on the screen. But instead of Copper Beach inviting me back via text, the name *Eric* appeared. Eric, as in San Francisco's vampire community leader; if there *was* a fixer, it would have been him. I gave the message a frantic skim, but thankfully he hadn't found out about my bloody tears already. Instead, he wrote about an upcoming meeting, something that I never bothered with.

I ignored the text, then resumed watching the practice space's front door. Another ten minutes passed before my phone flashed a reminder that my 9:00 p.m. shift started soon.

Time was up. And this band wasn't happening.

But it was more than that. I'd auditioned for three straight bands, three really good bands that offered the exact blend of melody and rage that I wanted. And each time, something caused it to fall apart. One band wanted to shoot for opening daytime slots at upcoming local festivals. Another was even worse—needing to meet for weekend daytime practices. And now, an accidental encounter with garlic.

Every time I found a good fit, being a vampire got in the way.

And with my last true band? Being a vampire didn't just get in the way, it destroyed everything.

Marshall didn't deserve what happened to him *or* what I said to him. Perhaps this was my karmic kickback, a purgatory where I never found another band again, let alone another best friend.

I shook off the thought, a conscious pushback at the guilt that had burned for three years. Right now, none of that mattered because I had to get to work. It was a blood day.

My car's battery-powered engine awoke with the lightest of hums while I thumbed through my saved library of music, a snapshot of all of the important stages of my life: Bowie, punk, postpunk, new wave, Madchester, lo-fi, and so on. All pieces of my identity; but for now, I needed a warm hug in the form of dance beats contradicting dark emotions. The bouncy synths and thumping bass of New Order's seven-minute classic, "Temptation," began blasting, a wall of melancholy lyrics disguised as pop music, enveloping me as I rolled away, still bandless, in my very practical hybrid car.

**VAMPIRE POWER MYTH #2:** We can bite into anything.

In movies, veins pop like a balloon hitting a nail. But in reality? Kids constantly bonk into sharp objects and get light scrapes. Construction workers work around nails and metal, but somehow buildings go up without anyone bleeding out. I worked in a hospital, so I saw this firsthand.

In practical terms, biting someone for blood was not easy. Newly turned vampires don't exactly have functional teeth. A gradual sharpening takes place over the course of a week, but we're not the instant kill machine from movies.

The so-called "vampire attacks" in the news? Sounded like algorithm-driven clickbait to me. And that was exactly how I thought about it—or *didn't* think about it—when I got to work.

Because today was a blood day. And blood days were literally life and death for me.

Not that I gave off that vibe. Instead, I went about my business, pushing my janitorial cart into the blood bank of San

Francisco General Hospital. The automatic door shut behind me, my cart's squeaking wheels announcing my arrival to Sam, the department's night manager, and some staffer who looked more on break than actually working. They leaned over a monitor, attention pulled away by whatever was on the screen. Which worked to my benefit.

Some vampires worked with blood volunteers—usually fetishists who gladly let someone feed off them, likely thinking it was a kink or a new obscure fad diet rather than real vampire sustenance. That still involved the wholly unhygienic and socially awkward process of drinking from a live human. Underground dealers also existed, pumping blood from their arms into a bottle for an in-person transaction.

Me? I went with blood bag theft.

Which, to be fair, I held zero guilt over. Did you know that hospitals waste about 25 percent of blood bags every year? Thus, my weekly pickup during my janitorial rounds hardly made a dent. It all fell within the normal range of lost, misplaced, or expired. In fact, the managers viewed me as helpful for bringing the soon-to-expire bags to disposal. If some happened to make it into my backpack along the way, no one was the wiser.

This, of course, assumed that there were actually blood bags to take.

Today, the usual inventory of expiring blood bags was empty.

As in, nothing on the shelves. Nothing to deliver. Nothing to steal.

Nothing to feed from.

In fact, even the main storage units for in-date blood bags appeared low.

Any stress from the Copper Beach audition evaporated, as things do when food sources suddenly disappear.

I paused the music on my phone and pulled the earbuds out. Some things required a little more professional behavior. I began scouring the other storage possibilities when I overheard the words the vampire community feared the most.

"I swear, it's a vampire."

Eric constantly preached that if humans *did* discover us, racists would find new reasons to fearmonger, while scientists would capture us for all sorts of poking and prodding. Given that we'd all managed to abide by this for centuries, it seemed like a pretty good suggestion to follow.

My hands squeezed the cart's handle tighter as I listened.

"That's ridiculous," Sam said, shaking his head.

"No, think about it." The man turned, the tag on his scrubs revealing the name Turner. "After everything we know about viruses these days, who would actually drink blood? Only vampires."

"Okay, look," Sam said, rubbing his cleft chin. "You're assuming someone drank this guy's blood—"

"Police said he's missing about ten ounces of blood. Same as the other two attacks."

"Alright. Let's assume someone—or some*thing*—drank ten ounces from that poor guy. They said his neck looked chewed, dozens of stitches needed. If you're gonna believe something ridiculous, go with a werewolf."

Suddenly, that headline didn't seem like simple clickbait. Ten ounces. Roughly the same amount my body needed daily, though half that offered cranky survival. So that *was* the typical amount a vampire needed to sustain until the next feeding. And the chewed neck like a werewolf bite? That was a real concern, not because werewolves were real (they're not), but because biting into a human was not easy.

In theory, you first had to properly locate the carotid artery, then make sure it was easily accessible by positioning the head and neck the right way. Then you needed a well-placed bite— millimeters of accuracy here, from an angle where things are hard to see. I challenge any human to try and bite precisely into a piece of Red Vines stuck on a loaf of sourdough to gauge its difficulty. This was in addition to the fangs' fairly mediocre ability to puncture.

Biting humans was messy. Factor in an especially scared nondonor human and tools to make the process smoother and, well, the result could easily be mistaken for werewolves.

With the hospital's blood shortage, their conversation ratcheted my anxiety enough for me to mutter, "Oh shit."

That little phrase pulled Sam and Turner away from the screen. Their desk chairs creaked as they turned my way, the headline—San Francisco's Latest "Vampire Attack" Victim Stable In Hospital—now clearly visible on their monitor.

If there *was* a fixer working in the community, they weren't doing a great job.

"Oh, hi, Louise," Sam said. "Need anything?"

Blood bags. A safe community, one without rogue vampires possibly revealing ourselves to humans. While I was at it, someone to play in a band with—human or vampire—though right now neither seemed to be working out.

"No pickups today," I managed as I pushed the cart through.

"What pickups?" Sam asked, his thick eyebrows furrowing.

"Expiring blood to pick up on second Fridays. You know," I said, switching to a very bad generic European accent, "because I'm a vampire and I need to drink it instead of biting people on the neck."

That joke always worked, but doubly so today.

Both men laughed, and I almost held up claw hands for emphasis. But no, that joke belonged only to me and Marshall. "I knew it," Sam said, "you're the vampire attacker."

"I thought you suspected a werewolf," Turner said, an Irish lilt to his gravelly voice.

"Sorry, boys. It's a little more boring than that. Management tallies these and I don't want to piss them off." That was a lie; I knew they didn't because otherwise I'd never get away with my theft.

"Right, right. Let me go check in on that." Sam stood and went to the computer on the far desk, his leg catching his chair enough to kick it over a foot. "You're right, our last delivery was low. Must not be as many donors. There's a note saying this might be a thing for a few weeks but it doesn't say why."

Just like that, my food supply went from "comfortably fed" to "empty."

"Cool, cool, no worries," I said despite the onslaught of emerging worries. I built my whole life around a job that provided blood—and that dried up? Maybe in a parallel universe, I might have my own recording studio with session time paid in blood bags. But here?

I loaded my email as soon as I stepped into the hallway. My fingers mashed over the virtual keys, autocorrect pulling all the wrong words and constantly changing *blood* to *brood*, which I supposed was fitting for a vampire. The message went to the local Red Cross chapter's volunteer manager, a request for shifts as a Volunteer Transportation Specialist.

Basically, someone who drove donated blood around.

I'd actually trained for the role when I was in between hospital gigs, but never took any actual shifts since most of them were during the day—which wasn't impossible with proper precautions, but still uncomfortable, and required a lot of extra effort, in addition to messing up my sleep cycle. Circadian rhythm still applied to vampire life.

But this was different. If the supply saw shortages, I'd need alternatives just like the early days when I first started and had no clue what I was doing.

Which really wasn't my fault. Because no guidebook existed for this life, and the woman who made me only came around a few times to check on me before disappearing forever. Despite the physical transformation to vampiredom creating several months of fuzzy memories, I still clearly pictured her during that last visit: a tall, pale woman with long brown hair in peak late-70s punk styling.

She'd brought weekly bottles, introduced me to a few Southern California sources for no-questions-asked back-alley blood, gave a very uncomfortable primer on feeding off farm animals in emergencies and offered a very dramatic lecture on the importance of not revealing ourselves to humans in any way. Yet, all of those came during surprise drop-ins and sudden departures, and even her final visit was nothing more than a quick hello before "You'll figure the rest out. You'll be fine."

In fact, she never bothered to tell me her name. Or maybe she did and I just forgot it in my fugue state. Whatever the case, I'd have to rely on those lessons now, to ride out any shortages. I spent the rest of my shift trying to recall how many bags remained in my fridge, and how best to ration them. Hours came and went, a low-level panic setting my night to fast-forward all the way until I stepped into an empty parking garage.

Then my phone buzzed. Multiple buzzes, actually. Though I hoped it was something about the Red Cross volunteer gig, that seemed impossible, given the late hour. No, a quick look showed another text from Eric. And this time, I bothered to read it.

I've received a few notes tonight about tomorrow evening's agenda. I share your concerns, but there is a plan to address this. Nothing is more important than the health and safety of our community.

Something was definitely up. A blood shortage, someone attacking humans in the wild, texts about "health and safety." A second message loaded up, words pushing the first message off the screen.

If you want to learn more, please come to the event. In the meantime, I encourage you all to download our new community app to stream the discussion. Do NOT discuss the media's 'vampire attack' headlines with anyone, not even jokingly. Blood will be served. Reply to RSVP for in-person attendance.

Did I want to learn more? Of course. Did I want an app that both invaded my privacy *and* knew I was a vampire? No. Did I want to get involved with the vampire community?

Not really. Especially given my history with Eric. But I needed blood, and this was a source, however fleeting.

Besides, maybe Eric had forgotten about our last encounter. Still, I refused to download his stupid app. On principle.

Count me in, I typed in a reply text, complete with a little white lie. By the way, I had trouble downloading the app. Maybe later.

On most work nights, I came home just before dawn, changed from scrubs to sweats, let my dog out, and drank blood. Today, that last part remained a sticking point. Lola greeted me as usual, a pitter-patter that told me she needed a potty break. I left the back door ajar for her to go into the small backyard, then checked my blood bag supply in the fridge.

If I'd been more responsible, thorough, careful, and whatever other descriptions my parents threw at me decades ago, I'd have a managed stockpile. Instead, three bags remained, a supply for about four or five days. I *could* stretch it to a week, though I'd be a grouchy, tired mess. After that? Movie vampires went on killing rampages when they needed blood, but in reality, it meant fatigue and delirium.

And if that went on long enough? Death by starvation.

No wonder someone got desperate enough to bite humans.

I grabbed a mug from the cabinet, white ceramic with a faded photo of a white schnauzer printed on it; Aunt Laura's old teacup, now used for blood. Mostly empty shelves stared back at me from the fridge, daring me to make a choice.

Did I take one now? Did I *really* need to drink or could I wait?

Lola returned from the backyard, hopping over the threshold with her short corgi legs, and her nails clacked on the floor as she ignored my mood and waddled past. The jingling of her collar faded as she went down the hall, and I told myself to do the smart thing. I shut the fridge door and left Aunt Laura's mug on the counter, then followed my dog.

Light flooded the space in my music room as I flipped the wall switch, illuminating everything from the guitars hanging on the walls to the drum kit and keyboard rig sitting in opposite corners. But no dog waited for me. Instead, her collar jingled from across the hall.

The bedroom.

The hour or so before bed normally saw me noodling on a guitar, playing with different pedal effects combinations or trying to work out a lingering melody while Lola stayed at my feet. But as I stood between the two rooms, a crushing fatigue washed over me, something that I knew had nothing to do with appetite.

I peeked in on Lola, the hallway light showing enough that I could see she'd skipped the circular dog bed on the floor to leap straight onto my spot. Usually she'd wait till I fell asleep to pull that off, and perhaps she took advantage of my vulnerable state today. She stretched her little legs into the air, then craned her neck to look at me with ears up, yawning before settling back down.

Maybe she just knew what I needed today.

Instead of going back into my music room, I stepped inside and shut the door, leaving the bedroom in a complete UV-protected blackout state as I crawled under soft sheets. I stayed still, the quiet silence of a moment without vampires, without humans, without blood shortages, just a happy corgi resting against my stomach and worries in my head.

# CHAPTER 3

THE NEXT NIGHT, SHOUTS greeted me as soon as I opened the door. I stepped in cautiously and took in the scene: a small crowd scattered about but focused on Eric holding court. Behind him, open windows let in the dark hues of late dusk, the normal meeting time so that night shift vampires could attend and still make it to work.

Normally I'd wear a band shirt to something like this, a type of bait to see if anyone might notice. But given the crowd, staying inconspicuous seemed like the better tactic, in case anyone recalled my community history.

Despite the noise, the room itself had space to move. Eric's text urged the community to come out, yet something held them back. Or maybe they ignored his texts, like I usually did, since I only counted some twenty people, though who knew how many watched the livestream.

I stood on tiptoe, and while I didn't see blood bags, the suite's corner had several tables with metal tubs holding bottles and ice. *That* was my target.

"People, people, please, I need you to take a breath and listen," Eric shouted, the *r* in *breath* rolling from his Scottish accent. He surveyed the scene, his hair forever captured in a perpetual state of curly salt-and-pepper, though the intensity of his gaze probably came from his life before becoming a vampire. Despite the fierce look, his plea carried proper concern. The shouting gradually dissipated, Eric's community status being enough for people to respectfully abide by his request. "If you need help, ask me for help. That's what the app is for."

Eric's words flew over me as I shuffled to the blood, pausing intentionally to look like I paid attention before taking more steps. "And other things are in the works. I'm asking for your patience," he continued, the same measured tone that I'd heard since meeting him when I first arrived in San Francisco around 1989. The guy seemed to be everywhere, or at least know everything and everyone, enough to lend some weight to the fixer rumor. He *looked* the part, like someone who graduated from punk days into something more respectable, with his boots and tight coat.

Several voices shouted out, one about blood, one about the attack, but the words intertwined, diluting any distinctive gripes. Eric nodded, as though he clearly heard each individual statement, simply waiting for the noise to contain itself.

"I'll say it again—do not attack humans. Under no circumstances. Do *not* attack humans. Community secrecy is our top priority."

"If anyone here knows the perpetrator, you need to speak up right now," a woman shouted. "You're putting us all at risk."

"We need to eat," another man yelled. "That's not their fault."

"Everyone's concerns are valid. That is why—" Eric pointed toward the back of the room "—we have blood back there. For those who need it." I stopped in place, then craned my neck along with everyone else, as if this was the first I'd noticed the tubs. "Centuries ago, feeding off humans was a way of life for our kind. The lack of technology necessitated live human drinking. But today, we can approach sustenance with a true morality. It has never been justified, but especially not today."

"That's not true," someone said. "Murderers, abusers."

"Yeah," another person shouted, "if we need to eat, we can do something to help society. We can organize it. Your app connects us—"

"No, no, no," Eric said, this time hands up. "Even with terrible people, it's simply not practical. Not with smartphones and cameras everywhere. Think this through. What happens if we get discovered? We all become science projects *and* the subject of prejudice. Secrecy is the key to—"

"What if we drink from a human friend? Swear them to secrecy?" I knew that suggestion would get shot down, but the ensuing screaming match provided cover to keep moving. Someone brought up that human friends could volunteer, then another retorted that humans shouldn't be trusted with our truths, which spawned further shouting about what was and wasn't acceptable. Questions and accusations were fired, from the practical-but-gross topic of using animals and wildlife to the ridiculous notion of asking for help from a supposedly secret society of ancient vampires. That rumor popped up about once a decade or so, and it was always more head-scratching than even the idea of vampire powers. The existence of such a society seemed as plausible as humans claiming the Illuminati ran the world. Some people just needed *any* conspiracy theory to give them hope.

Through it all, Eric somehow managed to answer each incoming question at a rapid-fire pace. More importantly, the chaos provided plenty of distraction as I moved to the tubs.

"No one's murdering. No one's turning to farm animals,"

Eric said, his voice direct despite the uncharacteristic irritation creeping into it. "I am leading an effort. So everyone will be able to get the blood they need. I am asking you to trust me."

"Bullshit. There's no way."

Political infighting and rumormongering among vampires wasn't what I'd bargained for tonight. This was why I'd avoided vampires for so long. On one hand, every region had people like Eric—they were necessary. On the other, it's not like vampires did a great job of caring for their own. My nonexistent relationship with my maker was the norm, not the exception. Most of us figured that was just the way it was, though I still felt bitter toward the woman who took off months after turning me.

"That's enough!" Eric yelled, a hint of ferocity finally breaking past his calm demeanor. "I want everyone to understand this—I am working for a world where every vampire gets the blood they need to live. Without compromising their morals. Without putting our community at risk. Without sacrificing their dignity. Equal access for all.

"Clean, safe blood bags can be obtained in many ways. Hospitals, blood banks, donation drives. Not every source is low right now. It's concentrated in various parts of the Bay Area. I promise you, I am working on a way to create transparency in all that. Data—" Eric held up his phone "—is the key."

He continued grandstanding, which was my cue to tune out. Data wasn't some magic wand to wave over everything; it pretty much destroyed the way musicians earned a living. The Bay Area was filled with tech bros trying to use data for the most random of applications, and I was pretty sure that "blood for vampires" would sit next to "smart juicing machines" in the Hall of Fame of bad Silicon Valley ideas.

Eric began talking about the community app, some soaring speech about how communities are better when they're connected and other such bullshit. I, on the other hand, was better when I had blood in my backpack. I reached the metal tubs and debated what to take.

How many bottles of blood were here? And how did each bottle compare to a hospital blood bag? I cursed my complete incompetence at math and eyeballed it, grabbing two bottles and shoving them into my backpack. No one seemed to notice, and though numbers definitely weren't my strong suit, it *seemed* like grabbing a few more wouldn't really upset the balance here. I put two more in my bag and was just about to zip it up when my back pocket buzzed.

Hey Louise, long time no chat. I got an extra ticket to see Active Child next week at Great American Music Hall. You want it?

My old bandmate, Pete, the on-again/off-again bassist that would sometimes jam with me and Marshall. "Long time" was subjective; he pinged every few months with things like this. If he'd been offering a gig, maybe I'd respond.

But I'd avoided shows for the last few years, and this wouldn't be any different, especially not while my food supply dwindled. I typed:

Appreciate it, but I'm busy. Maybe I'll see you at another show.

There. Nice and polite. And a lie. I hadn't been to a show since Marshall died, and didn't see any in my future. Even *thinking* about my favorite venues proved too painful. I slid my phone back in my pocket when it hit me that the room was silent.

And everyone stared my way.

Human interaction once again messing up my day.

"I said, can I help you with something?" Eric said, his voice projecting loud enough to match the fact that he looked directly at me.

"Me?"

"Yes, you."

"I, uh…" I started, feeling the weight of everyone's eyes. "No, I was just leaving. Have to go meet someone, but thanks for all the info and I'll try to remember to download—"

"Your name is Louise, right?" I gave a tentative nod, complete with a half smile. "I thought so. I remember the last time we ran into each other."

I was hoping he didn't, that the distance of several years wiped it from his recall. Because I had been out with Marshall, which on its own wasn't a big deal. But the *look* Eric gave me at the time told me he knew.

"It's been a few years, hasn't it? Back patio at Emperor's Kitchen, right? Good to see you again," Eric said. His eyebrow arched up, a knowing glint in his eye. Was he going to tell everyone about my clear rule breaking that night? It made enough of an impression that Eric cataloged it in his mind. And the way Marshall died, even some time after that encounter with Eric…well, it caused enough grief for me to sometimes stir in bed, questions swirling about the circumstances behind everything.

Either way, it was my fault—fixer or not. And we really didn't need to get into that in a room full of hungry vampires.

"There's something everyone here should know," Eric said.

"Look, I—" I started, though he held up a hand.

"Louise, we're asking everyone to only take two bottles."

"Oh," I said, suddenly nodding a lot. I looked at the tub of bottles, noticing the cartoon strawberry and grape characters on the labels for the first time. That was one way to blend into the human world. "Oh. Right. Got it, totally got it. My mistake, I thought it was four—"

"It's alright. You got here late. You probably just missed the announcement."

"Cool," I said, still nodding. I tossed two bottles back onto the stack, then offered a sheepish grin. "Yeah, I'm always late to stuff. My parents always harped on me about punctuality—"

"Thank you, Louise. Are you leaving now?"

"Yeah." The answer came like I was answering my parents about why my grades sucked while my brother aced everything. "I gotta give my dog a bath. She's a corgi and she sheds everywhere, so—"

"Do you want more blood?"

Was this a trick question? Who didn't? "Yes?" I said slowly.

"During this shortage, we'll have more meetings with handouts. You should find a way to download the app." He gestured to the bottles. "It's a good time to become more active in our community, so please use the app to inform when you encounter either surplus or shortages. And remember the rules we live by. It makes things safer for everyone." Each word carried an underlying tension, the same straddling of suggestion and menace as the first time I heard them.

Five or six years ago, Marshall and I sat on the back patio of a Chinese restaurant half a block away from the Warfield Theater, where we'd planned to see Japanese Breakfast a few hours later. He did the human thing of eating dinner, I did the vampire thing of *not* eating, though I'd requested we sit outside to avoid potential garlic exposure. Our debate about why the Rock & Roll Hall of Fame was bullshit turned into a spirited argument about who deserved a nomination and why it should be INXS. One hour became two, making us late for the gig. The final bill came, along with a lone fortune cookie. "Excuse me," Marshall called to the waiter, "can my friend get one too?"

"Of course," he said, scooting off.

"Dude," I said.

"I know. But the best part of eating with you is I get two of these." The waiter returned, handing me a fortune cookie, and I waited several seconds before I slid it over. "I love these. I wish they sold them at Costco," he said before cracking the second one open. "'You will live a long and prosperous life,'" he read before handing the slip of paper over to me. "I think I got yours."

"Very funny," I said, making claw hands complete with a vampire hiss. He laughed, then matched my gesture, completing our running gag.

Which would have been completely benign except for the vampire who saw it.

Eric had been crossing the patio when I made my joke, and it stood out enough in the quiet space that he stopped mid-stride, his intense stare turning our way.

"Oh shit," I said under my breath.

"What—" Marshall started when Eric appeared at our table.

His steely eyes darted between us, his mouth staying in a very serious straight line. No greetings or small talk, not even a hello. Eric simply stopped in front of us and planted his hands on the table. "I suggest you remember the rules we live by. It makes things safer for everyone." His line triggered a chain reaction: first Eric's knowing look at me, then my innocent, wide eyes that tried to say, "of course I haven't said anything," then Marshall's puzzled look, followed by my "don't" look back at him. Eric gave a simple nod before leaving the patio without a word.

After he gathered some distance, Marshall spoke up. "What was that?"

"I don't know who that was," I said quickly, though that was a lie. I'd known Eric for decades at that point.

"Was he a va—"

"I don't know who that was," I bit out quickly to cut him off. I locked eyes with my best friend, holding the look long enough to say otherwise. And neither of us brought it up again, though our silly hiss-and-claw goodbye stopped that night.

Had that been a threat from Eric? Was there a direct line between Marshall's car accident several years later to that very preshow meal, that discussion about fortune cookies?

I'd avoided vampires as much as possible since then, and though I didn't exactly have a more certain answer now, I at least knew Eric remembered that night. Which meant all I could do was silently nod while the entire room watched me. I slung my bag over my shoulder, then waited for him to resume his speech before leaving.

With a little while before my hospital shift started, I walked home, drowning in the sounds of the city, all sorts of feelings about Marshall resurfacing despite a few years of shoving them deep down. San Francisco itself was only seven miles by seven miles, and walking for thirty minutes got me halfway there when I spied a Muni bus heading in the right direction. Several minutes later, I stepped off the bus on my block and began walking between the rows of thin colorful houses crammed together like cans in a pantry.

The life of the city passed me by as I walked, each step a conscious attempt to focus on the songs blasting in my earbuds and *not* replay any events involving Eric or Marshall. And by the time I got to my block, it seemed to work, enough that I looked forward to a quiet night with a small ration of blood, my guitars, and my silly dog.

Except when I got to my door, a bland sedan sat idling at my house, the bobbing heads of two passengers in the front. The dim night made it hard to make out their details, and though they both held their phones up, one clearly moved fingers in a more crisp and competent way. When I got up my porch steps, Lola's alert pitter-patter and jingling collar tags started on the other side, followed by a bark.

She must have heard the car door open behind me.

"Excuse me," a weathered male voice called out.

I didn't need any further weirdness tonight, especially not from lost tourists. I fumbled in my pocket for keys, pretending to be too lost in thought to notice.

"Excuse me," the man said again. "I'm looking for Laura Wu."

*Laura Wu.*

I stared back at his curious eyes, wondering if I should tell him that she died more than twenty years ago.

# CHAPTER 4

"LAURA WU?" I ASKED, more to buy myself time than anything else. The man looked at me, tired eyes over aged tan jowls and sun spots, wisps of black and white hair poking out underneath a wool cap. He adjusted his glasses and squinted—at first, I thought this was at me, but no, I tracked his look over to the numbers on my house's siding. I held my keys tight, *not* wanting to get into a conversation with anyone, let alone someone who was probably a friend of my aunt.

"Yeah. Is this still her house? I have an old address but I didn't know if it was outdated. I know it's a long shot."

It *was* Laura's house—circa 1992, more than thirty years ago.

One night changed it all, and it wasn't a legal usurping or grand bequest or anything like that.

The moment was both quiet and loud, dramatic and still, and it appropriately happened with tinnitus ringing through my ears, the stinging thrum of a postshow hearing tunnel. This usually passed in a few hours, and while I didn't expect such things for a big-staged arena concert, I also didn't normally get to the front of the pit at large shows. And large shows didn't usually start with ear-piercing opening bands like the Pixies.

Then the ensuing sensory overload of U2's Zoo TV tour, the first to feature countless video walls blasting words and images and lights in a nonstop sensory overload. Even two hours after the arena lights went up and I shuffled out, every step came with a disorienting haze, like I'd done drugs that came in the form of flashes, delayed guitars, and Irish wail.

That feeling remained while I opened the door to Laura's house, my first time doing so with my own key. And my first time arriving with the intent of sleeping in my own room during the day—which meant the closet since I hadn't fully blacked out the windows yet, but same difference, because Laura had invited me to live with her. Rent-free, in exchange for helping out as her glaucoma reduced her vision to blurry blobs. And I'd started that first evening by hopping on BART across to Oakland to catch The Pixies and U2.

But when I came home, the door became a portal to another world. Not the sweaty loud mess of a concert, not the cold bite of a San Francisco night, but a time warp of overlapping eras. A lone corner lamp projected a yellow glow, and right underneath it sat Laura, her salt-and-pepper hair tied up and a cup of tea in hand. At her feet lay Howie, a neatly groomed white mini schnauzer. Next to her sat a large stereo born from the 1980s, a three-foot-high beast with different decks, including one for vinyl.

A record spun on the top deck, the speakers playing a live Joan Baez concert. I closed the door gently behind me, holding the knob so that the latch slid closed without its familiar click.

"How are you?" she asked, a genuine inquisitiveness rather than polite greeting, as she always did first thing when we saw each other.

"I'm sorry to wake you—"

"Nah," she said, waving her hand. Howie's ears perked up and he looked over at me, though he stayed glued to the floor, satisfied to be Laura's foot warmer. "I stayed up."

"You didn't have to do that," I said instinctively. Decades prior, that would have sounded like an indignant teenager. But for this moment, it came mostly out of concern for Laura's health at her age.

"Nonsense. Tonight is special." I'd wanted to head right to my stash, an ice chest with several hospital blood bags, until I could get my minifridge set up from my old place. But Laura's words kept me close, and I walked over to take her free hand. Howie set his head back down and huffed out a sigh, as if I was disturbing the peace. "It's your first night home."

Which wasn't accurate. Not even close. As her eyesight had started to wither, I'd spent more and more time here, helping out before work. "I've been here plenty of times," I said with a laugh. "It's not that different now. Let me take your tea—"

"Still drinking it. A toast," she said. "Come on, go grab a drink." When I didn't budge, she gestured again. "Go, go."

"Okay," I said, letting go of her hand. I looked Laura over, seemingly so content with the world in her comfy chair, warm tea, loyal dog, and Joan Baez in the air. Miraculous, really— life had taken so much from her, from her family to her vision to her longtime girlfriend, and yet her smile seemed the definition of *content*. "Alright." I walked into my room, the small bedroom that later became my music studio. I grabbed a blood bag from my cooler, then headed to the kitchen to pour some into the lone plastic cup I'd brought over.

My footsteps caught Laura's attention and she held up her teacup. "To living at your house?" I asked.

"It's not my house. It's *our* house now. To homes. Families. And," she said, nodding to the turntable, "to Joan. It's okay if I can't see, as long as I can hear her."

She called it "our house." And in that moment, I felt new ties weaving between us, like two links in a chain finally forged together. The level of trust Laura put in me—and I, in turn, put in her—it all meant something.

She deserved the truth.

As I held my cup of cold blood that night, I decided to take a leap of faith with that trust.

Despite keeping the vampire community at arm's length, their rules always lingered in my head. I knew Laura wouldn't break trust. The only risk came from whether it might change her opinion of me. Yet I decided right then that such a choice was up to her.

The moment was earned.

"There's something you should know about me. If we're being honest." I took her hand and wrapped it around the flimsy plastic of my cup. "I'm not drinking water here."

Laura had been fifty-eight when I did that, ten years away from dying at the age of sixty-eight. Decades had passed from that moment to this cold night standing outside of the same house.

I looked at the man in front of me—who was he? A friend of hers? A relative? But that didn't quite line up. The numbers crunched in my head slowly: if Laura died at sixty-eight, any friend of hers could be…like ninety-something right now. Something like that. A ninety-year-old person would not be driving around at all, especially not through the hills and narrow streets of San Francisco.

Especially not with a teenager in tow, a mopey-looking kid whose unkempt brown hair, tired eyes and pale skin told me that one of his parents was Asian and one of his parents was white.

The boy walked over from the sedan's passenger side, then leaned against the front hood. The whole time, his eyes stuck on his phone's screen and his fingers tapped away, the sour look on his face showing the whole situation annoyed him.

"Laura died a while ago," I said.

"Oh. That's terrible to hear. Not surprising, but still. I guess we all lost touch. She was a relative." Something about this man seemed familiar. Which I suppose made sense since he was somehow connected to my family, but other than Laura, I only had one very awkward late-night interaction with them several years after becoming a vampire. Which was decades and hairstyles ago. "I've seen a few photos of her when she was young—you look just like her. Are you her granddaughter? We didn't know she had any children."

"Oh." Children? They might have been related but this guy *really* didn't understand Laura. "Not my mom. I'm just—" I searched for the best, safest explanation "—a distant relative. No kids for her."

"Yeah. I didn't know that side of the family that well, so I never met her. We just were in town so we thought we'd stop by." The man looked back toward the boy, whose frame and scowl placed him at maybe twelve, thirteen years old? Right on the cusp of the age to really channel his angst. "Didn't we?"

"She kept to herself. Only trusted a few people," I said, considering how remarkable it had been to earn that trust—and for her to not freak out when I revealed what I was. "She'd been through a lot." I scanned the man's response to that to see if he knew what I meant, if he could even grasp the scope of the chasm that grew between Laura and her family. "She died peacefully, though." I considered the age difference and my twenty-something appearance. "When I was really young."

"I see."

"I'm sorry, I missed your name." Which I didn't, because he hadn't said it. But it was the polite way to dig for details.

"Oh," he said, sticking out a hand. "Right. I'm EJ. And this is my grandson, Ian."

EJ. Were there distant relatives named EJ? None that I could recall, though really, I suppose I wouldn't know, given how

I cut off my parents. I searched his face for clues, but with a whole family branch of possibilities, it seemed fruitless. One of the problems with only hanging out mostly with musicians over the past decade was that I'd totally lost the ability to judge age; everyone looked the same under dim bar lighting. I put EJ at somewhere between fifty and seventy, depending on his level of hard living, though he had the blessed agelessness of Asian genetics. And considering I only recalled meeting two female cousins once in my youth, chances were we'd never crossed paths before.

It was clear that EJ didn't spend an hour every day weight lifting, but aside from a mild case of granddad-bod, he looked like he took care of himself.

The kid, on the other hand, appeared pissed and/or tired as hell. Ian fired off a straight-ahead stare that warded off any attempt to decode his weary indifference.

"Look, I'm sorry to barge in. We were just in the area and, well…" EJ took in a hard breath. "We're in a situation where family might make things a little better. I had this address, but we didn't know if Laura still lived here. No one's talked to her in decades." That was true. Though EJ didn't mention *why*. That part, I knew—and I held a grudge, even if Laura let that go years before she passed.

The weight of my backpack pressed into my shoulder, chilled bottles inching closer to room temperature with every passing minute. "I'm sorry but I don't know what else to tell you. The house was eventually passed down to me, and, uh, well, it's where I live," I said with a mild shrug. "I really didn't know much about our extended family, so this is all new to me."

Ninety percent of that was true. I left out the part about carrying blood in my bag.

"Okay. Well," EJ said, "maybe we should just get going. I'm sorry we bothered you." Was it possible for the word *sorry* to be thrown around in every sentence in a conversation? It sure felt that way.

"No bother. I was just out for a walk tonight."

"I'm sorry." There it was again, this time with EJ extending his hand outward. "What was your name?"

In that split second, I considered my options. I could try to make up a new name, a new identity on the spot, sever any potential further family complications. But on the off chance EJ ever came around again, best to minimize confusion. Taking notes to sort out my lies was too much effort. "Louise," I said, taking his hand.

"Oh," he said with a chuckle, "that's funny. I wonder if you were named—"

"Are we done yet?" Ian said. "It's freezing and I gotta pee."

What was this kid's deal? I understood teen angst—I mean, I stayed in the corner of my room listening to Velvet Underground and The Stooges in gigantic earmuff headphones until my idiot little brother had ruined it all. But I still wouldn't be this rude to strangers. Maybe it was a generational thing? I know I *looked* in my early twenties, with the way I dressed and my asymmetrical A-line haircut, and my closest community was musicians, who tended to be without families or career paths, but even I knew better than to be a jerk like this.

"Ian. Settle down. That's just rude. You should put away the video games and say hi before we go."

"I told you, this isn't a game. I'm coding. It's called *homebrew*," he said, the last word loaded with teenage annoyance.

"You know what I mean. This is Louise and she's your..." His face scrunched up. "I'm not sure what she is, a cousin of some degree. I think."

"Hi." I offered a hand like a proper adult. "How are you?"

There. Nice and simple. And while Aunt Laura had passed on the notion that that question should always be asked—and answered—with sincerity rather than politeness, I really just wanted something throwaway in return here.

Ian looked at me, his eyes filled with the judgment only a young teen might bring. But something else lingered behind that, further than the battle that always happened at that age. The intensity of his stare betrayed an apathy that tugged harder than typical youthful indifference.

"My dad just died. My mom's gonna die soon," he said, straightening up. His phone screen dimmed, and without blinking, his eyes met mine. "So, you know, shit's fucked up." He took my hand with a loose grip.

So much for throwaway.

Now I'd lived a really long time, and I certainly had my own teen rebellion phase. You didn't gravitate toward Bowie and Iggy Pop and punk unless something existed to push back against. Even if that rebellion simply fought against a family hell-bent on conforming to the most normal of norms.

But I'd never had to deal with anything close to the magnitude of what Ian's young life must have faced.

"Oh," I said, unable to come up with anything else. Ian's hand dropped from mine and we stood like we existed in two different dimensions.

"I'm sorry about the language," EJ said hurriedly. "We're going through a difficult time right now."

"Why are we talking to random strangers about this?" Ian bit out. "You don't even know her."

"It's fine," I said to EJ, my voice low. "Really. I'm so sorry to hear that." It dawned on me that not only was Ian dealing with the loss of his parents, EJ was dealing with the loss as well. Pop culture showed vampires as cruel, cold beings disconnected from humanity and the world. But from what I'd seen, plenty of humans were colder, more selfish and disconnected than they acknowledged, regardless of what they ate. The flip side was that probably the majority of vampires felt that disconnect—but compounded by being in a world that changed while they did not.

So maybe being callous to the world arrived sometime *after* the first century of life. For now, I felt for Ian. I didn't know what kind of path he was on. I hoped the kid had a support system beyond EJ. And maybe, a sliver of kindness from a distant relative might help. "Look, you came all the way out here." From inside, Lola's nails shuffled against the entry tile at the sound of my keys. "You wanna come in and use the bathroom?"

# CHAPTER 5

LOLA GREETED THE GUESTS, and if having company confused her, she didn't show it. Instead, she rolled on her side like the worst guard dog of all time, and despite absolutely no commands from me, she performed the only trick I'd taught her: a single paw sticking up, waiting for a high five. I apologized for my ridiculous dog, a single scratch causing orange corgi fur to shed by their shoes, then pointed Ian to the bathroom.

My house had a functioning toilet even without my bodily need for it. I always offered it for occasional repair people—or, in another life, Marshall. But otherwise, it only got a once-a-week flush, a standard maintenance practice passed down by the vampire community.

My skills at talking with relatives atrophied years ago, and I nodded along to EJ's recap, a low voice and constant guard to see if his grandson had returned. His daughter, Sonya, Ian's mother, had been diagnosed with a rare and aggressive lung cancer about a year ago, and despite chemotherapy, it persisted. Then two months ago, Ian's father was killed when his car was hit by a drunk driver.

Just like that, Ian had nothing.

Hence, the anger.

With Sonya booked at a hospital south of San Francisco for an aggressive experimental treatment, EJ had taken Ian out of school for a road trip, driving up from San Diego for a few days. Even though the hospital was an hour away, Sonya and EJ agreed that a big city might be a good distraction for the boy. Turned out, he'd refused to leave the hotel room other than when they went down to the hospital, spending every second working on some coding project on his phone, though he apparently enjoyed room service.

I stepped back to make EJ some tea for the road—really just an excuse to dash to the kitchen and put my blood in the refrigerator. But the offer was sincere, since tea was one of the few human groceries I kept on hand. A little-known fact about vampires is that we can actually drink a little tea (lightly steeped) and I quite enjoyed both the taste and the smell, particularly of lemon tea. I poured hot water into a double-stacked paper cup for EJ, then a black mug for myself, bold white letters on the ceramic proclaiming Goth Is Undead.

Pretty sure neither of them would get the joke. Unless Ian was named after Ian Curtis, but I doubted there were any other music people on the family tree.

EJ took his, though he didn't drink. He held the cup with both hands, a harsh grimace on his face. "I just don't know what to do. There's no guidebook that prepares you for this sort of thing."

I understood that part.

Not with family catastrophes, but the chaos of stepping into the unknown, a complete life shift without any direction or tutorial. I started to reply when the sound of strummed guitar strings came from down the hall.

We both heard it, though I moved much faster to stop Ian from exploring further, something that wasn't exactly ideal in a vampire's house.

EJ followed, walking carefully not to spill his tea, and I moved with a determined "don't touch my shit" walk, only to pause at the doorway.

Ian crouched, one of my acoustics propped on his knee. This was Jeff, a sunburst Gibson L-series acoustic with a rich full tonal range—appropriately named after Jeff Buckley. But for Ian's purposes, the most important part was probably that Jeff sat closest to the door.

Ian didn't notice us, too enamored with the wall of hanging guitars. He'd probably already taken in the corner drum kit, two-keyboard setup, and mixing desk around the room, and as I reached behind me to shut the opposite door to my vampire resting chamber—really just a normal bedroom with the bookshelves and curtains blocking out the windows—EJ nudged me.

"I'm sorry he's intruded like this," EJ whispered. "But it's the first time I've seen him smile in weeks."

He *was* smiling as he observed the gear, though his face turned to a scrunch as he looked down at the guitar, fingers fumbling as he tried to form what looked to be either a C or a G chord.

I reminded myself that this kid was dealing with unfathomable family loss—so don't freak out. "Hey," I said with a knock.

He jolted with a start, knee banging hard enough against the body that the open strings rang out. My fang dug into my inner lip and I told myself to stay calm. "Sorry. I just saw this and—"

"It's cool," I said, even though it wasn't. I stifled an urge to grab the guitar out of his hands but composed my thoughts into much simpler—more polite—phrasing. "Just be careful."

"You have *so* many guitars," he said, a new enthusiasm coloring his words. "And drums! I've never seen drums in person."

"Mmm-hmm," I said, trying to figure out how to end the conversation besides nodding quickly.

"Is that," he started, pointing at the wall, "a Telecaster?"

The question threw me off. While Telecasters were popular among musicians, the name wasn't exactly commonly used.

A tiny smile came to my lips, and I didn't even try to hide it.

"It is," I said slowly. Hanna, a standard Fender named after Kathleen Hanna with the famous Telecaster shape, a rich blue body with clean lacquered mahogany fretboard.

"I've read about them. They look so fucking cool," he said, enunciating the f-bomb like he really wanted me to notice. He leaned over, bright eyes and raised cheeks in a way that urged more. "What types are the others?"

"You know guitars?" I asked.

"I've been reading about them. I always wanted to hold a guitar."

My first guitar came courtesy of a garage sale at age fifteen, a beat-up acoustic with nylon strings and a slightly bent neck so that it wouldn't hold tuning for more than twenty minutes—which only got worse as I poured all of my hours into it.

And I still remembered the power that suddenly emerged when holding it for the first time.

"He's been using a guitar app on his phone," EJ said. Ian's face fell instantly, like the old man had let out a secret.

"I mean, it's to learn chords," Ian spit out. "I know it's not the same. And it keeps crashing my phone." He looked up as his fingers pushed down on the frets again. "I'm saving up. To have something of my *own*."

I understood the pull in his eyes, the allure of shielding yourself with notes ringing out from strings. I got that. I didn't know what to tell him *about* it, but at least I understood.

"We should get going," EJ said quietly behind me. "We don't want to bother Louise and it's late."

A pause took over the room, and despite being surrounded by thousands of dollars of equipment built for cranking out really loud sounds, the only noise came from the sound of tea slurping.

"I made tea," I finally said. "In case you want some for the road."

"Oh." He looked at me, then shifted to EJ with narrowed eyes, then back down. "Oh. Okay. Got it." He set Jeff back on the stand in a gingerly motion, like he finally managed to escape his own thoughts and realize he sat in someone *else's* room of expensive musical gear. His head craned slowly, surveying the room and lingering on the drum kit before resetting to the floor. "It's really cool gear," he said. "You in a band?"

This wasn't exactly the time to discuss the garlic incident. "In between bands right now."

"We have an early morning," EJ said. "We have to drive down to University Hospital tomorrow. But thank you for the tea."

"No problem." What words did a situation like this deserve? "Good luck" seemed a bit too trivial. Same with "nice to meet you." Ian nodded, his eyes still fixated on the wall of instruments. He moved past Jeff, though his ankle brushed the stand, just enough to bump the instrument and cause the faintest ring from the strings. Ian missed it completely, moving past with posture slumped forward, and EJ put a hand on his shoulder.

Ian shrugged it off.

I walked in silence with them, uncertainty lingering between us. "Well, it was nice to discover some long-lost relatives," I said. A little more meaningful than the other option, without going overboard.

"We'll be in town for a week," EJ said. "We'll of course be spending time at the hospital, but hanging around here too.

If you have any suggestions for fun things to do. Can I have
your—"

"What he means," Ian said, "is that they want me to be distracted from what's happening."

"That's not it at all."

"Yes it is. God, you guys talk to me like I'm five." His pace
picked up to a defiant speed despite the narrow hallway. Lola
remained sprawled out on the entryway tile, but she glanced
up at the movement.

"It's been rough," EJ whispered.

"I'm right here," Ian called back.

This was definitely not how I planned my hour before work.
And despite the sheer surprise of these distant relations and their
catastrophic situation, uncertainty stewed. Did they really count
as family at this point? That term *kind of* shifted after walking
out decades ago, probably even more after turning into a vampire, and even further still after moving away without contact.

Did I owe them anything other than polite chatter and a functioning toilet at this point? I even provided a bonus cup of tea.

So, probably not.

Instead, I chose more deliberately: no hanging out on the
doorstep with endless final words, no hugs, no exchanging of
phone numbers—just a simple goodbye. My feelings for the
situation ended with a sympathy that landed somewhere between blip and surge, the universal kind that happened when
learning about someone's GoFundMe.

But I had my own crisis to deal with right now: blood, or
lack thereof.

Ian and EJ argued the entire way to the front door and even
on the path from the porch to their car. I said a final goodbye
and shut the door the instant they cleared the threshold.

Several minutes later, my home reset to its natural state for
Saturday nights before work; speakers playing songs to fit my

mood—a dreamy soundscape from the Cocteau Twins, Elizabeth Fraser's soaring vocals awash in an ocean of echoing reverb. It juxtaposed the gnawing anxiety in my gut, a delayed reaction to having people in my house, touching my stuff, *talking* to me.

I needed a drink.

Not just blood. A drink, in the traditional sense. Enough to take the edge off, but not enough to affect my drive to work.

In my cabinet of human consumables, right behind the boxes of tea, sat a bottle of vodka. I pulled that out, along with a glass. A few drops were enough for my purposes and mixed cleanly with blood; anything else hit way too hard, probably from the lack of breads and meats slowing down alcohol digestion. I learned "too much, too soon" the hard way—once and never again, on the first night I tried mixing alcohol into blood.

I had a good reason, though. It was the night Aunt Laura and I found out my mom died. Only flashes remained from that night, and that probably was for the better. Lesson learned.

My wrist twisted, letting just enough pour out for a proper chillout snack, then I opened the refrigerator door to grab a blood bag, a conscious dip into my rations after a fucked-up night. Except something was wrong: two bottles from Eric's event should have sat right next to the bags.

Yet there was only one.

My eyes darted in a frantic scan of the kitchen: counters, floor, island, the sink—did I leave it out when I was making tea? Had Ian or EJ seen it? Did I reveal anything, and if I did, what could that possibly mean for...

But no, it turned out simpler than that. My boot accidentally kicked the backpack sitting next to the fridge, and it slid with a weight that gave away its contents. "Damn it," I cursed to myself, opening the main pouch to find the missing bottle. Turned out that I didn't need to have any alcohol to lose my faculties—encountering some long-lost branch of my family punched with the same effect.

The time showed that nearly ninety minutes had passed since I left Eric's meeting, well past the roughly sixty-minute time limit for room-temp blood before it started to react to the environment. Storing it now would be pointless, and drinking it, well...

Did I want to tempt a day of nausea?

I considered this question, as well as the ticking clock. Every second that passed meant further coagulation in the bottled plasma.

*Drinking old blood is punk rock*, I told myself and unscrewed the cap, dumping its contents into the glass. I jammed a finger into the mix, stirring to resolve the blood and vodka until they became one.

Several minutes later, I stood over the sink rinsing the plastic bottle and considered the absurdities of the day. Would I have taken such a risk if there wasn't a blood shortage? Probably not, but what could be done about it? Eric was the community leader here, and if he acknowledged issues, then facts were facts. And I need an alternative source of food.

But what?

Nothing yet from the Red Cross's volunteer manager, though that might take a few days. And live donors? I cringed at the thought of the volunteers who got drained as a fetish. I mean, live and let live, but the actual process of biting (they *always* wanted to be bit) and draining was a skill I'd never mastered—and given the number of teeth and amount of fluids involved, the whole thing seemed both gross and impractical. Even worse, the few times I dipped into that community, the donors always wanted to chat afterward, which was actually more emotionally torturous than biting people. And there was no way I'd return to buying from blood pimps like my early days.

There had to be another way.

I stood, staring at my reflection in the kitchen window, a light flush coming to my cheeks and ears. One thing that vampirism definitely didn't cure was the way my Asian physiology turned my skin beet red with alcohol in mere minutes. Heat radiated off the curves of my ears while I stared and considered possible food sources.

In a way, I blamed pop culture for lying. Vampires seemed so cool in movies, but outside of the whole lack-of-aging thing, being a vampire made everything harder. There was no easy food source, no job board, and you barely received any guidance when you were turned. The trade-off for living longer was a weird schedule, inconvenient sustenance, and living with a bunch of deactivated internal organs.

The joys of food and drinks? Gone. Sex? Those body parts became inert, along with the hormones that drove them. Sure, we could have feelings and most of us still enjoyed *looking* sexy, but the actual urge for physical intimacy disappeared.

Marshall once called vampire life "depressing." And with inconvenient sustenance, he might have been right.

But then I hit an epiphany, something so obvious I chuckled out loud in my otherwise empty house, the walls rattling with continued drums and bass coming out of speakers in every room.

Eric acknowledged blood bag shortages depended on neighborhoods. San Francisco had been hit. But thirty, forty miles south? Those hospitals might have some supply.

With Ian's mother already checked in, I could pose as a visitor and find out for myself. I was, after all, family. And that was better than dealing with Eric's community of vampires.

I just had to show up.

# CHAPTER 6

AT THIS TIME OF year, sunset started around five thirty, or just about thirty minutes after driving became reasonably safe for vampires. Which meant waking up at the ungodly hour of 4:00 p.m. and letting Lola out to go potty in my small yard while I avoided any possible UV exposure in my dining room.

Like human skin, vampire skin got sunburned. Unlike human skin, vampire skin experienced damage in seconds, our physiology being extremely sensitive to UV. I'd heard of some vampires donning fully protective suits for an entire day as a form of extreme challenge, which probably resulted from people who enjoyed skydiving and other stunts becoming vampires. I preferred living, and my life was basically already nocturnal before I turned, so vampire life suited me.

Getting up, on the other hand, was never fun. But I had places to go.

The car ride itself required layered preparations, a technique I learned when sunrises coincided with my commute home from work. The movie vampire idea of using sunblock actually worked, but it was part of a formula. After that came a ski mask and sunglasses. Which probably looked weird to any passing drivers, but whatever—I lived in San Francisco, so weird was relative. On top of that lay 100 percent coverage: leather jacket, gloves, pants, shoes—not a single exposed area, all protected by a shade hat.

My car offered further protection. First, I put a sunshade fabric over the driver window. I'd also had UV-filtering film installed on all windows. And I chose white for my Prius—I had no idea if it actually helped, but since white absorbed the least heat, I came to the very unscientific conclusion that it somehow made me safer.

For tonight's specific task, I wore my work clothes underneath, including my work badge around my neck. This wasn't for my job, though I did intend on going in right after this. Instead, I planned to visit a certain extended family member. Of course, I'd never met Sonya Madson, but between what EJ had told me and some strategic googling, I knew enough to fake registering as a visitor. And since EJ and Ian had said they were heading to the hospital that morning, I figured my evening arrival would neatly miss them. I even took a quick detour to Harold's Guitar Shack in the Mission District to pick up my acoustic known as Emmylou after she needed the tuners replaced. And to pet the resident dog at Harold's. That part was always important.

A very straightforward plan lay ahead: 1) register as a visitor, 2) get some props to give me greater access, 3) get blood.

I arrived with a backpack large enough for a college student backpacking for a summer, a stash of ice packs weighing it down. Sunglasses still on my face, I walked through the underground parking garage to the massive doors of the hospital's main lobby. A minute later and I'd registered, now marching forward with a large red name tag that proclaimed VISITOR across the top.

I even invented an alibi in case EJ or Sonya herself checked the visitor log: I would tell them I was driving by the area, had a moment to say hello, but ultimately got pulled away by work. No one would be the wiser.

First step complete.

With greater access to the floors thanks to a visitor badge, I searched for a janitor closet. That included an inadvertent passing of Sonya's room. I'd only looked because of the sound of guitar strings, but my peek turned into a longer pause when I saw it was Ian.

He sat with Sonya, his grandfather nowhere around. The sound didn't come from a guitar but rather digital notes on his phone, all while his mother watched from the hospital bed. Though I only caught it at an angle, the harsh tension on his cheeks and brow from the other night no longer existed, replaced with both a buoyancy and a heaviness that lived in contradiction. He played an out-of-step melody, something that sounded halfway familiar, though his constant stopping and restarting prevented me from figuring it out.

I reminded myself of why I was there, how my presence would only add confusion, and I pushed forward, leaving my mystery relatives behind until I found the janitorial supply closet. Then I lingered, tapping away at my phone until someone on staff came and went. And right before the door's hydraulics pushed it shut, I stuck my foot out to hold it ajar. A good minute passed for an all clear before I reopened it and let myself in.

Step three: roll out a loaded cart with a convenient space in the middle to hide my icy backpack. At a glance, my own ID for SF General looked close enough to this hospital's badges. And that one time I left my badge in the break room provided invaluable experience for bullshitting my way through with a combination of smiles and saying "hold that door for me please." No one said no to a woman pushing a massive janitorial cart.

In fact, the whole thing went almost too smoothly, like I was being set up on camera for some kind of prank. But in this case, apparently I pulled off the role of hospital janitor on an extremely believable level. I didn't like my job but at least I knew I was good at it.

And to my relief, the hospital had blood. Not enough—the mainline stock appeared full, but the expiring bags left something to be desired. I filled my backpack with enough to tide me over, but I'd still need to ration. Survivalist articles explained how humans could subsist on like two apples a day for the short term; I wasn't sure how that scaled to vampires, but this supply at least gave me a few weeks.

My backpack slid into the middle of the cart, hidden behind a row of cleaners and industrial-grade toilet paper, its weight carried a far different momentum than the usual mix of supplies. Seventeen minutes from start to finish and I was almost out. I rolled the cart to a men's bathroom, then knocked on the door. "Janitorial," I yelled, and when no voices replied, I pushed the cart in far enough to be free from any hallway security cameras. I shoved a yellow bar that said Closed For Cleaning across the doorway, then gave myself a moment to breathe when my phone buzzed.

Another text from Eric.

I apologize for repeating myself, but given the increasing media hysteria about the "vampire assault" please avoid any humans right now unless absolutely necessary. I will keep you posted on blood supply.

Eric and his community rules. Still, I clearly was on his bad side. And if I was going to rely on his supply of blood, I needed to get involved, be a better vampire. Human musicians didn't seem to want to hang out with me anyway.

Heads up, I'm down at University Hospital and their blood supply is better.

I typed the words before tapping the Send icon.

From the cart's shelf, I grabbed my hoodie, putting it on to transform from "regular janitorial staff member" to "hospital employee ready to go home." I slid the backpack off the cart's shelf, and I hoisted it on my shoulder, the weight of the collective blood bags slamming into my back with a breath-stealing *oomph*.

Now incognito, all I had to do was get to the elevator, travel down several flights, and walk out to my car. And with light Sunday evening traffic, I'd get home with plenty of time to spare before work. But something rammed into me as soon as I stepped out, knocking me off-balance with a giant backpack of blood bags. I steadied, then locked eyes with the person who ran into me.

"Oh, sorry," a teen voice started. "Louise? What are you doing here?"

It was Ian, phone in hands.

*Fuck.*

"Oh, hey," I said, searching for an excuse. "Bathroom's closed." As if he couldn't tell from the huge Closed For Cleaning sign.

Ian frowned at the comment, then squinted. "Why are you coming out of a men's bathroom?"

"Oh." I laughed, like I totally knew what I was doing and *wasn't* carrying a giant backpack loaded with blood. "Wrong door."

"It says closed."

"Right, I know." I pointed at the sign. "I checked. Confirmed, totally closed."

Ian's eyes narrowed and he shoved his phone into his back pocket. "You're in the men's bathroom."

My inability to talk with anyone outside of my dog created a clear problem here. "So, what you probably don't know is that I'm on the janitorial staff at San Francisco General Hospital. I usually work nights. My shift starts in a few hours, actually." At that moment, I'd wondered if maybe I should have swapped out one musical instrument for, say, an improv class. It's not like I ever used my saxophone and I hated ska anyways. "The sign fell down," I said. "I put it back up."

There. A perfectly feasible and realistic explanation.

"You put it back up?"

"Yep. Janitorial protocol. Because no one was around. Oh—" I held up both hands "—and then I washed my hands. 'Cause, you know, bathroom floor. Kinda gross. So, anyway, I should go. There's another bathroom on the other side of this floor if you need it."

"Okay, but...did you come to visit?"

Good thing I had my previous alibi. "As a matter of fact, that's why I stopped by," I said, a smile trying to portray full confidence in my statement. "I was running an errand down the peninsula and thought I'd drop in before heading to work. But I didn't have a phone number for your grandpa, so I was just kind of wandering."

"Oh, okay. Well, Mom's resting now. We were going to leave soon."

"Ah," I said with a mock grimace. "That's too bad. Really unfortunate timing."

Ian nodded, though instead of replying, he pulled out his phone. His thumbs flew over the virtual keyboard. "Cool. I just let Grandpa know. What are you doing now?"

"Gonna head home," I said. Polite but curt.

"I was on the way to the bathroom. Then I was going to the café. Grandpa's talking to Mom and I just needed to be..."

His hands raised, a shaking gesture that translated to frustration. "Somewhere else." He swept his hair out of his face, and harsh lines framed his mouth in ways that shouldn't appear on someone so young. "You—" he sucked in a breath "—want a snack too?"

The question rolled out in an uneven tone, like he was asking someone out for a first date. But this stood as a much weightier, yet much simpler proposition. I must have been the only person besides his grandfather and his mom within his recent orbit, and something had to give.

"Maybe you can tell me about your guitars," he said after several empty seconds.

Fifteen minutes. Maybe thirty. I had some time before work, after all. I knew nothing about these extended relatives of mine, but lending a few minutes to a kid grasping for a lifeline seemed reasonable, no matter how awkward it might be.

And I did love to talk about my guitars. Especially since I hadn't had anyone to talk about music with since Marshall.

But *after* I dealt with the blood.

The backpack shifted on my shoulder, blood bags and ice packs sliding within. "I think I could use some tea. You know, I actually realized I don't need this big bag, so let me put it in my car first."

"Oh cool," he said, then stepped forward to match my position and looked at the floor. I took several steps, and Ian did the same. Then I slowed, and he adjusted to keep pace. I turned down a hallway, away from the elevator and he followed, like a computer-controlled drone.

This wasn't going to change unless I just started sprinting. It seemed like the more I gave humans a chance, the more I wished I had vampire powers. Instead, I walked briskly with the cool of an ice pack seeping through my backpack's nylon lining. Being a jerk about this was an option, but basic decency quickly struck that from the list.

"I'm in the parking garage," I said with a sigh that Ian ignored.

"No problem," Ian said, either ignorant or willfully ignorant of my intent to shake him. It's not like I had a good explanation for transferring blood bags into a cooler.

My teeth dug into my bottom lip, the sharpened fang poking harder than it should have. "Yeah. Sure." A new idea sprung up, a possible way out of the awkwardness. "Hey, how about you order for us and I'll meet you after I drop off my bag?"

Ian stopped, his shoes scuffing against the tile floor. His hands shoved in his pockets, and his eyes fell to the ground, unkempt hair falling over his eyes. "I…" he started, and I let air breathe between us. "I'd like to be with someone that's, like, not my grandpa."

Ian's voice came out so low, so small that it may as well have been a whisper from a room down the hall. Suddenly, his body appeared frail and weak, his earlier rage withering away and leaving only a thin frame that might blow to pieces if we went outside.

There was no losing him now or for the foreseeable future. Different ideas shifted in my head, and instead of coming up with white lies and excuses, I yielded to the moment.

I'd figure it out.

"Well," I said as we walked, going with the only type of small talk I cared about, "who are your favorite bands?"

**CHAPTER 7**

**VAMPIRE POWER MYTH #3:** Drinking blood is the greatest rush in the world, an untouchable euphoria.

Bullshit. The greatest rush in the world comes from live music, when the energy between the band onstage and the sweaty crowd in a too-small space erupted into something beyond drums and singing. For decades, I'd experienced this only from the audience, but after Aunt Laura died, I'd had my fill of it from the stage as well. *Very* small stages, of course, but still. Live music created a feedback loop of pure emotion, all captured into three or four minutes of sonic fury and ringing ears.

Blood, on the other hand, was just food. And right now, it all sat stacked in my backpack, sloshing around as Ian told me about his terrible taste in bands.

I did give him points on one thing: he really loved Stalks Chateau, a recent popular band with a by-the-numbers sound. And everyone had to start somewhere. I'd heard of them, of course; when human urges like food or sex didn't matter, brainpower went toward much more important things, like discovering new music.

But yeah, they were…well, *bad* was probably too harsh. Not my thing, and clearly groomed by record executives to tap into a potential crossover between a nostalgia emo sound and pop.

I'd asked him *why*, though—why that band, why those songs. He stewed on that while we walked, passing by nurses with stethoscopes, administrative workers with clipboards and regular people with the same bright VISITOR sticker I wore. He stayed silent to the elevator, during the wait, even on the ride down. As we stepped out of the lobby, he spoke with a quiet voice.

"I don't know."

"Is it the music? The lyrics?" I asked. "Like, the guitar or the beat?"

Ian bit down on his lip and we walked through the massive sliding doors to the underground garage. "I'm not sure," he said evenly. "I just—" he took in a breath "—*feel* something whenever I hear them. People look at me like I'm from another world when I say that. Mom does. Dad does." He winced, probably realizing his use of present tense, and his voice dropped. "Do you ever get that?"

*Did I get that?*

I *missed* live music desperately. And yet, I'd kept it at arm's length for so long, not because I wanted to, but because stepping back into a venue simply felt impossible, a chasm too massive to overcome.

Because on a rainy night in early 2020, live music was taken from me, in all its forms. Going to shows. Playing with a band. Connecting with people.

Erased, in moments.

"I'm worried," Marshall had said that night as we made our way down the stairs of the historic Fillmore auditorium, shuffling out after The Nineteen Twenty finished their encore.

Drops started to pelt our heads, taming Marshall's normally wild mop of dark brown hair.

"What?" I said, my ears still ringing with postshow tinnitus.

"I said 'I'm worried,'" he repeated as we walked farther into the rain. We stopped, his hand rubbing the stubble on his cheek as we waited at a crosswalk. "You've seen the news over the past few weeks?"

"Not really. I try to avoid it."

"You haven't heard about the disease? It hit Asia, and now Europe?" I had, of course. I'd seen passing headlines on my phone but vampires operated with different concerns than humans. Or, at least I did. "I'm worried this might be the last show we see for a while."

"That seems a little absurd."

"Look," he said, stepping around a gathering puddle on the sidewalk. "I know you don't, like, get colds or stuff. So maybe you don't keep up on these things. But it's some scary shit."

"Well, hey, I can always livestream from my home studio. Cool?"

Marshall didn't laugh. Raindrops intensified, and I put my hoodie over my head to blunt the soaking. "This whole thing just makes me think of my cousin. The one in Toronto. He almost died from SARS like twenty years ago. He caught it randomly. Wrong place, wrong time."

Of all the things we'd revealed about ourselves, from my vampire nature to Marshall's evangelical youth, we'd never touched on this, leaving me with little to say but "oh." He was my best friend, my bandmate, but the difference in our natural existence still created a disconnect, things where my level of empathy had to be faked.

Mostly because I didn't know what to say.

"So," he replied as we turned the corner to hit a cross street. "You don't worry about these things, right?"

"What do you mean? Like, the state of the world?"

"Disease. Viruses. You said yourself that you don't get sick."

"Yeah, I mean, our nature," I said, being careful to not use the *V* word, "is basically just a superpowered immune system."

"So something like this doesn't affect you."

"Well, my life isn't all great. I mean, you once told me it sounded depressing."

"Yeah, but..." He stopped, facing me. Rain had slicked his hair at this point, creating thick lines across his forehead. "You don't die. This can't kill you."

"Dude," I said, "what are you getting at?"

"Can you—" he started. His mannerisms told me where this was headed, from the half looks on the ground to the short, hesitant breaths. I'd seen enough vampire movies to know. "Can you make me like you? Can you—"

I don't know which stopped him, my groan or my palms slapping my face. Maybe both. Wind swept the rain, tossing it sideways as traffic passed us. "I can't. You know that."

"No, you said you didn't know how it worked and probably couldn't. That's not definitive."

"I'm telling you, I can't. Look, you're just freaking out because of the news—"

"Louise. I don't want to die," he said, a stark vulnerability to his words that shook me, his tall frame seemingly shrinking to my size. I'd seen every cycle of Marshall's emotions before, but nothing quite like the sheer dread on display now. "I don't want to die. This shit, it's really scary. It's caused me to rethink so many things. About me, about what we're doing here. About *you*," he said quickly, but before I could ask what that meant, he rushed by it with more words. "They're saying it's worse than what my cousin had and—"

"Wait, wait, wait. I can't do it." My hands wrung with exasperation. "I'm not saying I *won't* do it, I'm saying I physically *can't*."

"But try. You can try. There's no harm in that."

"Harm? You'd be stuck with me forever," I said with a laugh, anything to break the tension. But it didn't. Instead, his eyes softened, expression turning in a way that I'd never noticed before.

Seconds passed and his head tilted, rain rolling down his cheeks. "I would be okay with that."

Another car zoomed down the street, splashing gutter water at our feet. "Okay, stop joking around. What I mean—"

"I'm not joking. Louise, I'm telling you something that I should have—"

"Okay, look, I'll explain it again. My kind of people, most of us don't know how to—" I inhaled, looking for the right words "—pass this on. But I can't. I really can't, because it might kill me. That's what everyone says. I would if I could." I offered a smile, a toothy peace offering that bared some of my fangs. "Hanging out forever sounds great. Think of all the songs we could write. But I just can't." This veered way off from our usual postshow discussions of set lists or opening bands or assholes in the crowd, and right now, I would have given anything to be talking about some drunk who spilled their vodka tonic all over my pants. "Look, it's raining *really* bad. Can we discuss this tomorrow?"

Marshall looked at me, a quiet glare that lasted much longer than it should have. Despite the rain, his cheeks visibly burned and he held still. "Alright," he finally said, a wordless turn that told me he had more to say.

He moved with tentative steps, like those unsaid words interfered with his limbs. Something bothered him, though I couldn't tell if it was just the vampire business or something more. "Drive safe," I yelled, a verbal attempt at a pat on the back. "It's raining hard."

His decade-old hatchback beeped, its flashing lights causing the adjacent sidewalk to glow, and he stepped into the street to get on the driver's side.

It simply wasn't like my best friend to shut down like that. At that point we'd been through fifteen years of good shows and bad shows, bands that worked and bands that didn't, my reveal of vampiric nature, and so many of his breakups with women and men. None of that ever led to a silent treatment.

Something was wrong and I had to try. "Hey, Marshall?"

He looked up, squinting through the rain as he held the door half-open.

I raised my hands like claws and hissed loud enough for him to hear, a gesture that I hadn't used since that night Eric stumbled upon us. Seconds ticked by, but a matching gesture never came. Instead, he shook his head and ran a hand through his rain-slicked hair before getting in his car. Its lights came to life, and several seconds later, he disappeared around the corner.

Which was the last time I saw him. Because about thirty minutes later, his car hydroplaned straight into the divider going south on 880.

Sometimes, when I couldn't sleep, the mysteries of that night came back to me. Not just what else Marshall wanted to say, but what it meant, what might have been if I'd just tried to do things differently.

And whether a vampire fixer ran him off the road. Because he knew my true nature.

All of those feelings came back with Ian's question about understanding how he felt about music. Which made answering it all the more difficult. "Have you ever seen a live show?" I asked, my voice echoing through the parking garage.

"You mean, like a play?"

"No, a concert. Band onstage. Terrible opening act. Ringing in your ears for two days afterward."

"I've seen videos of Stalks Chateau concerts. They had really cool visuals."

I suppressed the urge to first cringe, then preach about the beauty of a small packed club with four people onstage, in-

struments loud enough to feel the room shake, about how the
larger the venue got, the worse the show usually became. The
need to proselytize scratched my skin and dried my throat, but
I focused; tonight was about getting blood, not making playl-
ists for a near stranger.

I let Ian go on about Stalks Chateau until we got to my car,
which had somehow gotten boxed in between a wide SUV and
a tiny MINI Cooper that parked far too close. "Goddamn it,"
I muttered under my breath. I stood behind my car, figuring
out the best way to get to the cooler on the folded rear seats
while Ian watched. "Just give me a sec," I said, slamming the
backpack down on the concrete in an effort to look casual but
delivering a much harder whack than necessary. The tight fit
would take some effort, and I shimmied between the driver side
and the adjacent SUV, only an elbow's length between them.
"Come on," I said as I pulled on the door handle. It clicked,
releasing from its latch, and I guided the door gently outward
before coming within an inch of the other car.

It was enough to jam my hand in and try to pry the cooler's
lid, but I merely brushed it. No way was I getting enough le-
verage to flip open the lid, hold it open, and unload my meals.
*And* somehow do it discreetly enough that Ian wouldn't notice
I carried bags of blood. That also ruled out pulling the bags
out one by one and shoving them through an open window.

I shimmied back to find Ian still there, staring silently. Maybe
the trunk? I could open up the hatchback and belly-crawl over
the hardshell guitar case containing a freshly repaired Emmylou. The cooler lid might not be able to open all the way and
that would make it awkward to reach but—

"Um, Louise?"

"Hold on a minute, I'm figuring something out here—" But
where to put the backpack? Maybe lug that in beside Emmylou and unload it that way?

"No, but seriously."

"Just a second," I said, clicking the button on the key fob to open the hatchback. "I gotta—"

"Louise, something's happening to your backpack. It looks like..." He hesitated, though I heard him swallow hard.

"It looks like blood."

# CHAPTER 8

I STOOD UP TO take in the sheer absurdity before me. My backpack sat, now oozing blood into a gradual pool next to my car, a scene that may have been interpreted by some to be a miracle akin to a weeping statue of the Virgin Mary or stigmata on a preacher.

Except that it came from the bottom of a dark green North Face backpack.

"Oh fuck," I let out, for so many reasons. The bottom blood bag must have punctured when it slammed down, and now Ian knelt to inspect the situation.

"Wait," he said, "this really *is* blood."

"No, it's…" Excuses ran through my mind, trying to come up with *something* similar to blood in color and texture. "Cranberry sauce." The second time might be the charm for that excuse. "I sometimes do Meals on Wheels. These are the leftovers."

Ian's eyes widened and his mouth twisted as he sniffed the

air. "It *smells* like blood. Like from my mom's transfusion when she developed anemia."

Now that just wasn't fair.

I forced out a laugh to buy a second to think. Except it probably wasn't great to laugh at a reference to transfusion. "I'm sorry," I said. "I mean, I'm not laughing about the transfusion. Seriously." The best way out of this was smashing the whole backpack into the cooler as fast as possible. I'd worry about the rest later. "What I mean is, this cranberry sauce is pretty bad. If it smells like blood." My eyes darted to the car, then the bloodstain pooling at the bottom of the bag, then at Ian, who started sniffing the air like he had something to prove.

Then back at the hardshell guitar case in the car.

"Hey," I said, grabbing the case's handle. "Can you hold this for me? I have a cooler filled with food—I'll just toss the bag in. I just have to climb through here." I thumbed at the gapping open trunk space.

"Wait," he said. "Why do—"

"Here," I said as quickly as possible, handing Emmylou over before Ian could get any further.

"Oh, cool." He took the case, then squinted at the name tag sticker across its side. "Who's Emmylou?"

"You're holding her," I said, picking up the backpack. Drips hung down as I supported the bag from underneath, a viscous flow that ran on my hand and left several drops on the trunk's upholstery. It didn't matter because Ian was suddenly taken with the guitar, rather than me or the blood oozing onto my fingers. "You can open the case, go ahead." Before he could reply, I turned my back to hide the visual of a bleeding bag. "Seriously, it's fine. I just had her repaired. I name all my guitars. Emmylou," I said with a grunt as I reached in and pulled on the cooler, "is named after Emmylou Harris. Country singer with a punk soul." Inside, ice cubes shuffled about with each tug, and once it got diagonal enough to open the lid, I shoved the backpack in.

"Can I try it? Her? It?"

I generally hated anyone touching my stuff, but the issue of a bleeding backpack took precedence—especially if the novelty would keep him occupied more than his phone. "Sure," I said, turning the backpack horizontally and trying to push it into the cooler. The backpack caught on the edge, the stitched North Face logo staring directly back at me and refusing to budge thanks to the bulk of the blood bags. Opening the backpack to individually unpack it remained an option, especially while Ian messed with the guitar.

But if he saw, then he'd *definitely* know it wasn't cranberry sauce.

I pushed again, more blood coming out of the bag's bottom, and now my fingers looked dipped in dark red paint. "Seriously?" I let out under my breath. From behind, Emmylou's strings rang out, the B string clearly out of tune. "Come on," I said, giving the backpack one more push to get through the narrow opening. It landed among the bed of convenience store ice cubes, and the lid finally dropped, though it stayed about an inch ajar. Several pushes later, the ice cubes reshuffled enough to close.

The inside of my car looked like a murder scene, despite me being a vampire who never hurt anyone and even drove an eco-friendly car.

I reverse-crawled out, and with my clean hand, yanked the trunk hatch closed, though a few drips managed to catch the edge of the bumper. The concrete held a blotchy stain, and I kicked myself for getting a white car. Wouldn't a red car have made much more sense in anticipation of blood accidents? Several feet away, Ian looked like he was trying to form a G chord but his fingers didn't quite cooperate. He strummed, and one of his fingers on the fretboard must have lacked the proper curl to let all the strings ring out. Instead, half of them muted, leaving mostly the out of tune B string playing with a mash of notes.

"There." I gave a thumbs-up and noticed the splotch of drying blood across the tip. "Well, that was going to be some leftovers but I guess not. Cranberry sauce is still good, though." *Good lie*, I told myself, then to provide further proof to Ian, I licked my thumb clean as proof that yes, this was edible human food and not actually blood.

Ian looked up from the guitar, then twisted his lips at me. But he quickly shifted back to his fumbling fingers, the guitar body balanced on a knee, as if there was *not* a small pool of drying blood right by his sneakered feet. He mumbled along, and though the sounds of tires squeaking echoed in from too-tight turns on slick parking garage floor, I locked into what he was trying to do.

A simple count. A melody played across single notes rather than a chord, and though his timing was a little off, I picked up the tune, the same one that he'd tried on his phone's app while sitting with his mom. Guess it took a real guitar to figure it out.

"Here Comes The Sun."

How did Ian go from Stalks Chateau to The Beatles?

I watched him try several more times, picking one string at a time with the side of his thumb. Emmylou's rich tone filled up the parking garage, its concrete walls and wide spaces providing surprisingly good reverb. His eyes narrowed in concentration and he changed from counting the beat to mumbling the lyrics along with the melody, his finger sliding only up and down the middle D string.

I looked at Ian, then the bloodstain on the concrete floor, then my car, then back at Ian, who still struggled on deciding where to go on the fretboard. I mentally urged him to jump down to the next string rather than sliding a finger up and down. It was like the guitar equivalent of a train slowly going off the rails. But with a Beatles song.

"Hey," I finally said after checking the time, "why don't we bring that inside? I'll show you a trick to playing that."

"You know this song?"

That seemed ridiculous to ask any musician, but then it hit me: in Ian's eyes, I wasn't someone who'd spent decades listening to, playing, living music. Instead, I was a long-lost relative about ten years older than him, someone born during the end of grunge—if he even knew what grunge was.

"Yeah. I know that song. Let me just—" I held up my hands while Ian kept plucking his uneven rhythm "—wash off this cranberry sauce."

# CHAPTER 9

BY THE TIME I caught up with Ian at the hospital café, he'd mastered the chorus to "Here Comes The Sun." Still one string, but at least he figured it out. In that time, I'd washed all the blood off my hands, though a few drops still remained on the knees of my scrubs.

The only noise in the café came from ambient chatter and Ian's attempts with Emmylou, alternating between playing that single melody and trying (but failing) to form chords. The staff and several other patrons ignored him; maybe tired, lonely musicians frequented hospital cafés more than I figured.

I never really had a need to go to the café at my hospital.

"I texted Grandpa," he said, sliding a white paper cup my way. "He's coming down."

I sat and gripped the cup, heat radiating through it. I looked anywhere but at Ian: the menu, the pastry display, the purple brushes of the dusk sky.

Just not at the boy playing my guitar.

What could I even say? Somewhere several floors up, his mom lay in a hospital bed dying. Somewhere hundreds of miles away, his dad lay buried in the ground. His poor grandfather seemed more flustered than anything else.

And then there was me. We both sat at this table, and *something* had to breach that gap. "So, how do you know 'Here Comes The Sun'?" I asked.

Ian looked up, but his face remained inscrutable with quiet eyes and mouth in a flat neutral line. He held himself frozen, long enough that the animated chord chart on his phone timed out and faded his screen to black.

"My mom."

*Way to bring up the dying mother.* "Oh. Does she like The Beatles?"

"I dunno. She doesn't really listen to a lot of music. But," he said, taking in a deep sigh, "when I was little, I had this tiny music box. Like, a metal thingy with gears. You wind it up and it would play this melody. My dad told me the name once. I had to look it up to hear the real song. I don't think my mom even knew what it was."

"Cool," I said while fighting a stunned expression. His words put together *why* he'd tried playing it for his mom in the hospital room. Such a connection between parent and child seemed impossible to me, a dimension away from my own childhood. No further words came; Ian played the chorus, except now I saw he actually got one of the notes wrong. He repeated the incorrect melody eight times before I held up a hand. "Hey," I finally said.

"Yeah?"

"You wanna learn the proper way to play that?"

Ian shrugged, then handed Emmylou over. I went first to the B string, bringing it into gradual tune, then strummed a few chords just to check. This wasn't a song that I played regularly or even specifically learned at some point, but one of those evergreen tunes that a bit of musical logic made easy. "See how I'm jumping to the other strings?" I said, plucking away. "Once you know the strings, this kind of stuff becomes natural. And you can also," I said, adding in a few hammer-on flourishes before letting it ring out, "mess around with it. So it's more than just straight notes. Give it life."

Ian leaned forward, his hands meshed in attention.

"You can also play the melody while using the bottom strings as bass," I said, thumb on the thick top string while fingers bounced around. "That's what blues players do. Or—" my hand moved around again, this time supporting the melody with chords at the same time "—something like this."

"So you know that song too?"

"Everyone knows that song," I said, before realizing that I sounded either condescending or like an old fart know-it-all. Which, I supposed I was, but still. "I mean, you hear it everywhere. And it's a really good song, so, you know, just one of those things."

"How long…" Ian started before looking off.

"How long what?"

"I mean, it's like…" His voice trailed off again, and a different kind of angst came off him, not the typical frustrations of his age but something that pulled deeper. "You're just playing, like, wow. And you were in a band."

*Were* was the operative word. But I didn't want to go into that now, not the past or what happened with Copper Beach. "Well…" I said, muting all of the strings with my palm. Funny thing was, it hadn't come naturally. I didn't have an instinct for putting together a melody, and my stubby fingers weren't the hands of a musician. My first guitar barely worked, and I bought it on a whim, more as revenge for what my parents and brother did to my record collection than anything else. "I mean, it takes practice. I started around your age. It just kind of…" I looked down at Emmylou in my hands, the texture of the mahogany body resting against my palm. "Sometimes you just work on it, and then a switch flips. It becomes second nature. You know?" I asked when my back pocket buzzed. A reply from Eric, though I shut off the screen. I had enough drama to deal with here.

"I think so. I just—" Ian stopped, then stood up. "Grandpa."

EJ shot a crooked look my way, though it probably had more to do with the blood spatter across my pants than anything else. His face appeared more sullen than last time, creases digging deeper trenches around eyes that sat narrower than the other night, and he arrived with a hefty sigh. "Your Mom is resting." He looked at us, hands shoved in pockets. "I've been standing too long today," he said, leaning back to stretch.

"I'll get you a drink," Ian said.

"I'm fine."

"Come on, Grandpa. Stop being stubborn."

EJ shook his head, and somewhere under the age and accumulated weight and stress, I saw features that distinctly stood out from my family, like the way one side of his mouth tilted higher when he smiled. "Fine. Just a tea. Maybe a pastry too." Ian nodded, then looked at the suddenly big line, perhaps the last rush before visiting hours ended.

"You brought a guitar?" he asked as he sat down.

"Picked up from a repair shop." That part was true, though the next part was a clear lie. "The shop isn't far from here. Thought I'd stop by."

"I'm relieved Ian's curious about it." EJ paused, lines crinkling his face. "He spends all day staring at his phone. He tried to explain what he's building on it, but you'd probably get it better than me." He gestured at me, surely assuming I was only about ten, fifteen years older than Ian. "He got that from his dad. Enrolled him in coding camp early on. I wonder if that's why he's so shut off. His mom's a school counselor, but even though she tells me what I should be doing with him, he doesn't follow any textbook. Meeting you was a pleasant surprise," he said with a groan. "We need all the help we can get. Honestly, I'd looked for any relatives that might still be around," he added grimly, "in case things..." His voice trailed off, eyes adrift over my shoulder. "That's why I was looking for Laura when I knew we'd be coming up north."

*Looking for Laura.* The urge came to throw that back in his face, to flip the table and make a big scene inside this quiet hospital café about how all of Aunt Laura's relatives cut her off, so the fact that no one had heard from her in generations might have been by her own choosing.

For me, blood was sustenance, like a slice of toast.

For Aunt Laura, it meant far less.

I squashed those feelings, fingerpicking an improvised tune while EJ continued. "And actually," he said, "I thought I might find my sister there. I heard a long time ago that she talked to Laura, but that was just a rumor. She might be on the other side of the world for all I know." He stopped, and shook his head with a snort. "Ran off with some rock band years ago. She'd probably like you."

*Some rock band.*

A coolness came to my face, probably causing my natural pale skin to bleach even further. Was there someone else in my family who'd followed my path?

"Ian tried to find her but there were too many people with her name. He said it's just harder to find people my age." EJ shook his head with a *tsk.* "She stayed away too. She must have had her reasons."

"I think..." My words came out carefully, each one selected with precision. I certainly didn't know anyone named EJ, but this stirred something weird. "I think my parents are several branches removed from you."

"What are your parents' names?"

"Patti and Lou." Which was metaphorically correct; I'd considered Patti Smith and Lou Reed more important in my early years than anyone I was related to.

"Don't know them. Ah, well," he said with a sigh.

Something still didn't add up, like the drums from one song played under the guitar from another. "I don't think Laura ever mentioned anyone named EJ either."

"Well, she may not have ever known me as that," he said. "My wife started calling me that when we were dating. She had an ex with my first name, so she went with my middle name as a joke. But she said Elijah was 'too biblical' so she started calling me EJ, and everyone else picked up on it." He smiled, the kind that mixed several emotions into one look, and I knew right away that his wife was no longer alive. "I like EJ better. She helped me loosen up as EJ. I was such a stick in the mud as Stephen."

Stephen.

As in my brother Stephen.

Every smirk, every argument, every moment of burning disdain coalesced into something both sharp and inscrutable. As I sat under the cheap hospital lighting with a guitar in my lap, suddenly everything made sense and yet none of it did at all.

Images of stacked records on a tiny suburban porch flashed through my mind, and that thought propagated into a white-hot fury.

That smirk.

I'd recognized it moments ago. Stephen, whom I last talked to when he was twenty or twenty-one, but came with a lifetime of animosity egged on by our parents from the moment he arrived. "Oh," I said, my throat suddenly dry. "Got it."

How did he not recognize me? But then of course he wouldn't. It'd make no sense for him to think his older sister still looked like a twenty-something. Besides, I had different hair now, a modern A-line cut beyond his years.

A reflexive tension crept in, and I glanced over at Ian in line, lost in his phone while he waited.

Diving into a device seemed like a good idea. Rather than go any further with EJ, I pulled my phone out and acted like some important message came. Messages *did* await me—several texts from Eric, apparently—but I loaded my email, staring intently at spam from music gear vendors on their latest discounts. The device vibrated again, another text from Eric that I swiped away without a glance. "Well, we should get going," EJ said as Ian walked back, tea in one hand and crinkled brown paper sack in the other. "Thanks for coming by."

"Good luck with the cranberry sauce," Ian said. EJ offered a wave and started his shuffle off, but Ian hesitated, bouncing his focus between Emmylou and my eyes. I replied with a nod, and when Ian didn't move, I gave a thumbs-up after several seconds, for no reason other than something had to break this stalemate.

Ian opened his mouth. "I..." he started, but then my phone lit up again with Eric across the top, this time a full-blown phone call. Ian shook his head before trotting off to match his grandfather—my long-lost, very estranged brother—and I looked at my glowing screen.

Did I get back in his good graces with one text? The phone continued buzzing, pausing only for the call to ring out before he tried again.

My finger slid across the screen to answer the call. "County Morgue," I said.

"Louise? Is that you?"

"Yeah, yeah, I'm just kidding around. I'm—"

"Are you safe? Has anyone noticed you?"

"I'm fine and—wait, what?" The first part of my answer came out instinctively, a polite expected response. The second part showed my real reaction.

That was a very strange question to take while sitting in a hospital café with a guitar.

"I want you to stay right where you are." A weird urgency carried his voice, a combination of clarity and frenzy that seemed completely unlike the guy who hosted community events. "I need to see it for myself. I'm almost there already. *Don't* talk to anyone."

# CHAPTER 10

MY FINGERS GRIPPED THE handle, the metal appropriately cold, given the dim light ahead. The door pushed open
with the weight of resistance, an unexpected hesitation cutting into the pace that had carried me from Eric along a direct
route here. I blinked, the sudden realization that I'd left Eric…

To get to this door. But which door was this?

Time slipped by as I took in slow breaths, grounding my
memory back in the place I stood, the path I took here, the
conversation with Eric—and the sudden realization I'd left him
at the blood bank without any clue what he actually planned
to do. Should I run back? I pulled out my phone, and as if he
anticipated the question, a single text awaited me: We're fine.
Go see your friend.

My friend, as in the dying distant relative that I'd never met.

The last few minutes started to come into focus. It started
innocently enough, with Eric arriving at the hospital café. I
plucked Emmylou's strings to play The Pixies' "Here Comes

Your Man." If this was a movie, my solo noodling would have switched to a slow-motion entrance while the full song kicked in, coattails swishing out as he pulled sunglasses off.

But this was real life, so rather than the dramatics, I played the riff a few times as he walked hurriedly in, distress on his face in ways he'd never shown at his events. Any weirdness from the meeting disappeared, and instead he'd asked about the hospital's blood bank, then asked me about anyone and everyone I'd encountered since I got here. Which amounted to the front registry admin, one nurse in passing, one half-asleep person at the blood bank, and my semiestranged family members. He'd nodded, taking notes in a very analog, very old-fashioned Moleskine notebook with a ballpoint pen, then his calm demeanor returned as if by a switch.

"You should go see whoever you'd registered to see."

"Oh, it's fine," I'd said, "I should get back to my dog and—"

"Louise," he said, his voice suddenly carrying a very steady, deliberate cadence, "you should go see your friend."

And then I was here.

I looked at my phone to check the time—still about two hours before my shift started. And right next to the bright white digits sat a new icon, something I'd never seen before— did I let Eric install his community app on my phone?

I blinked the fuzziness away, then realized I held a bottle, something he'd offered me and I'd apparently drunk given its half-empty state. A label wrapped it, a strawberry and a grape with cartoon eyes betraying the fact that it was clearly blood sloshing about inside.

Maybe it had sat too long, or had a rare blood type that my body didn't like. Could intolerances develop at my age? I shook those concerns away and looked ahead—I'd decided to use my visitor badge to get here, I might as well understand what brought my extended family into my life.

Sonya lay still, various tubes hooked into her arms, gadgets and display screens around her. The blankets tucked almost to her neck, and despite the state of things, her chest rose and fell with strong breaths.

As a young adult, the idea of death felt alluring, all goth vibes, black eyeliner, and punk bravado, reciting lyrics and romanticizing the end while sitting in dull suburbia. But the strange thing about being a vampire, despite the whole mythos of morbid gloom, was that the actual prospect of death proved to be quite frightening. Even at the hospital, I only emptied wastebaskets.

I never encountered death on this level.

Seeing Sonya up close conveyed something different, and suddenly, Ian's desire *not* to be there made sense. The stench of death wasn't some sort of spiritual gloom or dramatic decay. Death arrived cold and sterile, a neat small room filled with the low buzz of machines. It was a stasis, not a preservation, and the lack of any type of movement made me want to escape to my small house, burrowing deep into my guitars and drums, a place where the only risk came from my dog's accidental messes and blood supply issues.

"Are you just going to stand there?"

Sonya's voice caught me off guard, breaking me out of my stupor. It carried a surprising strength and clarity despite the slowed pace. "Oh," I managed, then scanned the room for the nearest wastebasket to empty. In the corner, a metal circular tin sat with a single crumpled wrapper for a granola bar, probably from EJ. It fit with the Boy Scout I knew decades ago. I gripped it, the plastic liner slipping under my fingers, and I held it up. "I'm just doing this."

Sonya started opening her eyes, blinking as she tracked me. "I'm on so many drugs, I might be hallucinating. I thought you were a visitor. Like," she said, her words slurring a little bit, "a mystery visitor."

"A mystery visitor?"

"Yeah, like maybe the Grim Reaper wears a visitor sticker."

I glanced down at the name tag pasted on me, then back at Sonya as we studied each other. Though she might have just stared through the fog of medication in her system. "Death is here with a hoodie and her name is—" she shifted in her place, eyes squinting "—Louise. Shouldn't your hood be up?"

Guess her vision was still twenty-twenty.

"I'm not Death," I said, realizing the irony of that statement. "I'm…" The word drifted in the air, lingering as Sonya's eyes gradually shut, and I considered leaving it at that. Several breaths passed, the only noise coming from a car honking outside. Her eyes snapped open, a quick scan of the room until they found me again. I put the wastebasket back where it should be. "It's a little late for visitors, isn't it? I should go."

"Meh," she said, the side of her lip curling up, "take what you can get these days."

Despite her state, a mischievous glint came to her eye, one that made me wonder how she could be Stephen's—that was, EJ's—kid. The EJ I knew, in full Stephen mode, was quiet, serious, standoffish. And maybe he was only that way with me, the Golden Child/Black Sheep model built by our parents, though his attitude certainly didn't help. Even now, just *knowing* EJ's true history, tension wrapped me, ready to roll my eyes and step away from it all.

The urge came and went, leaving me with a stranger in a hospital bed.

"I'm," I said, "a distant relative."

"Oh," she started before inhaling hard. "The musician. Ian mentioned you."

I looked at her face, eyes and cheeks that showed traces of her dad and her son. And, I supposed, me, though no other connections wove between us. It wasn't just generations that created distance. It was whole other worlds, like I belonged to a parallel dimension. My life existed within the confines of gut-trembling bass and earsplitting feedback, a loner urbanite with a goofy dog compared to her suburban worries about bills and school districts. And that had nothing to do with being a vampire, except that condition allowed me to stay where I wanted, as long as I wanted. "The musician. That's me."

"Well," she said, pausing long enough to show that something in her body wasn't right, "stay if you want. I'm kinda stuck here."

I did stay, in fact. Not too long, since I had to get to work, only about twenty minutes or so. Sonya seemed to enjoy the company despite having zero idea who I was—who I purported to be or my actual identity. Instead, it might have been that she needed to speak to someone who wasn't sticking needles in her, assessing her chances of survival, or walking through a shroud of unspeakable tragedy. I came to her as a simple visitor, a ship passing through the night thanks to the slightest of relations.

But rather than talk about myself, Sonya seemed much more curious about Laura. "She'd said she was born twenty years too early," I said, adjusting on the stiff plastic chair next to the bed. "She talked about her admiration for how her community turned the AIDS crisis into a political movement, something that unified them into becoming a voice. Becoming visible. Her late girlfriend was a very loud activist. But then she'd turn to me, unable to see but just knowing where I was. And she'd say, 'God bless 'em, but I'm too tired to do all that.'"

Sonya laughed—quiet, reserved, something that only created tiny ripples in her body rather than the crest and fall of hearty guffaws. But she smiled, and a sigh came with it. "She sounds," Sonya said, before closing her eyes, "fun."

"Yeah, she was," I said before realizing that my real age probably broke this story. "I mean, I was young. I only understood later. But I'm lucky I got to live with her."

"You met Ian?" Her eyes remained shut, and that simple distinction caused her voice to carry a disembodied quality.

"I did."

"He's a cool kid. Been through a lot. Probably tired of everyone telling him that. Me especially. Blame my child psych degree," she said, pausing for a breath halfway through the last sentence. "Also, he swears too much. Always eating, always swearing. That's my son."

My laugh came out in sync with hers, hers gradually fading away as she settled back into the bed. "Yeah, he really does, huh?"

I sat after, waiting for Sonya to reply, and in the passing seconds, I started putting together ways to gracefully exit before this got awkward.

But it turned out I didn't need to. Sonya's breath turned steady and deep, and her eyes remained shut. I watched her descend into rest, traces of our laughter still visible on the corners of her mouth. My phone showed two further texts from Eric, one thanking me for the tip.

And, of course, a reminder to stay in touch.

I stood, stretching out the stiffness in my back from the harsh chair, and walked to the room's door. On the other side of it was an escape back to the familiar. It felt comfortable despite the fact that I had an ice chest sitting in my car with bags of blood. I planned on dropping the blood at home, maybe giving Lola an extra hug too before heading into work. But first, I lingered for a few extra seconds, taking in the scene in front of me. Marshall and Laura hovered in my thoughts as I forced myself to confront what real death looked like: lonely, empty, and unfair.

# CHAPTER 11

**VAMPIRE POWER MYTH #4:** A vampire must be invited into your home.

The truth is actually much simpler. Any being can cross any threshold. No mystical force field existed other than societal politeness.

On your phone, though, you have to give permission—vampire or human.

I'd *thought* about deleting Eric's app since it'd been installed at the hospital last night, but staying up-to-date on the current blood situation overcame my technoparanoia. I'd kept my phone as app-free as possible, using a web browser and bookmarks more than any branded app to avoid companies peering into my life.

This, however, was different. Eric wouldn't have a public site for the vampire community. It'd be the app or nothing, and for now, I needed to know about possible blood distribution.

So I gave permission, as in, checking the permissions form when it appeared. I invited Eric's app into my life.

Actually getting access wound up being a bit of a chore, because the first screen brought up a form that required all sorts of info, including date turned, how many humans you regularly interacted with—the types of things that made me squirm as I typed. Eric's ability to dance around the word *vampire* or *blood* remained impressive, though—and probably smart in case someone stumbled upon the app. In fact, to the uninitiated, it probably would have seemed like a very odd dating app.

After all those hoops, it said I needed to be approved, which happened during my usual prework routine of changing into scrubs, walking and feeding Lola, and making myself hospital-presentable. Sometime during that, the full version of the app auto downloaded, the icon updated from a technical group of letters and numbers to a simple white triangle without any text below it.

I didn't know Eric very well, but this seemed considerably humorless, given the ridiculousness of vampires-meet-tech. Would it really hurt to use a blood drop or a bat or something fun as the icon?

But once I got past that, the actual app loaded considerably more data than I expected. No pixelated versions of Dracula came up. The first tab was simply a copy of his community texts, the second was an ongoing thread of conversation: people asking questions, people answering questions, people arguing about the question, then people arguing about the answers.

And after I opened the app, every time a new comment posted, my phone buzzed.

Which, given the speed of arguments within the community, meant 1) more people downloaded this thing than I thought, and 2) this arguing might as well have been shouting into the void. None of it helped the current situation, but it did prove just as irksome as human social media. Rumors kicked around, from speculation of the vampire assault's perpetrator to further theories about ancient powerful vampires with superpowers. I didn't know if Eric and his community leaders had fixers, but they sure could use a forum moderator.

After a deluge of nonstop notifications, the app didn't seem worth the trouble. My fingers swiped through my Settings menu to remove Eric's app. But shortly after the circular processing icon started swirling, a message appeared.

Unable to delete application. Contact the application's developer for further information.

Well, that wasn't fair. Eric never said feeding the community was in exchange for all of our private information—I really, really did not want targeted vampire ads based on his stupid app. Did I have to manually remove it? Learn to hack phones? Vaguely post about it on Reddit? I knew how to program drum loops but that skill wouldn't help here.

I shoved my phone in my pocket; this wasn't getting solved tonight. I didn't even know *how* to solve it. Between blood bags and surprise relative visits, a standard night of janitorial duties before coming home and zoning out sounded wonderful. Especially with a snoring corgi at my feet and a drop of vodka in my rationed glass of blood while Nick Cave serenaded me.

I was about to head to SFGH when the doorbell chimed. "Now what?" I said as Lola barked at our visitor. I pulled out my phone to check the security camera, one of the few apps that did exist on my phone.

The image loaded up, a real-time fish-eye lens pointing downward at what appeared to be two people: an older man and a teen.

With a guitar case in his hand.

That was new.

I hadn't seen or spoken to Ian or EJ/Stephen since parting ways at the parking garage. No phone calls or messages came, no acknowledgment of my visit with Sonya—though really, she may not have even remembered it, given the amount of chemicals that pumped through her body. In fact, I realized I never gave them my number, and they didn't seem the type to sleuth it for themselves.

Lola's objections continued until it devolved into a mix of barks and snorts, and the more agitated she became, the more her loose fur drifted into the air. I'd *just* vacuumed, so that was unacceptable; I opened the front door wearing my work scrubs, now washed and free of bloodstains. Lola's nose poked over the blockade of my leg as I held the door. "Oh, hey, you two."

EJ gave an awkward wave while Ian stared at the ground. "Is that your first real six-string?" I asked, laughing at my own bad reference.

"No, it's a guitar," EJ said. Of course they missed it. That was okay, since it was a terrible song. "We stopped by a used music shop this morning. Cheapest one they had."

"That's how you start," I said.

"They even gave us the bag for free."

Ian still didn't look at me, though he finally spoke. "There's a crack in the back." He unzipped the bag and held the instrument for me to see, from the jagged line across the back body to the nylon strings across the neck, something that probably curbed the guitar's sustain and thinned its tone.

But hey, it got him playing.

"That's punk rock. As long as you can form chords, you know?" Neither of them reacted, let alone answered. At my feet, Lola shuffled about, her curiosity causing her snout to jab at my leg. "Well, cool. Awesome that you finally got one and—"

"Will you teach me?" Ian blurted the question out so abruptly that EJ grimaced.

Plenty of musicians supplemented their income by teaching. But also, none of them were vampires, which came with all sorts of logistical problems. Still, given the capabilities of modern technology, long-distance lessons were certainly feasible. "Tell you what," I said, "let's swap email addresses. Start learning with an app, and then we can try to video chat and you can show—"

"No, I mean tonight. Will you teach me?"

"Tonight?" I said. My fingers gripped the door hard enough that it swung on its hinges an inch before I steadied myself.

"What he means is," EJ said in a soft gravel, "I was about to drive down to be with Sonya tonight. But Ian insisted we come by here."

"I've had enough of that place." Ian looked away as he spoke, and I knew *exactly* what he meant: the emptiness of Sonya's room, the cold rhythm of the machines and monitors, the unnerving peace of only doctors and nurses shuffling about through the hallways…

"I'm about to leave for work," I said, gesturing at my scrubs. Ian's face didn't quite fall, but the edges around his eyes softened, cracking at the bluntness of my statement. "I mean—"

"You see?" EJ said, patting his grandson on the shoulder. I looked at EJ, defeat carving into his expression. Was that defeat for him or Ian? Or maybe the weight of everything? He didn't look like the brother I knew. That simple act of tenderness, of empathy, that seemed completely out of my brother's realm of possibility.

Could people really change? The scars of our life together dug deep enough that I shrugged the thought off. His very presence sparked an instinctive defiance, a mental door shutting that would never let him back in.

Because nearly fifty years ago, he'd betrayed me. We were never best buds, but I had enough big sister instincts to look out for him during our early years. By the time I hit middle school, a change crept in, starting with the fact that grades and sports came more naturally to him. The disdain my parents gave me turned to praise for him, building a gradual splinter between us.

And on one high school afternoon, that splinter erupted into a chasm. I'd come home from school during my sophomore year after taking the long way around—the way that included a Tower Records at a nearby strip mall, my black 70s punk mullet buried beneath my hood as I walked quickly to avoid any unwanted attention across the rougher blocks. That extra effort proved to be worth it, just to thumb through the week's new releases, lines of large thin cardboard sleeves ready for perusal. Sifting through the options, listening to the overhead speakers, all of it became a meditation of sorts, something I continued doing until brick-and-mortar music stores ultimately died out in the early 2000s.

That day didn't start with anything particularly special. No new releases came out, no surprise discoveries grabbed my attention, no hidden treasures lay buried behind the wrong stack. The only reason that day stood out stemmed from what happened when I got home. Pre-EJ Stephen sat on the porch steps thumbing through a magazine when he noticed me coming down the sidewalk.

As I approached, his peculiar expression grew clearer. Not his usual neutral blankness, but crooked lips and a rare triumphant glint in his eye.

He *sneered*. A goddamn sneer. And before I had a chance to say a word, my little brother reached up to push open the door, letting my parents' voices float out. Even without their exact words, I knew the rhythm of when their Cantonese dialect carried anger. I slowed, taking in the expression on Stephen's face as he turned back to his magazine.

Then I stopped.

Not at the sneer, not at the bits of Cantonese I picked up and processed. But at the stack *behind* Stephen.

My records. About twenty of them, with the Kinks' *Lola Versus Powerman and the Moneygoround* at the top.

Everything that I had bought over the past year since discovering the power of Velvet Underground. "What did you do?" I let out, more a demand than a question. He ignored me, reading *Sports Illustrated* like I didn't exist, the growing sense of violation in my gut propelling me. "What did you do?" I repeated, this time, snatching the purple LA Kings cap off his head and tossing it like a Frisbee to the sidewalk.

"Louise!" my mom yelled from inside.

"What did I do?" he asked quietly. "I didn't do any drugs. That was you."

I turned to the entryway, and halfway down the hall, Mom stood holding a tiny baggie purchased a few weeks prior, in the back alley behind Tower Records. It had been an impulse decision. Hell, I didn't even know how to properly smoke it— the mere *idea* of owning something illegal, that was the actual allure.

"I haven't smoked it," I protested to anyone who would listen. My mind raced with excuses, but who could I blame without throwing one of my few friends under the bus? "I—"

"It's the music," my father said, coming into view. "Why you just can't be normal? Look at Stephen. He listens. He plays sports. He studies. Ever since you started listening to that music, you ignore your schoolwork."

That wasn't true. I'd ignored schoolwork basically since middle school started. School existed as a dimension of antagonism, with teachers who just wanted to retire, and girls who just talked shit, and boys who wouldn't even bother with me, given my black hair and Chinese features. Why *wouldn't* I ignore school?

I glared at Stephen, who'd retrieved his hat and put it back on, and it might as well have carried a halo for academics and a medal for using athletics to overcome any issues around looking different. And our parents certainly weren't shy about pointing that out.

"You waste your mind on this garbage?" Mom asked, each word of broken English laced with a sting. "You know what we do with garbage, we throw it out."

My mom stormed forward and put the small bag on the stack of records, something untouched since I'd stashed it behind a shoebox at the top of my closet, and yet it was as if my entire sense of self lay in a small bag of back-alley weed. "You put all of this in the garbage. Now."

"What?"

"Your music and your drugs. In the garbage."

"Wait—those are my records. I bought those."

"With allowance *we* give you. You get a job, you buy your own records."

Which I couldn't do at that age. I was fifteen, too old to babysit and a year too young to apply to Tower Records. Though I would, I'd already sworn that to myself.

"And it smells bad too," Stephen said with a look that told me *he'd* been the one to find it. *He* had snooped through my stuff. *He* had touched my shit.

What else had he gone through in my room?

That afternoon, I'd done as I'd been told, but everything shifted, an inner defiance surging strong enough to tilt my axis from feeling misunderstood to a deeper loathing that radiated around me. And the next day, it was as if nothing happened. Dad still watched baseball with my brother. Mom still took her long walks. The anger disappeared from their voices, but judgment remained with every look.

One week later, I'd set out on a walk, a journey for sheer physical distance. I returned, though, with a garage-sale guitar that wouldn't stay in tune. But that little defect didn't matter; the moment I saw the instrument, I simply knew.

If they wouldn't let me have my records, I would make my own goddamn music.

I looked at the guitar in Ian's hand, wondering if it gave him the same pull I had all those years ago.

"She works nights," EJ said. "Come on, we should go—"

"Actually," I said, causing them both to pause halfway through their first steps off my porch. "You know what? It's, um, unique circumstances. I can call in sick tonight."

Ian turned. His mouth started to curl into a smile, but his cheeks trembled, like they stifled the urge. But I didn't know if that was because he wanted to appear cool or if something in him wouldn't allow a breath for enjoying little victories. Either seemed possible.

"Fair warning, I don't have many snacks." Ian nodded at that, and though he tried to hide the beaming grin on his face, it slipped past any attempts to be cool. EJ nodded and mouthed a word of thanks. He went over some evening logistics with Ian while I nudged Lola back and considered if I had anything to hide. But as long as we focused on music, things would work out.

"Now," I said, opening the door wide as EJ returned to his car, "have you thought of a name for your guitar?" He shook his head no as I gestured inside.

I invited Ian in.

## CHAPTER 12

LOLA CONTINUED HER ROLE as the world's most inept guard dog, belly flopping as soon as we stepped inside the house. Ian still gripped his guitar by the neck, though he hadn't developed the spatial awareness to avoid knocking its body against the doorframe on his way in. This didn't slow him down, and I watched him pause to take in my home.

He'd been here earlier, of course. But that involved a dash down the hallway, then arguing with his grandfather before returning. I tracked his eyes as he moved from the framed Fillmore concert posters to the three-picture frame sitting on an end table.

"Is that Laura?" he asked. "The person who used to live here?"

"Yeah." The confluence of Ian, his grandfather, my own family history, and Laura's rift with her relatives all coalesced into one very strange moment, one that I figured Laura would have appreciated. She'd appreciate anyone holding a guitar, really. I took in the sight, the silhouette of a boy and a guitar at my altar of Laura, until I realized one age-defying problem.

One photo was Laura sitting on the front porch of this house with Howie. One was her standing at Alcatraz circa 1993, a tiny Joan Baez onstage behind her.

Another showed us on the pier—not the tourist side, but farther south where it sat quietly, the perfect spot to just exist.

Also, I looked exactly the same in the photo except for a '90s Winona Ryder-esque pixie haircut.

"So, let's get in my studio room," I said, taking steps down the hallway. I shut the living room lights off too, hiding the photos in the dark. "It's soundproofed."

"Who are those bands?" he said, finally breaking from the photo frame.

Ian was behind me, which meant that my grin remained hidden from him, fangs and all. "They're all very good. You should check them out."

We set up in my home studio, Ian sitting on the stool that normally went under my KORG keyboard rig. From his fumbling fingers, it was clear he'd been practicing, his pinkie still working to get the final string on the G chord, but at least it sounded mostly correct when he strummed with his thumb. He glanced up, though he quickly looked back down when he saw me looking.

I tried to play it cool, of course.

"You've been practicing?" I picked Emmylou off the wall—might as well start with someone he was familiar with.

"A little. I read to start with G and C because they're pretty close to each other." He tried again, fingers fumbling the transition. "And I tried D because it's kind of there too. Oh, and I almost learned barre chords." His words sped up, the moodiness from earlier transformed into a tangible giddiness that he couldn't hold back. "I looked them up, and I can kind of get F, so it's almost there. And I looked up the chords for—"

"Okay, that's great," I said, trying to stop his freight train without being dismissive. "Let me just see where you're at. Follow me." Clean chords on acoustic strings reverberated out, a simple pattern of eight strums as I tapped my foot to keep time. My head nodded with each beat, and I watched as Ian matched me from G to C and back several times, his cheeks lifted in a smile.

I knew that look.

"Let's try that D," I said after a few minutes, moving my fingers. "You're getting this."

Ian's strings caught, his fingers muting his strings. His knuckles bent, the grip not quite there, and the grin disappeared from his face. His lip curled with visible teeth and a sudden "Goddamn it" came out, loud enough to stop me. "Sorry," he said after several blank seconds, "I just want to get it right. I had it earlier, I swear." Before I could offer any hints, he started up again, only for the same scene to repeat; this time his cursing raised the bar to a full "Fuck."

The word came out with enough venom that it clearly had nothing to do with forming a guitar chord. His scowl remained, and I wondered which direction his rage really went.

Maybe every direction.

"Hey, it's okay. There's one song, 'When Doves Cry' by Prince—I've tried to play it for years. The opening riff is impossible. I try and my hands slip off. It happens," I said. "D can be a little tricky at first—your fingers have to squish in. Forget the bottom string, just play the first two." Emmylou rang out as I showed him. "And wrap your thumb around the top to mute out the big string." Ian shook his head, focusing back on the moment. The pressure building in him seemed to subside, releasing with every successful strum of a D chord.

His success evolved gradually, C to D to G, and then again

and again. They rang out slightly out of time and with the buzz that came when fingers failed to cleanly hold frets, yet for the most part, it worked. I played with him, taking the lead on changes and rhythm until he instinctively moved between the formations.

"Hey," I said, a new idea coming to mind. "Do you want to play a song?"

He gave a nod, a quicker and smaller one than normal, like he tried to cover up his excitement.

"Now, if you were paying me like a regular guitar teacher, I'd make you start with something like 'Hot Cross Buns.' But we're just hanging out. So here are some easy punk songs, only three or four chords. Have you ever heard of the Ramones?"

He shook his head.

"Okay, then," I said, my mind cycling through bands that would probably have songs with a combination of C, D and G in their songs. "Black Flag?"

He shook his head again. Which songs did I learn first?

"The Stooges? The Kinks?"

More headshakes, then a deflated sigh.

"Okay, look." The fingers of my left hand rested across the fretboard, muting Emmylou's strings. "I agreed to teach you guitar. But tonight's going to be a full musical education." I debated whether to go to my vinyl collection, but for simplicity tonight, I pulled out my phone. "These songs will change your life."

"Disco?" Ian asked several hours later, a derogatory chuckle that told me he only knew of disco from stereotypes.

"You laugh," I said, pausing the Bee Gees' "Stayin' Alive" after ten seconds. Perhaps I shouldn't have gone with such a well-known song. "Okay, look. When I was growing up, I laughed at disco too. All punks did." We'd been at it a while now, most of the time Ian's fingers fumbling through basic major chords while I played him a select mix of punk and indie rock from the '70s onward, with a dip into the '60s for early Bowie and Velvet Underground. But the Bee Gees threw him off. "I mean, anyone who is into rock probably mocks disco. But you dig deeper to see how important it is. Without disco, there's no dance music, there's no new wave. There's no hip-hop. There's no electronica, there's no pop music from the aughts. Everything in music is just pieces and genres mashing together. One thing becomes another. It's really cool that way. Listen to the bass line. I know the song's cheesy but just listen to that part," I said as "Stayin' Alive" started playing again. "See how it drives the melody?"

From the Bee Gees, we went to The Clash. From The Clash, I pulled up Duran Duran to show how they brought those sounds together. From there, I pulled up Throwing Muses to show how rhythm and key could shift midsong, then I capped it with 2000s dance-punk. Songs blended together, a playlist that answered Ian's questions, all leading to him sitting up at the end of David Bowie mashing styles together in "Sound and Vision," a glint in his eye. "I get it," he said, a sudden spark to his voice. "The drums and bass and all the stuff on top of it. It's all numbers and objects."

This time, it was my turn for a furrowed brow with a question. "Numbers and objects?"

"In programming. Everything in an algorithm is really just a number. Objects are, like, pieces of it. Sections." He leaned back, his guitar still on his lap this whole time. "Songs are just like code put together."

"I, um," I said, stretching my arms above my head, "I always thought of it more as a vibe."

"I think, like, the vibe is *how* you put it together. But *what* you put together, it's like numbers and objects in code."

For the first time since our disco discussion, Ian began strumming his guitar before stopping and pointing at the bass sitting in the corner. "Can I try that?" Despite usually being precious about my instruments, I pulled Gail—named after bassist extraordinaire Gail Greenwood—off the wall and handed her over. Another hour passed, this time with Ian on the bass while I switched between guitar and drums. Though when he asked why blue painters tape was wrapped around the bottom of each drumstick, I said it was for grip rather than the mild contact allergy vampires got with non-lacquered wood (which made splinters *really* annoying). All the while, I watched as he moved between simple root note rhythms to trying something more melodic, even a little funky. He struggled, of course, given that he'd only really picked up a guitar a few days ago, and I wasn't even going to try to explain how slap bass worked.

But during this, all the different things we tried, from my punk-speed chord progressions to lazy acoustic strumming to drumming a disco beat with my hi-hats, he adapted to it all, his mind working in ways that his fingers couldn't quite grasp yet. The whole time, I kept thinking about what he said: "It's all numbers and objects."

That still didn't make sense to me, but it didn't matter—the part of his brain wired for all that coding stuff now connected to the tapestry of musical possibilities. And for one evening, we didn't talk about his angst or his parents or his fears. Instead, this distant relative, this teen that I barely knew, absorbed everything I said about all forms of music, processing it in his own way—a way that maybe I didn't get, but it was pretty punk rock of him to do it himself.

Halfway through an impromptu drum-and-bass jam, Ian stopped and pulled his phone out of his pocket. I paused my beat, hands, reaching over to silence the hi-hat. "It's Grandpa," he said, "I forgot to check in."

"Guess we were too hard-core. I'll drive you to the hotel." I flipped devil horns with my hands, but he didn't quite understand the gesture. "Sorry we didn't learn more chords."

"It's okay. I got a little more out of it." He looked at his phone again. "Grandpa's always checking in on me."

The brother I knew, he did the same thing. Through extra looks and overheard conversations, through nudges from our parents about what trouble I might have been up to. An instinctive annoyance burned at me, and I forced myself to take a moment, reset.

Same person. Different lifetime. My brother's habit of butting in seemed to stay with him, but the motivation for it? His concerns about Ian came from somewhere else completely.

In fact, standing there, watching Ian fumble through tuning his guitar, brought a similar feeling. "I don't know what you're doing tomorrow," I said while loading a map, "but we can jam again." The screen flashed before displaying a twelve-minute route to their hotel. "If you want," I said, tapping the big button to confirm that he was ready to go.

I glanced over at Ian, who focused on plucking a string while he turned the tuning pegs. Even though he seemed to be trying to avoid looking back at me, I saw his cheeks rise in what had to be a smile.

This sparked the most surprising revelation of the day: like Ian, I felt the urge to smile. And like Ian, I tried to hide it.

**CHAPTER 13**

**VAMPIRE POWER MYTH #5:** Vampires live a glamorous, alluring, *sexy* life.

I suppose that was all relative, but I was pretty sure my recent days wouldn't draw anyone to immortality. Normally, I'd spend my weekends in my music studio—weekends, as in Tuesday and Wednesday, given my out-of-sync work schedule. So having Ian drop by to discover guitar chords and good bands, well, other than the company, it wasn't that different. On Tuesday, he visited with Sonya during daylight hours. Then, EJ dropped him off in the evening, my estranged would-be brother seemingly relieved to be free from his grandson's burdens for a few hours.

By the time Tuesday night turned to Wednesday morning, Ian developed some muscle memory in his chord changes. Better still, we didn't talk about death or family secrets or anything like that. We played music, and though it was rudimentary at best, the groove of a live partner strumming along meant conversation came in notes and beats, not words and feelings. This made everything work out far better.

The boy even seemed to have practiced a little by the time he came by on Thursday. "I found out something this morning."

"What's that?" I asked as I popped on my amp.

"Did you know New Order used to be a band called Joy Division? They're really good. Like, unique." The question came out so earnestly I turned to avoid laughing in his face, and instead I wound up looking at a framed photo of Laura. She stood, posing in front of a lit hotel on Market Street while I snapped the picture, the people around us oblivious to the in-joke that an actual vampire was at the site of the opening scene from the movie *Interview with the Vampire*.

"I did," I said after a second. "In fact—" I tapped on the photo "—I had to explain it to her. Laura. She always got them confused about which came first. But that's okay. She introduced me to political folk."

"Political folks. Like, a senator?"

"No, no," I said with a laugh that prompted him to defensively scowl. "Political folk music. Like, songs that are angry. But pretty. Here," I said, loading up my music app. I looked over at Laura in the photo, thinking she would have loved this conversation. "This song is about two people who were executed for political purposes." The opening piano to "Here's To You" chimed through my studio's speakers, and as Ian listened to the layers of instruments coming in to lift Joan Baez's voice, I closed my eyes, the song taking me back to a different time with Laura.

The last time with her, in fact.

"How are you?" Laura had asked, her voice barely audible from the hospital bed. Her right hand slowly rose, finger pointed at the window. "It's late."

Her grasp of time, of the oncoming daylight surprised me, given that she'd been in and out all evening. But perhaps this was one of those unexpected bursts of adrenaline, and I'd decided to take her lucidity for all it was worth at the moment.

"You're here?" I asked.

"Of course I am. I'm not hanging out with John Lennon yet. Should I say hi for you when I get there?" She smiled and her chest rose like a laugh coiled up for release but dissolved into her bones. "Or who is that fellow you like, the one with the deep voice?"

"Ian Curtis," I said, taking her hand. My eyes welled, and I reached into my bag for a pack of wet wipes, ready to clean any blood-tinted tears.

"I'll look for him," she said, a surprising strength in her sudden squeeze. That single gesture ignited a storm of despair at what I was losing, and a new idea appeared, desperation in the form of one last impossible idea.

"Aunt Laura, what if…" My voice quivered with a few mere words, and I tried again. "What if… I mean, there might be a way to—" I stopped, my fang digging into my lip hard enough to pierce. I dabbed the blood that oozed and tried again. "I mean, the way I am, you know there's no harm in—"

"Louise, you're being silly. I don't want that," she said with eyes closed.

"Listen. Maybe I'm not clear. I'm talking about—"

"I know what you're saying. The *V* word." She put a finger to her lips, the corners curled up in sly reference to our secrecy over my condition.

My free hand joined our clasped fingers, wrapping them over tight. "Yeah. That."

"You said you couldn't do it."

That wasn't necessarily true. I said that supposedly it had a slim chance of success, along with a high probability that it would kill me. But those were rumors, I'd never known anyone who'd actually attempted it. Maybe it always worked and we are all just too afraid to try it. "Well, that's what everyone says but I mean, I remember the woman who did it. *Something* has to work."

"But she never told you. You said no one knows," she said with a cough. "Besides, your rules."

"No, *fuck* the rules," I spit out instinctively.

"Even if you figured out a way, wouldn't I just be frozen like this?"

"I mean…" I started, excuses filling up my head. "I think you'd heal. Our immune systems are much stronger. Look, my hay fever doesn't bother me anymore—"

"Does it take forty years off my age?"

"No." That part, I was certain of. Even though I didn't know—hell, no one really seemed to know—how we were turned, there was plenty of evidence showing the plain truth of being frozen at whatever age you turned.

"Well, I can barely move. And everything hurts. That sounds terrible. If I can't fly or hypnotize people, I don't want any of it."

Damn it. Why did we go see *Interview with the Vampire* together? "There's gotta be a way."

"Louise. I hate rules too, but this time you should follow them. Stop this bullshit and be happy. Think of," she said, drawing in a deep breath, "all the great bands you'll be lucky enough to see. Even if I was like you, I couldn't do that. In fact, maybe you'll listen to me now. Because I always hear you."

I blinked, then tried reading her face for clarity. Were the drugs making her spout fortune-cookie wisdom? "I'm not sure what you mean."

"I hear you, every damn day in your room playing your guitar. And I'm telling you, stop hiding. Go find a band to play with."

She'd told me that off and on over the previous year, and I always argued with the very obvious fact that I was a vampire. Slight detail that prevented public engagement. "I can't, I'm a—"

"I know what you're going to say. And I was being polite before, but fuck it. I'm dying. You say you can't, but I know it's not because of *V*," she said, stopping to take in a breath. I leaned forward, though I already knew what she was going to say.

Because the reason had always been there. It would always be there, about everything, and I needed someone—I needed Aunt Laura—to kick it down.

"It's because," she said, "of what your parents said to you. Everything my sister told you. It's everything they said to me. And you know what I say—fuck 'em. Go play in a band. Be happy. If *V* gets in the way, figure it out later. Maybe even find someone. All respect to you and Howie, but I was happiest when Natalie was around."

Natalie being Laura's partner, who died of a stroke shortly before I moved to San Francisco. "You know I can't— I mean—" I paused, searching for the right words "—my hardware doesn't work anymore."

"Love is more than that," she said with a heavy breath. "If you let it. That's the trick."

I came to prop up Aunt Laura when her body betrayed her. And here she was, pep-talking me at the very end, perfecting her ability to zing me in the ways I never expected, but usually needed.

"Just listen to me, alright?" she asked slowly. "Just listen. Now I'm tired. Do me a favor."

I leaned over, my head in the lap of a frail old woman who did more than my mother ever did. "What's that, Aunt Laura?"

"The CD player in the corner." She referred to the Discman sitting in the corner attached to portable speakers. I'd set it up for her the day before, though the hospital staff must have been playing DJ with the small stack of CDs next to it. "The last track. Put it on Repeat, please."

I nodded and quietly turned it on, the speakers coming to life with an initial *pop*. The CD spun up, and soon, piano

chords rang into the room. I adjusted the volume enough for
it to become background noise as the song ramped up. I knew
it, of course; "Here's to You" was Joan Baez's collaboration
with Ennio Morricone, a repeating refrain of four lines over
and over, a celebration of resistance over injustice. Joan's voice
pierced with clarity, a paradox of calm and rage. I looked out
the window at the encroaching sunrise, the gradual blend from
blue to purple as daylight hinted at its return.

"Ah." The room seemed to shift with her deep breath. "Joan
is the best."

An urge pulled me, an instinct to defy her, grab *something*
to slice open my wrist, a call so clear I pictured myself dripping blood over her lips, all in the blind hope that everything
I'd learned was wrong, that I *could* find some way to bring her
back from the brink. But that would be for me, not her.

Aunt Laura asked that I follow the rules. And move on.

I stood at the foot of the bed, Joan Baez singing about final
moments and triumph while Aunt Laura lay under the sheets,
a quiet smile on her face.

I didn't say goodbye then. I had told myself that I didn't want
to presume, and another day might pass—hell, some sort of
miracle might have snapped her back to herself, and then I'd
have to become a superreligious vampire.

But deep down, I knew: it was simply because I *couldn't* say
goodbye to the first, possibly only person to really know me.
Forming those words proved impossible.

Instead, I let Joan Baez talk for me.

That morning, I went home and crashed, keeping the portable phone's brick-sized handset with me in my darkened space.
It woke me up at some unknown time during daylight hours,
though the nurse's dry voice and soft tone told me everything
before she finished her first sentence. I'd lain in bed, thinking
about the very song Ian was listening to now, how that singu-

lar refrain carried Laura off, a combination of pride and "fuck you" and empathy wrapped into four lines.

A "fuck you" to the disease eating away Laura's body. Or a "fuck you" to the way family had treated us.

Maybe both. And in the days after Laura passed, I did exactly what she asked and started looking for other musicians. Because she was right.

She was always right.

"This lady's just saying the same thing over and over," Ian said about Joan Baez halfway through the song.

"Sometimes that's all you need," I said, feeling some blood tears coming to my eyes. I turned away, glancing at the side of my hand after wiping my face. A hint of red smeared across— not the full-blown allergy attack I'd had during the session with Copper Beach, but enough that I needed cleaning up. "Hey, I, uh…" I started, looking for an excuse to suddenly leave. "I forgot to feed Lola," I said. "You can hop on the drums if you wanna try them."

Several seconds later came the *clack-clack-clack* of corgi nails and soon Lola arrived. Despite already having eaten her dinner, I said the magic phrase "feed Lola," which meant I was now morally obligated in her dog mind. She followed me from room to room, first down the hall, then to the bathroom where I washed my face and hands, then back out to the hall. "Alright, *only* a snack," I said, pulling out my phone at the sudden buzz in my back pocket. A blinking envelope icon indicated a new text message, though my corgi didn't care. "Hold on," I said to Lola, her collar jingling as I opened the cabinet with dog treats. "Jeez, let me check my—"

It *looked* like spam at first, or the type of automated message you get for two-factor authentication or that tried to steal your private information by announcing you've won some giant cash prize *and* free health care.

But after a second, I let it process. This was much better than that.

Call for volunteers—delivery driver needed for emergency blood bag transportation. Requires large trunk space or back seat for safe storage. Driver must provide own cooler. Pickup time tomorrow at noon.

A blood delivery gig—it *seemed* enticing, except I'd never attempted to skim off the top from one of these deliveries before. Hell, I'd never actually done one of these gigs before, and didn't they usually require a Red Cross truck with special equipment in the back? It seemed really, really strange for it to say "bring your own cooler" like it was asking people to bringing beer and potato salad to a normal human barbecue.

Also, the whole noon pickup created a bit of an issue given the whole UV-sensitivity thing. Blood or no blood, this made zero sense to try. Especially without any guaranteed returns. I'd be putting myself in front of a UV firing squad for nothing.

Still, my meager supply wasn't exactly holding strong. Despite the rationing, the headaches and fatigue had started to kick in. I just hid it from Ian as best as I could.

At my feet, Lola hopped and grumbled.

"Right, right. Priorities," I said, opening the cabinet. I shook the box of dehydrated chicken treats, and Lola immediately rolled over and stuck out a paw to high-five. "Showing off now?" I asked when my phone buzzed again.

We highly encourage drivers for the job. You will be rewarded. Thank you for being part of the community.

Now that sort of thing didn't usually come from the Red Cross.

This was a new number, an anonymous five-digit series that meant nothing. Was this ridiculously timed spam? Or was someone skimming the Red Cross's volunteer database? And especially for vampires, that was really strange for it—

*Community.*

All *Eric* talked about was community, and he'd mentioned finding new means of blood distribution. This must have been one of his initiatives, and it wouldn't be surprising if he'd somehow built a connection with a blood drive. So while I didn't appreciate the invasion of privacy, it proved its worth here.

Still, that didn't really overcome the "driving at high noon" problem. But given that this text probably went out widely, I opted to act first and strategize later. The phone's haptic feedback punched while I typed my volunteer response, pausing only to pull up my volunteer ID from an email several years old. The message sailed off, a green check icon confirming it flew across cyberspace, and seconds later a confirmation came in.

I exhaled. The blood was mine. I just had to get to it.

"Louise? You okay?"

I turned to find Ian standing there, along with the sudden realization that the out-of-time drumming stopped some time ago. Lola grumbled again, and though I tried to gently open the sealed, interior plastic treat bag, a lack of blood threw off my motor skills. My fingers tugged with enough force to split it open, the box slipping out of my hands, and Lola charging for the open spill. "Oh, goddamn it." I swooped down to pick up the mess as Lola charged in. "Lola, don't—" I said, reaching for the dustpan next to my garbage can. "Forget it. Enjoy your crumbs."

"You need help?" Ian asked again.

"No, no, I'm fine."

"Just telling you Grandpa texted. He asked if you could drive me back soon. He's going to bed." He squinted, looking down at my dog licking up an already-clean laminate floor, something that was either adorably gross or just gross depending on how much you loved dogs.

"Yeah, sure. One second. Lemme just finish cleaning up."

"You sure you don't need help?"

"I'm good. Keep drumming. I'll get the map ready." He turned away, and while I stared at the texts on my phone, ill-timed kick-and-snare hits started from my studio room, and the combination of the two sparked a new idea in my head.

I couldn't walk in the sun. But I knew someone who could.

As I walked down the hall, questions and ideas coalesced in my mind, Plan Bs and Plan Cs popping in between the sheer audacity of my request. After all, I'd just met this kid a few days ago, and even if he *were* willing to go with me to some industrial park, I'd need some rational cover story for what we'd attempt. And did this break any vampire rules? I didn't think so, since I wasn't revealing or explaining anything.

And besides, I needed to eat.

I stopped, several paces shy of the door, the amateurish drumbeat rolling together like a car trying to turn over. Ian had switched from attempting a standard kick-snare rock beat to using the kit's toms, a sound that almost mimicked...

Was Ian playing *Joy Division*?

I paused, listening to the offbeat drumming. "Fuck," I heard from the room as he abruptly stopped, then it started again. "Goddamn it," he said, repeating the process. He *was* playing Joy Division; somehow, he'd figured out the opening beats to "Transmission." Which meant that he'd *listened* to "Transmission" intensely enough to try and pick up its unique opening rhythm.

I wasn't a parent, but I imagined watching children take their first steps or graduate high school felt similar to this, or maybe similar to when I taught Lola to high-five. I approached the music room, the drumming paused after another curse word, and I heard "Transmission" playing through a tinny phone speaker.

"You almost got it," I said. Ian stopped, red-faced as he looked up.

"Oh. Yeah. I've been listening to the songs we talked about." The snare rattled as he set the drumsticks on them. "You know, one thing they don't tell you about hospitals is that there's just so much waiting. Like, I want to see Mom but I hate waiting in hospitals. It's too much. So I plug in. And just listen."

*Just listen.*

I'd come from completely different life circumstances than Ian, completely different eras. Completely different musical educations. Ian lived in a world of playing any song ever recorded on demand, of learning virtual instruments before playing real ones. We may not have overlapped in anything else, but in those few words, I understood Ian's feelings down to his very core.

"Yeah," I said softly, "I get it." I pointed to the drumsticks sitting on the snare. "But hey, you're picking that up quick."

"It seems easier than figuring out frets."

"Well, then, keep at it." I tried; I really tried not to grin. The last thing Ian probably wanted to feel was some adult projecting grown-up admiration—and that was the last thing I wanted to do. I was cooler than that. "Anyway, we should get going. But I wanted to check something first. Are you going to the hospital tomorrow morning?"

"Not if I can help it."

A different kind of smile came, not one of pride, but opportunity. "Wanna help me with something?" I asked.

**CHAPTER 14**

THERE WAS NO FUNCTIONAL reason to be awake during daytime hours. Except for maybe an all-day music festival, and even I had never risked that, regardless of the lineup. Otherwise, shows never started with the sun overhead. And urban living meant plenty of twenty-four-hour places when needed, as well as online ordering.

Only one thing was worth venturing out into skin-destroying UV rays:

Blood. A blood bag pickup, from a volunteer transport position that may or may not actually be connected to Eric's cagily vampire-not-vampire app.

Not starving was the reason to go out. Even at noon. Which was going to be different from driving at dusk.

As soon as Ian left last night, I searched for coverings available by next-morning shipping, which led to a box of one-size-too-large motorcycle pants waiting for me when I dragged myself out of bed at 10:00 a.m. As I unboxed them, I took down a full serving of blood, and I even wondered if mixing an espresso shot might work, though that would require actually having it available. Without caffeine or sleep, I started my day by steering clear of any potential direct UV contact in my house, all the heavy drapes drawn.

First, I applied a slather of sunblock everywhere, SPF 100. Extra layers on my face, enough to make any exposed skin look like I'd painted whipped cream on my cheeks and nose. Leggings, then the motorcycle pants on top, which, despite their decorative red lines, fit far better over other clothing than the standard "I'm going to see a band" leather pants in my closet. On my feet went two pairs of socks, then my tallest Doc Martens. On my upper half, progressive layers offered more protection: a tank top, then a T-shirt (a Bauhaus one, for luck), then a turtleneck for maximum coverage. Over that was *supposed* to be a balaclava, but none of those shipped overnight. On top of that went a leather jacket, which *was* part of my standard rotation of clothes—emotional armor that doubled as physical armor today. Then thick neon-colored snow gloves circa the 1980s dug out from a box of Laura's things I'd been too reluctant to donate.

The finishing piece came with a helmet—not a motorcycle helmet, but a fairly cheap Daft Punk cosplay of Guy-Manuel used for a concert in Berkeley circa 2007, cheap enough that colored glitter stickers adorned the sides instead of actual LED lights. Which, for my purposes, probably added another layer of blocking out UV.

The doorbell rang, and despite wearing the getup for the past twenty minutes, the combined bulkiness gave me a stiff gait, like a marionette dipped in glue. I took the helmet off and did a mental check of explanations before grabbing the doorknob. As I threw the door open, I jumped back in case any ambient sunlight put me at risk.

Ian didn't say anything at first. Instead, he just looked me over while I waved him in and kicked the door closed.

"Remember what I said about having sensitive skin? That's why I asked you to come," I said. "Burn super easily."

"Okay," he said, with a very noticeable side-eye.

"Oh, but this," I held up the helmet, a sudden burst of inspiration to explain my ridiculous getup, "this is just to show you something cool. Something a little different from guitars and drums. Have you heard of Daft Punk?"

Bass thumped through my car as I disobeyed the navigation route displayed on my phone, the Recalculating icon showing up every few turns as I tried to minimize any direct hits from the sun. My getup did the trick, though; even with the occasional sunbeam, it landed safely on my outer shields. I wouldn't know for sure until I removed everything, but the usual, immediate burning pain of UV exposure wasn't there, though I instinctively flinched a few times.

At which, Ian would ask if I was okay. "Of course," I said, then I'd deflect by saying I was just dancing to the Daft Punk tracks blasting in my car. I'd given Ian a crash course in many genres over the past few days, but mostly to teach different elements of live music. This was his first real foray into electronic music outside of video games and movie trailers, and I kept pointing out how Daft Punk brought bits and pieces from genres together, a bass line from "Voyager" or the 70s-influenced guitar of "Get Lucky."

I did all this with my helmet on, which might have looked like the most elaborate performance art to a passerby. It also meant driving with extra care: slower speeds, minimal lane changes, and excessive checking of mirrors. To Ian, well, he wore an unreadable expression but he asked a lot of questions about programming electronic drums and loops, so that at least distracted from the whole "vampire trying to survive the noon sun" bit. Despite cranking the car's AC as much as possible, my outfit barely breathed, the natural discomfort of "too many layers of clothing plus a cushy helmet with a fogged-up visor" began creeping in.

Still, better safe than sorry. Sorry, as in torched by the sun.

The pickup spot was in a Daly City building nested among a whole hub of business parks, the decay of decades visible on faded street signs and chipped paint. "So where is it?" Ian asked as we rolled into the parking lot. The map on my phone planted an icon squarely in the middle of the very dull, very 1980s-looking structure, but that generic location meant little for the several two-story buildings stacked in rows under the noon sun. Luck was on my side—a filled parking lot meant I had the perfect excuse to pull into the fire lane and hit the emergency lights.

"I'm not sure. Suite F-thirty-three. I guess…" I squinted, though my semifogged, semitinted visor made it difficult to get details. "I guess just look around? Here." I handed over the volunteer badge I'd earned after delivery driver training a few years ago, my twisting leather apparel squeaking as I moved. "Show them this. Lemme call them and give a heads-up."

Ian nodded, examining the badge, then turning to the dull buildings burning in daylight. "Isn't this where those vampire murders happened?"

Shit, he'd been reading the news. "Those were assaults, not murders," I said, like that made it any better. "And they happened a few miles away. At night. Sunlight, you know?" He shrugged as I flipped open my helmet's visor, the overwhelming brightness seemingly harsher than in my memory, and I squinted as I punched in the donation center's phone number. "Hi, this is Louise Chao. I'm the volunteer driver for the day," I said extra loud when the reception picked up. "I'm in the parking lot but I'm in the fire lane right now. I have someone with me. Can they grab the package?" I'd called earlier and the reception person claimed it wouldn't be an issue as long as I gave them my badge, but asking here played along with Ian's expectations.

"Sure, that's fine," the voice said, a slight echo from the speakerphone's projection. "Please give them your badge and your driver's license."

"Great, thanks." I took in a breath of clean air, then flipped down my visor. "Good to go," I told Ian.

His face crinkled as he held up the badge. "I need your driver's license."

"What?"

"She said badge *and* driver's license."

"Did she?" Physically handing my license over to Ian created zero problems. But, if he happened to look at the dates on the shiny plastic card, *that* might be a problem.

It'd been updated, of course, no longer carrying my original birth year of 1956. When I'd moved out to San Francisco, I kept my original until stumbling into Eric, who suggested updating a driver's license every ten years or so, with plans to move or change jobs being the perfect opportunity. He'd revealed that a vampire worked at the main DMV office in Sacramento, rotating positions every six or seven years so no one noticed his lack of aging but staying in the organization as a service to California vampires.

Apparently he loved the vampire community way more than I did, committing to eternity at the DMV.

Problem was, I'd lived in Laura's house since the early 1990s. I'd gotten a new birthdate for my ID in the early 2000s. I'd been at the same hospital job for eleven years, with my boss changing every few years. Staff clamored to get out of the night shift but I didn't, so the people around me lasted only a year or two at best.

So I'd intended to update my ID. It just never seemed necessary, one of those perennial things I'd set reminders for before pushing it out another six months.

Until now.

Because according to my ID, I was in my midforties. Claiming good genetics only went so far. "Oh, right," I said, the car's emergency lights playing a continuous rhythm of blinking and clicking. The top of my helmet bonked into the car's ceiling as I reached for the small backpack behind the passenger seat. I unclasped the top and grabbed my wallet, a black rectangle of fake textured leather with David Bowie's signature lightning bolt printed across it. "Good call."

The car continued humming and Ian turned to his phone, tapping away at the screen.

My ID sat in the first slot of the wallet, my forehead and eyebrows peeking out over the fold. I slid the card out with my thumb, the false birthdate of 1980 and decades-old photo staring back at me. Despite the age of the image, the facial features were all the same—pale complexion, brown eyes, round cheeks, and a crooked smile that, for anyone who looked close enough, showed a hint of fangs.

It would have to do. I flipped the plastic card facedown and handed it over. "Office F-thirty-three. Use the dolly in the back seat, then load the blood into the cooler," I said, thumbing to the folded dolly behind Ian's seat.

"Okay. Guess I'll look around," he said, taking the ID without a second glance. Ian did what was impossible for vampires, stepping directly out into the midday sun. Wind kicked up, blowing the strings of his hoodie over his shoulders, the brightness of direct sunlight causing him to squint. He gave a short wave, grabbed the dolly from the back, and walked into the complex's courtyard.

All I could do was wait.

# CHAPTER 15

**VAMPIRE POWER MYTH #6:** Vampires have magical eyesight, can see in the dark at great distances, and can maybe even gauge heat signatures.

My eyesight was very, very ordinary. Preserved when I turned, so probably not quite 20/20, but still good enough not to need glasses. Definitely without the ability to extract tiny details or sense auras or anything else along those lines.

Though really, in that moment, everything did seem kind of magical. Daylight didn't translate differently for vampire eyes, but I took in things unseen for *decades*. Shadows, reflections; the overwhelming *brightness* of things caused me to squint as I waited, double-parked with emergency blinkers clicking on and off. With my Daft Punk helmet on, I leaned into the moment by blasting a best-of playlist—for fun, yeah, but if anyone knowledgeable passed, at least they'd understand instead of calling security on the strange woman having a car rave.

Time passed, the space filled with four songs and counting.

The opening beats of "Around the World" kicked in while I watched for Ian. My phone buzzed, and I held it up to see a text notification.

My ex-bandmate Pete. I tapped it open, expecting to see a simple check-in hello or another offer for free tickets.

What I got, though, was far more interesting.

> Hey, sorry about the short notice, but are you busy coming up? My band just lost a guitarist and we have a gig in a week. Would you be willing to learn some songs and fill in? After that, who knows? Come by our practice space this weekend. We'll work with your schedule. Yes, I remember you work nights. :)

A no-strings-attached practice and gig? With the possibility of more?

I stared at my phone, images of blood all over David coming to mind, followed by echoes of Sally's freakout. In some ways, this worked even better than Copper Beach—I knew Pete, I could dip my toe in the situation, and maybe it'd be a perfect fit. I'd just need to squeeze it into my work schedule, maybe swap a shift this weekend to prepare, then see how I got on with the rest of the band.

Maybe the fourth time would be the charm. I typed:

> I think so. Lemme take care of one thing and then confirm.

"One thing" was a really mild way to put "survive a delivery under the midday sun" for a vampire, but I kept it simple and watched as a thumbs-up icon came in reply. From there, all I could do was breathe and watch the occasional non-Ian person walk by. Which proved hard to do in my helmet, so, given the safety of my car, I took it off and checked the mirror. Sweat didn't produce the hint of blood like tears did, but it still made me look like hell, with matted hair and running sunblock.

But then it sank in: that was *me* in the rearview mirror. Face tinted white from an excess of sunblock, hair in damp tendrils, and deep lines under my fatigued eyes. Yet in the middle of the day, hanging out during times when UV rays should have killed me.

Except I was very much alive, very much *not* on fire. I sat in the driver's seat of my affordable hybrid car, marveling at the way the sunbeams cut through tree branches and leaves, the way passing birds cast shadows on the pavement, the extreme *blue* of the sky above. I sat for minutes, simply enjoying the miracle of the daytime world in a bland industrial park.

But then I felt it. Not a sharp pain, definitely not like being on fire or getting stabbed or whatever. Instead, it was a tingle— not even really pain, just the sense of contact, a light pressure activating the nerves at the top of my head, like an itch or an irritation. After several minutes, the feeling crept from a tingling to discomfort, a light sense of—

Burning.

My scalp. I hadn't applied sunblock to my scalp.

"Oh fuck," I said, looking again at the rearview mirror. No one had poured hot oil on top of my head, but it was beginning to feel that way. The dot of feverish heat soon swelled into a searing burn at the crown of my head, despite my hair. This was what I got for admiring the day for too long. I made a mental note that if I ever wanted to do this again, make sure the balaclava was actually in stock first. Ian appeared before I could put my helmet back on—and without any blood. Instead, a woman behind him kept pace as she lugged the dolly carrying a white metal box. As they approached, their voices became clearer and I heard Ian say, "she's my, like, third cousin."

"Well, she should know better," the woman said.

Uh-oh.

Despite the searing pain atop my head, I forced a smile and a wave, then popped open the hatchback to see if politeness might speed things up. Ian shrugged in acknowledgment and reached over to open the passenger door.

"Hey," I said as a draft of wind hit me. "Just pop it in the back."

"Louise Chao?" the woman asked, the metal box rumbling as the dolly bounced over pavement cracks. I leaned over the car's console, an elbow resting on the cosplay helmet between seats. "I need to verify your ID." She held up the driver's license in her hand, and knelt down to lean into the open passenger door.

"That's me," I said, pushing my smile wider as I locked eyes with the woman. The brightness of the midday sun really kicked in with the open door, and suddenly I realized that new burning sensations started. The more I held her gaze, the more my eyes felt the sear, and even though I'd muddled my way through high school science, I put together that the glare from the sidewalk must have been reflecting some UV into my unprotected corneas. "Sorry, we couldn't find a place to park, so I sent Ian."

"I see that. Next time, park there," she said, pointing at the loading spots along the curb. The woman looked at my ID again, then back at me. "We shouldn't let a minor take the delivery." I nodded several times, blinking as I felt the blood tears starting to well up from the pain. "This needs to be delivered within an hour to maintain temperature."

"We're already on our way." I thumbed to the trunk area. "Just pack it into the cooler."

"Cooler? This is properly packed. It can't go in a home cooler."

That contradicted the text. But whatever, I wasn't going to argue now. "Oh. Right. Okay, load it up."

"Alright. Thanks for the pickup," the woman said in a tone that showed more irritation than gratitude. I took my ID back from her. "Daft Punk, huh?"

"Oh. Yeah, I'm a big fan. Still sad about their breakup. Sometimes it's, uh, fun to pretend it's a racing helmet—"

"My ex was super into them. They never did it for me." And with that, she closed the passenger door, my eyes feeling immediate relief as the layers of metal and glass protected me from the UV rays bouncing off the sidewalk. Guess that protective film I'd applied to the windows really *did* work. I glanced back at Ian, who'd rolled the dolly around back and picked up the metal box when I let out a cry.

It took several seconds to realize what had happened: when Ian lifted the metal container, it tilted at an angle that caught the sun, firing a ray right into my face. Which prompted my shriek, which *then* prompted the stare from Ian through the car's open hatchback.

"Are you...okay?"

Was I? I wasn't sure—I'd never encountered direct sunlight before. Popular vampire lore said enough about the sun's potential damage that I'd never risked it. The community had various theories about things like makers and turning, but we all agreed on the sun.

Sun equaled bad.

Now I knew *how* bad. One look in the rearview showed a patch of singed skin about the size of a quarter.

Also, it was smoking.

"Oh yeah, I'm fine. Just, um, caught my neck on the seat belt. Clumsy mistake." The inner foam of my cheap helmet brushed against the wound like barbed wire scraping my face, though I suppressed screams enough to get it on. "Let's get to the drop-off," I said, my voice muffled by the closed visor. "Clock's ticking."

# CHAPTER 16

BLOOD DONATIONS WERE USUALLY dropped off at hospitals. I'd seen for myself at my own hospital's blood bank storage. But today's destination pulled us into the warehouse district across the Bay Bridge by Oakland's harbor, closer to where bands practiced and shipping companies organized than cutting-edge hospitals. Through nondescript rows of metal buildings and dirty streets, Ian saw parts of the Bay Area that were definitely *not* on any tourist guide.

The map's guide listed the final turn and we pulled into a small alley between buildings, a space thin enough to trap us in—but also shield us from direct sunlight. Ian kept glancing behind us and I caught his eyes through my helmet visor. "Ah, it's fine," I said. "Those metal delivery boxes are tough."

"It's not that," he said, looking back, but this time wrinkling his nose with a sniff. "Do you smell that?"

I knew *exactly* what he meant: the odor of singed skin. Of

course I knew, because that smell was trapped in my closed helmet. "Smell what?"

"Something smells like burning. Ever since we left the pickup. I keep checking the box to make sure there's nothing wrong with it."

"Huh." I loudly sniffed the air behind my helmet. "I don't smell anything. Maybe it's just my car and I'm used to it. Okay," I said, craning my neck to assess the scene in front. "I guess we just knock?" In front of us sat a metal door within a metal wall; no windows, no entry with large glass walls, no sliding doors that indicated professional health care or biotechnology or anything else that might have remotely used blood. Instead it looked more like the warehouses emptied out for raves.

And near the top of it sat a little black dot, likely a security camera.

My phone buzzed with a notification.

Bring the blood to the front door. You will be protected from the sun.

This *did* involve vampires. And likely Eric, with his creepy app. I looked at the sky above, the sun now angled to hide behind the buildings. Unlike before, no direct rays hit pavement or walls or anything else that might have created a reflection. And my motorcycle getup covered me, which probably offered enough protection—overprotection, really, but it settled my nerves. One blistering skin wound was enough for today.

"I'll be a minute," I said, unbuckling and opening the door. I put a hand out into the air outside. My limb did *not* immediately catch on fire, and no creeping burning sensation arrived under my snow gloves or leather sleeves.

"Sure," Ian said, like this was a totally normal afternoon for him. Though, given what he'd been through, maybe he welcomed anything away from hospitals and illness. The hatchback door clicked as it opened, and I stepped out with more confidence than I actually felt. A quick look at the passenger seat and Ian clearly wasn't paying attention. Instead, he held his phone horizontally and little metallic noises came from it. I tilted to see if he secretly coded a bomb or something, but his screen offered a bigger surprise:

A drum loop app. I didn't get too close a look, but I saw the stack of lines, each representing a different piece of a drum kit. Then the green highlight running from left to right as it played through a synthesized repeating beat.

Programming meets music. Of course Ian would get it.

And that particular beat, it took several seconds for me to recognize it, but the pattern of the toms and kick hit me—it wasn't perfect, but he'd tried to re-create the opening of Joy Division's "Transmission."

Behind the visor of my sweaty Daft Punk helmet, a huge grin came over my face. Maybe this kid was more rhythm than melody. And that was alright.

"I'll be quick," I said. A drop-off, then the drive home with some more blood, then I'd text Pete back, possibly even start listening to tracks before work to get ready. This bizarre deviation from my life would stabilize, floating back into its intended path of playing in a band.

Ian grunted in acknowledgment, tilting the phone's screen away from my view. I stepped to the back, loading the heavier-than-expected metal box onto the dolly that once belonged to Aunt Laura. I walked with one hand over the box, keeping it steady as I pulled it down the alleyway. It rattled with each bump despite my careful steps.

I paused, scoping out the roofs of the buildings around us. All that talk about vampire anonymity—were they tracking my situation here? I hadn't said anything, and Ian was just a kid, *and* I had the delivery. It seemed to check all the boxes for playing by the rules. Without anything suspicious in my view, I moved forward.

A metal door slid open, its wheels riding on rusted rails. A figure stood several feet back, a silhouette safely out of the sun's reach. "Come in," his voice called out, and even though my helmet muffled my hearing, I recognized the Scottish accent. The metal box clanged as the dolly rolled over the door's tracks, and once I stood safely within the loading bay, the person stepped forward.

Eric.

He waited, hands folded across his waist, the same tight coat he had on at the community meeting, his eyes, bright and aware for this time of day.

"Louise. Thank you so much for doing this. It's great to see our community participate in gathering resources." He leaned down to undo the metal clasps securing the box's lid before opening it. I watched his lips move, mouthing numbers as he counted up the estimate. "Looks good." He pulled out his phone, then tapped an icon on the lit screen. "We're good out here. Can you please drop off the sustenance donation?" A voice squawked through with an affirmative, and Eric looked back my way. "Just a minute for your cut. Oh, you can take off your helmet if you need a breath. You're safe here." His head tilted, one eyebrow raised. "Who's your passenger?"

I pretended to struggle with my helmet, buying myself some time to come up with the answer to such a pointed question. "Distant relative for some daytime support." Eric nodded, his expression blank. "He doesn't know anything, he just thinks I'm—" I took in a breath as the helmet popped off "—quirky."

"We all have those," he said without any of the cold animosity from the meeting. "Your outfit looks effective against the sun." Eric complimented the functionality of my getup without noting that it was Daft Punk cosplay. Despite being an effective community organizer and all of that stuff, he clearly didn't have good taste in music.

"Still got burned," I said. "Reflection off metal."

"Ah," Eric said. "You mind if I take a look?"

Vampire doctors existed in the community to do things like set broken bones and handle wounds with our unique physiology. Was Eric that as well as a community organizer and tech guy? If so, he clearly set the bar for making the most of immortality, at least in terms of societal productivity. "Sure. I've never had sun damage before. I wasn't sure if I should put, like, ointment on it."

A door slid open from behind Eric and a woman appeared with a disposable insulated bag in one hand. She paused to look me over, and my forced-but-polite smile received a smirk in return. The single fluorescent light overhead and natural daylight behind me reflected off her glasses and the arrowhead-shaped lapel pin, then she set the cooler bag at Eric's feet before leaving out the same door. "Your cut of the blood. That's about a three-week supply. How is your rationing?"

"It, um," I said, searching for the right word, "sucks."

"Headaches, weakness, fatigue?"

"Yeah. Along those lines. But this will help."

"Frustrating, isn't it?" Eric asked, his posture tensing. "Fighting just to live each day? So many of us have to worry about our next meals. It shouldn't be that way. But—" he pointed to the bag "—this should tide you over. You brought a cooler?"

So that's what that was for. "I did."

"Use that. There's some ice packs in there but you should get it into a fridge in the next hour or so. And treat yourself to full servings. Too much rationing damages your body. Now, let's see what you got here," he said, squinting at the wound. "It'll heal on its own over the next week. But if you want, I have something that can help get it back to normal in about a day or two."

"Something" that magically healed vampire skin? I forced my expression to be neutral despite the internal swirling of questions. But, I *did* have to go back to work tonight and anything that helped maintain a low profile would be welcome. "Sure. As long as it's not too gross."

"It's not. Really simple." Eric followed that with a quick grin. "One second." He disappeared through the back door, and I glanced at the car. Ian still appeared to be enamored with his drum app, which was good enough for me. "Here you go," Eric said, returning after a few minutes. He held up a vial of deep red liquid, its twist-off cap doubling as an eyedropper.

"Is that blood?"

"Yes and no. Our bodies absorb everything best through blood. That's just our physiology. Put five drops on the wound today and again tomorrow. That'll help the healing."

"So, what is this?"

Subtle changes shifted through Eric's face, from his lips to his brow. His lips pursed before hesitating, and the light in his eyes shifted. "Science," he said with the smallest of smiles. "Combined with ancient wisdom. Think of it as Neosporin for vampires. You'll know more soon. Everyone will. Keep watching the app."

This was all too weird, and who was the smirky glasses woman with the blood? The whole thing gave me the wrong vibes, especially with how it was all connected to the app that refused to uninstall. I considered asking about that little bit of privacy invasion, but before I had a chance, Eric looked at his phone and grimaced. "Sorry, I have to run. But thank you again for the delivery."

And with that, he disappeared into the back, the door rattling behind him. It shut with a click, then the whir of mechanisms churned into what sounded like a very locked door. I looked back at Ian again, who still stared at his phone, completely unaware that two vampires had just exchanged containers of blood about twenty feet in front of him.

Helmet snug on my head, I started back toward my Prius, vial tucked in my pocket. The external door began rolling shut as I loaded the cooler with bottles, the same cartoon fruit label as before, then slammed the hatchback hard enough that Ian looked over. In the driver's seat, I put my phone in the clasps of its windshield mount and set to punch in the map directions to my house. Right below the map icon sat the simple white triangle icon for Eric's vampire app, a little piece of software that seemed like a benign community tool a few hours ago. But now… "Keep watching the app" sounded far too ominous for my liking.

Besides, what had this so-called community done for me? Their rules prevented me from helping Laura. And they caused my rift with Marshall, perhaps even worse.

I didn't need more of that in my life.

"All done?" Ian asked, stopping the out-of-rhythm beat on his phone. I caught his glance, and he quickly closed the app. My helmet visor tinted the world's color, but I swear a flush came to his cheeks. "I was just working on a project while you were gone."

"Yeah," I said, craning my neck to catch the multicolored text now displayed on his screen.

The car came to life, quiet rumbles before a low hum rang through. I looked at my lit phone, the screen bright as the map spun, the word Recalculating at the bottom. Sitting between two hunks of metal in an industrial sector must have confused the GPS.

Even though a fresh supply of blood sat in the back of my car, the way this unfolded didn't sit right. The mystery text, the location tracking, the vial, this warehouse in the docks. There had to be better ways to get blood.

I shifted the car into Reverse and we started to roll backward in silence, a mood that carried over the next few minutes while a plan gathered in my head. Above us, the early afternoon sun shone, and when I emerged from the industrial neighborhood to head to the Bay Bridge, a sunbeam pierced the windshield and landed on my arm. I looked down at the layers protecting my skin, from the anti-UV film on the glass to the leather and cotton over my skin.

I didn't feel a thing.

The car lurched around paths and through light traffic, and when we hit the Bay Bridge, I reached up to turn my phone off. Ian looked up from his coding. "Everything okay?"

"Yeah." The map disappeared and the screen went dark as we pulled ahead. "So look, you're a tech guy. Can you help me get something off my phone?"

# CHAPTER 17

WE RETURNED TO MY house, which was remarkably dark despite the late afternoon sun. And though Lola slept during the day as she always did, Ian's presence stirred her. She followed him to the kitchen table, a move probably more to do with his bag of fast food than a sudden canine schedule adjustment.

"The best I could do was mute the app. But it's making everything slow," I said, which felt like a good cover story, "so if you can remove it, that'd be great." Ian planted down at the table so I could finally remove my helmet. "You can give her a fry if you're feeling generous. *One* fry," I said from the hallway, my burn scar safely hidden from his view. I took one last peek as Ian tore into his grease bag, and Lola seemed to understand my words, hopping then sitting at Ian's feet with wide eyes and straight ears. Ian grunted a teenage affirmative, and I left him to both eat *and* figure out why Eric's app stubbornly refused to be deleted.

I marched off to the shower, layers of sweat waiting to be

washed off, though first I pulled out Eric's vial of mystery healing blood. I unscrewed the vial's eyedropper, and when I put drops on the burn, the area stung.

The wound tingled, blood absorbing into it, and I stared at the absurdity of what I'd just been through. All because the blood I was *supposed* to get at my job was no longer available. It's not like I planned to fill my potentially infinite lifespan with janitorial work but I needed to eat, and cleaning toilets was better than risking sun damage.

Ian's voice echoed through the hall, breaking my concentration. Even through the door his annoyed "No, Grandpa" told me more than enough about his conversation. I shut it again, The shower knob squeaked as I turned it on, and soon steam filled up the space, all the grime and sweat of the day ready to be washed off. But when I finished some ten minutes later, Ian was still on the phone, his voice getting louder, complete with an irritated snarl. I cracked the bathroom door while toweling off just to make sure he wasn't chatting with my dog about fries.

Nope. Nor was he grumbling to himself about my phone's operating system.

No, his words carried more weight, an urgency in his tone, and a crack in voice. "That's bullshit," he said as I wiped steam off the mirror to inspect the burn on my face—had Eric's mixture helped already? Because now it looked like a patch of dermatitis instead of an oozing wound. "That's bullshit and you know it." I dug through the bottom bathroom drawer to put the vial in a bag of Laura's first-aid stuff—Band-Aids, ointment, and gauze, all more than twenty years old, one of those things that still hung around as years became decades simply because I'd forgotten about it.

Or chose to forget about it enough *not* to throw it out.

Now dressed in very normal clothes without layers of UV protection, I made my way back out to find Ian tensely perched, phone to his ear.

"No. I'm not ready to yet." And with that, Ian's finger tapped the screen hard, the modern way of slamming the phone in anger. He sighed, head in hands, and I watched as Lola rolled on her back with a single paw up. "High five," he said softly, meeting the paw.

I took careful barefoot steps forward, quiet enough that not even my dog turned to attention. "How are you?" I finally managed, hoping for a real answer in return.

"Yeah, I'm *fine*," he said, a clear lie compounded by the extra teenage emphasis on the last word. I would have laughed at the sheer indignation if rage and worry weren't carved into his taut cheeks and narrow eyes. I needed to respond somewhere between prying and caring and being aloof in a cool twenty-something sort of way.

Nothing came to mind, so instead, I stood there and nodded until I finally managed an "Okay."

"Wait," he said quickly before his phone came back to life. I wasn't sure if that was directed at me or Lola or life in general, but his screen blinked and loaded until he finally held it up for me to see. "Do you know this band?"

Playground Fight. I knew of them, but not for the right reasons. "Eh, they're, um, okay." Perhaps I should have been more polite about it, but after getting up in the middle of the day *and* driving around the Bay Area, fatigue removed any false pretenses when it came to music.

Ian squinted again at his phone. "What about Iceberg?"

"Not bad?"

"Damn it." Ian scrolled through his screen. "Hormone Attack?"

Lola must have sensed the growing frustration from both of us, as she rolled onto her paws and shuffled off to the living room. The familiar jingling of her tags and a *thump* told me that she'd jumped onto her favorite couch spot. "Are you going through a playlist or something?"

"No."

"Okay, help me out. I'm usually asleep right now, so my brain's not working." Ian's mouth twisted into a scowl long enough for his phone to time out. "So, if it's not a playlist, is it..." I searched for anything that might prompt a list of mediocre bands, "songs that are simple to learn?"

Ian leaned forward, the shift in his weight causing the floorboards to creak.

"Look, if you want to learn one of those songs, we can. They have chords for pretty much every song—"

"They're moving Mom to hospice."

Ian's words came out flat, but they stopped me quicker than any band or song title could have. Things locked into place, from the angry phone conversation to the angrier expressions on his face.

But why was he bringing up random bands?

"How, um," I said, searching very carefully for the right words, "how do you know what hospice is?"

Ian shot a look that immediately told me I'd asked the wrong question.

"See, now you're doing it too." More stereotypical teenage moves came: a huff, a headshake, muttering under his breath.

"Doing what?" I asked, trying my best to sound sincere and sympathetic but without edging into patronizing.

"Talking to me like I'm five. Of course I know what hospice is."

How *did* he know what hospice was? At his age, many things concerned me: getting enough money to buy records, my brother getting into my shit, the way my dad was treated at work. But that particular word never entered my sphere at all; in fact, I probably didn't even know how to pronounce it until I'd seen it on TV in the '80s or '90s.

Then it hit me: of course Ian had heard it. His mother was dying. It *had* to be part of the discussion. I tried a semilogical turn despite the fact that it started with a complete lie. "Sorry, that's not what I meant. I meant, how do you know that your mom is going to hospice?" Ian's mouth twisted into a skeptical line. "And," I added, throwing him further questions to distance myself from my pivot, "I'm not sure what that has to do with those bands."

My tone worked well enough that he didn't fire back. Head in hands, Ian let out a deep sigh and waited, long enough that I got up and fixed a drape that had been letting a poke of afternoon sunlight through. "They're sending Mom home."

"Home isn't hospice," I said, trying to reassure him.

"They're sending her home to 'rest,'" he said, fingers in air quotes.

"Well, that could mean anything." His look cut right through my thinly veiled attempt at comfort. He was right—I *was* talking to him like a little kid.

"This was an experimental treatment that was gonna take at least three weeks. Possibly six *months*. You don't end a treatment unless it's, like, not working." I wasn't sure how much Ian knew about cancer treatments, experimental or otherwise, but he spoke with enough self-assuredness that it certainly made sense. At the same time, all of his inflated talk and dagger eyes built a clear barrier to protect something else. "They're flying home tomorrow."

"They?"

Ian bit down on his lip as he stared at the floor. "I told them I'm not going."

I knelt down, brushing wet hair out of my face. "What are you thinking?" I asked. The question came with a very real possibility of pushing him over the edge, despite its gentle sincerity. My shoulders tensed, bracing for a response, and I realized that the tension had less to do with my discomfort and way more with concern for how Ian might actually get through this.

"Can I stay here for the weekend?" he finally asked.

Things finally connected. He wanted an excuse to stay. But still, I was a vampire. I couldn't let him stay here. There were bags of blood in my refrigerator and my room doubled as a really large, comfy coffin during daytime hours. I had zero plans on telling him the truth, but if he found out, what kind of risk would that create—especially with Eric's app stuck on my phone?

Plus, there was the opportunity with Pete this weekend.

"I'm not sure," I finally said, trying to consolidate all of those things against the eyes staring back at me.

"Okay, fine. Fuck you too," he said, his words seething. "I'm so—"

"No, it's not that. It's just," I started, justifications bubbling to the surface. "I work at night. I mean, I'm a night janitor at a hospital. I can't just decide. I have to plan in advance." Which wasn't technically true, trading shifts with coworkers was easy when jobs paid overtime.

"You can't call in sick again? Take the day off?" Ian's eyes widened, his tone turning to desperation. "Maybe I can just stay here with Lola. You know, take care of her while you work. I have coding projects. I can work on those. Or I can clean your backyard." He finally exhaled, shoulders deflating. "I just don't want to think about them for a few days." His hands pressed against his temples, and though he tried to hide it, his eyes gave away the fact that his armor was cracking. "Before I," he said quietly, "you know, actually have to."

On the other end of a trip home was the possibility of life taking another harsh turn for him. He simply wanted to delay it. And being away from it must have felt like the easiest escape.

"Please," he said, "give me this weekend."

Lola must have sensed it too; she hopped down from the couch and approached. We silently watched as she waddled into the room before plopping on Ian's feet, several stray corgi hairs tossing into the air for me to vacuum later. She rested her head on Ian's shoes.

Perhaps she lobbied on the kid's behalf.

So while I understood him, practicality got in the way. I played out a mental checklist in my head: Blood sat in the fridge. He'd also need to eat. And sleep. The curtains had to stay drawn, but my daysleeper work schedule could explain that. I considered each room for any vampirisms that might give myself away, but it all came back to my blood supply and the security of my bedroom.

Turned out, living like a vampire was actually pretty mundane as long as he respected my schedule. My dog required more maintenance than me. The issue really did stem more from the prospect of potentially letting someone get too close to my day-to-day secrets.

But then there was also the issue of the audition with Pete, of one more shot at making it work with a band. I'd need all weekend to get competent on a full set list, especially if they had a gig a few days after.

This wasn't something to half-ass.

"I was looking up bands in town," he said quietly. "I was thinking, maybe... It'd be my first show."

A first show. That first discovery, the swirl of ear-bleeding noise and bright lights and a thick mass of humanity moving in unison—he'd gone from being curious about guitars to exploring bands on his own, a full-body immersion that broke free of the real world's troubles.

That part, I understood.

I'd been a little older than Ian when I'd hit that moment. Sixteen to be exact, and just old enough to drive. That night, I was supposed to have been studying for a history exam, which, in a way, I was. I'd driven two hours to witness David Bowie, which was life's ultimate education. My slight frame helped me wiggle my way up near the stage—not the front, but probably a third of the way back, enough that Bowie and Mick Ronson and the others stood clear onstage, light reflecting off their costumes. The opening rush toward the stage as they jumped right into "Hang on to Yourself" created a visceral stir, a dizziness as I tried to comprehend what was happening between the lights and the sound and the ocean of bodies around.

Then the opening chords of "Ziggy Stardust" hit, the drumbeat carrying my legs, my voice projecting in a full body roar that blended into the swirl around me. Every single line came out of me; every single snare hit swayed my body, an experience that seemed equal parts blissful delirium and hypnosis. It drove itself, song after song, my mind and body united in autopilot, and when the proper set finished, Bowie and his band stormed offstage, the crowd shimmering from the experience. That break in connectivity returned me to my own body, a realization that songs and minutes had passed and though I'd heard it, seen it, *felt* it, somehow it floated through me while carrying me at the same time.

Every show I'd been to, even the bad ones, they all carried that tangible sense of combustion, a liftoff that only came with live music.

Ian sought that. He sought stability and peace in a cacophony of drums and guitar. He didn't quite understand what he was looking for, yet somehow he felt this pull.

And though I hadn't been to a show since Marshall died, I could give this to him.

But this weekend was my shot with Pete's band. They even promised to work with my weird schedule to get me into their practice space. If I didn't take it, they'd get someone else. They *had* a gig; they couldn't wait.

I looked Ian over one more time as I reached over to scratch Lola's neck. She pulled away, then turned to me with big eyes followed by a whimper, and I wondered if Ian possibly trained her to do this while I'd been in the shower.

Because damn it, it worked.

I grabbed the phone off the table and typed a quick reply to Pete.

Sorry, turns out I have family in town. Let me know if your new guitarist doesn't work out later.

"Tell you what," I said. Lola's collar jingled as she turned to look at me. "Let me talk to your grandpa."

Several seconds passed, as if Ian needed time to properly absorb what I meant. Which was good, because I needed that same time to fully grasp the commitment I was about to make. "Are you serious?" he finally asked, his voice lifted.

"I am. But I gotta get some stuff done first. I'll figure out my work schedule but I'm not changing my sleep schedule. Got it?"

"Yeah, yeah, of course."

"Maybe you can work on that while I talk to your grandpa," I said, pointing at my phone, which still awaited a fix to remove Eric's app. A show, without Marshall—but with Ian.

If I was going to go back into the hallowed space of live music, Ian's first show seemed a good enough reason. "And one more thing—if we're going to a show, *I'm* picking the band."

## CHAPTER 18

**VAMPIRE POWER MYTH #7:** Vampires have the ability to bend people to their will.

This clearly wasn't the case. I couldn't force EJ into letting Ian stay. In fact, I was probably making it worse. As EJ's voice rose in irritation, my own nerves steeled up, a flood of rebuttals and insults surfacing.

Arguing with my brother again awoke long-dormant instincts. Closing my eyes created a form of time travel, his weathered old voice suddenly the young tween arguing with me on the porch of a postwar house, the sun from a too-hot summer giving the memory the yellow tint of a faded photograph. All of it created a full-body muscle memory, even changing the way I held my posture to avoid him looking over my shoulder before yelling at him.

But no, this wasn't about verbally beating my younger brother over something that ultimately didn't matter. This was about Ian, who sat at the table squinting at my phone, my dog now following him everywhere because of a single French fry and a high five.

"He should be with his mother," EJ said, while I held Ian's phone up to my ear. "Every second counts."

"Look, I get that." My tone tipped into levels of irritation only family might activate, and it took several breaths to temper further urges. "But he needs space too."

"You just met him." Maybe EJ recognized our relationship on a subconscious level too, because his voice took a similar turn. "What makes you his advocate?"

Which was a good question. Because really, I'd only known him for a few days. But that rage he embodied, and his catharsis through music, that thread overcame the decades of life experience between us. "Because I remember what anger felt like at that age." My brother had grown up, the belligerent smarm of Stephen evolving through rites of passage like getting married and having kids into EJ. Whereas time passed for me but I didn't age, freezing me in a perpetual cycle of playing punk songs and going to shows, my worldview much closer to Ian's life. "He doesn't need hope. Or false hope. He needs a pressure release."

The line went quiet, the only noise coming from Ian mumbling to himself while he tapped on my phone.

"It's a few days," I said, quickly crossing and uncrossing my fingers. "I'll take him to the airport myself Sunday night."

EJ sighed loud enough to make the phone's audio crackle. "Alright. But tell him to help me pack now." EJ listed off a few other scheduling things, all of which I agreed to quickly; I needed time to humanproof my house.

The line went silent as we signed off with each other, and I took a step back to scan my home, a place that had suddenly become a bed-and-breakfast for nonvampires.

The rough checklist in my head came back, and my pulse thumped with the velocity of anxiety, the kind that triggered when a semibad idea edged on reality. Where would I get groceries? Would Lola be weirded out? Should I store my blood in a cooler in my room? I looked around my house, every piece of furniture and decor becoming individual pieces of a giant burning question, my sudden willingness to empathize with a troubled teen now colliding with the fact that I lived off blood rather than sandwiches.

On the other side of the room, Ian still sat while squinting at my phone, Lola resting on her side at his feet.

Maybe I didn't have to answer all those questions perfectly. I could just give a teen a place to couch-crash after his first gig, with access to fast food as needed.

How very punk rock.

"Hey, good news," I said, walking over to the kitchen table. Ian remained hunched over my phone's glowing screen, tapping with both speed and intensity. "I worked it out with your grandpa. He asked for you to meet up with him now, though. I know I was originally gonna drop you off at the hotel on my way to work, but I'll get you a rideshare now—"

"Wait," he said, looking up at me. A different shade of concern projected from his eyes, not the life-altering blend of fury and fear he'd had when he discovered his mom's circumstances. The knobs were dialed down on this look, more the creased brows of concern and a squint of frustration. "I've been looking at your phone—"

"It can wait. I really need a nap before work."

"I don't know if it should. There's something very weird with this app on your phone. It's supposed to just be, like, community messages, right? But it's not." He held it up, the screen split between Eric's app and some diagnostic code below it. "It's the most invasive app I've ever seen."

# CHAPTER 19

JUST HOW INVASIVE WAS Eric's app?

According to Ian, it wormed its way into accessing everything on my phone. Which, at first didn't seem like much, given how few apps I put on my phone. But right when Ian left, realizations hit, one by one.

My browser history, with every band I'd researched for auditions. My photos. Lyrics I'd whispered into the audio recorder during late-night inspirations. Vampire jokes I made to Lola. The sun protection I'd bought, the "vampire or werewolf" discussion at work, my every move as I trekked around looking for blood between my hospital, University Hospital, and Eric's delivery question.

Ian found that Eric's app hooked into all of that, exploiting every existing app and function to spy. My not-very-exciting vampire *life*, all encoded in bits and bytes for... What purpose? I didn't quite grasp how any of this could unify the community or get us more blood.

Did they put all of this data in the context of being a vampire? Because if it tracked everything I said and did, then how would it reconcile the human food I just ordered?

A notification came across the screen, a message stating that my grocery order was being prepared. A slew of nonvampire things was set to arrive: bananas, corn chips, bread, a packet of sliced ham, milk. All of this information flowed across digital streams to Eric's servers.

And for now, there was nothing I could do about it. Though maybe the groceries would at least throw off their algorithm. In the meantime, I had to shake off the fatigue tugging at my eyelids and consider my fridge.

How did you make a refrigerator accessible to a guest when it was filled with blood?

The last time I considered this, I went with the direct route. As in, I bypassed any pretense and just said it. Marshall was, after all, my best friend and my bandmate of a decade at the time, logic dictated that at some point he *should* have come over, and if anyone earned the right to my true identity, it would be my songwriting partner. "You realize this is the first time I've been in your house?" Marshall had asked as he stepped in and scanned the framed concert posters lining the wall.

"Are you sure?" I said, scooping up the scampering corgi puppy before she started leaping onto Marshall's ankles.

The question was intentionally misleading because of course it was. I don't know why I'd finally told Marshall to come by. Functionally, his text of: I'm close by, can I pick up my kit? led to the convenience of geography. But he'd asked before, and those times, I'd come up with excuses, sometimes legitimate and sometimes a white lie to hide my vampire lair.

Yet this time, I'd said yes. Without any fuss. And why *should* there be a fuss? He needed a little TLC after a bad breakup and I had no plans for the night. Lola furiously licked my cheeks as I let him in, and I guided her back to her crate to continue training her for my nocturnal schedule. Her attention turned to the rubber toy stuffed with peanut butter, leaving me to give Marshall a brief tour of the house. Somehow, it felt far less intimidating than expected.

Living with Laura had been different. It had been *her* house, after all, and I was the one who moved in. But other than the contractors who mounted my new TV on the wall, no one else had stepped inside for years.

I'd put Marshall's electric drum kit out in the hall for him to pick up, but five minutes was all it took for us to veer off on a tangent. "You know," he said, grabbing Gail from the wall to once again show off that he could play slap-bass and I couldn't, "what confuses me about this breakup is she said I care about music too much for someone in his thirties. But she's a DJ! She spins at the Cat Club every Thursday night."

"Women," I said, hopping on my drum kit.

"Men too," he said, continuing his impromptu funk riffs. "No luck there when I tried. How hard can it be to find someone that you just *sit* with while you listen to a Siouxsie remaster on vinyl? Forget sex. There's your sign of true love."

"People are the worst. That's my conclusion." I kicked into a disco beat, open hi-hats alternating between a tight snare beat, and our improvisation became the worst funk song of all time, something that lasted for a good five minutes before I gave up and moved to my keyboard rig.

"You know, this really isn't fair," he said, moving to a popping slap-bass solo.

"What's that?"

"This space. You have a whole studio we've never used before."

"I inherited it from my aunt."

"You could seriously book this for recording time. Make a whole side gig out of it." He laughed, and I was half-surprised he didn't make some reference to his day job as a bookkeeper for a CPA. He looked around, taking in the soundproofing I'd put up by hand. "Seriously, all of this would be a tax write-off. Your gear would practically be free."

There it was.

I let myself dream for a moment, of a life where something like that *was* possible and I didn't have to steal blood from SFGH's blood bank. I pressed down on Nancy, my keyboard rig named in honor of Nancy Whang of LCD Soundsystem, and I started synthesized choral chants, a faux-goth melody to play opposite Marshall's faux P-funk lines. The groove went on for several minutes, soon joined by a generic preset dance beat, a logic defying culture-clash that wouldn't have existed anywhere else.

But then again, a vampire and an accountant being best friends and playing in punk clubs for a decade didn't make much sense either.

Except the vampire part was secret. Community rules dictated it be that way.

The song continued on, Marshall adding dramatic vocals without a live mic, the words melting into the wall of bad sound around it. We went for several more minutes until the goth-funk jam ran its course, eventually ending with his laughter and, "Okay, seriously, enough of that."

We looked at each other, indulging the simple comfort of our presence. And right then, I realized it was really dumb that I hadn't invited him in until now. If I couldn't trust Marshall, who could I trust? And at some point in our friendship, he'd probably notice I wasn't aging.

Fuck the rules.

"Hey, since you're here," I said, tapping a light synth-pop riff to combat my nerves, "there's something really wild I should tell you."

"Yeah?" he asked, and though he kept playing notes on

Gail, his whole demeanor shifted, an unexpected glow coming to him.

"You know how I can't do any daytime gigs?"

A puzzled scrunch took over his face. "Yeah, what, are you finally changing work shifts?" Our improvising continued, juxtaposing a poppy New Wave soundtrack to the most serious conversation topic in the world.

"No, it's not that." My left hand started playing on the lower keyboard, chords to give breadth to our jam. "So, I have this, um, chronic condition. It's why I have to work nights. And eat a special diet."

"Oh shit." The bass went silent, and my keyboard soon followed. "Why didn't you tell me you had health issues? We've been friends for how long? Are you okay?"

His concern brought a smile, toothy enough that my fangs grazed the inside of my bottom lip.

"So this condition. I'm kind of like..." I took in a breath, my hand against the side of my keyboard rig to steady myself. It was too late now; I had to say it, rules be damned. "A vampire?" I meant to say it with more authority, but nerves pushed it out as a question.

Marshall's lips twisted in a way that showed my explanation created further confusion. "You mean your skin sensitivity? You already told me about that."

"No. I mean, like, literally a vampire. Like, Dracula. *'Bla, bla, I drink blood and hiss.'*" My hands shot up, fingers curled in mock claws while I pushed out a hiss. "Just kidding, I don't actually hiss."

"Okay," Marshall said, "you're being weird. Did you have some strong edibles before I came here?"

"No, no, no. Seriously, look at my teeth." I opened my mouth and pointed at my fangs. Talking while my mouth remained open proved difficult, though I tried my best. "See?

Real fangs," I got out in muffled words. "Yes, you still have to brush vampire teeth for good hygiene."

Marshall squinted, his whole body leaning forward while the bass hung from his neck and shoulders. "Okay. So let's assume that you really are a vampire and not just superhigh on edibles. Did you bring me here to eat me?"

"What? No, I brought you here so you could pick up your gear." Marshall's glib question stung. We'd been friends for a decade and he jumped right into murder? "Jeez, you think I'm a killer?"

"I dunno. You said you're a vampire. Don't vampires immediately grow fangs and start eating people?"

I considered going into a long explanation about how the transition was a little more complicated than that, and killing people was very frowned upon. But I went simpler. "No. Well, yes. I mean, we need blood. That's why I have blood bags." Marshall's eyebrow arched. "Really. Go check out my fridge. But I don't fly or murder people. I just kind of…hang out indefinitely. At night. No jobs during sunlight. No gigs during sunlight. That's pretty much it."

His brow furrowed and his gradual nod hopefully meant a gradual acceptance. "Is your dog a vampire too?"

"Lola? No, she's not a vampire." The corgi pup must have heard her name, her collar jingling from a distance until she sprinted into the room, head tilted and oversize ears alert. I knelt down and she bounded toward me with the chaos of a puppy unsure of her four stubby legs. "She's just the best dog *ever*," I said in a high-pitched voice before I started singing The Kinks. *"La-la-la-la Lola."*

"So…" Marshall looked me up and down, trying to read my face. But he already knew my expressions, so maybe he looked for sudden differences to check if I'd lost my mind. "You're serious?"

"Of course I am." I turned Lola to face Marshall. "Doesn't she look like the best dog ever?"

"You know what I mean."

"Yes. One hundred-percent, swear-on-the-grave-of-David-Bowie serious." Which, given that David Bowie had died only a month prior to this discussion, demonstrated the sheer importance of my words.

He took Gail off his shoulders and hung the bass on the wall, then simply stared. Several minutes passed, and I decided to give him the space to process it all. "Dude."

"I know. But, like, don't tell anyone. We have rules about secrecy." My voice dropped as I realized that Lola had suddenly fallen asleep in my arms. So much for nocturnal training. "I mean, I barely know any others."

"Oh, that's fine. I just mean, you must be the least scary vampire in history. You make it sound kind of..." He paused, lips twisted in thought.

"Depressing."

I'd never exactly thought of my life as depressing. I mean, it definitely wasn't *exciting*, especially considering most people's assumptions about vampires. But then I tallied up the things I'd lost over the last four decades or so—my family, the physical ability to eat, the practical ability to connect with nearly everyone on a normal basis except for a handful of night owls (and thus, musicians), Laura. At some point, Lola would be a distant memory too, and how many "best dog evers" would I have? Laura didn't approach vampirism with that kind of melancholy, which might have been a reflection of her age more than anything else. But he did make a good point.

And at least I had him.

"Well," I finally said, "are we still cool?"

"You're still you," he said, his voice unexpectedly soft before turning to a wry grin. "Besides, check out this studio you've got here."

On that night, I'd let my best friend *into* my home and my life—and look how that ended. Blood tears started to gather, something I really didn't need right now. I made a promise to myself that I'd help Ian through this weekend, I'd blow his mind with the magic of live gigs, and then I'd leave the rest to his family.

Anything further was simply out of my league. It was too *human* for me to deal with.

That thought carried me off to an unintentional nap, only to be shaken awake at dusk by a notification on my phone. But instead of an update to say my groceries were on the way, it was a text.

From Eric. Well, not explicitly from him, but from the same five-digit anonymous number that commented on my prior delivery.

> There is another opportunity this Sunday for those that wish to make a difference in the community. It requires several hours of driving and some manual labor. It starts in the early evening and will be paid in blood bottles. More importantly, it will mark the start of a significant change for the community. Are you interested? You did a great job. I'll need to know ASAP please.

Even if I hadn't committed to babysitting over the next few days, I'd probably turn it down. The whole massive-invasion-of-privacy thing continued to irk me, and combined with the massive hassle of getting up in the daytime and risking skin-melting burns?

I flopped back on my living room couch, the sun safely descending on the other side of the house, and Lola jumped up without asking. Her short legs found footholds between my arms and elbows, and I lay there, enjoying bits of color from the afternoon-turned-dusk.

I stared at the device in my hand, the mix of plastic and circuitry that let him monitor my life. He probably even knew that my dog's sharp elbows and stumpy claws lay uncomfortably across my stomach while she gave me big sad eyes. Pillar of the community or not, something didn't click. Not with all of the weirdness of today. And until I got his app off my phone, I intended to stay away from anything to do with Eric.

Sorry, I typed, I have plans this weekend.

As the message swapped out with a confirmation icon, I opened a browser and looked up who was playing in town that weekend, unsure of whether this live show was going to mean more to Ian or me.

## CHAPTER 20

**VAMPIRE POWER MYTH #8:** Vampires have super hearing, like predators in the wild.

This was false, but also kind of unnecessary in the modern world. Why have superhearing when you could be around drunk people who talked too loud in public spaces?

Having successfully swapped shifts for the weekend with my fellow night workers, I stood with Ian across the street from the Fillmore, quite possibly the greatest music venue in existence. I had seen so many bands in that historic building spanning decades: The Clash, Blondie, Pavement, Bikini Kill, The National, and so many other memories mashed into a giant blur of loud noises, sweaty bodies, and bright lights.

The Fillmore, though, was also where I saw The Nineteen Twenty *that night* with Marshall. And when Ian asked about the last time I came here for a show, I danced around the question. He didn't need to know specifics about what happened on that rain-soaked evening; my reply was a simple "I don't remember—it's been a while."

As I approached the building, a personal weight came over me, and not just the long history of the venue. Ian, however, simply asked, "That place?"

We waited for the crosswalk signal to turn, cars whizzing by on Geary Boulevard, a range of people behind us, from the semi-intoxicated group discussing their after-show plans to an older couple who were probably *not* heading to a punk show. "Yes, it's that place. The sign that says, The Fillmore." I pointed to the large sign hanging from the building.

Ian shook his head, pointing to the bottom floor. "That looks like a food mart."

"It *is* a food mart. On the bottom floor. Welcome to big cities."

The crosswalk icons switched, and though it was only a white stick figure beckoning us across, every step echoed with thoughts of Marshall's last night. A clear sky sat above us, yet I could practically feel *that* night's rain pelting my forehead. I reset, staying in the moment with Ian as he spouted off all sorts of random details he'd looked up about the bands on tonight's bill, a familiar teenage know-it-all-ness to his tone.

Another Marshall thought crossed my mind, and this one came in equal parts epiphany and pressure release:

He would have appreciated me bringing someone like Ian here for his first show.

We hurried across, Ian doing a double take at the car that zoomed through with complete disregard for traffic laws. It was early enough that people milled about the theater's entrance, as punk legends Grape Ape wouldn't take the stage for two hours or so. But while few lined up to get in this early, a step inside gave Ian his introduction to another great rock tradition: the bouncer.

We waited in line halfway up the stairwell, the huge man sitting on a stool kept cool, while a tall guy in a man-bun got agitated over something, probably an ID issue. Curiosity usually would have prompted me to listen closer, but several too-loud voices got in the way.

Because I heard the members of Copper Beach behind us, and they were *loud*. Their we've-been-pre-partying voices carried farther than they should have, arguing about another failed guitarist audition. That offered enough to catch my suspicions, but a quick look confirmed it.

Of course. A small, insular community meant a high likelihood of bumping into *someone* familiar. Ian stood shoulder to shoulder with me, face buried in his phone, though when I moved up a step, he stayed glued to his spot.

I turned to nudge him, a quick elbow and "hey" that got him to move, but must have shown enough of my profile. From the corner of my eye, I caught Sally looking at me, double take lingering long enough to make the connection in return.

With that, vampire rules were suddenly at risk.

I didn't need supernatural hearing to zero in on their chatter, their own drunken voices took care of that. "Dude. It's the woman with bleeding eyes."

"What? No, that's a totally different person," said their drummer, Josh.

I scanned around the small entrance hallway for signs that *other* vampires may have come to see Grape Ape. Of course, that would require me actually knowing other vampires.

"No, I swear."

Further shuffling came from behind, but I didn't turn to check it out. Though a third voice entered the conversation, who I took to be the remaining member of Copper Beach. "What? Her? The one with the white guitar?"

"Yes. Bleeding eyes. She's gonna get us all sick."

I resisted the urge to check to see if Ian picked up on any of this. Instead, I craned my neck to check the holdup ahead—they still argued over a real vs. fake ID at the wristband station.

"You're overreacting."

"Lucy, right? That was her name?"

Well, that was good. If anyone overheard this, at least they'd have the wrong name.

"Come on," I said under my breath, though Ian either noticed my mouth move or heard my quiet plea, as his eyes shifted my way. "Oh," I said at a normal volume, "they're just checking IDs if you want to drink at the bar. But I don't drink and you're underage, so we'll pass right through."

"What's the holdup?" he asked.

"Probably a fake ID or something," I answered, staring straight ahead despite the urge to turn and check on anything going on behind me. My phone. Was it listening in and transmitting to Eric? I reached into my pocket and powered it down.

"No, her name was Louise. Lou-ise. Not Lucy." Her slurred enunciation still convinced everyone around us, tickling my anxiety. "With the white guitar. And the bleeding fucking eyes. Said it was garlic allergies."

Ian stepped up next to me, and while he still held his phone in his hands, his shoulders tensed at the mention of my name. He tried to hide it, but he shot a very obvious glance my way.

Well, it couldn't get more clear than that.

"Next in line," the bouncer yelled, holding up a stack of wristbands.

"That's us," I said, shaking my head to decline access to the bar. The burly man waved us in, and I searched for anything to distract Ian from discussions of bleeding eyes, starting with the hall of psychedelic posters spanning decades of shows. "Welcome to the Fillmore." I pointed to the bin of bright red apples sitting in front of the wall of posters. "Free apple if you want one. It's a tradition."

Ian looked at me, then at the apples before picking one up and staring at it far longer than most people examined fruit. "You want one?" he asked me with squinted eyes. I shook my head and he took a bite before moving on. He scanned the room as he chomped, hopefully absorbing the timelessness of the venue, though he might have just people-watched the incoming flood of hipsters and punks.

"Hey," he said as I motioned him into the main hall, "did you know those people behind us?" By my estimate, we had about fifteen minutes before the first of three bands, which meant plenty of space to claim a spot. I pretended not to hear the question, instead weaving us through the light crowd underneath the main chandeliers.

"This is good." I said, sticking us right center-left of the stage, close enough that we could read the printed set list taped on the floor. "Set list. Soundboard." I pointed to the far side stage. "There's the drum kit for the opening band. You can see the main drum riser behind it. This is where it all happens."

"Cool," he said, taking out his phone to snap a picture. "But you didn't answer my question. Did you know those people behind us? They mentioned a Louise with a white guitar."

Ian thankfully stopped there without any mention of bleeding eyes. Good thing I'd shut off my phone. "Oh. Maybe. Local musician community is pretty small," I said with a nonchalant wave. "We see each other everywhere."

There was one moment when I knew I got it right.

The evening unfolded with a tension different than most. Shows usually came with the concern of "maybe I'm wasting my time and money," or the possibility that it might be overhyped and underwhelming, or the sound mix was bad. But on *this* night, I kept shooting nervous glances, and it wasn't because I was worried about the members of Copper Beach outing my true identity.

No, this was because I wanted Ian to have an *experience*.

Not just enjoy a live band. Not just get away from his troubles. I wanted him to have a sense of liftoff only offered by live music, the mix of euphoria and hypnosis that I first experienced seeing David Bowie.

Not everyone had the privilege of seeing David Bowie for their first show, but Grape Ape were a fantastic punk band to indoctrinate Ian. It didn't start that way. When the lights dimmed, Ian had his first encounter with an opening band—perfectly decent but forgettable. I kept leaning over, pointing out things like how the guitarist used a capo for one song. For their short set, once the novelty of loud live music wore off, he stood with polite disinterest, occasionally checking his phone.

Things shifted when Grape Ape took the stage, and at least Ian had done some homework to be familiar with their songs. That, combined with the thickening crowd and gradually building energy, created a surge of enthusiasm as the four women walked onstage. The first song punched with the strength of a solid opener, the second was a fast-paced older song, and the third was their single that worked its way through digital streams into the ears of hipsters around the world. That got Ian into a groove, locking his head bobbing to the beat while, even mouthing the words to the chorus.

But the next tune, that's where it happened. I'd recognized it as "Autonomous," the opener from their latest album. Ian's movement changed, from a slight bobbing of his head to full shoulders-bouncing-in-time to the opening drums. His eyes, however, stayed fixated, and he gradually changed from mouthing all the words to full-on screaming along, mesmerized by the band without any self-consciousness.

And even though I may have been a sixty-something vampire born of punk and raised in the faded Southern California suburbs, I let myself sink into the moment as well, singing along with the final chorus, an affirmation that if I'd done nothing else for this kid, at least I pushed his first step on the right path.

About two hours later, as we shuffled out the door, the doorman handed out the traditional commemorative posters for Fillmore shows. Ian took one, holding it up to see his first piece of gig merchandise. "Is every show like that?"

Grape Ape. He'd remember them forever because of this moment. "No. Some are even better."

We broke past the threshold, the sting of the night air welcoming us back to the land of traffic and smog, and I pulled out the rubber bands I always brought for a night at the Fillmore.

"So what do you do after a show?" he asked as I rolled up our posters and snapped them tight with the rubber bands.

Back when I went with Marshall, we'd go to a bar or an all-night diner, something within walking distance of the venue. I'd claim that I was straightedge and have a water while chatting with other local musicians who showed up. Which usually went better than the random vampires at one of Eric's community meetings.

In this context? I wasn't sure where to go.

We stood in the middle of the sidewalk, an obstacle in the current of people that flowed all around us. Ian awaited my response, an eagerness in his eyes that never existed with my own family.

He looked to me for an answer.

How about that?

"Well," I said, turning my phone back on. "Normally we'd go to a bar. Which you can't do. But, we could get a bite."

Ian's head tilted at this, a hesitation to his entire demeanor. "What do you mean, 'a bite'?"

This was weird, but if I acted weird, then he'd be even weirder, and weirdness was the last thing I needed. Especially if Eric listened in after I turned my phone back on. "A bite," I said, loading up a map of nearby places that were still open. "Like, greasy diner food surrounded by tired drunk people? It'll be like a glimpse into your twenties. So, you hungry?"

"Yeah. I'm always hungry. You?"

"No," I said, "just some water for me. Come on, there's a place a few blocks away."

# CHAPTER 21

WE DREW SIDE-EYES AND strange looks as we stepped into Chester's, a standard open-too-late greasy spoon within walking distance of the Fillmore. Second glances shot at Ian, who was by far the youngest person in the building.

Ian either didn't notice or didn't care, and instead stared at the chalkboard menu written over the bar. We waited behind a short line at the register: patrons ordering first before sitting down, a smattering of late-night dates, postconcert fans, and random individuals nursing drinks. Most of the patrons sipped from tall glasses and nibbled on things like chicken wings and nachos, but from the way he studied the menu, Ian clearly wanted a full meal. I watched, considering the strange reality of simply being able to order something to eat. But a tickle in my nose interrupted, one of the usual dangers of hanging out with humans in restaurants.

The building was an aromatic minefield, garlic potentially anywhere. Even at the entrance, my nose caught a hint of it, and without Marshall around to scope it out and give the all clear, I had to play it safe. "Let's sit by the window," I said, pointing to a table next to an open breeze. "Fresh air after being cooped up inside for a few hours. Get whatever you want." I gave the menu a quick sanity review. "Except the cheesy garlic bread."

"Wait, what?"

"Oh, we're up," I said, quick enough to avoid the question. The woman at the register motioned for us to move forward, and I let Ian order a massive carne asada burrito with a side of guacamole while I requested a simple lemon tea to sip on. If he brought up the cheesy garlic bread, at least I'd have some time to come up with an excuse.

We walked through the dim orange lighting between a smattering of faded sports photos and a single lit TV in the corner, cross chatter from the half-filled diner helping drown out the standard postshow tinnitus. "Shouldn't be too long," I said, and as we sat down, I pondered what to say. Should I check in on his family situation? Ask him his thoughts on Grape Ape?

But he chose for us. "Hey, I thought of something with your phone. Can I check it out?"

No hard questions and no small talk. Sounded like the right choice to me. "Sure. That app is still on there." I unlocked my phone and slid it over as the waitress by the register caught my eye with her waving arm. "Oh, we forgot the stand thingy with our order number. I'll grab it."

"Sure," Ian said, tapping away at the glowing screen. I moved through scooted chairs and half-drunk customers to reach the register and grab the chrome pole holding a laminated number eleven. A waiter yelled "excuse me" as he barreled by with a large tray propped up with one hand. He moved past, leaving me with Ian in my sights, though instead of looking at my phone, he had angled his neck to peek in the far corner. I watched as he adjusted in his seat, shifting to get a better look at…something before returning to the still-glowing phone, but then another look back.

I looked too, though the handful of customers at beat-up tables didn't prove remarkable. "Something interesting?" I asked when I returned to our table.

"Huh? No. I still can't delete the app. It's really stubborn."

"Ah. Weird," I said, scooting in, one eye on the corner he checked out. "Well, I suppose I could factory reset it."

"Yeah," he said. I debated pressing him on whatever caught his attention when the waiter appeared with his burrito, and suddenly the only thing that mattered sat on his plate.

Several years had passed since I last set foot in a restaurant. I inhaled, trying to take in the *humanness* of the aroma. I knew the individual pieces—the cooked steak, the melted cheese, the refried beans, the sting of cilantro and onion. But even smelling with purpose failed to produce a physiological response. No hunger tickled, nothing salivated, and I may as well have identified the different odors of various bathroom cleaners.

Tea still worked for me. Everything else came in bright, clear, and lifeless.

Ian tore through the burrito in silence, and I slid my phone back. It unlocked to the last screen he'd been in—Eric's app in the map view, where a blue dot clearly showed me.

And a purple dot flashed in proximity. I zoomed in closer until I realized that this wasn't just somewhere close by or even on the same block.

That dot belonged to someone in the restaurant. Was that what Ian looked for? Did he figure out what it meant? Eric's app used acronyms and other coded identifiers, so it's not like each blip carried a caption of NOSFERATU on it.

I scanned the room again, except instead of taking in decor, I searched for other vampires. Problem was, my antisocial nature meant that I barely knew anyone in our transient community.

Ian's appetite was satiated about halfway through his burrito, slowing him down to the side of chips and salsa. He started looking around again, though this time his eyes tracked to the window between the cooks and the waitstaff.

Was this kid *still* hungry?

"Yeah," I said in a really terrible attempt at restarting conversation, "think I'll just download my photos and do a factory reset. I hardly have any apps anyway. All they do is spy on you—"

Ian stood up, his knees bumping the table. "I, uh, have to use the bathroom," he said, eyes fixated past me.

"Um, sure. Okay. I'll just wait here. Mind if I have some chips?" Which, of course, I wasn't actually going to eat, but the question helped with keeping up the whole human appearance thing.

"That's fine. I'll be right back."

Ian dashed off, though instead of going to the back restroom, he hovered by the swinging door of the restaurant counter before walking over to a table of drunk hipsters, one wearing a Grape Ape shirt. A fierceness took over his expression, an odd determination that hadn't appeared during anything we'd done together, not even during the show. He spoke to them, though my nonsupernatural hearing failed to pick up any words.

Something he said must have struck a nerve because the table laughed at him.

He chuckled too, though with a shoulder shrug that gave away its lack of sincerity. And in one quick gesture, he reached down and grabbed...

Did he just steal something from their table?

Tension crept along my shoulders as I watched Ian march forward, his eyes fixated on the corner he'd watched before. He moved quickly, almost to the corner booth. He paused several feet away, first looking at the basket of stolen food in his hand, then at his own feet. He sucked in a breath before muttering to himself and stepping forward. But instead of a normal step, his arms flailed as if he'd tripped over something, enough to toss...

Bread? Fired outward at the two seated people in the corner.

The table braced his impact, hands slapping down loud enough that I heard the clanging silverware, and he let out a rapid-fire apology to the patrons, one who nodded and tried to usher him away.

And another who began sneezing wildly while covering his eyes. Ian's apology refrain continued, but he angled low at the sneezing man, someone who looked human, but I knew better. I played the last minute back in my head, from Ian's leaving our table, to grabbing a basket off the table, to his faux fall, putting together what he knew.

He must have been listening to Copper Beach behind us after all.

Because that wasn't just bread. It was an order of cheesy *garlic* bread.

And it was a *vampire* he'd launched them at.

"Oh shit," I said under my breath, standing up and looking straight at the exit.

**CHAPTER 22**

"IT WAS AN ACCIDENT," Ian said as we huffed our way out of the diner and back on the street. "I tripped, I swear." I didn't say anything—I didn't know *what* to say. One wrong thing and I might give away my true identity, and we were in enough potential trouble as it was. For now, I played it as simple as possible, not even bringing up the fact that he'd stolen garlic bread off a table. The sooner we got past this, the better. After all, Ian could have figured out the app was about vampires or he might have made some giant assumption about garlic intolerance. "It's okay," I said, despite it not being okay. "We're both tired. Long night. Big night. Accidents happen. Worse things happen. You know?"

We took a rideshare back to my house even though it was only a twenty-minute walk. Most of it passed in silence, Ian only relaying the voice mail EJ had left him: they'd made it back to San Diego and were gradually getting "set up."

That last part came out with broken hesitation, and though

part of me wanted to say a knee-jerk "that could mean any-thing" response, we both knew the truth. I let Ian take the space he needed. Which meant that when we got back to my house, he gave Lola a few pets, then walked down the hall. He moved with purpose, and though he locked himself in the bathroom, this had nothing to do with biology.

The intent of his stride, the pace of his steps—I recognized it. I knew that it meant something shifted in him, a conscious decision to move into something new. What that was, I sup-posed I'd find out. But it was likely to be significant.

I knew because I'd done something quite similar years ago.

Back then, my journey started with laundry. First the pile of clothes on my bed, then the thought of "how often do they do laundry on the road?" The question lingered longer than it should have, a practical anchor that blocked me from just throwing shit in a bag and leaving. But after a minute of star-ing at *laundry*, the source of my hesitation became clear. It had chipped away at me ever since I started holing up in my room with my guitar. It echoed through my life, rippling out at differ-ent times: when I got a job as a bartender, when I dropped out of community college, when I spent my money on guitar stuff.

It was *guilt*, formed piece by piece across a lifetime of being chastised for failing my family's expectations.

Our suburban home was far from picturesque. Nestled in the small and cramped sprawl of stucco and fencing, it offered my parents a comfortable commute and little else. It "fit in" simply by being real estate, which seemed to be their whole purpose of existence. Whenever I'd complained about the sprawlish hell, I'd get a trio of *tsks* and a story of how I needed to learn to appreciate why my parents immigrated, how every moment was an opportunity to "build something" and "fit in" for "a better life" than what they had.

Even when my dad would come home radiating a silent anger, it dissipated in a flash. At most, he'd slip a quick whisper about the "lazy and stupid" people who got promoted over him. But then he'd quickly revert to being appreciative of what they had, what they built, a blind patriotism to this life, as if criticizing any element of it was a personal affront to the effort of their American life.

From the waist-high speakers, the kicking bass drum of Blondie's "One Way or Another" thumped along, a stinging attack of guitar chords whipping the air. Debbie Harry's angry snarl announced itself, burrowing within me so deeply that I found my fist clenched.

"One way or another," I muttered under my breath. I looked at the packed duffel bag sitting next to the open backpack, a lumpy stack of T-shirts and socks ready to be packed in. Four weeks on an impromptu gig as a roadie for a mildly successful touring band called 11 Hours might not have been the same as taking science classes or volunteering, but this was *life* experience. I stuffed clothes into the backpack until the song ended and a noise from downstairs caught my attention. I pulled the needle off the record, though it continued spinning while the familiar *ding-ding-ding* of the phone interrupted.

The ringing refusing to go away until I finally stomped down the stairs to the mustard-yellow phone on the counter. "Hello," I said to the person who just wouldn't give up.

"Oh. Hey. It's, uh, Stephen." Of course I knew that. I'd heard Stephen's voice every day of his life until he'd left for his freshman year of college two months prior. The way he took stuttered breaths in between words, the way he tripped on his own name, all of that was built in with reflex. Introducing himself when our familiarity gave a completely clear definition of who Stephen was. "Mom or Dad home?"

"They went to lunch."

"Okay. Tell them I'm leaving now, I'll be there in an hour and a half."

I looked at the clock on the counter, thin black arms ticking across a wood panel with painted numbers, the orange price tag still on its corner. "Exactly an hour and a half?"

"Pretty close. I mean, depending on traffic and stuff."

"But what if you have to pee?"

Stephen paused, then huffed into the phone. Mission accomplished—I asked him a question just reasonable enough for him to consider the answer, though he probably knew I didn't actually care. "Lou—"

"It's fine. I don't know when they'll be back. They might go to the grocery store after. But I'll be gone."

"Oh. Okay."

"Actually," I said. Breaking it to him now would probably make more sense. They'd all find out anyway. "I'll be gone for a few weeks. Leaving a note for Mom and Dad." I glanced upstairs. "Don't touch my shit." Which really meant my pair of guitars, one electric and one acoustic, neither worth much in practical value, but they meant *everything* to me. So that constituted "my shit."

"Where are you going?"

Options flashed in my head. I could tell them that I'd signed up for the Peace Corps, that would check the box on their intellectual standards. Or I could say I was following some sports team around—what sports were even being played right now, and how often did they do it? Or I could *really* needle them and say that I'd been talking to Aunt Laura and decided to stay with her for a few weeks.

In the end, I offered a half-truth. "I got a temp job."

"A temp job?" Stephen snorted, a "huh huh" laced with mockery. "Uh, what about your regular job?"

This was a trap. I knew it. I knew exactly how he'd execute it because it was the same way Mom and Dad lobbed verbal blows until you wound up punching yourself in the face. I went with the easiest answer. "I got the time off." Which was a lie. I told the bar about it, they fired me and said they might—*might*—

take me back part-time when I returned. But whatever, Stephen would be back working on his fancy degree by the time that all came around. And though I wasn't necessarily on a time-table, suddenly leaving seemed much more pressing. "Anyway, I gotta go." I almost included a condescending "little brother" in there. Except such a jab lost all its power by the time he hit middle school, when it became clear that Stephen's interests lined up exactly with my parents' vision of acceptance and success. That always compared to his sister's spiral into being the dumbass who sneaked in weed, tended bar, and cared too much about music. "Don't touch my shit," I said again, hanging up before he replied with something better.

I scribbled a note on the pad next to the rotary phone, a quick blip about Stephen's imminent visit along with "I'll be gone a few weeks, check in soon." I reminded myself to un-clench my teeth before running back upstairs to finish pack-ing. As I pulled the zipper closed, a car door slammed outside, quickly followed by another *thunk*.

Then the front door opened.

My heart did that terrible thing where it beat harder and faster than it should over something completely trivial. A sim-ple lie might get me out of it and give several weeks to come up with an explanation, especially since I'd already started one track with Stephen.

I shut the door to my room, then grabbed my bags, poised to time my escape with the hope that they hadn't seen my note and wouldn't cross my path in the hallway.

"Louise!" Mom's voice came from downstairs.

Shit.

Bags in hand, I opened the door and marched swiftly, a di-rect line to the front door.

"Where are you going?" Dad asked the instant I reached the bottom of the stairs, his tone laced with suspicion. "You gone a few weeks without telling us?"

"Work," I said.

"Bartenders travel for work?"

Despite facing the front door, their glares dug claws in, killing my forward momentum and drawing me back. Normally, this would be where I'd turn around, mumble an answer, then slink upstairs to my cave of drums and guitars. But maybe it was Debbie Harry demanding an escape, or this opportunity with 11 Hours, or everything crashing together into a single moment. Something held me steady, fighting back against their words.

I stepped forward.

"You make another bad decision?"

A breath. *One way or another,* I told myself.

And then another step forward.

Normally, their scrutiny ran me over. Today, I would stand up.

"It's work. On the road."

*"Diu nei!"* Mom only threw out Cantonese when she really meant business. And it was usually followed by a cutting remark under her breath. Her formula came so predictably, yet it always worked.

Not this time. I refused.

"I always knew boys were smarter." There it was. *Just* loud enough to hear. Words sharp enough to angle me and Stephen into direct competition, a fight to the death despite my seniority. He'd elevated himself on their scorecard the moment he got straight A's in sixth grade—something I'd never been able to pull off—and he overtook me soon after.

"By the way," I said, my mind exploding with the most perfect lie that I couldn't stop myself from grinning. "While I'm gone, I'm gonna see Aunt Laura."

*"Diu nei!* We do *not* talk about her."

"And I'll meet her girlfriend." The year 1977 was long before I connected with her, but the effectiveness of this partic-

ular retort planted the seeds. At that moment, all I wanted to
do was fire back in a way that I *knew* would break past their
defenses. "Not roommate. Girlfriend. You know, she tells me
they have sex all the time." I finally turned, a sudden power in
my words, and I let myself take in their expressions for a sliver
of victory. "Should I describe how two women have sex?"

Both my parents started shouting indecipherable words, but
it didn't matter. I walked upstairs, "One Way or Another" playing in my head, my boots moving to the fast rhythm. Though
I carried a backpack, I hung the duffel bag over my left shoulder, then grabbed my two guitars.

Stephen wouldn't get a chance to touch my shit.

"Louise!" Mom yelled, the smoothness in her trained words
decaying to broken English as her agitation elevated. "You talk
to Laura and you are disowned from this family. You think
you such a smart girl, you find out on your own."

"Not smart. *Tough*," I yelled back. A flood of words jammed
up against the dam in my head, seeking a single crack to find
a way out. But they weren't coherent enough to easily translate into "I want this" or "You said that." Instead, they were
something far more dangerous and chaotic:

Feelings. Shapeless, directionless, a crackling ball of emotions unable to take form into something sensible.

Even if I wanted to say something more, I didn't know how
to.

Mom gave her cold stare, the one she fired off when disap-
proving—which was different from the one she used when she
conveyed disappointment. Dad shook his head and walked to
the living room, his sigh accompanied by the rustle of newspaper. Mom maintained her glare, unblinking eyes tracking
me as I walked with purpose, every step seeming to echo out
into the suburban landscape. And even though the walk only
covered from the inside of the house to my shitty Volkswagen
Rabbit parked along the sidewalk, it may as well have been a

march into a different country, a different life. It represented a fundamental turn away from everything I knew, even leaving my records behind.

Everything except my guitars.

Back in my small San Francisco house, the bathroom door down the hall squeaked on its hinges as it opened. And now Ian showed that walk again, some five minutes after he'd disappeared, he returned with purpose, steps causing the old floorboards to creak under his weight. By now, Lola had gone from being mildly interested in him to full-on adoration, a handful of French fries converting my dog into a complete traitor.

Ian came up to me in straight steps, a direct line without pausing to pet a dog.

"I know what you are," he announced.

My mind moved to the most legit-sounding excuse possible. "Yeah, I'm a dog person. Some people are cat people but I just love dogs better. They—"

"No, I know what you are. Sleeping during the day," he said, starting a count on his fingers. "The people behind us in line. The stuff you wore to protect yourself from the sun. The weird app. The burn on your cheek. When you talk about Laura, something about your age doesn't add up. And your birthday on your driver's license." So he *did* look at that. Shit. "You're different."

"I already told you. I'm a janitor at a hospital. I work nightshift. So I'll probably be asleep when you wake up—"

"Stop lying." His words came out as direct as I'd heard in our short time together—not angry, not emotional, more of a forceful plea. "Come on, if I threw garlic bread on you, wouldn't your eyes start bleeding?"

"Not…necessarily." This was true, actually. Vampire allergies to garlic ranged in severity, which was probably why the guy in the corner was able to be in a restaurant in the first place while I tended to avoid them.

"Is it called 'vampire'?" he said, pausing only to pet Lola when she waddled over. "Or is there, like, a technical term?"

"Okay, this is ridiculous." My phone. What if Eric heard us talking about vampire stuff out loud? I pulled it out of my pocket and powered it off. "Look, lots of people work nights."

"Stop that." This time, the words came laced with anger. "That way you're talking to me. My grandpa talks to me like I'm a kid. My mom does too. I thought you were *cooler* than that."

My breath held, Ian's words hitting harder than I wanted to admit. This whole thing started as a favor, then a kindness. Then a commitment. Each of those tangled together into a need for honesty.

It's what I would have wanted in return.

"Alright. Let's just talk this through. So what if I was…that?" I asked. "You think I'm gonna bite you, drink your blood?" I shrugged my shoulders, trying to look as inconsequential as possible. "Turn you?"

Ian shook his head right away at that last question. "No. I don't want to be turned," he said, prompting an immediate enough relief that I may have even exhaled. Which didn't help my cover-up. But given the building pressure, this made for a significantly easier conversation, no matter where it led.

"Okay, that's good. *If* I was that, I wouldn't—"

"It's not me. I want you to turn my mom." Ian looked right at me, his brown eyes staring with a wide-eyed connection. "I want you to save her."

# CHAPTER 23

**I WANTED TO SAY** YES.

Not because I dreamed of turning people into vampires. Far from it. The urge to say yes came with a simple appeal, an acknowledgment and confirmation of Ian's desperation. But it wasn't that easy. And I didn't know how to explain that to Ian without coming off as dismissive or condescending or just plain cruel.

I had to say *something,* but the disaster of that night with Marshall loomed over my thoughts. Though the words I came up with tonight weren't any better than before. "I...can't?"

A silence grew between us, and Ian shot a look that lacked definition, as if he couldn't comprehend my reply. "What do you mean, you can't?" he asked, both anger and confusion tinting his words.

"I just can't."

Ian seemed to leap past the whole confirmation of 1) vampires exist, and 2) I was one of them. Which meant that at some point, I'd need to have to talk with him about community rules. "Of course you can," he said, his voice becoming increasingly frustrated. "That's how it works."

"Actually, that's *not* how it works." This marked the third time a human learned my true identity, and between this, Laura's "it's fine" response and Marshall's "that sounds depressing" reaction, I wondered if I simply wasn't very good at being a vampire. Definitely a poor representative for the community if nothing else.

"That makes no sense." His hands went up in a shrug, a full-body rejection of my statement.

"No, seriously. I can't," I said, mirroring Ian's frustration for completely different reasons.

"You mean you weren't made? Were you born a vampire?" Ian squinted, mind clearly churning. "Like, is my grandpa secretly one too?"

"What? No, of course not."

"So you *were* made a vampire."

"Yeah, I mean, that's basically how it works," I said, an exasperated sigh slipping out.

"So then you can turn my mom." He pointed with the cadence of his words, as if that would prove his point further.

"No, that's the thing." My hands went up, the universal sign of slow-the-fuck-down. "Okay, let's reset. Yes, someone turned me. No, I can't turn other vampires."

"This makes no sense," he said again. But repeating it wouldn't flip reality. "You're, like, contradicting yourself."

Lola waddled between us and plopped down. She looked with ears back, seemingly pleading for us to stop arguing or at least give her a bone.

"So, here's what I know about turning," I said. "The rumor—standard assumption, really—is that it can kill you if you try."

"Didn't you have, like, a master vampire or something?"

In my head, the chorus to Depeche Mode's *"Master and Ser-*

*vant"* began playing. "This is what I know for sure—like, I know this because everyone has the same story. I went out to a show. Iggy Pop—seventies punk guy. I went to his show in LA, have no real memory of the show and kind of came to about two weeks later in a closet in my apartment." Senses came in flashes: the lights from the stage, the heat of bodies mashing together, and the intense stare of a tall woman in a leather jacket (we all had leather jackets), torn white T-shirt, and pleated skirt, an outfit that looked so of-the-moment that it might have come from a scrapbook. "For a few months afterward, my maker would just randomly show up to help me learn the ropes, and then she disappeared completely. I don't remember much about it. That whole period was like a really intense drug trip." I cocked my head sideways at Ian. "Hopefully you don't know what an intense drug trip feels like."

"I saw you get burned in the car. If you were tripping for months, you would have stepped into the sun. Or got stuck outdoors."

"No, see, here's the thing." Too bad I didn't have that article of vampire power myths to show Ian how wrong pop culture got us. "So in movies, you see people get turned into vampires in, like, seconds. Maybe minutes. But it's really a gradual process. First, you kind of go feral and eat a ton of protein for a few days. I think calories for the transformation. Then your body starts changing on the inside." Was there a technical description for this besides "most of your organs shut down"? Others probably knew better than me, but that required going to community mixers and that really wasn't my scene. "Like, basically making your body capable of surviving on blood instead of food. And your fangs sharpen." I omitted the part about how gross and difficult biting into a human actually was. "You come out of that after about two weeks, and over that time, your body becomes more and more sensitive to sun until you can't take it anymore. Most of us reported our maker helping us learn the ropes during that hazy time." I shrugged, though a bitterness lay underneath. "Some even learned their names. But I didn't."

Ian sat, lips pursed, before pulling up his phone and tapping at the search bar. "Okay, what you just told me makes even less sense than the movies. You were eating meat but you're feral? That sounds more like a werewolf." He sat up, the chair bumping underneath him. "Wait, there's werewolves too, right?"

Why did people always lump the two together? Vampires represented a change in the way human organs operated. Werewolves were people that freaking transformed into giant dogs. Now that *really* didn't make sense. "No way. Werewolves are a ridiculous fiction."

"How do you know? When there's vampires, there's *always* werewolves."

"Okay, look. When you're in the meat-eating stage, you're not like *rabid* feral, you're more like...drunk on instinct. So you'll go buy a bunch of hot dogs and rotisserie chickens and just sit and eat them. But not, like, eating live raccoons off the street. Though you *could* live off wild animals if you really needed to. They're just really hard to catch." I stopped, rubbing my face at how this flew off the rails.

"Is that what happened with the attacks in the news?"

"I'm not even sure," I said, though I avoided that the only reason I *didn't* know was because I never hung out with vampires. "My point is, the process is pretty mysterious to all of us. I don't know why. You're right—*someone* somewhere has to know. But instead, everyone says that you could die if you try to turn someone, and it probably won't work anyway. So I can't turn your mom. I just can't."

"You don't know for sure."

"Yeah. Okay, look. You're right about that. I don't know for sure. But I'm like 99.999 percent sure that I can't. It's what everyone says. And as for that point-oh-whatever chance that I can? It still might kill me. So I can't. I really can't." My stance suddenly softened, shoulders dropping like I carried all of Ian's hopes on them. "I'm sorry. It's just not something I can do."

Ian stayed quiet, tapping through search engine results on his phone, as if someone somewhere might have posted the secret to this and if he *just* found it, he'd be able to convince me. But internet vampire lore came solely from pop culture. Real vampire facts had been filtered out through a combination of community coaxing and probably tech people like Eric scrubbing for any authenticities. I sat on the kitchen floor with legs crossed and waited, giving Ian all the possible space he might need. Lola took advantage of my position and hopped onto me, her head winding up on my lap but her long body hanging off. Despite the awkwardness—and her right elbow jabbing into my inner thigh—I stroked her oversize ears and waited.

Ian needed time to process the fact that he couldn't save his mom. And maybe the vampire stuff too, though all of that probably came in a far second.

Several more minutes passed, Lola content with ear rubs while Ian continued searching for whatever obscure epiphany he needed. But finally, he let out a full-body exhale. It took the weight off my shoulders, though it seemed to put it back on his. He shook his head, biting down on his bottom lip, and his gaze stayed down.

"Well," he said, a new dry gravel to his voice, "I can't find anything about vampires eating a bunch of protein before they turn."

Guess he still didn't believe me. But that lack of online information also meant that vampires everywhere kept the informal credo of staying quiet on the topic. Movies and TV provided enough disinformation for us. "Yeah, we're really encouraged not to post anything online. Secret identities and all that. Which is too bad because a tutorial video would be superhelpful during those first few years."

"You could be making it up."

"I could be—" I started in a gentle voice to counter his accusatory tone "—but look at me. Look at everything you've seen. You know I'm not. Hey," I said, looking him straight in the eye.

"I wouldn't lie to you."

Ian finally met my gaze, crinkles forming around his eyes as he fought back welling tears. The tears eventually won out, a small streak down each side and he shut his eyes, holding himself static until everything recalibrated. The screen in his hands timed out, search results disappearing, but rather than awaken the device, he let it sit. He finally took a deep breath, then released it, though the biggest change came from the ashen expression on his face. He set his phone on the table and opened his eyes, staring straight ahead.

"I'm really sorry," I said, "I wish I could help." Saying the words stung, an echo of what happened with Marshall, except in a way, this carried so much more weight. With Marshall, it had been a request—a desperate one, sure, but a request without any sense of legit impending doom. "Trust me, if I could, there'd still be a few more people in my life."

Fear drove his request, terror from the way the pandemic infiltrated every nook and cranny of human lives, and he had taken that idea too far.

Here, Ian was still driven by fear—fear of a life where he might lose both parents within a year of each other. But his solution came in the form of a desperate bargain. The only problem was, he placed his faith in the wrong person, the wrong kind of people.

"Look, you can be mad at me if you want. I mean, if I didn't know it firsthand, I'd find the whole inability-to-turn thing pretty ridiculous too. Blame every vampire on TV for that one."

"So it can really kill the person doing the turning?"

I thought of Marshall, betrayal written into his eyes on that last night before he shut his car door. "That's what everyone says."

"The movies really missed the mark, huh?"

"I wish I didn't have to disappoint you. But look, you wanted to escape *everything* for a few days. We at least did that, right? I mean, come on, Grape Ape is a pretty badass first show. And you know," I said, my tone softening, "that was actually my first show in a while too."

"Yeah? I thought you went all the time."

"I did. For the longest time, that's what I did." I looked at my blank phone screen, and somewhere in that small device was the life I used to lead. Photos, recordings, text messages, not just of Marshall, but Pete and the rest of the musicians I'd see on a regular basis, either before shows or at gigs or at bars before or after gigs. That was the thing with musicians—they lived a very similar life to vampires outside of the whole "drinking blood" thing. "Then my best friend died and I hadn't really felt like returning since. Until you wanted to go."

Ian looked at me, the light in his eyes shifting. I wondered how he saw me now. Did that simple admission reframe his view of me? He'd met me as this standoffish distant relative with a strange obsession for naming guitars, which then became someone who shielded him from the pain of his world.

And now someone who, in a way, shared that pain.

"How was it?" he finally asked. "Going back?"

"It was," I said after several breaths, "just like I remembered. Our minds are funny that way, you know? We get all worked up about stuff when really, the simple thing to do is just go ahead. The best thing to do, really."

"Yeah." He bit down on his lip and looked beyond me, as if we were back under the blinding spotlights at the Fillmore. "The best thing to do."

At this point, my back ached, my butt muscles were asleep,

and Lola lay like a rock on my crossed legs. But I still reached over as best as I could and gave him a light punch in the leg. "Hey, I've got an idea."

"What's that?"

"Well, look. Now you know, right? No more hiding who I am. So first off, this can never, ever get out. We have rules about that. But…" I pushed out a large toothy grin, something forced to move the conversation into a more upbeat realm. "Wanna see how a vampire actually lives?"

# CHAPTER 24

**VAMPIRE POWER MYTH #9:** Vampires have vicious claws, a natural defense that turns their fingernails into deadly weapons.

If that was the case, I'd be able to open cardboard boxes more easily. Instead, I asked Ian for help with the brown shipping box I'd hidden my blood in. He dug through a drawer for scissors as I grabbed the package out of the fridge, layers of packing tape sealing the bottles in and the words Protein Shakes scribbled in big black marker on all sides.

"More like platelet shakes," I said, laughing to myself. The joke either flew over his head or didn't land and he hadn't learned enough social graces to react accordingly. After several further seconds of silence, I reached in and grabbed the box farthest to the left. "I drink about a cup and a half a day. This stock will last me a few weeks, longer if I ration it. They expire, though. You wanna see? I'm hungry and don't have to hide it anymore."

Another hour had passed since our big talk about turning humans, pushing us well past two in the morning. Ian had no shortage of questions about vampire life, mostly answered with "No, it's not like that." His biggest disappointment seemed to be my room, where he'd been expecting a full-fledged coffin adorned with skulls. Instead, he got a bed straight from the IKEA catalog, and three layers of sunlight protection over the two windows: shutters, blackout curtains, and bookshelves—also from IKEA, and specifically placed to progressively block out any possible stray beams of light.

The blood part, however, provoked his curiosity. "Come on, let's have a snack," I said. I pulled out one expiring blood bag from the box, then poured it into a Count Chocula coffee mug while Ian dug out a bag of chips from the cabinet.

Such a simple way of feeding: open the fridge and pour—the complete opposite from those early years, when finding a source required way too much planning. In my very early days, once my anonymous maker stopped giving me safety tips and handouts, I stumbled around meat-processing plants and farms, getting my face and hands far dirtier than I wanted with both official night shifts and unofficial break-ins of slaughterhouses in the middle-of-nowhere, California. But, to my credit, I never killed an animal myself.

Once I moved to Los Angeles, though, I needed an urban source. And it came in the form of a blood pimp—my term, not theirs. Which didn't make getting blood from an unhygienic person any less gross, but at least I knew I'd be safe. More importantly, I'd learned that blood pimps were surprisingly easy to find if you went to the right places and asked the right questions. Either there were way more vampires around or more humans fetishized blood than I realized.

Knowing this made my 1989 move to San Francisco possible. I only needed a few days of discreetly asking around to locate one. Blood pimps were equal parts volatile, reliable, and gross, but eating was eating, and it played within the vampire community rules.

I watched as the tube dripped blood into a third mason jar. "That's good," the blood pimp said, a woman I'd come to know as Wendy. Wendy stood over the donor with eyes that stabbed and a fierce tattoo that ran up and down her shoulder. When the donor nodded, Wendy handed him a juice box, the usual process for these donations. The donor grunted, a raggedy-looking man whose details I didn't want to cement in memory, then unhooked the catheter himself. Whatever he did with it, I didn't want to know; I sealed up my mason jar and stuffed it into my backpack with the rest of the blood.

"Want dessert?" Wendy asked. She held up the catheter tube, blood still sitting in most of it.

"Sure," I said, taking it quickly and sucking down one end.

"On the house."

I finished as fast as I could, my knuckles rapping against my lips to wipe them off. Transaction complete, Wendy handed me two more jars—one supposedly of her blood and one of another donor's, though she could have filled them both with livestock blood and I honestly wouldn't know. I gave a cursory thanks, then turned, trying to move quickly without looking like I hurried. My backpack—an oversize bit of army surplus gear—jostled with every step, and I turned the corner from the alley, then huffed my way uphill on Kearny Street. Walking through the edge of Chinatown and North Beach, I moved through the cross-pollination of bars, strip clubs, and all-night activity, hustling to my car and counting the seconds until I got to some measure of contained safety.

Behind me, a silhouette moved, and my pace picked up. My anonymous maker had arrived this way when she actually both-ered to show up, but this was also rough terrain in a new city. And I hadn't figured out how to get in touch with the local community's vampire doctors yet, so I did the smart thing by keeping my mouth shut and pressing forward.

I didn't need any trouble.

Then a voice called out. A deep voice with a Scottish accent, someone who definitely was *not* my maker. "Excuse me," he asked, "are you alright?"

"Yeah, I'm fine." Given the circumstances, I wasn't, but engaging with strangers felt like a markedly bad idea, not just because of the neighborhood, but with a giant bag filled with mason jars and Tupperware.

"That's a lot of blood in your bag," the man said. "About two weeks of feeding?"

I stopped, the question creating instant hesitation. Had he been watching? What could his purpose be in saying that? His tone carried both concern and curiosity, something that seemed out of time and out of place for this neighborhood.

Despite my better judgment, I turned around.

"You're safe?" he asked with a wave. "These sources aren't always the kindest bunch." He curled his lip, and at first, the gesture threw me off—what did that expression even mean?

But then it hit me: it *wasn't* an expression.

He was showing his fangs.

"It's fine," I said, realizing that this might be a most polite attempt at a mugging for my blood. "We're consenting adults doing a thing. Just heading home now."

The figure stood, hands folded and back straight, a silhouette from his tight jacket and windswept curly hair standing tall. "Wouldn't it be easier if you knew where your meals came from? Clean, safe. Without—" he gestured around us "—all this?"

"Look, I don't know how long you've been, um, like *this*, but sometimes you gotta do shit you don't want to do. To eat." I stepped forward, wondering how much experience I had over him. "It's not like the movies. Fangs don't puncture easily."

"Oh, I know that. And I always follow community rules. Even when they change over the years."

"What are you, one of those ancient vampires people talk about?" I said before cursing my hipster urge to always seem more knowledgeable than I was.

The man laughed, shaking his head. "You should know the difference between rumor and fact." He let out a short laugh. "Listen, you're new here. I'm trying to organize a little bit. Give us resources to get basic things, like more easily obtaining meals. But also housing, jobs, that sort of thing. Making sure everyone is working toward our best interests."

"Are you running for president of vamp—"

He put a finger to his mouth with a quick shake of his head. "Never that word. Not in public. Secrecy is safety."

"Okay." Which made sense, but still seemed weird, especially by the glowing yellow signs and loud music from Larry Flynt's Hustler Club on Kearny Street. "Well, I was gonna ask if you were running for...community president. But the timing on that joke is probably gone." The man still chuckled, a soft laugh probably out of pity. "You get blood bags from the hospital or something?"

"No. But someone in the community might. I host monthly get-togethers for our kind. Food distribution, resource discussion. A medical clinic if you need it. We need to support each other." Lines formed across his brow, a very serious look for the strangest of situations. "We're trying to build something better. Someday our lives won't just be focused on our next meal." He gestured at the alley with a sigh. "Or doing this..."

Those early days—aimless, desperate, and hustling on the street for blood. Compared to the present, sitting with Ian while sipping on blood warmed by microwave. I wondered what this might have looked like to someone from the outside, a woman drinking a thick, dark-red sludge out of a Count Chocula mug far past midnight while a young teen ate an entire bag of chips, a snoring corgi in between. In a way, it might have appeared normal.

Because it *felt* normal. Or what normal might have been. This was different from playing music with a band or going to a show. This was a simple act of sharing space with another person, discussing the most inane things as seconds expanded to fill the space of hours.

The same way things used to be with Aunt Laura. With Marshall.

Ian didn't reveal any significant details or purge any deeply guarded feelings. Instead, I found out about his favorite brand of chips, why he thought protein shakes were disgusting, how he wanted a dog as a child but their house's landlord wouldn't allow it, why programming felt like a logical tether in an illogical world. He even admitted that while he liked a lot of the music I'd introduced, he still didn't quite "get" David Bowie.

I'd give him a pass on that last one. He had plenty of time to learn.

"You tired?" I asked. "I'm getting there. Maybe we can both be daysleepers today." To prove the point, I loaded up R.E.M.'s "Daysleeper" to play over the speakers.

Though lines began to etch under sagging eyes, he shook his head. "Not yet."

Maybe he just needed time to digest the world-changing day he'd just had. Or maybe he wanted to be a teenager staying up until sunrise, eating greasy chips and playing games on his phone.

"Suit yourself. The couch is yours," I said, snapping my fingers twice to get Lola's attention before pointing to the bedroom. "See you around five-ish." My dog led the way down the hall, my pace keeping up with her tired short legs. "Oh, you can *try* blood if you're really curious, but I promise you're not missing anything. Just don't take too much."

"No, thanks. Hey, if I'm going to be up," he said, "you want me to keep working on your phone?"

The question caused an immediate pause in my step. I turned, my hesitant expression delivering an unintentional response, something that Ian immediately frowned at. But he *did* just use my phone to test a theory about vampires, so my feelings were justified.

"I, uh," he started, his voice an unlikely quiet, "could use something to take my mind off everything."

Still, after the talk we just had, what harm might come of it?

"Alright. See what you can do. But when I get up, we'll have to talk about community rules and stuff." Lola offered an annoyed grunt while waiting. "Humans can't know about us," I emphasized, nudging Lola with my foot to get into the bedroom. Her collar jingled until a familiar *thump* told me she'd hopped onto the bed, probably sprawled out right in the middle of it. "But we'll cover that more tomorrow."

Ian walked over and grabbed the device. "Cool," he said, his eyes drilling into the dim screen. "I'll see what I can do."

I nodded, stepped into the bathroom to apply Eric's "Neosporin for vampires" on my almost-healed burn, then let myself exhale from the madness of the last few days.

# CHAPTER 25

EVEN WITH COMMUNITY RISKS, telling Ian the truth must have been a bigger relief than I imagined. Either that or the overwhelming fatigue of recent days finally caught up to me. Whatever the reason, sleep came in an all-encompassing wave, even my snoring corgi's occasional position shifts failing to nudge me awake. Also, Ian had my phone, so my usual alarm didn't go off, leaving me completely disoriented when I finally opened my eyes.

Waking up in pitch-black was pretty standard for me, and Lola must have sensed my stirring, as she went from lying by my feet to nudging me. "Okay, okay," I said, wet nose pushing my cheek. "You gotta go potty?" The question was soon followed by a *thump-thump* as she hopped off the bed, and I blinked the sleep out of my eyes to focus on the end table's clock.

Seven in the evening?

I fumbled out of bed, feet searching for solid ground until I eventually reached the door and swung it open to let in the

overhead hallway light. "Hey, Ian?" I called out. "Sorry I
overslept. You could have knocked if you needed me," I said
through a yawn. "Vampires don't murder people for interrupting their sleep. That myth is also bullshit." Lola's nails
clacked as she hustled over to the back patio. I glanced into
the dark, front room, the shadows of lumpy blankets on the
couch. "Okay, okay. You first." Lola hopped down the short
steps, bursting through the back door before I even finished
opening it. I turned to the stars above, bright constellations
on a clear night as my dog dashed over to her usual pee spot.

I couldn't make things right for Ian, couldn't save Sonya.
But maybe having an ear for venting and a pipeline for good
music might tip the scales during some rough years.

Lola finished, stopping to sniff a small weed sprouting
through a pavement crack before looking up at me. "Come
on," I said. "Probably hungry, huh?" She scooted through the
door and headed straight to her food bowl in the corner of the
dining room.

Not even a second glance to the living room.

"Hey, Ian, time to get up," I called out. "Sorry I turned you
into a night person. Welcome to musician life. Very similar
to vampire life." Still nothing from the living room, and after
filling Lola's bowl, I went into the dark room. "I'm gonna turn
the lights on. Prepare yourself," I said to the darkened space.
"Three, two, one."

The wall switch flipped with my finger nudge and a low light
brought the living room to life, the same corner lamp that kept
Laura company while she listened to Joan Baez: an ugly yellow
column with a weathered lampshade circa the 1980s. It worked
more for mood than visibility, but it told one clear story here.

Ian was not on the couch.

Not asleep, not sitting up on his phone. The blanket I'd left
folded for him lay rumpled and tossed to one side, but other
than that, no signs of his stay existed.

"Hey, Ian?" I tried again as I began stomping through the house. He wasn't in the music room, and I slid open the closet door in case internet searches sparked any wild notions of possibly turning into a vampire by hiding there. But my house wasn't big to begin with, so searching quickly concluded across my studio, the office that I barely ever used, and my own bedroom. The door to the unlit front bathroom sat open, and a quick look at the shower felt necessary, just in case he hit his head and passed out in the tub or something.

Nothing.

Where else? He might have been hungry and didn't want anything in my cupboards. Or he might have simply taken a walk to clear his head. Or maybe there was some tourist thing he wanted to check out. Or...

Or maybe the whole fixer thing *was* true. And they had come for him.

I forced myself to stop, grinding panic to a halt. I needed practical solutions, not random questions. Which led me to my next check—I marched to the front hall, Lola trotting along, probably with the thought we were going for a walk. I was about to nudge her away when I saw my first piece of solid evidence:

The front door was unlocked.

As in, he must have left without any ability to lock the door behind him. So he didn't take my keys, and one look at the oversize mug by my front table showed that yes, car and house keys sat in black ceramic, protected by a Ramones logo.

Then it dawned on me: I didn't have my phone.

Did he take it with him?

"Shit, shit, shit," I said under my breath, and my bare feet echoed with each step on the cold, solid floor. If he was going to leave it *and* be thoughtful about it, it probably would have been someplace practical, like plugged into the charging station in the kitchen or on the kitchen table or on the coffee table or someplace really obvious. But I stormed around my house, looking back and forth on otherwise blank surfaces, no phone in sight.

So he may not have been thoughtful, but being thirteen, I'd give him a pass on that.

Another thought arrived—if he'd been working on it while lounging on the couch, he may have fallen asleep and it slipped into the cushions, and *then* he woke up and left the house. I went back into the living room and turned on a second lamp, a much more practical modern one than Laura's, all sleek design and lumen output. Light flooded the space, and my hands dug through couch crevices, a gesture rare enough that Lola ran over and waited by my side, her little back legs pumping to try and jump on the cushion. "No, not now," I said, throwing one hand out to dissuade her. But she failed to listen or understand or just didn't care, and instead she bolted under my hand, the sound of paper crinkling as she passed by. The dog angled, then looked up and powered her way onto the couch. "That's not what I meant," I said with a shake of my head, pausing to grab whatever she stepped on. I reached down for the sheet that somehow fell to the floor, crinkles spidering out from paw steps, then squinted at the scrawled words.

Suddenly, everything made sense.

*I'm gonna find a way to save my mom. Because it's the best thing to do. It's punk rock.*

Save his mom? We'd already established that I couldn't turn her. And whatever experimental treatment at the hospital failed to deliver. So what else might?

Also, I couldn't tell if that last part was sincere or mockery. The kid was impossible to read.

I sat on the couch, my still-sleepy brain trying to connect facts and thoughts in the wake of all this. Lola didn't seem to notice and instead inched over to rest her head on my lap while I stared at the paper.

He didn't know San Francisco. He didn't have much, if any, money. At least I didn't think so. He didn't have a car or even a bike, so his modes of transportation were limited.

But he did have my phone. And instead of working to take Eric's app off, he likely dug under the surface, not to figure out a way to remove it, but to understand what it actively tracked—and how that could help him. The restaurant, that may have been a bit of a right-place-right-time situation.

I cursed whoever decided to order garlic bread that night, then focused on what seemed likeliest: Ian wandering around San Francisco using Eric's app to track other vampires. And then what? He couldn't bribe them, and it wasn't like he had wonderful people skills.

And if he *did* find vampires...well, if Eric found out, things could get much worse. But I told myself to focus and not worry about that for now. Maybe it wouldn't even come to that. "Ian?" I yelled, a last-ditch attempt in case he somehow managed to hide or fall asleep somewhere that I missed. "Come on, this isn't cool."

Nothing.

Ian was out in a city that he didn't know, looking for creatures he didn't understand, in a community that prized secrecy. And while most of us found reasonable ways to get our daily blood, some vampires—just like people—were just dicks. And at least one of them had turned up the dial to attacking humans over the past few weeks.

I'd brought Ian into the world of vampires. I was going to have to get him out of it.

And that meant one thing: if I didn't have my phone or any ability to track him, I'd have to talk to the one vampire who did.

# CHAPTER 26

THERE WAS A NIGHT, several decades ago, that led me on a quest for my relatives. But so many things here contrasted to that moment: instead of the Bay Area, it was Southern California; instead of San Francisco fog, it was in a sleepy suburb; instead of looking for clues on a smartphone, I broke into a house the old-fashioned way.

That night came about five years after the storm-out from my parents' house, and several after my humanity ended. Turned out vampirism wasn't a cure for childhood grudges, and five years wasn't enough to make my journey feel unfamiliar; every step on the sidewalk echoed the past, from the location of each crack to the way a sliver of moonlight fought past the yellow streetlights for visibility. I'd been up for a few hours at that point, which meant that my parents were in bed, likely asleep. I pushed open the back gate, its loose latch giving way with a forceful yet silent shove. I closed it with more care, guiding it back flush with the post by hand to prevent it from slamming shut.

Even in the dark, I knew the backyard hadn't changed at all. Despite Stephen being away for probably his final year of college—or hell, maybe grad school at this point—my parents failed to put any effort into escaping the mold they'd built for themselves. In fact, the plastic chairs on the small patio may not have moved since I'd left, the only difference being the way the elements wore away at the plastic coating.

I moved to the sliding glass door, fingers wrapped around the handle. Muscle memory activated, the way that lifting the door up while pushing outward bypassed the lock thanks to the weak doorframe and shoddy construction. Did Stephen know this secret? Did my parents ever discover it? I figured not, as neither had any reason to even try it. The door slid just wide enough for me to scooch through the slim opening, the pocket zippers on my leather jacket brushing the frame. I pushed the door, closing it to the point where the latch connected but didn't quite lock.

I was in. And though curiosity needled me to turn on the lights and see if anything had changed, I resisted. I told myself that I probably wasn't missing anything, that my parents hadn't changed a single thing in their lives, so it's not like they would have remodeled or anything.

Instead, I stepped quietly across the carpet to the full-length cabinets that sat across the dining table. My fingers slid under the third one, propping it open just enough to get a solid grip before slowly pulling the whole thing open. If there was one thing I'd hoped my parents *did* change, it was actually applying some WD-40 to the hinges.

But of course they didn't. Around the halfway mark, the hinges began squeaking, a high-pitched yowl that caused me to stop. I waved my arm around to gauge its clearance—enough for me to stick an arm in there, hand feeling past the loose papers, small boxes of paper clips, and cup of pencils to find...

Nothing.

Nothing significant, anyway. What I came for was gone.

The cabinet shelf used to hold a small toaster-sized combination safe, something that stashed away a mix of cash for emergency purposes, sometimes up to a hundred dollars in various bills. My plan had been to open the safe and leave only a single dollar bill. If they'd somehow changed the combination of six-eleven-fifteen, then I'd just take the damn thing and carry it to my car a block away.

Some might have called that stealing. But for every paycheck I got in high school, my parents took half of it "for the bank." The money still belonged to me, regardless of whether I lived with them or not. So this had nothing to do with theft and was more about me collecting on past dues, possibly with interest. How much, I wasn't sure. Math wasn't really my strong suit other than counting out beats before key changes.

Except this plan required the safe to be there. I closed the cabinet harder than I intended, the light *thump* causing me to freeze. The hallway clock ticked, counting off the seconds until probably two or three minutes passed by. No noises came from upstairs, and I exhaled, trying to get back into the logic of my parents. If they hadn't left the safe in its normal spot, where could it be?

I scanned through the dark, memories filling in the colors and shapes of what existed in the house. My parents never changed anything, so moving that safe? That didn't make sense. I moved forward, arms out to feel in front of me, stepping slowly enough that even when I kicked the corner of the kitchen chair, it only wobbled—not nearly enough to wake up anyone upstairs.

"Who's there?" a woman's voice called out.

Downstairs, it turned out, was a different matter.

I stopped, holding my breath to remain as still as possible. If I succeeded, perhaps this mystery person in the adjacent living room would think the silhouette of a woman in a leather jacket was simply a bizarre dream.

Then the lights flipped on, the chandelier above the dining

room table coming to life. I squinted, my eyes adjusting at some random woman in flannel pajamas wrapped in *my* old bedspread on the couch.

"Who are you?" she started, before her voice got louder. "Stephen?"

"Who am I?" I straightened up, the one time in my life I really wanted to claim space in this house. "Who the hell are you?"

Rapid-fire steps came from above, followed by the rhythmic *thunk-thunk-thunk* of a dash down the stairs. "Annie?"

My brother. A single word from him lit my nerves on fire. Suddenly we became our teenage selves, an instinctive belligerence ready to lash out within these four walls.

"What's the—" he started, running a hand through his messed-up hair before following her look to me. "Louise?"

More noises came from upstairs, and as if they descended from the moon to lecture me, Mom and Dad now stood in the hallway. "What you doing here?" Mom asked, her ability to go from asleep to stinging tongue as easy as flipping a switch.

Dad fumbled his glasses on, then blinked at the scene in front of him, as if my appearance seemed impossible. "You look bad."

"Thanks," I said, a clear indicator that I'd made the right choice in leaving.

"Why you here?" Mom moved her words into a position to attack. "You here for money?"

Out of context, such words might have been an offer. But even if her tone came gently—which it didn't—I knew her better than that. "I don't want your money," I said, in a complete lie. I *did* want their money, though *want* felt like the wrong word for it. It felt more like I demanded retribution or tax for the box they forced me into—not so much a proverbial round peg, but more like water spilled over their expectations, barely contained if not overflowing. "I just came for this." I grabbed the first thing my fingers found on the shelf: a thin spiral note-book, pages smaller than my palm.

There they stood: my mom, with her robe. My dad, in loose pajama pants and a worn tank top. Stephen, a look on his face that seemed the perfect blend of Mom's contempt and Dad's silent exasperation. And this mystery girlfriend/friend of his—it would be like Stephen to make her sleep on the couch. I fought back the temptation to ask if they'd had sex yet or if they were still in the "holding hands" phase, and instead improvised *something* regarding the notebook. The pages flipped by, a history of addresses and phone numbers: old neighbors, former coworkers, exterminator services from the onetime rats nested in our backyard retaining wall—a snapshot of decades, captured in the form of faded ink and frayed paper.

I stopped at a page I'd somehow never seen before. Or the details may have just eluded me until this moment. The lines of the paper showed the name Laura, followed by some Cantonese characters. Both were written in blue ink, as if merely her first name held enough power. Below it sat an address in San Francisco.

And across it all, straight and precise pencil lines striking through each part. Not the scribbles of chaotic dismissal, but a dedicated and conscious elimination, first through Laura's name, then her street address, then the city of San Francisco, as if crossing it off with such care rejected her from their lives.

I tore the page out. And with the frayed sheet in my hand, a realization hit me. Years ago, I'd used Laura's name as an emotional grenade at them, knowing that her very mention was one of the few things that broke past their stoic exterior. But now her name was with me—by happenstance, sure, but it seemed appropriate that the two outcasts from this family wound up together.

I looked at the address underneath the scribbled lines.

602 Moraga Street, San Francisco.

Maybe I'd need it someday.

"This," I said, holding it up. "I needed Aunt Laura's address."

No one in the room responded. No one even moved. The standoff remained, seconds stretching into a far greater gulf. Finally, I made the choice to end it.

"I'm going now," I said, folding the page and putting it in my pocket. "Don't worry. You won't see me again."

I left, going out the same front door I'd marched out years prior, though instead of moving in a rushed fury, I walked with a methodical calmness, pausing for an extra breath to see if they might try to stop me.

None of them did, of course. And though I didn't actually knock on Aunt Laura's door until nearly a decade later, that first step took me toward a sense of belonging.

Laura had let me in. And in turn, I had let Ian in. This succession of family outcasts *meant* something, perhaps a simple acknowledgment that we belonged, that we mattered.

I had to find him. I had to *protect* him.

From the city. From vampires in search of more blood. From *himself*.

Before leaving my house, I checked the news—no further "vampire attacks" had happened. On the other hand, no arrests were made. So either the attacker was a human at large, or a vampire still roaming the streets for blood.

Or possibly a fixer had taken care of the perpetrator.

In all situations, Ian was at risk.

I drove around San Francisco, hoping that Ian's familiarity with my car would be enough that he'd come sprinting in relief at the sight of a vampire driving a white Prius. I rolled around the city, from my quiet streets in the Inner Sunset to other neighborhoods, even through the tourist areas of Golden Gate Park and the Presidio, just in case he'd decided to go there. The entire city might have been possible—forty-seven square miles of risky decisions. After two fruitless hours of driving all over, including a stop at The Fillmore in case he'd had a sudden desire to check out the evening's gig, I pulled over by the south end of the Embarcadero and stepped out onto the pier.

Wind kicked at my hair, blowing it in all directions as I hugged my leather jacket tight. That jacket had seen me through a lot, from my final days in Los Angeles to exploring San Francisco with Laura to playing shows with Marshall, all the way to now, as the Bay air whipped against my cheeks. Water lapped against the pier, the waves providing a rhythmic hum only eclipsed by the occasional car driving by. Lights from the Bay Bridge floated against the dark sky, and across the water, Oakland sat waiting, the mix of high-rises and traffic beneath the hulking metal cranes at the base of the city's port.

Somewhere in there, Eric's warehouse. And a bunch of vampires who probably could track my phone.

Not that long ago, the idea of reaching out to a community of vampires felt strange—not just foreign, but bordering on impossible. Eric knew I'd broken the rules before; what kind of punishment might I face for this? All of those unknowns formed a creeping dread, an acknowledgment that all the times I'd flouted guidelines and connected with humans might come back to haunt me.

Yet here, it all came down to one question: would I face that for Ian?

I found the answer right away.

Because even though we'd only known each other for about a week, Ian had grown into much more than a distant relative who needed a break. In him, I saw a kindred spirit, someone who understood the need to hide within drums and bass, who wanted that same fury I felt in a screaming punk chorus, who managed to find peace through the loudest of guitars.

He needed me. In so many ways. And I wanted to give that to him.

In that way, I needed him too.

I took one last look at my destination across the Bay, then got into my car to face the leader of the vampire community.

## CHAPTER 27

**VAMPIRE POWER MYTH #10:** Vampires have the ability to transform into mist and just, like, *mist* through stuff.

I never understood the logic behind this one. Superstrength? Sure, like maybe the theoretical vampire body extracted some nutrition from blood that accelerated muscle building. Not true, but at least somewhat reasonable.

But turning flesh and bone into a mist, and then floating around, even sneaking through keyholes? Beyond ridiculous. How much mist could I actually be? If some of my mist-ness got contained in a jar, would I reform without my leg? Was my mist flammable?

It all sounded extra-bullshitty to me. Which was too bad because I really could have used it right now. Another hour had passed before I got to Eric's warehouse, having been slowed down by the fact that many of Oakland's warehouses looked similar. And it turned out that my sense of direction was terrible without my phone. But the slim alley between two taller buildings *seemed* right, though by the time I parked and got out, I realized that I'd only seen this in the abnormal situation of the midday sun.

Right now, only orange-yellow industrial lights dotted the buildings. But as I approached, I recognized the security camera bolted above a metal door. Which is where the whole trans-form-into-mist ability would have worked, allowing an easy slither through crevices to find Eric *before* politely explaining what happened.

Instead of misting, only one option remained. "Hello?" I called out. "Hey, I'm a vam—" I started before catching myself midsentence. "I'm one of you. I was here the other day doing a drop-off. Remember?" I thumbed back toward my car. "Same car. It should be on your security footage."

The door remained shut, the only noise coming from the night wind whipping all around me. I waited another min-ute, looking for any signs of movement anywhere. Behind me, a torn newspaper page kicked up and floated across the path. Above me, clouds moved in a slow drift past the bright sliver of a crescent moon.

No Eric. Or his mystery assistant.

"Hello?" I looked around, scanning for any security that might take out any polite-but-desperate vampires. "My name is Louise Chao. I wore a helmet and suit here the other day? It was a Daft Punk helmet."

No answer came. Only the still night air, and farther away, the beeping from a car in Reverse.

"You know Daft Punk? 'One More Time'? 'Around The World'?"

I looked behind me, only the deep black of night layered against the false oranges of cheap industrial lighting. I squinted, letting my eyes adjust in case something escaped my attention, and some thirty or forty seconds passed. Still nothing.

Exasperation forced out a sigh, and I reached in my back

pocket to check my phone, a move driven by instinct more than anything else. But of course, Ian had my phone, its missing weight a constant reminder, not just of its absence but the fact that I'd put him in danger by association.

Still nothing.

"Hello?" I called out once again before marching to the metal door. "Hello? Come on." My bare palm slapped against the door, clanging hard enough to linger in the surrounding space. "Hey! I'm one of you. I just need to talk to Eric." I hit the metal several more times, the sound echoing enough for my musician brain to identify that this very spot would be great for recording drums. "Hey, look, I'd text but my phone—"

"Please stop hitting the door," a woman's voice said from… somewhere. It came through tinny and contained enough that it sounded out-of-body. And also a bit annoyed.

"Hey," I said, my voice lowering to a normal-but-projected level, "I'm looking for Eric. My name is Louise Chao and I don't have my phone—"

The sound of a latch interrupted me. Then another click, then a muffled whirring sound, and one final latch, all from behind the door. The door slid on its rails, the noise rattling across the otherwise quiet space. A sliver of bright light gradually became a flood, stinging my eyes for several seconds.

And in the middle of the light, the silhouette of a woman. She stepped forward, her features coming into focus: black hair in a tight bun, light brown skin that carried the familiar dull vampire tint, and very serious eyes framed by glasses.

I knew her—the woman who handled the blood during the drop-off.

"I'm looking for Eric," I said.

"I heard you the first time."

"I'm a…" I hesitated, then showed my fangs. "I'm a…you know," I said, rolling my hand with my words.

Despite the fact that we were both about five foot three,

something about her oozed intimidation as we stood side by side. She turned away from her tablet, then scanned me up and down, eyes peeking over her glasses. "It's really bad practice to go around telling strangers that. You never know who's listening these days." She touched an arrowhead-shaped pin on her lapel, prompting a chirp-like beep. "I've got her. Bringing her in."

The woman turned before I managed a better look at the pin, though its distinctive shape seemed awfully cultlike to me. And the way that it acted like a walkie-talkie, the layers of devices listening, transmitting, chirping—all of it carried a superunnerving vibe.

"Come on, Louise Chao. Not another word till we get inside. You've drawn enough attention as it is." Despite our paler skin, vampires can very much blush with embarrassment, and in the bright light of the front entryway, my flushed cheeks must have been very obvious to this woman. In return, her expression carried an amused smirk—which was better than threatening looks, so at least I wasn't in too much trouble yet. We waited for the door behind us to fully close, locks snapping into place one by one. In front of us, she pressed a button on a touch screen panel. "Serena Cabrera," she said in an even cadence. Two beeps chimed, then a hydraulic hissed and another large metal door slid open—not quite as smooth as what movies portrayed. This door slid on rickety wheels, clunky electronics and squeaking motors pushing the thick slab into place. "Sorry. It's not quite a starship, is it?"

We stepped through into something that looked more like start-up schtick: six or seven desks set up, each with multiple wide monitors. Each had two people sitting and staring, clicking mouse buttons or scrolling through tablets adjacent to everything. Lines of code whirled by, along with various line graphs, dashboards, and workflow shapes, connected by arrows—one monitor even had a bunch of photos of a gigantic estate surrounded by trees. Maybe vampire office workers spent their days checking out vacation spots too.

In the center of it sat the largest monitor, something that looked very similar to the app's hidden map but bigger—not just the size of the city, but with more icons across more shapes. Dots, diamonds, squares, across a spectrum of rainbow colors, littered the section of San Francisco. Against the wall, hardware sat on racks, constellations of LED lights blinking in different colors, and in the back, several metal roll-up doors sat closed. In the small space in between all that were two leather couches, a coffee table, and a refrigerator.

Which, I presumed, was for blood.

The woman led the way to a far-off office, flimsy temporary cubicle walls built into modular rectangles, hanging lights keeping the industrial nature of the place. Really, getting rid of the desks and computers for a stage and speakers would have made this a great place for a show, definitely a rave. The blinking racks of hardware could stay for atmosphere.

I made my way into a small room with a plant in one corner, an end table with charging docks in the other, and two plastic chairs set too deep for anyone to be comfortable, though I tried. "Is, um, Eric busy?"

"Guy barely sleeps. Wish I could learn that trick." She sat on a tall stool against the large window looking into the space, still tapping on her tablet. I shifted in my chair, trying to find a position on the plastic seat, but it was as if the designer wanted whoever sat in it to *not* relax—perfect for an office. The woman must have sensed the shift in the air, and she resumed her work, an intense focus compared to me sitting there, aimless nerves coursing through my body. I looked around, taking in the makeshift office's details, from the probably fake plant's arching leaves to the reflection off the table's thin chrome legs.

Without my phone in my pocket or a guitar in my arms, my body ached to do *something*, a fidgetiness that failed to channel itself into anything beyond a feedback loop of anxiety. "So," I said, only the hum of ventilation above us to go along with the sound of her tapping foot, "everyone here is a vampire too?"

Her eyes went wide. "Wait, what? Vampire? What are you talking about?" she asked, a hurried panic taking over her words.

My stomach dropped at the question, and a different kind of urgency took over. "I mean, like…work ethic. Everyone's working at night. Real vampire energy."

"I'm gonna let you in on a little secret." Her voice lowered to a whisper and she leaned forward. I matched her pose, even though it proved difficult from my deep-set chair.

"What's that?" I whispered back.

"We're actually," she said, her words hanging while she looked around, "we're all *werewolves* here. Even Eric."

The confession wrapped around my brain, breaking any processes and pausing my breath.

Werewolves?

My hands tightened around the arms of the chair as the revelation sunk in. Werewolves? But…that didn't make any sense. And I'd just told Ian that werewolves were bullshit. What possible harm did I throw him into? What *else* didn't I know? What the hell kind of—

"The look on your face," she said with a laugh, tension releasing until I slumped back into my chair. I buried my face in my hands, and suddenly my lack of recent socialization probably explained so much more about me, especially given that this building likely held all of the data about my life. "I'm sorry. I shouldn't have joked like that."

"It's okay," I said, putting on a nonembarrassed front for my obvious embarrassment.

"I mean, the very idea of werewolves is kind of ridiculous, isn't it? Humans that turn into dogs? How would the body actually be able to transform like that? Physically, organs would get moved and bones would break. No way it's medically possible. Yes, we're all vampires here, and yes, we're all working with Eric. He's trying to do a lot of good for our community."

I bit my tongue on the fact that he'd invaded the privacy of every vampire that downloaded his app.

"My name's Serena, by the way." I nodded, unsure of what to do with this information. "You mind if I play some music while we wait?"

Music—finally something I could work with. "No, not at all."

"Thanks. It's kind of obscure stuff, so I always ask." Her tablet screen shifted colors until the line-itemed display of a playlist came up. I craned my neck to see if she was a fellow music nerd.

"Oh, don't worry," I said, relishing in the pressure release of talking music instead of freaking out about Ian. "I like the obscure stuff too. Actually, the reason why I need to talk with Eric is kind of related to—"

By obscure, I'd expected a punk band from the '70s that never broke through, or maybe a '90s indie band that toiled on the college radio circuit. Maybe early '70s European electronic like one of Kraftwerk's lesser-known contemporaries, or even some early rockabilly stuff from the '50s. But instead, I was interrupted by men harmonizing over the crackle of an early 1900s recording, something that had to be prejazz or at least pre-Louise's-knowledge-of-music.

She smirked again. "I told you—it's kind of obscure."

"No, no, it's cool." A forced smile emerged, a simple gesture to deflect my confusion. "I've, um, come to appreciate all types of music in my time."

"This *was* the music of my time," Serena said, and even though her statement came with an edge, a wistful tone arrived as well. I'd been around decades, yet she'd seen an entire century come and go, perhaps growing up in a world without cars, and now she held a tablet with all the knowledge—and music—of the world.

Probably not the easiest to wrap one's head around.

"I can't listen to modern stuff," she continued. "It's just soulless noise. Screaming and electronics. There's no beauty in it."

I nodded, like I completely agreed with her take even though I instantly thought of artists and songs to demonstrate that soul and noise *could* coexist. Instead, I kept that inside and let the discussion drop. Past her, Eric's staff continued their work within the warehouse, half of them sitting at computers, typing away, and the other half hauling carts like this was the back storage of a big box store. I sat for several songs that sounded like four guys singing in aluminum foil, and my mind drifted, deconstructing the musicianship of the singing and quality of the recording. Which helped me project a somewhat forced sense of calm.

Minutes passed, the songs offering the only noise between us. "I'm sorry, but is Eric going to be long?"

"He should be here soon," she said without missing a beat.

"You don't need to babysit me. It's cool." I stretched my arms overhead, my leather jacket squeaking at the movement. "No need to worry about me."

"You *did* come here screaming at our door."

"I wasn't really screaming," I said, straightening up. Through the window, a lone figure marched this way. I tracked him as he paused only for brief interactions, saying hello to someone at a workstation or chatting with someone hauling a dolly of bins. "I just didn't know how to get your attention."

Step by step, the silhouette approached until warehouse lighting confirmed that it was indeed Eric. And in one hand, he carried a bottle, blood sloshing around with each step. In the other, he balanced an open laptop. Serena opened the door for him and he entered. Through serious creases lining his face, he flashed a quiet smile when he said hello before offering me the bottle.

I took it, examining the same cartoonish fruit on the label as the previous bottles he'd given me.

"For you," Eric said. "In case you're hungry. You look tired."

I'd been prepared for Eric to come out with fury for my rule breaking, so a meal and a calm demeanor were a pleasant surprise. "It's been a night."

"You know you can mix some espresso in there, right?" He grinned, his head cocked at an angle. "I'm serious. It's how I start my day."

Once all of this was over, I might have to try that. Someday.

Eric and Serena talked quietly, a quick discussion about inventory and equipment, including gloves and wineglasses. Though he ended it with the strangest question:

"Have you rehearsed?"

She laughed, then glanced back at me. "Not enough. But it is what it is."

"You're gonna be great. I know you got this."

"Enough with the relentless positivity." Her voice changed into vaudevillian melodrama. "Or I *won't* do it." Eric's chuckle came with a headshake, and they came off as two chummy coworkers, not vampires doing some sort of clandestine data-mining operation in a remote warehouse. "Thanks for indulging my taste in music. No one else here likes it," Serena said to me before tapping an icon to stop it. She waved and walked out the door, all while Eric stared at the laptop he'd set on the small table.

"So," Eric said, "tell me. What rules have you broken?"

I looked him directly in the eye as I considered all the possible things to say to him that *wouldn't* wind up getting myself and/or Ian in a whole mess of vampire-related trouble. But I needed to find Ian and to protect him.

And that meant no surprises.

# CHAPTER 28

**SEVERAL MINUTES PASSED AS** I sped through my recent history, going through everything from my audition with Copper Beach to our disaster meal at Chester's to this evening. Each time I revealed another layer, Eric's expression grew grimmer, but I needed to connect all the dots to paint Ian in a sympathetic light. "I need to find him," I finally said.

I gave Eric space to process, though I watched for any undercurrent of fury. What happened with Ian marked some pretty major cardinal sins, and I prepared myself for some sort of trial, or at least scolding. "I know this broke a bunch of rules. But I'm asking that we find Ian first before you, um, deal with me. He's just a kid. And dealing with a lot of terrible things."

"I understand. And I agree, we'll prioritize the boy and discuss those other matters later," Eric finally said. He tented his fingers while looking ahead, then creases formed on his forehead, fingers stroking his chin. Outside of the office, everything seemed normal. No extra security formed, Serena didn't arrive with stakes or whips or anything else typically used for punishing movie vampires. "And you're not sure which direction he may have gone?"

"No."

"Well," he said. He tapped at his laptop, then glanced behind him. My pulse thumped hard in my chest, dual tension between concern about Ian *and* my current situation: in a warehouse, surrounded by vampires.

"We should try to locate him," Eric said.

That part was good. But Eric didn't say *why* they wanted to locate him.

"It's not his fault," I said.

"Life has not dealt him a fair hand," he said without looking up. "But our top priority remains community secrecy." The typing paused, then his finger tapped aimlessly as he pursed his thin lips. "Is he capable? Smart?"

That was unexpected. "Yeah," I answered, though worries quickly arrived about whether the answer dug him into a deeper hole. "Do you think the person from the headlines is still out there?" I asked. "Are they a danger?"

Eric shook his head, then resumed clicking away at his computer. "His situation is under control." Though I sat still, internal panic fluttered as I wondered what "under control" meant. And would that apply to me? "Does Ian still have your phone?"

"I think so. But it might be out of battery by now. Unless he charged it while I was sleeping."

"Let's think this through." Eric tapped his screen, which flashed to a larger view of the San Francisco map on the app. Except instead of just purple dots, his display was just like the monitor outside, with multiple colors and shapes scattered around the city. I had no clue what it all represented, though it did beg the question of what exactly Eric pulled from everyone's phone.

More importantly, why?

When it became clear that he didn't mind me watching over his shoulder, I watched closer as the different colored shapes moved around the map, some following streets and some merely shifting in place. He loaded a side menu, then checked some boxes before he typed numbers into a field.

My phone number.

The program's loading icon appeared, dots chasing each other in a never-ending circle while we waited. "So you auditioned for a band?"

"Yes, but they don't know a thing," I spit out quickly, my tone probably more defensive than I should have used.

"Interesting," he let out, lips pursing before he tapped several more keys. Why he thought so, he didn't say, and soon the map flashed, all of the other shapes and colors disappearing. In their place came a line trailing throughout the city, and as Eric zoomed out to reveal the tracked mix of ups and downs, lefts and rights, the origination point became clear.

Pointing at the screen seemed like the quickest way to change the subject from me playing music with humans. "That's the start."

"That end?"

"Yeah," I said with a nod. "That's my house on Moraga Street." Part of me wanted to withhold that information, but given the trail displayed on screen—and the fact that my phone was always there for long periods of time—finding my address wouldn't be difficult for Eric's team. Might as well turn it to my advantage.

From the display of icons and digits, Eric drilled down without a word, data shifting and changing as he quickly filtered it. Several minutes passed while he worked in silence, and though I didn't know exactly *how* he did it, Ian's trail gradually built on the map.

Which was good, but also confirmed a lot of my suspicions about his app.

Ian had left my house right before sunset and walked with seemingly random turns all across the Inner Sunset district, pausing at various places until eventually crossing 19th Avenue.

Eric clicked on one of the areas where Ian lingered, then hit a few more keys, changing the map once more. A handful of purple dots appeared on Ian's path, and then it hit me:

Vampires.

But on that path, the timeline showed the vampires scattered when he approached. Eric fast-forwarded the vampire movement and scrolled Ian's path to the end of the tracked timeline. The line simply stopped with a time stamp from about fifteen minutes ago. "Battery must have died there. But," he said, pointing at the map, "my guess is he's going to meet this group. He's still on foot. You should try to intercept him." Before I could answer, he tapped a button on his phone. "Serena, can you come help out for a little bit?"

My car rolled forward, moving through the streets of Oakland back to the Bay Bridge like the least-threatening patrol car of all time. I wondered if Serena detected a hint of blood from the backpack incident; though I'd cleaned it, the chaos of recent days stole my time to thoroughly care for upholstery.

She didn't seem to notice, though I did catch her looking at Eric's bottle, which remained unopened, rattling around the cupholder between us. "You gonna drink that?" she asked, her face illuminated by her tablet tracking Ian's path.

"That?" Though hunger tickled at me and my fridge wasn't exactly overflowing, I hesitated at a bottle directly from Eric, at least in this situation. "No, you can have it."

"Thanks. Sorry, I didn't have enough today." The cap popped with a twist and she took a long drink before focusing back on her tablet. No signs of brainwashing or delirium came over her as she nudged the map ahead. "I can't say for sure but I think if he follows the same pattern of behavior as his last few stops, he's lingering for a bit everywhere he goes."

"You search for many kids hunting vampires?"

"No, but my third degree was in behavioral psychology. Works well with my computer science and artificial intelligence degrees."

"Wait, how many degrees do you have?"

"Seven now. I try to get one every fifteen or twenty years or so," she said, like getting that many degrees was totally normal. Where did she even get the money for it? "Yeah, I mean, if you're going to live this long, why not do something with your time? That's why I got my black belt in aikido last year. You gotta keep busy, right? And knowledge is how we get a better life." I nodded like I totally understood her even though I did not. "Hey, can I put some music on? Helps me think."

"Sure," I said, suddenly reconsidering my last two decades spent building my entire life around a career that provided blood.

Serena tapped the arrowhead pin on her lapel, which chirped back to her. "Computer, play my playlist for thinking."

The car soon flooded with men's voices singing in harmony over the crackle of century-old recordings. Serena nudged me to turn here and there, getting us closer to her projected path for Ian based on his previous movements and the marked vampires on the map.

"Is that pin part of what you and Eric are building?"

She looked up from her tablet, meeting me with a quizzical look. "Pin? You mean this?" She pointed to the arrowhead. "It's just a Bluetooth thing that connects to my tablet. It's from *Star Trek*."

"Oh," I said in a way that was meant to hide my embarrassment but clearly didn't. "I don't watch much TV."

"You don't know *Star Trek*?" she asked. I recognized the tone of her question—replace *Star Trek* with the name of a band and the question may as well have come from me.

"I mean, I know it, I've just never watched it. It's kind of surprising you like it. Since you were born after the Civil War."

"I dunno. I think it kind of makes sense." She stopped, the tablet screen flashing. "Oh weird, it just loaded a final set of pings. I keep telling Eric we have to upgrade the infrastructure if we want to scale up. The latency is still an issue," she said with a sigh. "You grow up with carts and buggies and horse poop everywhere, suddenly anything with starships is the best thing ever. If they let vampires into NASA, I'd sign up right now. Just have to deal with that whole UV exposure thing."

We moved forward without speaking, ten minutes of barber-shop serenades while the lights of the Bay Bridge whizzed by. Whether it was the rhythm of the drive or just the sheer dispar-ity between my life and Serena's, my thoughts wandered from Ian's dilemma. It wasn't that Serena's seven degrees shamed me for being an underachiever; rather, the way she said "if you're going to live this long, why not do something with your time" so simply, stating it as a fact of vampire life rather than an otherworldly credo. Eric's "do something" had been community, ever since I stumbled upon him. Serena's was ap-parently getting every degree on the planet while watching *Star Trek*. In my head, all sorts of justifications manifested, listing off all the pivotal bands I'd seen before they got big or the shows I'd played in half-empty bars, or hey, I was a really good dog owner.

But then also what Marshall said to me years ago: "You make it sound kind of depressing."

Was I just living a depressing vampire life with a really ex-cellent soundtrack? My parents had talked about having a bet-ter life, but Serena presented the same idea without the words dripping in shame.

That made it a little easier to understand.

"Okay, this time stamp from the last ping is about fifteen minutes ago," Serena said as we descended into the city limits. "We should wind up close to him. Unless he suddenly made some unpredictable moves."

"Well, teenagers, you know?"

"Actually, I don't. I probably haven't talked with a real teenager in a hundred years. You don't meet many as a vampire. It's not like my friends have kids."

"Good point." We wove through streets, Serena continuing to direct me until we approached Ian's last known position. "There's a trio of vampires up ahead, and it looks like they're sitting in a park. Makes sense for Ian to go there—it's public enough to be safe, private enough for him to try and talk with them. Smart kid." Her posture shifted as she fired several glances my way, then a look down at the tablet before looking ahead. Her neck angled this way and that as if she scouted the dark street ahead. "Hey," she said, the pace of her words slowing down. "I'm going to do something, but you don't know about this, okay? You didn't see it happen."

Holy shit. Vampire secrets. Was Serena a *fixer*?

My fingers tightened on the steering wheel, reminding me that crashing right now definitely wouldn't help Ian. "Uh..." was the only reply I managed.

"Do you want me to help you?"

"Of course."

"I'm trying *not* to get in trouble with my boss. While helping you. Understood? So you did *not* see what I'm about to do."

"Sure," I said, unsure of what I just casually committed to. "I'm just watching the road."

"Okay." Serena tapped at her screen, until a pop in the tablet's speakers came. The music lowered, followed by a shuffling sound and muffled conversation, a slight echo to each voice. Then another noise, something that gave it all away and made my stomach drop.

A police siren. Which wasn't important in the big scheme of things, but it did reveal something much more practical and much more dangerous—and increased my motivation to do a factory reset of my phone the instant I got it back.

That was live audio, a stream direct from the phone of each vampire.

I'd figured Eric's app sifted through the data in our phones. But a live listen-in, all at the touch of a button from Serena's tablet? That had been my worst-case scenario.

I was pretty sure the community didn't know about this. Yet, despite the problematic nature of the app, it still represented my best chance of finding Ian right now. Another voice came through the broken audio stream, unintelligible, but one word made it through clearly enough:

*Vampire.*

"That's him," Serena said. "The community knows better than to use that word." I looked over to see her fingers pinching on the tablet map, zooming in for a closer look as the dots scooted around. "Go forward another three blocks, then right." More voices came, jumbled together but laced with irritation. The voices grew louder, overdriving the tablet's speaker, though the audio continued to be wrapped in a muffled gauze, probably from sitting in pockets. The yelling intensified, a desperation painting Ian's tone, though his words remained unclear.

One vampire, though, spoke loudly and fiercely enough for her words to come right through the mic.

"What are you doing, kid? Do you wanna die?"

Then the audio streams abruptly cut out.

# CHAPTER 29

"GODDAMN IT," SERENA SAID, tapping her tablet.

"What's happening?" My grip tightened on the steering wheel and I reminded myself to keep my eyes on the road, especially in the unpredictable cross traffic of San Francisco. Immortality didn't shield us from the repercussions of bad driving.

Still, when you hear vampires threaten the teenage relative you're supposed to be watching for the weekend, tensions escalate a bit.

"It's this app. Live audio streams overload the server's processors. Causes it to stall. It's a bug, not a feature. We really need to upgrade to high-performance hardware." Despite the anxiety of the moment, I smiled, probably matching her smirk from earlier. Maybe she could talk computer stuff with Ian. If we recovered him safely, that was. "Just keep driving."

Scattered audio burst through the tablet's speaker, though it offered little more than white noise. "My map still works. It looks like they're on the move."

"Okay, but what do we do when we get there?"

"I'll talk to them. You just tend to your friend. Turn right here."

We pulled into a quiet part of the Inner Sunset, and though my headlights beamed forward, they didn't reveal the silhouette of any angsty teens or people-who-were-likely-vampires. "Come on," Serena said, pulling a small vial out of her coat pocket. She twisted the rubber top off, poured it into the larger bottle in my cup holder, then swirled the liquid around. As she drank the mixture, her tablet chimed again, and she set the half-full bottle back down. "We should go," she said, undoing her seat belt.

We stepped outside, car doors slamming in unison.

"What was that?" I asked, scanning the street for movement.

"What?"

"The vial."

"Oh that? Just a little pick-me-up to mix in."

"Like espresso blood?" I asked.

"Something like that," she said, a quick laugh to herself before focusing on the tablet screen.

In the distance, several voices shouted. Serena held her tablet, the brightness of the screen floating through the dim night air, and she pointed at the dots. "Look for him on the side streets." She thumbed at the cross street, one side going uphill and the other down. "I'll handle these folks."

"Folks" felt like too light a term for potentially murderous vampires, but her logic made sense. I nodded an affirmative and began a light jog to the left. "Ian?" I called out at a careful volume. Living in San Francisco normalized voices outside your window at all hours of the day, but community secrecy and all that probably meant it was best to avoid anyone calling the police. I called his name again, but other than catching the attention of someone getting in a car, the words got absorbed into the city night. "Nothing here," I said, looking over my shoulder. Serena was already gone; I jogged back down to the empty intersection.

Her voice pierced the quiet, faint enough to be at least a block or so down. I gauged the area, sidewalks clear of bystanders, only cars parked against sidewalks. What kind of runner was Serena that she got down there so fast? Was she a former Olympic athlete in addition to her college degrees? I jogged forward, cursing myself for clearly not being in the same shape as her, and kept calling Ian's name. The air weighed heavier as I picked up my pace; even though much of vampire physiology froze upon turning, getting fit remained an individual choice, and right now I questioned my lack of exercise other than drumming. "Ian?" I yelled again with a huff.

Some distance down, a silhouette moved on the horizon, arms up, and the wind carried what sounded like Serena's voice. It started with urgency, a yell that echoed.

Then silence. If Serena spoke with the vampires down there, it was too quiet for me to hear.

Suddenly, another voice entered from behind me. "Louise?"

I turned to see Ian—hard lines under his eyes, his shirt dirty and hair a mess, a mix of relief and weariness colored his expression.

"Holy shit!" I cried, running over. Though I also wanted to throttle him like Paul Simonon smashing his bass on the cover of The Clash's *London Calling*, I hugged the kid, the zipper pulls of my leather jacket cramming into his face as I held him tight. "I told you. I fucking told you. I told you we can't turn anyone." My arms squeezed his lanky frame while I chastised him. "Did you think I was lying?"

"I need to save my mom," he said into my shoulder.

"Well, you *don't* do that by looking for vam—you know. Especially in a big city." I let him go at arm's length. In return, he gave an awkward brush-off that tried to play it cool, but relief clearly shone in his eyes. "Are you okay?" I asked.

"I'm fine," he said, though the tremble in his voice told me that statement was more teenage bravado than honesty.

"I'm not your grandfather. No need to bullshit me," I said with a scoff. "What did you find?" I pictured movie vampires, fangs out and chins dripping with blood while hissing at prey sprinting away. But life experience taught me better, and I assumed something else shook him. Ian continued staring at the ground, a slight headshake the only response to my question. "Come on, I've been honest with you. Did you meet a bunch of them?"

"A few," he finally said.

"Did they hurt you? Try to bite you?"

"No, not at all. Most just denied what they were. They just walked away." He exhaled, disappointment weighing on slumped shoulders. "Even when I said I needed help." His eyes met mine, a wide-eyed stare revealing something shifted in his worldview, an axis-tilting event that couldn't be undone. Learning that vampires existed didn't spawn this look. Neither did the finality of his mom's condition.

No, Ian's stare carried a mix of anger, regret, and disappointment, the kind that only arrived when you realized what truly drove people.

"We're taught to care about secrecy, so public searches are kind of frowned upon," I offered, though I knew that probably wasn't the reason they shied away.

"I think that's what sucked the most," he finally said, his voice dry. "They didn't care. They didn't even try." He pointed down the street, where the silhouette of Serena still stood. "It's like they thought they'd scare me off by pretending to mug me or something. Instead of just listening."

"Yeah," was all I could say. We nodded in unison, an unintentional agreement at the shittiness of people. "Did any of them hurt you?"

"No. Some just walked away. The last group yelled a bunch of stuff until they realized I wasn't afraid of them."

"Look, I know *I'm* not scary, but you should be afraid of them, okay? Or, at least, of random people in big cities in the middle of the night. It's not a good idea."

"My dad died. My mom's dying. I'm not afraid of anything."

Behind Serena, a car came to life, taillights and engine interrupting the dark and quiet of the nighttime street. It pulled away from the curb faster than it should have and disappeared around the corner. Serena's silhouette gradually filled in as she approached, her lit tablet floating through the night. "Hey look," I said, searching for words to fill the void. Laura's final moments came back to me, Joan Baez serenading her in compact disc form, but I shook that away, knowing full well Laura wouldn't want that from me. Instead, I thought back to all the *other* times I'd listened to Joan Baez with her: in the car, in the living room, in our small backyard, at the Warfield. "You can't save her," I said, a quiet calm wrapping my words. "That just won't happen. But you can fill her remaining time with things worth remembering."

Ian's stance broke, posture dipping so slightly that a view from a different angle would have hidden it. Had Ian been older, more mature, more in tune with life experiences, I would have looked for a bigger reaction. But here, the young teenager next to me shifted as much as he could. "Come on," I said, "let's get you something to eat."

I put my arm around Ian's lanky frame, giving him a squeeze. He didn't shrug it off.

Back in the car, Serena avoided most of our questions, instead merely saying that she "talked to them." We headed east toward the city's inner edge, and she asked if we'd mind her music again. And though I'd met her in the body of a bright-eyed young adult wearing a Bluetooth-enabled *Star Trek* pin, she carried an air of exhaustion now. Her head tilted back into the seat, black hair no longer neatly tied back, eyes closed and shoulders slumped while we boarded the Bay Bridge. Her fatigue seemed catching, a wave of tired hitting me as well, and without asking, I finished the bottle of espresso blood sitting in the cupholder. In Serena's lap, her tablet remained active, and though Ian *should* have been fully seat-belted in, he leaned forward enough to peek at the glowing device.

"What are those blue icons?" he asked. Serena's eyes fluttered open, an annoyed crease across her brow.

"It's nothing," she said, tapping her *Star Trek* pin and telling the tablet to play her music. A barbershop quartet began singing about bright skies and lovely days, though Ian responded with a burst of laughter. Though I drove steady onto the bridge, Serena's reaction kicked strong enough to catch my peripheral vision: clenched jaw, pursed lips, and the crease across her brow deepening into a harsh line.

"What is this?" he said, his laugh obnoxious enough that I wanted to smack him for reasons far different from running off to save his dying mom.

"This is music with soul," Serena deadpanned back.

"Uh-huh. Louise, have you played her any punk yet?"

Serena's groan came out louder than the song, and my fang dug into my inner lip. "You know, I think this music is actually cool," I said, even though I clearly didn't. But anything to ease the sudden tension in my car. "Like, they didn't have pedals and amps for their instruments. So they're working with what they got." I kept going: 1) to be blatant enough that Ian might take the hint, 2) to teach him that gratitude didn't usually come in the form of insults. "I know I can't harmonize that well. It's a skill."

That blunted Ian's snark and we rode in relative quiet, only serenaded by four voices harmonizing from the tiny speaker of Serena's tablet. "So what are those blue icons?" Ian asked again. "They're not on the phone app."

Serena remained silent and flipped the device over, its display now facedown.

"Come on, I've seen the app. I'm curious what you're having the machine-learning algorithm look for."

"What do you know about machine learning?"

"I'm taking classes."

Serena turned to me, lip curled on one side. "I feel like they barely taught us arithmetic in school and now this. Funny what a difference a century makes." The word *century* caught Ian's ear, prompting a raised eyebrow. "Your school got you into this? Shouldn't you be, I don't know, playing baseball?"

"My dad taught me," Ian said. All the energy dropped from his voice, and though I knew why, Serena didn't. I wanted to jump in again, but for wholly different reasons. Redirect the conversation, maybe with some pithy comment about her music just to needle her. Anything to stop the oncoming disaster from Ian's words. "That is, before he died."

Serena's face went blank. A hundred years of being frozen in that state, what level of loss did she see? Did she hide among her own kind, timeless as the world shifted and evolved? Did she watch her own family grow old and die? A sudden curiosity grew, not just about her but about every vampire, with the realization that there were many reasons why Marshall might have been right at calling our lives "depressing."

"Ah," she said, contrition weighing down that single syllable. She looked down at the tablet, then glanced at me as Ian settled back into his seat. The lights from the bridge continued passing us, a steady rhythm creating an infinite loop of shadow and brightness. Serena's barbershop quartet finished and a quieter song played, a single vocalist over a piano. "Well, you two have already seen this in action. Do you want to know how the app is calling queries from our data cloud?"

## CHAPTER 30

GETTING BACK TO THE warehouse proved remarkably less chaotic this time. Perhaps driving without the stress of a missing teenager or the glaring sun made it easier to navigate the twists and turns, and despite my newly returned phone charging on the console, I didn't even need any maps for it.

Calm apparently did wonders for my sense of direction.

We pulled into the same alley as before, though this time Serena led us without any of the fanfare the last trip required. The car idled quietly, and she tapped on her tablet. "Eric wants to chat but needs a few minutes first," she said. "They're finishing something up. Just wait."

*Consequences.* Earlier in the night, Eric agreed to table that until later. Except later was now, and he wanted to talk, probably not just about tonight but a lengthier history of rule breaking.

So a few more minutes to avoid that? Fine by me.

The fatigue I'd felt earlier seemed like a comedown, but slamming the half-full blood bottle hadn't helped. I thought

Serena caffeinated the drink with espresso or something, but "something like that" might have actually been a chill-out tea instead.

Whatever it was, something new washed over me—not the familiar pull of end-of-night fatigue, but a different sort of calming effect, my eyes closing in a strange state of zen.

And then I remembered something.

I remembered the night I was turned.

More specifically, I remembered *her*.

Who was she? She didn't look like she belonged at an Iggy Pop show, despite dressing like a punk. But she felt more glam, maybe, though not the sort of gender-bending, rule breaking glam of David Bowie. No, this person radiated *odd* in a way that couldn't be encapsulated, like she picked her worst trait and leaned into it just to unnerve.

Also, she was really tall. Which made for a problem at shows where people packed together in suffocating density.

My boots pushed to the rhythm of the drums and bass. The opening thumps of "Lust For Life" kicked in, and though I flailed in ways that seemed fitting for how Iggy Pop himself moved, a clear view of the stage still proved difficult given this tall creature planting herself in the middle. The song's guitar kicked in, a strumming rhythm that punched into the air and while elbows poked at my shoulders, the crush of humanity lifted both my body and mind, a collective roar that built a hive-like joy.

With, of course, Iggy Pop as its current patriarch.

Iggy Pop gyrated and swayed, his lithe body flinging sweat and whiplike hair tossing. Words flew from my mouth at top volume, locking into the surrounding crowd, the music, and the stage in a hypnotic balance. The cacophony of drums and guitar buried my worries one by one: the terrible drunks at my bartending job, the accidental cigarette burn marks on my forearms *from* those terrible drunk customers, the last time I bothered to attend community college, the last time I talked to Stephen, the last time my parents crowed about Stephen's exciting internship for NASA.

The last time for this, the last time for that, the last time for *anything*. Because *everything* carried its own collateral damage in my life.

None of it mattered in the moment. The sounds of the bass drum thumped loud enough that it overtook the beating of my heart, the screech of Iggy Pop screaming the song's final words over and over as he fell to the stage, kicking in the air.

This was existence.

When the song's final cymbal crash died off, the houselights came up to pull me back into the real world. Sweaty punks, all limbs and tank tops and boots, shuffled around, some pushing and some meandering, some shoving their way to the bathroom and others sliding between the throngs heading to the bar for one last order.

All around that strange woman, who planted herself like a rock in a river of humanity. A really tall rock.

I caught her eye, curiosity lingering for a second, and the woman looked back. She…smiled? It seemed like that, a curl of the lip revealing what looked like extra large, extra pointy teeth.

This lady really needed to see a dentist.

"Did you enjoy the show?" she asked, a weird diction like she'd stepped out of a 1930s film. Or maybe the pill I'd taken hours before still fizzled. Sometimes that shit came from a bad batch and did things you wished it hadn't.

"Me?" I asked, pointing to myself.

"You seem like something is bothering you. Trouble at work?" The woman smiled and nodded, her voice coming through clearly despite the postshow ringing in my ears. "Trouble with your family?"

This *had* to be the pill. Something about it probably made

me accidentally blab about my personal life in between songs. And pretty much every drug on the planet messed with memory in some way.

"I get it," the woman said. "I understand. We come here and lose ourselves." Maybe she was on drugs too. "And sometimes, there's a little bit more. Are you curious about what's out there?"

As a bartender, I'd had all sorts of strange questions about the meaning of life, religion, aliens, or anything else. So if she sought to weird me out, it wasn't happening.

I quickly crossed and uncrossed my fingers, then took in a breath. "Sure. Why not?"

The woman reached into her back pocket and—

"Okay, we can go in now." Serena's words poked through and jolted me back to the present. My body shook, a startled wave that rippled through my arms and shook my neck. "You okay?"

"Yeah," I said. "I was just...remembering something." I glanced back at Ian, who looked too consumed with his phone screen to notice. "Something I thought I'd lost."

"Serena." Eric's voice came through her fancy Bluetooth badge. "We're ready. I'd like to talk with our new friends. I also need you to check on the supply quality."

"Time for the day job," she said, with a pause long enough to insert a reaction for her joke. I mustered as much of a smile as I could, but that uncovered memory was still draped over my thoughts. "Wait, that was—" Serena started, first looking at the bottle, then me. "Did you drink that?"

"Oh yeah. On the drive over. Espresso blood, right?" I asked, wiping my mouth with my hand.

"Sort of. Well, um..." She eyed me up and down before returning to her tablet. "Kind of a custom formula."

The metal door cranked open with a familiar grinding sound, though the long shadows and security cameras came across as much less dramatic this time around, even with the gradual reveal of Eric. He waved us in, which seemed odd, given we had a human with us. But Ian's teenage impulsivity got the better of him, and he stepped out of the car without any hesitation.

I *should* have pulled him back, doubled down on being careful, given Eric's emphasis on community secrecy. But Ian was already halfway there by the time I unbuckled my seat belt, and I caught Serena shaking her head, a little side-to-side gesture that might have been overlooked had she not huffed in amusement. We caught glances and she mouthed an exasperated "kids."

"You're okay? You're safe?" Eric asked, as he walked to the small office I'd been in earlier. Ian brushed those aside and started asking about the app, questions about real-time this and database that and acronyms that flew over my head. This must have been what it was like when I talked to Lola—or back during my childhood when I tried to explain music to my family. "You're very curious about this," Eric said as we made our way back to the same office I'd sat in earlier that night.

"I'm learning to code. With data, you can do anything."

Eric nodded with a wide grin, smile lines framing his eyes. "Yes. It's remarkable, isn't it? For so many years, everything was disconnected, isolated. And now we're linked together. Even people like us. Listen," Eric said, taking in a breath, "I'm very sorry to hear about your mother. Unfortunately, there's nothing here that can help her. And I hope this hasn't been too strange for you, learning about our existence and everything. You weren't supposed to." His eyes softened, a short laugh coming out. "Technically, there are rules about this," he said, sitting down on a stool.

"Punk rock," I said, holding up a fist.

"It's weird," Ian said. "But, you know, there's a lot of weird shit in our world."

Eric raised an eyebrow at the curse word. Guess he didn't

spend a lot of time with teens. "That's one way to put it. So, tell me, how did you get access to the underlying data?"

Ian shot a look my way, which Eric and Serena picked up on. All eyes turned to me, like I'd committed some sort of crime. Which, I suppose, I did. Informal, unofficial, but still clear rule breaking. "I wanted to remove the app from my phone," I finally said. "Uninstalling it didn't work, so I asked him. He likes computer stuff."

"And why'd you want it removed?"

"Well, it's like you said—data. I *don't* want to be linked with everyone. No community, no shenanigans, no weird vampireness. Once the blood supply gets back to normal, just, like, leave me and my dog alone, you know?" No one spoke, though Eric inhaled, like words caught in his chest. It changed into a stifled sigh, as if he thought better of it.

"Her dog is really cool," Ian chimed in, his turn to run interference. "She can high-five."

"Well, the community will find out about this soon anyway." Eric nodded, then tapped the window. "You see that cart he's pushing? The bottles we've provided? That's going to change things. It's a semisynthetic mixture. In the back, we've got processing and bottling. With that, a single blood bag can produce ten times as much blood. Not pure enough for human medical use but compatible with our bodies. No more struggling to eat. We create a centralized resource for this, and then the app—" he tapped his laptop screen "—lets vampires order it as needed. And we hire vampires as delivery people." The app, the mysterious text—all a test for his delivery system. Eric always talked about community, and now he was intent on bringing the vampire community into the modern world, whether it wanted that or not. "Your job," he said. "You're a night janitor at the hospital, right?" I nodded, thinking back to that moment all those years ago when he intercepted me by the Hustler Club, his speech about getting vampire feeding away from the streets, about building something better. "You've based your career—your *time*—around getting food. But what if you didn't need to build your life that way?" The stool creaked as Eric leaned forward, his voice a near whisper, as if the weight of his words would be enough to connect them. "What would you choose to do then?"

I sat, blinking for who knows how long. A choice? From hiring blood pimps to coordinated theft of expiring blood bags, choice never existed before—only ends justifying means. Only a few seconds, but during that span a world of possibilities lit my mind. Without being tethered to some crummy job as a means to eat, what would I do with my immortality? "Get back onstage somehow. After that, I..." I hesitated, suddenly unsure. "I guess I don't know."

"You don't know. And that's the point. A world of possibility instead of survival. So many of us have built our lives around the simple act of daily sustenance." Eric turned to Ian. "It's not like in the movies."

"You'd be surprised at how hard it is to actually bite a human," Serena said to Ian. "It's messy and kind of disgusting."

"Yeah," Ian said with a short laugh. "I've heard."

"So, I understand your concerns about data privacy. But what we're creating here is not just an equal world for vampires. We're talking about giving vampires the chance to live their lives, truly live their lives. And provide security in a world that's making it increasingly difficult to stay secret. Serena," he said, "how many degrees do you have?"

"Western civilization, biology, biochemistry, aeronautical science, psychology, statistics, and computer science."

A ping of irritation flashed through me, though to be fair, I liked Serena much more than my overachieving brother.

"How did you eat while getting them?"

"Oh jeez. Depends on the decade. So many blood donors. A few accidental murders, which sucks, but you know, kind of an era-specific thing. Cows. Blood bank theft. Rats. Rat blood is the worst, but it works," she said. "And those." She pointed out the office window. "For the past two years, I've been drinking those."

"Has that made your life easier? More stable?"

"I mean, I guess so, if you call hunting for rats in alleys behind restaurants difficult. But I will say—" she chuckled enough that her shoulders bobbed "—you don't know difficult until you've tried scheduling with a blood volunteer *before* smartphones. My god, that was a lot of work."

"You see? We are going to remove those limitations. We'll provide supply, then the means to fulfill demand. We'll let vampires deliver to earn money, or they can simply order bottles as needed. Data and technology," he said, pointing first at his laptop screen, then at the office floor of people sitting at computers, "are creating a new society for us. A chance to really live. Do you still want to remove the app from your phone? Because I can do it for you now if you really want— no strings attached."

During his speech, all sorts of different things percolated, including the simple freedom of *not* having to work in the hospital. How many doors would that open? I pictured myself behind the controls of a recording studio, or maybe traveling for a few months as a roadie, or even guitar repair. All possibilities that had been shut off with the week-to-week practicality of recovering blood. And my life already had the advantage of inheriting my house from Laura—what about those who had to deal with finding blood *and* paying rent? What might they do if Eric simply removed one of those burdens from their lives?

"I still don't understand why you need to listen in on everything," I said slowly. "If this is just a food delivery service."

"Ah, that. It's precautionary. That's all I'll say for now. But worth it. And necessary."

Serena nodded. "I don't like it," she said quietly, "but he's right. It's necessary. For now."

The idea of Eric listening in, of tracking all of my comings and goings, all of the useless music news and guitar gear I looked at on my phone—was that worth it for this blood-ordering app and whatever other mysterious purpose he had? His side of the scale presented a weighty argument, though a lifetime of "don't touch my shit" held its ground.

I wasn't opposed to it. Food *was* food. Eventually. But not today.

"I'll delete it for now," I said. "Maybe put it back later."

"Fair enough. No offense taken." Eric held out his hand, and I put my phone in his palm. Ian leaned forward, matching my curiosity but probably for different reasons. Eric swiped through some screens and tapped away before finally entering a password, and several seconds later, he handed it back. "There you go. Let me know when you want it back."

The phone sat in my hand, a world of opportunities in a palm-sized device. I stared at it, doubt creeping in at my choice. And yet, one other question lurked, something that just clicked for me:

Eric said that the formula turned one blood bag into ten bottles. But those blood bags had to come from somewhere.

"The blood bag shortage," I said. Eric raised a single eyebrow at my statement. "You took those for your manufacturing."

"We did," he said. "I won't lie about that."

"But why? You're endangering the community."

"We needed to scale up. To ensure we could produce a high volume of bottles, large enough to support everyone in a timely fashion. We'd fallen just short of our goals, but then you told us about University Hospital. That put us over the top."

I caught Ian looking our way, and before I could respond, he butted in. "A stress test."

"That's right." Eric nodded.

"I—what?" I asked, suddenly feeling like the least-smart person in the conversation. Which I probably was, but I bet none of them could play drums as well as I could.

"It's a thing we learned in programming," Ian said in a tone that clearly reaffirmed that point. "To test something, you push it beyond its normal limits."

"The boy's correct. This is food supply. It cannot stall. We needed to know it could grow and still be sustainable."

"But," I said with a breath, "humans got attacked because of this."

Eric's face scrunched, the lines around his eyes and brow creasing deeper. "That was—" Eric took in a deep breath before continuing "—unfortunate. Anytime someone gets hurt because of our needs, it's unfortunate. This, particularly so. But the perpetrator made the decision, not us."

Eric's words didn't come with the lecturing condescension of my parents, but that same sense of justification existed. I may have been in a vampire start-up office instead of my old suburban house listening to Blondie, but the same urge surfaced: a need to say something.

"That's true," I said. "But *you* forced the need. You created the demand so you could increase your supply."

Serena grimaced at my words, in a way that told me she agreed. Eric winced as well, though his expression shifted, lips pursed and eyes shut.

"Look," I said, now diving into therapist territory that I clearly wasn't trained for. "I mean, I know you didn't intend this. But bad things are going to happen if you only look at the big picture and not what happens to real people."

Eric's fang dug into his bottom lip. "We have contributed to the victim's medical fund. Anonymously, of course. And we are accelerating things to ensure this doesn't happen again. Short-term and long-term." His voice shifted, any guilt melting back into lobbying mode. "You must—you must understand. Our lives have been built around blood for so long. What happened is unfortunate. I'm relieved that the latest victim is recovering. But what is possible—that could change everything. To be free of our tether."

"This guy," Serena said, looking at me before turning to Ian. "Always pushing for progress." She nodded at the exit. "We've gotta get back to work."

We walked in single file, Eric and Serena leading us. Over to the left, a massive roll-up door buzzed and began to pull up inch by inch. Though most of it remained obscured by the sea of desks and monitors around us, enough clearance existed to show a forklift rolling by, and farther behind, industrial fluorescent lamps gave the warehouse a dull light. In front of us, another person wheeled a cart. Eric stopped the person and opened the cart. The lid popped open, like an ice-cream cart for vampires, and Eric pulled out several bottles of manufactured blood. "The strawberry label is a little silly, I know. But it's the easiest way to not draw attention. Can't exactly have a syringe or a bat on it, you know?" he said as he handed them over. "Sorry they're chilled. The nice thing about manufactured blood is that it's stable longer than natural blood, so you don't have to rush to get it into the fridge. You can warm it up when you get home if you want."

"Still selling me on the app, huh?" I said, taking the bottles.

"It's a good thing, I promise."

"*Everything* is a good thing to you," Serena snarked at Eric. "Mr. Positivity over here," she said to me. "The only thing that riles him up is when people break our rules and when people don't use the oxford comma."

"The oxford comma is very important for grammatical clarity."

"You see?" she said with a laugh. "You two get going."

Eric led us out the front entrance, the heavy metal doors acting like an air lock between a warehouse full of computer-science vampires and the grime of Oakland's industrial sector. Perhaps there weren't any consequences after all; the final metal slab opened, its mechanical locks clicking and whirring after he punched in six digits on the number pad. The outside night air greeted us, the distinct odor of nearby traffic exhaust mixed with the Bay water.

"One last thing. Two, actually."

So close.

We paused, both turning to face Eric. Serena's head ticked crooked, one eyebrow raised, and though she opened her mouth to say something, she hesitated. Her lips remained parted, the sharpness of her fangs exposed.

"Both of you must understand that secrecy is the key to our community. If we discover someone is being careless with our existence, well," Eric said with a grimace, "appropriate action must be taken."

So there *was* a fixer.

"However, mutually beneficial arrangements can always be made. In lieu of consequences. Are you interested?"

"Um," I said. The question was directed at me, but I tried to gauge Ian's response as well. "Possibly?"

Eric nodded in full community-organizer mode. "What I said earlier was true—there's nothing here that will help your mother." The mere cadence of Eric's words teased something more. Ian clearly felt it too, from his sharp inhale to the way his fingers balled into fists. "But, there *is* a way to turn her." His words gathered momentum, both in tone and in pace. "You'll need something special. And there's a way to get it. Tomorrow night. But *only* tomorrow night. After that, supply may be…uncertain."

Tomorrow night?

I pulled out my phone and loaded up the last text he sent about an emergency blood delivery:

There is another opportunity this Sunday for those that wish to make a difference in the community. It requires several

hours of driving and some manual labor. It starts in the
early evening and will be paid in blood bottles. More importantly, it will mark the start of a significant change for
the community. Are you interested? You did a great job.
I'll need to know ASAP please.

"Yes, it's that. That was a general request. But now that I
know you two better, I realized there's very specific help I
could use." A single eyebrow rose as he looked at me, then
his eyes shifted over to Ian. "From both of you. This is so important that I'm offering you exactly what you want. For you,
young man, a chance to turn your mother. And for you," he
said, returning to my gaze, "all those rules you've broken?
Consider them forgiven."

Ian's face barely managed to capture his expression, and I
spoke up before he committed himself to any further vampire
shenanigans. "Hold up. 'Specific help'? What's that mean?"

"I can't say unless I have a commitment."

I looked at Ian, who met my eyes for a flash but without the
level of skepticism I'd hoped for. "I think we're going to need
a little more to go on," I said.

Eric shook his head, teeth digging into his bottom lip.
"There are details that need to remain confidential until we
know you are fully committed. For safety. I think—" A buzz
interrupted him, and he pulled out his lit phone. "I'm sorry,
I must go. A lot of moving parts right now. But let me know
as soon as possible. Your skills could significantly benefit the
community." He took in a quick breath while typing a reply.
"This could be life-changing. Not just for you two, but all
of us."

Before either of us could muster a response, he walked off,
phone up to his ear. The door shut behind him, eating the last
evidence of artificial light, locks snapping into place one by
one with audible clacks until all that remained was the sound
of the wind.

# CHAPTER 31

IAN STAYED SILENT, RIGHT up until the moment we began the descent off the Bay Bridge into San Francisco. "We need to talk," he said, breaking the quiet. I wasn't sure what to expect—everything from a complete shutdown to nonstop pleading seemed feasible, so a contemplative and sullen statement caught me off guard.

"Sure," I said, hitting the turn signal. "I'll find a spot to pull over." Though I already knew where to go for a life-or-death contemplation like this. It was the same view I'd seen a few hours ago, and the same place I frequented in the weeks following Laura's death.

I pulled to the curb, the meter blinking to tell us that parking was free at this near-midnight hour. "Have you seen the pier?" I asked as we got out, but he already took in the view.

We stood, the wind kicking with a cold that stung, waves that lapped gently several hours earlier now hitting the pier with a matching ferocity. In the distance, the lights of Oakland blinked at us, and somewhere within that mass of concrete and technology sat Eric and whatever he was planning.

"We went to Fisherman's Wharf for dinner. It was very loud. Not like here."

"Yeah. This is a good spot to think." My options involved being straightforward, being dissuasive, or playing dumb. I opted for the last one. "So," I started, "what did you—"

"Fuck it," Ian said, staring straight ahead. "I want to do it. If you don't go, then tell him I'll go."

"Whoa, whoa, whoa." Ian remained staring ahead, though I stepped into his line of sight, palms up. "Let's think this through."

"There's nothing to think through. He says there's a way. I have to take it."

"He also thinks it's necessary to listen in on everyone's phone, so I don't know if I totally trust him."

"I don't hear you coming up with any other solutions." His eyes showed a fierceness alongside his sharp words that broke what little momentum I had. He must have caught this change right away, and his posture took a more contrite stance. "Sorry. That was mean."

"Okay, well, you're right about that. I don't have a plan B." The toe of my Doc Martens scuffed against the pavement as I searched for the right thing to say. "Look, there's some weird shit going on there. When we were searching for you, Serena mixed a vial of something right before she ran off. I thought it was caffeinated blood but I had a…" My voice trailed off, dancing around the fact that I'd learned something about the night I was turned. "Well, I felt a bit off. And I had, like, drug flashbacks. When I jolted in the car. Probably shouldn't have tried that while driving."

Ian blinked blankly at me. "You jolted in the car?"

"Yeah, right outside the warehouse." He really *was* into that phone. Kids and their damn tech. "And she looked exhausted.

I thought that she was just tired, but whatever she mixed in there messed with me too."

"What does that have to do with turning my mom?"

"The point is, they're up to some strange shit. You can't just promise the world, and then withhold all the important stuff. That's supershady. Especially the part about forgiving my rule breaking? That's like borderline blackmail. For all we know, 'consequences' are empty threats."

"You don't trust anyone." Ian adjusted, hands now on hips in full-on accusatory stance. "That's what this is."

"Eric? You're right. I don't."

"No. I mean, like—" he waved his arms in a giant circle over his head "—all of them. Maybe not just vampires. You don't trust people. You know what?" In the dim light, his expression changed, the softness that came with epiphany. "You've been alone too long."

This whole time with Ian, I hadn't lost my cool. But hearing a teenager say those words came pretty close to tripping that particular wire. "What does *that* have to do with anything? Besides, I live with Lola."

"No, I mean, you're like, broken off from anyone else. How exactly are we related? Why don't you talk to family anymore?"

"I *had* family. Laura. She died." That statement had been part of my reality for decades, and yet, saying it this time stung more than it had in years. "And she went peacefully. Gracefully. Listening to a good song on Repeat."

"Okay, fine. Then after that. Why come out here? All you do is hide in your house with your guitars. You even said yourself, you haven't been to a concert since your friend died. I'd expect you to see other friends *more* after one died, not less. All those vampires working with Eric? I bet they're living normal lives."

*Normal.* So many emotional scabs crusted over the wound caused by that word, and yet the way Ian said it exposed the hurt again with an unknowing surgical precision. *"Why you can't just be normal?"* My dad had asked that same question the afternoon they'd thrown out my records, six words loaded up with equal parts anger, disappointment, and taunt. What did *normal* even mean? We were never going to be normal in that neighborhood at that time. *He* was never going to be normal to his neighbors and coworkers, and his unending aspiration to meet some buttoned-down standard was never, ever going to happen. He'd put such *value* into such an artificial thing, as if he *wanted* me to break away to rock and punk, like the harder he jammed the normalcy button, the faster he'd accelerate my decisions. And my mom, with her stinging tongue and dagger eyes, like needling me would somehow pull me back to them rather than push me away.

Even Laura, as much as I loved her—more than any other human, vampire, or dog I'd ever met—she'd push this topic away whenever family outside of *us* were mentioned, a stand-offishness that lurked even on the night we learned of my mom's death. At least, from what I could remember; I *did* get pretty drunk that night.

"Hey, my guitars are awesome," I finally said, a poor joke in a weaker voice, giving away the recent flips and turns of my psyche.

Immortality didn't help with childhood issues, apparently. It only took me nearly fifty years of vampiredom to realize that.

Ian kept at it, regardless of my attempt at humor to derail his intent. "But they're just *stuff.* You can't replace people with stuff." He let out a sigh, his breath visibly rolling out into the cool night air. "Look, my mom's a school counselor. When Dad died, she told me that, like, every day. Sometimes multiple times a day."

"Probably for different reasons than why we're arguing now."

"Yeah."

But the knot in my gut went beyond my mom and dad, beyond what Laura couldn't bring herself to talk about. One more person existed in the family equation, someone with his own polite wrecking ball swung at my life choices. "There's something you should know."

"I knew it. There *had* to be something."

"No, it's not about vampires." I held Ian's gaze, knowing that the revelation I was about to drop did little to change how he felt about his mom's situation.

Though it might bring him closer to mine.

"Your grandpa, his real first name is Stephen."

"I already know that."

"I have a brother named Stephen."

Ian squinted, at first not connecting what my words meant. Right before I was going to spell it out for him, his brow lifted and his mouth dropped, pieces coming together several seconds later than they should have. "Oh."

"Yep."

"Wow. Okay. Whoa."

"I left when he'd just started college. We weren't always enemies. I looked out for him when he was little. But when we hit middle school, he just became more of what my parents wanted. And they sensed that. They egged it on." Each revelation uncovered layers I'd buried deep, things that stayed detached even after I knew EJ's real identity. But saying it now gave it an impossible power, a bright and clear mirror to the pains of my family history. "They wanted some weird version of our lives. And when I refused, Stephen leaned into it. I never forgave him for that. He never earned it. The only good thing is that it brought me here. I would have never gone to Laura without that. I suppose I should thank him."

Ian nodded, a surprisingly agreeable reaction to the pileup of life-changing revelations hitting his young life. "So you don't trust people because my grandpa was a jerk when he was young," he said, quicker than I expected. "And because of that, my mom's gonna die."

Smart kid. Always bringing it back to the main point. "That's a bit of a stretch you're making."

"But it's true. You're just scared to give them a chance." I wanted to interrupt, to point out that I took a chance on Laura, I took a chance on Marshall, I took a chance on *him*. But then he'd probably point out that that only amounted to three people over thirty-some years, which wasn't a good ratio any way you looked at it. "Thing is, you're selfish."

"Excuse me? I just saved you from vampires and muggers *and* I let you into my house to pee the first time I met you."

"Doesn't matter," he said with a headshake. "I'm not forcing *you* to turn my mom. I'm asking you to give her a choice. Because her body is *not* giving her a choice right now, which means *I* don't have a choice. I didn't have a choice when my dad died. I don't have a choice with *anything* right now. So yeah, maybe if you say 'no' that might work with whatever you're feeling, but it's being selfish. It's not fair. It stopped being fair when you decided to tell me what you were. When you let me into your life. When you taught me guitar and took me to see Grape Ape and showed me punk. You don't get to do all that, bring me into this life—your life—and then just shut off. That sucks. And it's not right."

How had only a few days passed since I'd met Ian? That cold night after Eric's community meeting seemed like a lifetime ago. Since then, we'd jammed, we'd been to a show, we'd fed fries to my dog. And he'd bared his soul to me, as much as a thirteen-year-old boy could. Probably more than I did when I showed up on Laura's doorstep—broke, aimless, and the complete opposite of glamorous vampire life. And yet Laura invited me into her home, giving me a shoulder to lean on and a soul to connect with while I got my life in San Francisco sorted out—and then she *gave* me her home.

I couldn't shut Ian out. Not now.

Because Aunt Laura wouldn't.

"Come on." I pulled my keys out of my pocket. "We should go."

"That's it? You're just giving up?"

"Did I say that?" My car beeped and its lights flashed. I took the first step to the driver's side, then waved him along.

"So you're going to do it."

"I'm not promising anything. Not yet," I said. He followed, opening the passenger door first. By the time I got in, he'd already buckled up, seemingly carried by an understanding of my tone. "But I don't want to be selfish. There's enough of that in my family. Aunt Laura taught me that. And—" I turned the key "—she had good taste in music. Always trust someone with good taste in music."

# CHAPTER 32

IAN'S PREVIOUS URGENCY TURNED to quiet patience, perhaps consciously backing off unless I really needed to be pushed. By now, the clock ticked well past midnight, and though this was the middle of the day for me, his internal rhythm likely suffered from the past few days. He still hadn't told me if he'd slept at all, though from my occasional glances his way, the bags under his eyes seemed to grow deeper with each passing minute.

We made our way back to my house, with only a quick stop at a drive-through. I didn't know how often Sonya or EJ let him subsist solely on fast food, so maybe it was a treat for him and *that* prompted his quiet. The fact that we'd just discussed paths to immortality while I bought him artery-busting grease wasn't lost on me.

Lola greeted us when we got home, following Ian and his bag of deep-fried tacos. They went straight to the kitchen, but I pulled out my phone and paused to consider my choices:

not just this choice, but all of the choices I'd made leading up to this.

Specifically, the one that ended with a visit to a cemetery.

It wasn't lost on me, the irony of a vampire breaking into a cemetery. But I had driven to Marshall's hometown of Davis, a sleepy college town about two hours east of San Francisco.

"Hey, dude," I said, sitting down next to his tombstone. "How are you?" I asked, as if the night air could answer me. Marshall Lee Waite, the marker read, with dates etched above a simple inscription:

Beloved Son, Brother, Friend.

That was it. No mention of his music, of his life, no fitting quotes from Nick Cave. Of all the times minutes turn into hours between laughs and debates, I was certain that we would have broached the topic of what belonged on our tombstones, presuming I got hit by a car or something. Even standing there, I came up with several: "Someone to Die For" by Belly, "Anti-Pleasure Dissertation" by Bikini Kill, "Monkey Gone to Heaven" by the Pixies, "In Undertow" by Alvvays.

All of those would have made for better epitaphs than the catalog blurb staring back at me. I reached over and touched the smooth stone, not the chipped and grimy old tombstones in vampire movies but something that looked like it fell off the display of countertops at the home store. It was clean, neat, and it barely existed—the opposite of Marshall. Our musical journeys may have only been for audiences of ten or twenty people, some of them half-drunk or apathetic, but they were always markedly *us*. Regardless of the constant rotation of drummers, the sound, the vibe, the *messy* way our spirits overlapped.

That was Marshall. Not this rectangular slab of semivaluable minerals, a few pithy words carved across them. My joints burned as I knelt down, examining the sight in front of me, from the neatly manicured grass to the dew forming across the head of the tombstone. Proximity revealed further details, things hidden from the lack of light but now visible up close:

An angel.

A stereotypical cherubic angel, stenciled adjacent to the first letter of Marshall's name, something that probably would have stood out in broad daylight but blended in here. An angel, for the man who hated organized religion even more than he hated ska. I stared at the etching, the curve of the wings and the brightness of the cheeks designed to deliver calm and comfort in a time of grief.

But not for me.

Had my life played out like a pop-culture vampire's, the religious symbolism would have caused me to hiss, turn away, possibly spark a spontaneous combustion. But reality proved far different. It still prompted a physical reaction, a full-body tension that tightened my fingers into fists and my teeth into a tight clamp, the bite so driven that the tips of my fangs grazed my inner lip.

Who the hell did this to Marshall?

But I knew. They were *relatives*—people that assumed things about him, about their relationship to him. They didn't know him at all. Despite our practical lives separated by the gulf between human and vampire physiology, I knew him far better than his family.

I took the soft guitar case off my back, setting it down to unzip it. I settled in against the tombstone and set Joan, an acoustic/electric Seagull guitar with easy action and a rich tone, across my lap. Soft chords played instinctively, and though I had grabbed her on a whim, it seemed fitting that the guitar named after Joan Baez was with me. "Sorry it's acoustic. Couldn't bring an amp in. I know you deserve tremolo and chorus instead of this," I said, strumming aimlessly, all the while a single thought repeating in my head:

*Marshall would have hated all of this.*

The more the thought circled, the more defiance gathered in me, a gradual escalation from justified indignation to fuck-you anger. I was mad—not just mad at his relatives for making these choices, but for him coming to me in desperation, for putting an impossible decision on me that all led to this ridiculous slab of bland font and neat comfort.

For holding back when he clearly had something more to say to me.

None of it should have happened. Not only should Marshall not have been in the cemetery, he didn't *belong* here on any level.

My fingers formed chords, changing the shape and sound without any intention. Major went to minor, from in key to something new; it moved like a free-flowing conversation over the course of probably ten minutes or so, the strings quiet enough to avoid any late-night attention but loud enough to ring through the air as hair tossed against my cheeks.

I'd come all this way to say something to Marshall. To have a moment of some kind, some sense of ethereal connection or an epiphany or at least several seconds of inner calm. But all of that proved elusive, and instead, the stewing anger failed to burn off in any way. Each strum, each chord change, each foot tap, every individual motion added to the intensity building inside, accelerating agents that added to my inner combustion until I could have broken the headstone with a single look.

"You know what?" I finally said, clapping my fingers against the strings to stop them. "Fuck you. Fuck you for driving off in the rain. Fuck you for asking me for something I couldn't do. Fuck the rules for being there. Fuck your family for putting you here. Fuck the *world* for fucking up everything during this." I shut my eyes but they didn't stop what had been unleashed. Months had passed since Marshall's death and somehow the moment felt as raw and real as the moment the door closed behind him.

"I think I know what you were going to say. That night. And I've thought about it. As much as a vampire can," I said, unafraid of using the *V* word given the circumstances. "And I would have tried. As much as a vampire can. Because two people who can listen to a Siouxsie remaster in comfortable silence?" I picked at the strings. "You're right. That's true love."

I closed my eyes harder, tears escaping with the urgency that only came when pain mixed with guilt. I wiped at my cheeks with the top of my hand, a hint of blood smearing across my knuckles, but I didn't care. "I miss you," I finally pushed out. "You're supposed to be here. You're supposed to be telling me that I'm singing harmonies wrong. Or that naming guitars is dumb. Or just *listening* to stuff with me. I can't be honest with anyone else. I can't let them into my house."

Perhaps it came from instinct, my hands knowing that the left pressing against frets and the right strumming with a pick was the best, most obvious, most natural thing for them to do. Whatever the reason, I played several chords in progression, a random mix of emotion burned in the form of major and minor chords.

Until I realized what the last few were. I played them again, changing the rhythm slightly to match a song.

Only so many combinations of chords existed. The timing behind them, the pauses and rhythm, that made each song totally unique.

And in this case, D to B minor, something that rang familiar. I played them again, an instinctive shuffle that reminded me of a very distinctive, very formative moment of my life:

The day I left my parents.

I continued, singing the lyrics to "One Way or Another" in a way opposite of how Debbie Harry did it on the recording. She was angry, and I was angry too, but her fury represented a punch at someone specific.

Mine was a punch at everyone. Including myself.

The song played out to an empty graveyard, the only witness a security guard in the distance and the stars overhead. I let the final chord ring out, returning me to a late night and an empty ceremony. Blood tears remained on my cheeks, a combination of time and wind drying them against my skin.

I stood, trying to conjure a final farewell. But nothing came to mind, and instead I held up my hands like claws and hissed like a vampire.

In my head, I saw him do the same in return.

I shoved Joan back in the soft case and slung it on my shoulder. Soft grass bent under my boots with each step, marking my exit from the cemetery.

And the last time I visited Marshall's grave.

As I crossed through the gate and hit the stone steps leading to the front cemetery's sidewalk, a decision came to me, an epiphany sent by fate or maybe Marshall—or maybe just myself:

I decided then and there that I wouldn't let anyone else in.

*That* was the fallout from the last time someone asked me about getting turned. Yet here in my dining room, Ian running Lola through her small set of tricks to earn a fry, I stared at my phone. The screen showed Eric's contact, the virtual keyboard ready to type a message.

"Good girl," Ian said, soon followed by the sounds of a dog eating a single French fry with too much enthusiasm. Maybe when all of this was behind us, I'd pick up some fries just for her. I might live forever, but corgis didn't, and good dogs deserved their share of fries.

"Ian?" I called out, the first words we'd exchanged directly since getting back to my house.

"Yeah?"

"Look, I still don't know how this all works." My eyes shut, trying to pull back details of that sudden flashback of the Iggy Pop show. But while details now *existed*, they remained fragmented, specific puzzle pieces with chunks missing. "So I can't promise you anything. But I'm gonna text Eric now."

I peered into the dining room, eyeing his reaction to gauge whether or not I'd done the right thing. He sat stone-faced, unmoving lips and frozen cheeks, but that in itself felt like a mask. Because the look in his eyes said something different— sharper, brighter, with a *longing* in them.

"Unless you don't want me to." That was just messing with him.

"No, no, of course not. Do it." He walked over with a purposeful stomp, and before I could stop him, he hugged me. His skinny arms pulled me in tight, a much stronger hold than expected. "Thank you."

"Look," I said, patting him on the back, "I don't know what Eric needs from us. Or wants us to do. And I don't know what your mom is going to say. It's still her choice. Okay? So let's keep all expectations in check."

He pulled back, his brown pupils caught beneath the welling of tears. He blinked for several seconds, his teenage pride probably trying to will away anything close to emotion.

I didn't say anything. Rather, I chose to wait until he was ready.

"You're giving her a chance," he finally said. "That's all I want."

"Well, you should also get some rest. If we're going to—oh no," I said, the sound of rustling paper coming from the other room. "Lola!" I yelled, and an orange blur crossed our path, a trail of spilled fries and a chewed-up container on the floor.

"I'll clean it," Ian said, "I got it." He dashed off, picking up dropped greasy potatoes along the way and leaving me alone with my phone.

Whether Ian was tired or not, I didn't know. But the weight of recent days caught up to me, and though I normally wouldn't go to bed for another few hours, every muscle moved at half speed, even the simple act of pulling out my phone.

The screen lit up as I pulled up Eric's name from the contact list.

Okay, I typed.

We're in. What do you need from us?

An icon appeared, confirming the message sent, and Ian returned with Lola trotting beside him, a guilty pace to her shuffle. She refused to look at me—an admission of guilt in the simple language of wonderful-but-greedy dogs. "I'm going to crash early. Rest before tomorrow. You should too."

"Yeah. I'm beat," Ian said, this time only giving scratches, not treats to my dog.

I leaned against the hallway wall and called out Lola's name. "Time for bed," I said, which prompted the dog to break away from Ian's neck scratches and hustle my way. Her furry abdomen brushed against my shins, and I started to tell Ian goodnight when my phone buzzed.

Eric's response brightened the display.

Great. I'll come tomorrow. Get up early. I'll be there by dusk.

# CHAPTER 33

**FIRST CAME THE KNOCK** on my door.

Then a muffled "Louise, time to get up."

Then a thirty-pound corgi tromping all over me, complete with face licks and paws catching on sheets.

"Alright," I said to Lola, before repeating myself louder for Ian. The bedroom's blackout curtains hid almost all of the UV, though a hint of dusk streaked through the very top of the windows, visible only to eyes adjusted to the dark. Lola hopped onto the floor with a *thump-thump* and I checked the time:

Four-thirty in the afternoon. Way too early for a vampire to be waking up, and yet, ever since Ian walked into my life, *something* always pulled me at this absurd hour. My bare feet slapped against the cold slats of solid flooring, prompting Lola to surround me with little hops of wake-up excitement.

The door opened and I shuffled out. "Hey," I said to Ian. Lola pushed past me, a direct trot to Ian before plopping on the floor for belly rubs. "Traitor."

She didn't listen, though, and instead held up a paw, awaiting a high five. But Ian wasn't the one who met her paw.

A thin man with a tight coat, wavy salt-and-pepper hair, and a Scottish burr rolling through his words, reached out. "Aren't you a pretty doggy?" he said, taking her paw.

Ian looked at me. "He got here about ten minutes ago. I guess I have the power to invite him in."

Eric's eyes snapped upward, his mouth tilting in a wry grin. "Many of the things you've heard about us aren't true." He stood up, hands in pockets and back straight. "I got here a little early. I thought we'd better prepare."

"Prepare? I'm going to take my dog to go potty," I said, checking the windows to see how much sunlight still hit my backyard. "And then we need a full explanation about what's happening."

"Fair enough. You'll need to wear something...nicer...than a leather jacket. But we don't have much time." Eric tapped his phone, and a knock came at the door several seconds later. "There's a lot in store for tonight."

Ian looked at the door, audible murmurs coming from behind it. "Should I invite *them* in?"

The physical transformation of a human to vampire was actually quite simple: give the blood to a human, have them drink it, and its contents overcame the human immune system enough to replicate and take over.

Vampirism, it turned out, was just a virus. With claws.

The rest of it, though, was quite wild.

The process didn't happen the way movies portrayed it, at least based on what Eric said. Not with a vampire's *own* blood, but with a special mixture. His explanation came with a cold technicality, breaking down properties of blood and blood cells in ways that went way over my head, though maybe Serena and her thousand college degrees could appreciate it. Apparently, it required a blend, a brew of blood sourced from vampires with exact genetics. All bottled up and kept in secret for authorized use.

Certain rumors had long circulated around our community. But the one about a secret society of ancient vampires?

I never would have guessed *that* one to be true.

Because where this special blood came from, who mixed it to unlock its special properties, who stored it, who *chose* the recipients—it all pointed to these Ancients. Who lived removed from us everyday vampires, but used people like Eric to monitor the communities across regions.

Mind you, Eric explained all of this while Serena and several other vampires came in—for some reason, we all had to dress like a cocktail party was on the agenda. They shuffled around with bags and tablets, Serena only slowing down to ask if my gear was ready.

"What do you mean?" I asked.

"Your guitar. Can you bring it?" Serena said, still tapping away at her tablet despite her long fancy gloves. "We really need to get moving."

"Wait, but it's not just the guitar. I mean, do you need my amp too? My pedals? If so, which pedals? Do I need a capo, ebow—"

"You're going to be backing me." Serena's words came out with a flat disdain that rang opposite to her styled hair, and suddenly I remembered Eric ribbing her about practicing in the warehouse. She shook her head, lips pursed and eyes narrowed. "I'll be singing. So whatever you'll need for that."

I stood in white knee-high go-go boots, which went perfectly with the black-and-white checkerboard dress that I'd dug out of storage, a bin of Aunt Laura's stuff from her more adventurous days. My outfit didn't look as fancy as Serena's, but I'd say that my mod aesthetic won more cool points, despite going against my punk sensibilities. "Backing you?" I assumed that Serena's taste in music hadn't modernized overnight, so this wasn't going to involve a bunch of Yeah Yeah Yeahs covers. "All this is about…a gig?"

"You said you wanted to get back onstage, right? You're the entertainment," Eric said with a knowing nod. He pulled out his phone, then flipped the screen over to his app. "And in a way, security. For some very special guests. And you—" he pointed to Ian "—I have a special task for you. A *human* task." His screen showed a zoomed-out map of the Bay Area, on which he then scrolled up north into wine country.

In a remote patch of green, a cluster of red dots blinked.

Despite being nearly a century old, Eric was still a tech guy. And tech guys probably didn't use blinking red icons unless the subject *warranted* blinking red icons.

"What the actual fuck…" I whispered as Ian leaned forward to peer at the screen.

"But first, you need to grab your guitar," Serena said, pulling my attention back to more immediate issues.

"About that." Serena's eyebrow rose before shooting a worried look at Eric. "I have a lot of guitars. And several bass guitars. And a ukelele." I pointed down to my music room. "Which one?"

"I don't care. They all sound the same to me. Pick one and we'll rehearse in the van."

Her bold claim was about to unleash a ten-minute tirade about the nuances of guitars, from the body to the pickups, but given the intense half frowns everywhere, I opted to march down the hallway.

There was only one choice.

After all, if I was going to do something ridiculous, possibly dangerous with a bunch of vampires, I needed the spirit of Aunt Laura with me. Besides, I was already wearing her dress.

We sat in a darkened van, like special agents on a mission rolling up across the Golden Gate Bridge and then deeper past Marin County. During that time, Eric went deeper into the

Ancients. Though at times the ridiculous facts sounded almost like trolling. At this point, I didn't know what to believe.

"So, everything we've ever been told is a lie?" I asked, tuning up Joan. In the row behind me, Serena did vocal warm-ups, sounding more like a youth theater production of *Annie* than a performer for some mysterious group of ancient vampires.

"That's...subjective," Eric said.

"I just learned all this vampire stuff a few days ago and it's all wrong," Ian said. "That's bullshit." A smirk fought its way onto my lips, and I kept it from sneaking out by concentrating on tuning Joan. Ian was right, though.

"Not necessarily." Eric leaned over from the front passenger seat, his seat belt pulling forward with his movement. In his hands sat that same Moleskine notebook he'd pulled out nearly every time I saw him. "The community was told that they can't create more vampires. That's true. They were also told that the act of turning is an act of suicide, which is mostly true. The amount of blood necessary to naturally turn a human can kill a vampire. It can also injure a human. This is why the Ancients' mixture is needed to turn. It's also a narrative for safety."

"Safety?"

"If a human drinks directly from a vampire, they get very ill. Nausea, fever, all of that. Sometimes it overwhelms their body. They can pass out, possibly die. The wrong person stumbles upon them and they might call nine-one-one. You know what happens when hospitals get mystery conditions?"

A snarky response came to mind, but I hesitated, aware of Ian's own dealing with difficult medical problems. He, however, didn't seem to carry that same concern. "They investigate," he said in between bites of a double cheeseburger dripping with sauce, something Eric graciously agreed to pick up on the way.

"That's right. So we cut it off at the source to keep things safe. The few times we've had to deal with human officials led to—" he took in a breath "—messy situations."

"Oh shit," I said, muting the guitar strings. "There *are* fixers."

I immediately thought of the last time I saw Marshall, rain pouring over him.

"Not as many as you'd think," Serena said. "Rumors work well to hold the line." She pursed her lips for a moment before turning back to me. "That's a secret too. Tell anyone and maybe we'll send one after your guitars."

"Okay, okay, point taken," I said, resuming tuning the strings. "So fixers. Ancients. And a magic blood mixture hoarded by a bunch of secret asshole vampires who hang out once a year in a compound in the woods."

"Correct."

"Sometimes the compound is on an island," Serena said.

"But they like live music, so they can't be all bad," I said, shooting a look at Ian.

"Do you remember what I asked you in the warehouse?" Eric asked. "The idea that you could do anything with your immortality—travel anywhere, learn anything, without the need to worry about a blood supply?" I nodded, all of the ideas rushing back to me. "We all live in a system with currency. For humans, their lives are controlled by money—the people who earn it and the people who hand it out, and in between is the invisible class system—" Eric stopped, then glanced at Serena. I turned her way to catch the tail end of an eye roll. "Go ahead and say it, Serena."

"I didn't say anything."

"You're thinking it. I don't need mental powers to know."

Serena looked at me, smirk still plastered on her face. "If only they let vampires run for President, right? Here's your best candidate. He'd win all the debates."

"What about president of vampires?" I asked.

"Well…" Serena said, then returned to the list of songs on her tablet. "I'll let him explain."

"As I was saying—" Eric cleared his throat "—the vampire

community is governed by the Ancients. Hundreds of years old. They took us from wild, roaming murderous creatures living in dirt and shadows, to a community secretly integrated into human society. This brought us structure and safety, laws and unwritten rules, all driven by blood. Who gets blood, how they get it, our infrastructure. And," he said, a pause that may or may not have been for dramatic effect, "who gets turned. They maintain this hierarchy. They're hidden, several dozen vampires steering the entirety of our culture and society. Some of us work for them. I provide community oversight, technological support, things of that nature. This balance has remained for centuries. The only difference between now and a hundred years ago is communication. And data."

*That's* why he was so pushy about the app.

"My job is to watch over the community. But in doing so, I see this power imbalance. I see the importance of community engagement. Data is the great equalizer. The Ancients, they don't understand technology at all. The world has moved past them. This app is just the start. The bottles, the manufactured blood—something much bigger is coming for vampires. If we're successful tonight."

"They sound like assholes," Ian said. Eric's quick chuckle was drowned out by Serena's loud guffaw, complete with spit-take.

"Successful?" I asked. "Are you, like, organizing a union or something like that?"

Eric and Serena locked eyes for a glance. "That's a good analogy," he said. "Every year, they have a gathering. To discuss matters from the human world affecting our world, to go over requests for turning humans, among other things. This year's is here, in Northern California. And I have something to present. Besides entertainment. Now, Ian, your role is critical."

"Me?" Ian looked up from his phone and pointed at the ill-fitting shirt and slacks they brought for him.

"I'll need your help in the kitchen." Eric turned back, settling into the passenger seat as the van rumbled forward. "There are some things humans can do that vampires can't."

"That sounds ominous," I said, playing a few quick chords on my now-tuned guitar. Joan's strings rang off the van's walls, surprisingly good reverb for a metal box on wheels.

"It's for the better. You help Serena. Ian helps me. Ian gets a vial for his mother. And your history of rule breaking goes away."

So both ancient vampires *and* my parents considered me a rule breaker. "My parents always punished me for not listening. The Ancients can't be worse than them," I said with a chuckle.

Except mine was the only laugh in the van. I looked up from Joan to see Eric and Serena eyeing each other, worried creases across both their brows.

"I think you should practice your set," Eric finally said before turning back to his tablet.

# CHAPTER 34

A WORLD WITHOUT THE search for blood.

The next hour wove us far beyond the Golden Gate, through two-way highways and past closed wineries and small vacation towns, before ultimately veering off onto a dirt road. And while Serena and I practiced through her short set list of decades-old songs, my mind considered the possibilities of such freedoms.

The simplicity of Serena's picks helped in that regard, songs that became elementary school fodder: "The Band Played On," "Ida, Sweet as Apple Cider," "My Wild Irish Rose," "Mighty Lak' A Rose," and others.

Given just how dated they were, it only took minutes for me to jot down a list of chord changes on a sheet of paper. We went through each song once or twice, sometimes stifling my laugh at the corny lyrics sung with her earnest performance. This continued in the van all the way until we made it through the gates of a compound tucked within an endless row of trees and hills. The van lurched to a halt alongside a row of other vans, with a few cars sprinkled in.

Then we walked.

Beyond the ornate designs of the outer gates, we paused at a fork in the path, a giant unused fountain sitting under the night sky. Eric gathered his small entourage in tuxedos with Ian in his ill-fitting getup, complete with slicked-back hair. Opposite them, Serena and I stood, her staring at her tablet of song lyrics while I carried Joan.

With each of us ready to break apart, Eric held up a hand and gave a quick refresher of his plan, though his speech centered on logistics of a schedule, like we were only there for the reception rather than with any intention of forming a union or whatever he had planned. He paused after listing times, places, and cues, then turned his head to scan the area.

"There's just one thing I'll need you to do," Eric said to Ian.

"Whatever you need. I'm all in."

"Good, good. Then listen." Eric looked at me, then back at Ian with intense eyes. "You'll need to drink some vampire blood."

A gust of wind kicked up between us as we each processed the meaning of Eric's words. Serena looked up from her tablet and even the other vampires preparing paused and watched.

Ian, usually primed and ready for an inappropriate response, fell quiet, though his face remained inscrutable.

So I spoke for him.

"Drink," I said, "blood?" I faced Ian, and his eyes were already there to meet mine. They lacked the teen bravado that had become commonplace with every glance and peek, and instead, Ian's expression was, if not a cry for help, at least a "what the hell" question.

"Not a lot," Eric said. Behind him, lights from the estate flickered, bursts of yellow-white lights poking through the horizon. "Just a spoonful. It can be Louise's even. If you prefer. This is necessary to mask his scent. Humans would be identified very quickly." Human and vampire scents lacked any clear difference to me, and my own sense of smell was clearly dismal, given how I usually missed when Lola's favorite blankets needed a wash. "I think one thing you'll find is that every vampire is a little different," he said, as if he read my mind. "But believe me, some would notice his presence and ask questions. We need to be cautious."

"I'm still not sure—" I started.

"It's fine. I'll do it." Ian moved directly in front of me and nodded. "Like from the wrist?"

"Ew, no. That's gross."

"That's easiest," Eric said, pulling out a knife in one hand, then reaching into his inner coat pocket for a small vial. "Cut your wrist, then he drinks for five seconds, then we put a drop of this on to heal it up." His eyes locked onto mine. "Neosporin for vampires."

When Ian asked to stay for the weekend, the last thing I think either of us expected was *him* drinking blood. Especially from me. "This sounds like a terrible idea," I said, the few maternal instincts I had kicking in.

"It's the safest way," Eric said with a nod. "It'll cycle out of his system in a day, he shouldn't be too nauseated from it and it'll mask him."

"I'll be fine." *There* was that naive teen swagger, the kind that bordered on stupidity. I stared at him, my own doubt tempered by his fierce determination. But the way his eyes gleamed told me that I'd taken this whole situation the wrong way; his boldness wasn't about an age-appropriate "nothing will hurt me" attitude.

Instead, he understood the weight of his decision, and his confidence was born from a desperation to reclaim his family.

"Alright," I said quietly before I held my arm out. "I'm a wimp with pain, though. Be gentle."

"We should hurry," Eric said with a nod. A sliver of moonlight beamed through the passing clouds, a bright reflection off the blade as he held it up.

## CHAPTER 35

**VAMPIRE POWER MYTH #11:** Vampires have impenetrable skin.

Absolutely not true. Not only was my skin pierceable by a blade fit for hunting alligators, the half-inch incision *hurt.* "Ow!" I yelped, in a completely undignified burst. Despite drinking blood on a regular basis, a deep nausea grew from the actual sight of blood oozing out of my wrist, and when Ian latched on, I had to shut my eyes while Eric counted down from five.

"You never drank from rats, did you?" Serena said in a deadpan voice.

"Let's patch you up," Eric said, pointing over to me. He poured the small vial over my wrist, and after the initial sting, the blood was absorbed into the wound to kickstart the healing process. "Both of you sit for a minute while we do final checks." Despite the chilly wind, my nausea continued to stir, and the opportunity to sit down was much appreciated. Ian plopped down next to me, his twisted lips showing that he felt something similar, though he certainly wouldn't admit to it.

Several feet from us, Eric talked with his small team of tuxedoed vampires as they opened their rolling suitcases, though what they contained lay beyond my view. In the opposite direction, Serena started the same vocal warm-ups from the van, though the strained expression on her face seemed to match my nausea.

"You alright?" I asked Serena. For all her deadpanning, organizing, and handling of difficult circumstances, her posture betrayed her sudden apprehension, an inward shrivel across her whole body despite nailing practice notes perfectly on pitch.

"Eric's asked me to do a lot of different things for him. This," she said, pointing to herself, "is probably the worst of all."

"Playing a gig is the worst?" I asked with a scrunched brow. So much education, so much *living*, all across wholesale changes in technology, culture, and communication—and yet, Serena's apparent battle with stage fright topped her "things to be scared of" list.

"You try standing in front of all those people."

I had, of course. A reception for ancient eternal vampires probably was different from indifferent bar patrons, but still, same idea on principle.

Several years after Aunt Laura's urging, I finally got the nerve to audition for bands. Like Serena, it didn't matter how much I'd mastered technique or had fancy gear, the very act of presenting *myself* before people was different; it meant finally putting myself out there.

Bands came and went, sometimes existing only for a few weeks before splitting for whatever reasons. Despite all the searching, auditioning, bedroom noodling, learning songs, and recording demos, it took a few years and three bands to actually fulfill my promise to Aunt Laura. But there we were, the five members of a band called The Scream Queens, arriving first at a dingy Mission District bar—the first of four bands on the bill, with a set time of only thirty minutes. Up front, a handful of people sat at the bar, staring at the baseball game playing on corner TV screens. In the back, one of the other bands sat together, a member offering a mild wave while the rest talked among themselves.

I'd attended enough local shows to know that opening bands on small bills usually got zero attention. And even though we were ignored by both the patrons and the other bands sitting in the back by the pool table, nerves tingled my entire body, from my toes to my fangs.

"Hi!" said Marcy, our lead singer and bassist, feedback ringing out over the PA. She stepped back to turn to us, a what-the-hell smile that prompted nods all around. The low buzz from my amp filled my ears, and as sound popped with my fingers adjusting on still strings, I waited for the countdown from Jake, our drummer. Not necessarily for the song to start, but for me to live up to what Aunt Laura had said so many years prior:

*Fuck 'em. Go play in a band. Be happy.*

"Good?" Jake asked. We all nodded and he began his four-count to kick off the song.

*One.*

I did it. With an audience of a single bartender watching baseball instead of us. On a PA that constantly pierced with feedback. With the wrong pedals activated due to nerves. All of those head-shaking things, but they didn't matter because I did it.

*Two.*

So many things flashed through my mind: not just my promise to Aunt Laura, but all the years of being on the *other* side of the stage as a fan, all of the music I'd funneled directly into my brain with headphones. My left hand pressed against the frets, ready for the opening chord, the weight and form of the guitar neck so different from my first garage-sale guitar.

*Three.*

It all coalesced on that tiny stage with shitty lighting. Every choice I had ever made led to this moment.

*Four.*

A sudden kick-snare combo exploded behind me, and I hit a fuzzy B flat chord, strumming it with a staccato pace until switching to G minor, going through two progressions before the bouncing bass line kicked in. During that time, all my tingling nerves translated into a buoyant electricity, an overwhelming surge of body and soul projected outward into a wall of sound.

The set, of course, didn't go well. We all had our mistakes: forgotten lyrics, a missed chorus, a missed cue by our drummer. But by the time the final cymbal crash hit, we'd powered through our short set of six songs.

This set from an unknown opening band on a local bill proved completely unmemorable to anyone that heard it. But for me, it was etched into my memories, a chronicle of something I'd aspired to my whole life.

And I was close to fifty years old at that point, despite my youthful appearance. So "my whole life" involved a *lot*.

Cursory applause met our final moments, and we all quickly tore down our gear to make space for the next band. As I pulled the cords from my pedal board, I took in the scene in front of me—three people sitting at the bar clapped without looking our way, the bartender continued watching the baseball game above and the guitarist from the headliner, Breaking Lights, rolled in her massive amp.

In the scheme of things, it snapshotted the most incidental of musician moments, coupled with the stink of spilled beer and cigarettes wafting in from outside. But the milestone of simply having *done* it, and the fact that such a thing may not have ever occurred without Laura's final push—that made time collapse into feelings from past and present.

Laura was right.

She was always right, and part of me kicked myself—frustration that I waited this long to do something, that I held myself back for the perfect situation instead of just jumping in.

Which is what she would have done. And if I had done it, maybe this first gig would have happened earlier—much earlier.

Perhaps Laura could have been around to witness it.

I blinked, trying to force away any blood tears before they possibly gave me away. I turned, head down as I wound my cord.

"Good set," a voice said, "is that a Gretsch Hollow Body?"

It was. Some musicians cared about that level of detail, while others simply saw six strings and a pickup. I immediately appreciated this person, though I wouldn't reveal that this guitar's name was Johnny, after the legendary Johnny Marr. Not yet, anyway.

"Thanks," I said, quickly wiping my eyes clear in case blood leaked out of them.

"Hey, I'm in the next band up. My amp's been cutting out. Do you mind if I use yours?"

I looked up at the guy, messy dyed-black hair falling over brown eyes and pale cheeks. He offered a quiet smile as he rolled up the sleeves on his red flannel shirt—more importantly, he didn't wince at any potential blood streaming down my cheeks.

Apparently I'd caught it before any disaster.

"Yeah," I said, patting my amp. "Knock yourself out. I'll be hanging around all night anyway."

"Cool. Yeah, I'm also sticking around," he said. "I'm a bit of a night owl."

"Me too." I stuck my right hand out. "I'm Louise."

"Marshall," he said. "I owe you a beer for this."

"Eh, I don't like beer. But you can get me a hot tea." I glanced over my shoulder at the bar. "If they have it."

Turned out that bar did, in fact, serve hot tea, which he got me immediately after his band's set. We sat together for the third and fourth bands, talking about our worst concerts ever, all while deconstructing the gear we saw onstage. And when our respective bands broke apart a few months later, it made perfect sense for us to start playing together.

After all, I was looking for someone who was the right fit.

All that happened because I took a chance to step onstage.

Cool stinging wind brought me back to the present, my nausea over the incision on my wrist finally passed. Serena's face, however, hadn't changed, a sour twist on her lips. I considered what she'd just said:

"You try standing in front of all those people."

"You love to sing?" I asked her.

"In the shower. While I drive," she said, sighing as she hugged herself. "That doesn't really count."

"It does," I said, bringing myself upright. "You love it. You're on key. That's all that really matters."

"Yes, but," she said, "all those people out there. What if I'm terrible?"

"That's right. All those people out there. They'll be listening to you." Such a question confused me—the confidence, the *willpower* to accomplish what she had done over her century, and she worried she might suck? But only one answer worked for this. "But what if you're not?" I took a step forward, then put a hand on her cold shoulder. "You might *not* suck. And who knows what that might lead to?" I glanced over at Ian, who stood up straight after battling his own wave of postblood nausea. "Especially if Eric's right about not worrying about blood anymore."

From behind us, Eric called out. "Are you feeling better? We should get moving."

"I'm good," I said in reply. To my left, Ian stood straight up, then raised a thumbs-up for all to see. He seemed fine, despite ingesting blood directly from my wrist.

"He's absolutely right about the blood. As long as you've got my back, we'll change everything," she said, with a toothy grin. "I'd say this goes beyond clearing you of rule breaking. Maybe it's time for you to start thinking about what you'd like to do with your life."

# CHAPTER 36

LOADING IN HERE WAS nothing like a bar gig. And it wasn't just the go-go dress I wore.

Everything stored neatly in my hardshell guitar case: Joan, two cables tightly wrapped up, and one distortion pedal in the storage compartment on the off chance Serena needed a little extra oomph to back her up. No amp, as that would be provided and ready, so at least I didn't have to lug that around.

The biggest difference, however, came from the fact that I walked into a massive compound filled with vampires instead of a dirty San Francisco bar. I followed Serena in, slightly stumbling from the heeled boots, the muscles necessary for stability being just a little different than the ones I used for my well-worn Docs. We took the path to the back, every guard and staffer apparently recruited by Eric and familiar with Serena. The main building itself looked cut-and-pasted from a country club stock photo, and maybe that was the intent of it: a getaway owned and operated by vampires, and if they wanted to, they could even put in a lighted golf course.

Serena pointed to a back entrance, a single service door without the decor of the rest of the structure. We marched in, and I took extra care with my guitar case—whatever Eric's agenda was, *I* didn't want to be on the hook for possibly dinging a wall or doorframe with the hardshell case. This place looked expensive, and though I wasn't sure if the real estate holdings of ancient vampires dealt with human insurance companies and contractors, I didn't need anything more on my plate right now.

"Your job is pretty simple," Serena said, her cadence more like the confident woman with too many college degrees than the uncertain songstress needing a pep talk. "Just back me up the whole time. I have to keep an eye out on things so I might signal you to stretch things out during some songs." So that was it. They needed a musician they could trust. "At one point, Eric will signal us and then we'll stop," she said, walking in between two guys pushing a large cart across our path.

"That's it? And then what?"

"Then if everything works as planned, you two will get your rewards."

At this point, I learned to not ask further questions about their cryptic vampire bullshit, even when several people passed by Serena with oddly stilted greetings and responses. Not even when she grabbed a pouch with her gloved hand from her purse, then handed it off midstride, full-on spy-movie style.

*Just a few hours*, I told myself. If everyone kept their promises, I'd have regular access to blood, Ian would have a vial for Sonya, and both of us could start thinking *possibilities*. Regardless of whatever goal Eric and Serena had in mind.

We walked through a kitchen area, and though none of the stove burners were lit, a line of people stirred pots of blood. Others passed by carrying trays of empty wineglasses while some wore thick dishwashing gloves over their elegant attire as they lugged plastic totes. Serena moved down a tight hallway leading to a small storage room. She stopped, tapping on her phone, and as the rumble of passing wheeled carts drummed through the space, a muffled sound floated in from beyond the room's side door.

Was that singer doing...a Leonard Cohen song?

Serena spoke in hushed tones to the other person in the room, and while they discussed what I assumed were the details of forming a vampire union, I stepped closer to the door, ignoring that my guitar case did, in fact, bonk into the wood-trimmed walls.

I listened.

"Dance me..." the woman sang, "to the end of love."

I gripped the doorknob, then turned and cracked it open. The view revealed a platform staged at the end of a ballroom, and on the floor sat fifteen or twenty circular tables draped with white tablecloths. The blend of bright stage lights and simple distance caused these so-called Ancients to look like blurry glimpses of tuxedos and dresses—no details, but enough to show that this whole night wasn't just a fever dream.

Eric's staff wore similar outfits, of course. But the differences came in the actions. The Ancients sat at their tables, probably forty or fifty of them gathered and awaiting service. They sat relaxed like doctors at SFGH on their lunch break, talking casually and half-watching the stage, some checking their phones or simply staring off.

On the other hand, the staff dashed back and forth with purpose. One woman carried trays of wineglasses filled with blood. Another cleared them from tables. One man ran from the side stage to check electrical connections on the soundboard. Yet another fast-walked across the back of the ballroom, carrying a stack of folded napkins in from the back.

This *would* have looked like any human reception, except the ages betrayed the truth. The seated young man, looking barely out of his teens, was likely hundreds of years old, turned in a chaotic era where begging and violence led to meals. And the man who looked fifty-something distributing wineglasses, he may have been close to his human age, perhaps an engineer or a lawyer, whatever education and experience he'd earned now swapped for focusing on his next meal.

I thought of all of the ways I'd scrounged for blood: farm animals, blood pimps, begging and pleading, my whole *career*. Not just me, but even Serena, who'd once hunted rats. And yet, despite countless vampires like myself, scavenging in hospital basements and donation clinics and even assaulting humans over recent weeks, these Ancients acted like their lives were fine, that the blood would always be there.

Because for them, it probably always would be.

Suddenly, I understood why Eric wanted to form a union.

"Assholes," I said under my breath.

"Yeah," Serena said, stepping over my way, "they are. But well-dressed."

And from above, a spotlight shone down on the woman singing, one far brighter and more focused than at the dive bars I played. Her tall, thin frame broke the light, a combination of shadow and silhouette wrapped in a flowing green dress, pale skin, and long brown hair. My eyes focused, trying to consolidate past and present, because even though her outfit matched the timeless formality of everyone on the compound, something about her radiated a familiarity, like a rhythm buried under white noise.

She sang out, repeating the title of the song in its dying verse, a vampire behind her playing a single cello in the dark. Her arms waved slowly, a showman's gesture with curves and flair, and her deep voice belted out the melody in a series of *la-la-las* before spinning around to the final notes of the cello. The music stopped, and polite applause came from the ballroom floor, sounding closer to a half-empty bar for a local band than a revelatory performance for a full floor.

The woman's arms remained up, taking in the applause for another few seconds before she bowed, her hair dropping past her shoulders.

But when she stood up, instead of looking at the audience, she did something wholly unexpected:

She looked at me.

"Oh," Serena said, "that's Madeline. She performs at this every year. Superdramatic, if you couldn't tell." She snorted to herself, then glanced over her shoulder before returning to me. "I mean, she's nice. In that unwittingly-part-of-the-oppressive-machine kind of way."

"What does that mean?"

"It means she's a very nice person who sings well and looks good doing it. But," Serena said with a smirk, "she's coming around."

But she didn't just sing well. She sang Leonard Cohen, which meant that regardless of her age or where she came from or what she did, there was already an unspoken bond between us. That single strand that connected us created more of a bond than any blood ties I had with my brother. Because a bond of music meant *understanding*.

Before Madeline turned back to the audience, her eyebrow arched my way, a single gesture of recognition. Our gazes held, and I pictured her in a leather jacket and pleated skirt at an Iggy Pop show, her features captured perfectly and transplanted into this time and place.

She was the vampire that turned me.

But why?

The door slammed shut, and Serena's voice broke my concentration. "We're up next." She sucked in a deep breath, her cheeks puffed out like she wanted to vomit. Or at least, the vampire equivalent of it. One hand was planted against the wall to steady herself, then she turned to the lone vampire working the backstage. They nodded at each other in a way that seemed to be more than just "good luck at this thing that petrifies you," and she tapped my shoulder. "Don't let anyone pull us offstage. Follow my lead. And wait for Eric's signal," she said, then the other vampire knocked twice on the far wall. A wall panel slid open and Serena led me to a dim corridor that eventually took us to the far side of the stage.

She didn't explain why she stopped to pick up a small pouch with her gloved hand.

I let myself dream about possibilities. Or perhaps it really was a life without excuses. Because Serena's songs were slow and simple, I strummed along, thinking of a world without scrounging and scheming for blood.

Never mind the fact that shortly after we took the stage, a pair of servants walked out with a scraggly-looking man with unkempt hair, weathered clothes, and wild eyes. His hands were held behind him, and he sat by himself, static in a lone chair.

We played through a bunch of standards that sounded like sexy versions of songs for elementary school students, and for a few of them, Serena would nod at me and I'd draw out beats with arpeggiated picking and improvised riffs. And while I had my distortion pedal hooked up, I stayed with a clean acoustic sound, the amplified strings echoing with the ballroom's reverb, dreaming of new life.

During this, Serena would sway to the music, but I saw her true intentions. She was *analyzing* the crowd in front of her, but for what reason? Something seemed to be off about their plan, because when I managed to catch a glimpse of her face, concern framed her expression, lines that grew deeper only as the night wore on.

During the third song—"Red River Valley"—the wheels

were set in motion. Quite literally, in fact, as I saw a side door open and Eric come through leading Ian as he pushed a cart of…

Wineglasses?

They *were* wineglasses. Just like the ones being passed out by other waiters, yet they didn't arrive on a tray. Instead they sat stacked on top of the plastic cart, Ian pushing them carefully enough that the blood in them barely sloshed around. And in the shelf below them, vials of test tubes, all presumably filled with some other kind of blood, though for what, I didn't know. Perhaps one of those would be the thing to save Sonya?

They paused right before they hit the first table on the ballroom floor, Eric whispering something in Ian's ear. The boy nodded emphatically, then gave a thumbs-up, which seemed far less dignified than the environment called for, given that this was essentially a state dinner.

Eric nodded in return, and as Ian turned away, I spied Eric reach into his pocket and drink a small vial before pushing the cart forward. Ian, though, either didn't notice or didn't care; he looked up at the stage as he stepped away and caught my eye, then pointed to the drum kit set up on the stage behind me.

And while I certainly enjoyed bonding with Ian, and he played drums better than expected, given his very limited experience, I mouthed the word *no* to him. He shrugged his shoulders, then disappeared through the same door he came from.

Four more songs finished, Eric serving the murmuring crowd from the cart the whole time. I watched as he gestured to the selection, each person at a table taking both a glass and then selecting from the vials below. Even watching Eric serve glass after glass began to ignite my ire, how this guy who tried so hard to give the community a foundation—some living on the street scraping for blood in the most dangerous situations—all while trying to keep us protected from humans, well…

Turns out that even for a guy like that, the best he could hope for in this world was being skipped over for promotion.

But unlike my dad, Eric carried a confident air about him, the way he looked as he handed each wineglass and vial over showed that something stirred inside him.

Serena hit the final notes of "A Hot Time in the Old Town," and while the same tepid applause bounced across the room, Eric pulled the cart back enough to linger behind the last row of tables.

And from there, he raised his arm, fingers balled in a fist.

Though Serena waved at the clapping coming her way, her own fist formed for a moment, flashing the same gesture before her arm dropped back down at her side. She turned my way before glancing back at Eric, then finally stepping toward me, her voice low. "We're out of time but someone's still not here. I've gotta check the back. Create a distraction and hopefully the commotion will get them in the room."

My blank look must have conveyed my utter confusion. "Wait, what? I thought I was playing backup."

"Right now, I need you to play a song. Any song. Make some noise. Get the attention in here. That's the only way any of this works."

Whatever this was, it went far beyond voting to unionize. Yet before I had a chance to clarify, Serena returned to the front mic. "I hope you've all had a lovely evening tonight, and of course, we're only just getting started," she said in a singsong tone that was definitely *not* her normal voice. "I'm going to step away for just a second, but I'm going to leave you in the very capable arms of the best musician I know. Please welcome Louise to the stage."

With that, the raised cheeks and toothy smile she'd projected outward dropped as soon as she turned. Instead, her intense eyes and quick nod were my signal to get up to the microphone.

I was up. And with Ian watching me from afar and our futures on the line, I needed to create a distraction.

I needed to play a song.

**CHAPTER 37**

NOT THAT LONG AGO, I let myself be vulnerable again. It started with a search for fellow musicians and ended in me sneezing blood all over my white guitar. I searched for bands to play with. In between, I emailed and texted, practiced for auditions, and spent far too long wrapping my head around the idea of finding a way back to being a live musician, of playing gigs again. All to search for that rush that I knew only came with standing onstage and playing those strings, something I'd lost with Marshall.

So it wasn't lost on me that despite the twisty road of recent days, I'd actually managed to get here. There was a stage, of course, and I was on it. Joan's straps slung over my neck and right shoulder, and the empty amplifier hissing behind me, waiting to blast out whatever notes I sent its way.

And just like my first gig, no one in the audience seemed to care.

Granted, that dingy San Francisco bar was filled with a

handful of after-work baseball fans rather than a gathering of ancient vampires. But still.

I stood, fingers forming an E chord with my left hand even though I didn't know what song I should play. The slight pressure against the frets caused tones to pop out of the amp, and I scanned the crowd again.

They didn't see a performer up here. They didn't see an artist or a creative; I wondered if they even saw a person, or if it was all a commodity to them, background noise for their gala. And while that normally wouldn't bother me—a gig was a gig, after all—knowing that the people sitting in the ballroom somehow controlled the fates of people like me, people who had to trudge and bargain through shitty day jobs and back alley means just for daily sustenance, well, that irritated me.

For vampires, they represented exactly what pushed my parents into striving for a normalization that they never asked for. That sent Aunt Laura into hiding in San Francisco. That forced Marshall into a strained relationship with his evangelical family.

It was all the same thing, just dressed up differently: a blunt force that shoved people down instead of letting them become who they should be.

Also, the Ancients didn't seem to be moved by Serena, despite her excellent performance. That also bugged me, because a voice like hers deserved to be heard.

I may have just been some loser vampire who worked as a hospital janitor, played in the occasional band, and spent my immortality hanging out with corgis, but I finally had something to say. Things were going to be different and I'd be the one to kick it off.

I stared at the crowd as they sipped blood from wineglasses, Eric pushing his cart to an empty corner while Serena remained...elsewhere. In fact, a quick glance showed no signs of her.

She needed a distraction? I'd give her a distraction. I'd give them all a distraction. And one song came to mind.

My foot activated my distortion pedal, the low natural hiss flowing through the amp, transforming into the stinging buzz that came from punk fuzz.

"Hey!" I yelled into the microphone at a volume that caused the PA to feedback. "Here's something different tonight!" My fingers rested against the strings to mute the noise and I raked my pick quickly over them for a percussive countdown. "One, two, three, four!"

My fingers formed a D chord and I began the staccato strums of the same Blondie song that played on the day I walked out of my parents' house, that night I sat at Marshall's grave. "One way or another," I started, trying my best to channel the fury of Debbie Harry's growl. I sang through the first verse, words she'd originally written about a stalker who harassed her in New Jersey, then moved to the chorus, a low aggression that crowed about driving past unlit houses. Despite the lack of percussion, I soared from the chorus back into the verse, eyes closed as I strummed with rapid-fire speed, my toe tapping out the rhythm.

Then a cymbal crashed.

Soon followed by a kick-snare combo that *almost* kept pace. I turned to see Ian in the shadows, smashing away at the drum kit behind me. Just like in my home studio, he managed to keep the kick-snare basics, but his rhythm hiccuped whenever he hit a random tom or crash.

But it didn't matter. There we were, playing "One Way Or Another" in front of a bunch of ancient vampires. On the other side of the song, Eric and Serena promised a new life, in many different ways. Despite all of the misadventures I'd had as a disaffected teen, as a confused new vampire, as a guitarist for many failed local bands, this clearly claimed the title of the most bizarre thing I'd ever done.

I had no idea what was really happening with this vampire unionization, but I drilled my focus down on the song. I wanted a band, I got a band—something beyond simply backing Serena while she sang standards. Perhaps just for one song, one slightly out-of-time song with no bass or second guitar or backing vocals, but it was a band.

And it was just as good as I remembered. The only thing missing was Marshall. I closed my eyes, my voice screaming and my hands strumming, and all the while, I imagined him playing several feet away, the sheer invisible presence of knowing he was locked in alongside me.

In a way, he really was. He'd always be there. Anytime I strummed my guitar or played my drums or simply sat in comfortable silence listening to a song, he'd be there.

One way or another.

I shouted the final line of the second verse, then poked in a transition riff. As I did, I glanced at Ian, though he didn't meet my gaze.

He was too locked into his out-of-rhythm groove.

And I was determined to keep him there.

My fingers flew, playing an impromptu facsimile of Chris Stein's solo, going from dissonant crashing to frenetic tones, all building back up to the final verse. Ian kept up, slightly confused by the transitions but when he seemed unsure of where to go, he just flooded the space with a wave of cymbals until he saw me return to the microphone. During this time, I checked the crowd. A few amused grins. Some chatter between occupants at their table. Others sipping from their glasses or looking at their phones or simply staring off in some other direction.

The lone disheveled man stayed seated by himself, hands behind his back, though at least he watched with a curious expression.

And Eric, who stepped forward and broke free from the shadows. He moved to the front of the ballroom floor, staring at the Moleskine notebook he always carried. He turned through several pages as I sprinted through the song, then it went back into his jacket pocket. His back straightened and his hands crossed as he approached the disheveled man, eyes now watching Ian and I as we headed into the outro.

The back entrance door swung open, a beam of hallway light breaking into the dimmed entertainment space. In walked a line of vampires, all dressed in their cocktail attire but walking in single file until they spread out in a semicircle across the back of the ballroom.

Including Madeline.

Serena had said something about her being "unwittingly-part-of-the-oppressive-machine," and yet she posed with a fuck-you stance that seemed to echo the same punk spirit I projected from the stage.

Maybe this went with her supposed flair for the dramatic.

I started into the song's outro, totally mangling my attempt at recreating Debbie Harry's quick switch from ferocious "one way or another" to rapid-fire spoken word and back again. We hit this several times, chaos created from my selection and Ian's complete unfamiliarity of the song, and I turned with Joan's neck tilted upward in an exaggerated pose to show Ian that we'd tumbled to the end. The cymbal crashed as I hit the final chord, the distorted mesh of strings ringing out. Ian got a little too into the moment, hitting everything on the kit multiple times at full speed until he finally slammed on the crash four times. A full eight count passed before he hit it again.

Turns out Ian had a flair for the dramatic too.

My shoulders heaved, lungs sucking in deep gulps of air. A mix of tepid applause and murmurs greeted me. I'd channeled the spirit of Debbie Harry's rage at this group of ancient vampires, yet they responded the same as they had to Madeline and Serena and whoever else performed tonight.

Nothing bothered them. Maybe because they'd existed for centuries. Or maybe because they knew it simply didn't matter.

"Yeah, well, fuck you too," I said under my breath.

Eric remained stone-faced by the lone man, and from the darkened wings of the stage, Serena finally returned.

I stepped away from the microphone and looked at Serena for next steps when a voice called out from the ballroom floor. "Excuse me?" an Ancient in a long black coat asked, his voice projecting enough to be heard over the din.

Uh-oh.

"Did you say something?" he asked.

"Uhhh…" I offered, drawing out the single syllable back at the microphone, "I said 'thank you'?"

"It sounded like," the Ancient said, boyish features contradicting a weathered voice, "you said, 'fuck you.'" He stood and stepped forward, a stiffness to his gait, and he glanced down at himself before smoothing his coat, a grimace suddenly coming over his face. "You are lucky that we have bigger things to deal with than your insolence." The Ancient turned, then looked at the disheveled man still seated beyond the tables. "Like those who dare expose us. Who risk our safety by attacking humans, drinking their blood."

Oh shit. *That* was what they did to rule breakers.

"They deserve punishment," the man continued, "and we will make an example—"

"This 'insolence' as you call it…" Eric said, interrupting at raised volume. A certain glee wove into his voice, a combination of orator's cadence from community meetings and a shit-is-going-down excitement that matched his eyes. "It's simple. It's one thing and one thing only. Louise," he called out to me, "can you repeat that, please?"

"Uhhh…" I said, pretty sure honesty was *not* the best policy here. I glanced back at Ian, who showed a shocking amount of teenage giddiness on his face rather than the fear typically associated with a situation as bonkers as this. And another look around showed Serena disappeared again without any clue why or if she found what she'd searched for.

"Go ahead. Be honest. We all want to hear it. We all should hear it. He," Eric said, pointing to the man, who I noticed for the first time was shackled, "should hear it."

Did Eric bring me here just to throw me under the bus in front of the Ancients? Suddenly, all of that internal guile of any righteous fury in the form of a Blondie song disappeared, and I really, really, really just wanted to be home petting my dog.

"Because it deserves to be said. It's absolutely true. We all believe it. From all of us, who do your dirty work, who keep the community safe, who keep the common vampires in line, who follow your rules while getting zero input or representation, we all say, as this, punk rocker—" Eric took in a breath, his Scottish burr fully rolling on the last word "—so eloquently put it."

He pointed to me.

And I leaned into the microphone, Joan still hanging off my shoulders. "Fuck...you?"

"'Fuck you,'" Eric said. "Fuck your rules. Fuck your traditions. Fuck your hidden agenda. Fuck your lies that you've kept from every vampire on the planet." He reached into a pocket, then held up a small key for everyone to see. "The prisoner's punishment will *not* be death. It will be penance. Rejoining society, knowing the mistake he made." Eric walked over and inserted the key into the shackles that bound his hands behind him. A low *click-click* sound came, then the restraints dropped to the floor. The man looked at his hands, then Eric, then up at all the eyes that stared at him. So, pretty much everyone in the room.

Eric paced in a circle around the standing Ancient, walking past his seated tablemates. "This man deserves a second chance. He was just trying to eat," he said, now directly behind the Ancient. He leaned over, speaking directly into his ear. "And searching for food is something he will not have to worry about anymore. No one will."

"You..." the Ancient said, now visibly struggling to speak. A tremble rippled through his raised hand, though his eyes went wide. I quickly scanned the rest of the room, and suddenly, it appeared that all of the seated Ancients fought to move as well. The line of service vampires bordering the room all waited, Madeline standing out with her dramatic pose of one leg forward and hand on hip. "You should know your pl...pl...pla—"

But before his shaky voice could finish, his words swallowed into a gurgle, and a choking sound echoed loud enough to fill the ballroom's tall space. His head jerked up and down and his eyes went wide before slowly looking down at his own chest.

Where a red stain emerged on his white shirt.

It grew quickly, a bloody circle becoming a dark running blob that soon trailed down the neatly tailored seams framing the shirt's buttons.

Then his head and limbs exploded.

Slushy, fibrous remains flew through the air, drips of deep red spraying all the way to the chandelier above. When it all settled, there stood Eric, the man's blood-soaked shirt and coat hanging off the stake gripped by his gloved hand.

I took Joan off my shoulder, holding the instrument by the neck as the strap grazed the floor. "Holy shit," I said, loud enough for the microphone to broadcast it to the entire room.

# CHAPTER 38

SEVERAL SECONDS AGO, THE entire room had been quiet, all eyes and ears on Eric.

Now? Not so much. But it wasn't quite the pandemonium you'd expect following the grisly and explosive death of a vampire who went from "dude in a tuxedo" to "explosive dissolving meat bits." Instead, voices filled the space. But what they actually said bordered on indecipherable, and it wasn't because of overlapping shouts and yells.

No, this sounded muffled, slurred words all melting into one another. In fact, all of the seated Ancients struggled to move, arms and legs trembling, some even unable to turn their heads to the commotion. And while several managed full-volume yells, others remained slack-jawed or frozen shut, only grunts and groans, something causing a total paralysis in their muscles.

"Oh," Ian said, loud enough for my ears to pick up. "The wood powder I put in the drinks."

I turned to him, eyes wide. So many thoughts sprinted through my mind, though two emerged as the most pressing:

First, was this what happened when wood entered our bloodstream? Because the occasional epidermal exposure left me with hives, but actually ingested? That had to be a systemic allergic reaction, something that caused an immobilizing level of inflammation.

Or was this death?

Second, had I just involved a thirteen-year-old in a mass-murder situation? Granted, the Ancients didn't seem to be good people in the first place, but still, I just wanted to show Ian how to play barre chords and the different phases of David Bowie's career. This wasn't a morality lesson I felt authorized to teach.

But none of the vampires on the floor exploded in similar fashion, and their slurred and muffled words continued, the use of jaw and mouth muscles probably dependent on just how much of this wood/blood mixture they ingested.

"This," Eric shouted, his gloved left hand holding up the bloody stake, "is a stake, embedded with silver, a natural anti-viral. Creates an unstable exothermic reaction in our blood." The remaining blood-soaked clothes slid back onto the floor, and Eric slowly turned for everyone to see. "Now, I want everyone sitting to take a good look around. Take a look at the people standing behind you. You wanted to murder this prisoner for being a victim of the system. To that, we all say one thing:

"We refuse."

I wasn't sure how the Ancients could actually look around, given their neck muscles probably tensed to the point of immobility, but in my own view, I now noticed that all of the workers wore gloves. And thanks to Madeline's theatrical movie-poster pose, it became clear that all of those gloves were meant to hold these silver-lined stakes.

"Now, you're probably wondering why you're all paralyzed. That—"

A yell interrupted him, and from the side of the stage emerged a woman in a simple black dress that somehow made her look superthreatening in the moment. Her red hair swirled with each step, eyes growing wider as she took in the scene.

Then she pulled out a vial.

Its blood contents disappeared quickly down her throat, the glass vial shattering on the floor as she tossed it on the ground. She took a second to assess her surroundings, then she blinked, a newfound fire in her expression as she started charging toward Eric on the ballroom floor.

This must have been who Serena was looking for.

One obstacle lay in her direct path: Ian sitting at the drum kit.

As she took each step, her speed seemed to accelerate, going from "fairly athletic angry speed" to something that moved well beyond that, more like...

Vampire power myths.

With only a fraction of a second before she ran over Ian— or attacked him, depending on her intent—I adjusted my grip on Joan, both hands gripping the guitar's lacquered wood neck like a baseball bat.

Then I jumped.

And I swung the guitar named after Aunt Laura's favorite musician.

Joan exploded into pieces, even the metal strings snapping upon impact. Chunks of wood flew as shards shattered, the woman's screams accompanied by a very appropriate "what the fuck" from Ian. I landed, ankle twisting slightly upon impact thanks to these stupid boots, and I looked up to see fragments of wood embedded in the woman's face, faint smoke coming from the wounds.

Joan's sacrifice slowed her down. And now that she looked at me, it might have saved Ian.

As for me? The fact that this woman picked up a full-stack amplifier easily, lifting about sixty pounds like a paperback book? I didn't like my odds.

"You," she said, her fingers gripping the amp's handle. "Insolent, ridiculous child." She wound up her arm, the massive amp getting loaded to be tossed like a ball. "You have no idea who—" she started, when another yell came from behind me.

Before I could turn to see who it was, Serena soared—literally, about five feet over me—and tackled the woman. The amp was tossed into a wall, the front face of the cabinet shattering, probably permanently ruining the amp's natural reverb. Serena landed on top of the woman, and their collective momentum sent them into the side stage's wall, leaving a huge indent that would cause all sorts of grief with insurance assessors. The mystery woman gripped Serena's arm and tossed her, but Serena landed on her feet—high heels staying on—and then dipped her shoulder. The woman lunged again, but despite her magically (or scientifically, I wasn't totally sure at this point) enhanced speed and strength, Serena's black belt in aikido gave her the advantage. She angled back, the woman's arm flying forward, and Serena gripped her by the wrist before pushing her shoulder forward and flipping the woman on her back.

The woman's strength took over, a two-armed shove that launched Serena straight into the ceiling above the ballroom. Dented metal beams rained tiny shards over us, but Serena crashed down, landing on her knees before springing upward. The woman charged again, and though Serena probably could have done some sort of cool, flippy move, she twirled on her back leg, and then used a simple, hard kick to the woman's gut. And while she recoiled, Serena's gloved hand reached over for a dagger-shaped shard that had once been part of Joan's neck. Guitar strings whipped around from the top of the piece, and

Serena held it forward like a spear before launching herself straight ahead.

My guitar—or part of it, anyway—pierced the assailant in the heart. She stumbled back, blood spurting from her wound. And here, I finally put it all together: the myth about the stake to the heart came from our allergic reaction to wood. With the wood firmly in the heart, its particles circulated on a systemic level, creating a paralysis that wouldn't allow the vampire to move or get help while they bled out.

But in this case, the woman didn't get to that stage of the dying process. Serena pulled out one of Eric's silver-lined stakes from a pouch and threw it directly into the woman's throat. Several seconds later, her body exploded, scattering blood in a radius that landed just outside of Serena's feet.

The woman's soaked dress dropped to the floor, Joan's wooden neck and guitar strings hitting with a *thud*. Aunt Laura had often talked about her love of Joan Baez's ability to use music and lyrics for a cause, to show virtuous anger for the oppressed. So she probably would appreciate a guitar I'd named Joan doubling as a weapon to destroy an Ancient who oversaw an oppressive system while trying to murder both me and Ian. Serena looked at me, a sheepish grin as she shrugged her shoulders, like that was the only way to explain her superhero actions.

But I'd seen this before. Not the combat, but when we tried to find Ian in San Francisco, she'd sprinted off with surprising speed. And right before that, poured a vial of something into the bottle of blood.

Just like the assailant's vial.

Not quite espresso.

"As I was saying," Eric yelled, like nothing murdery had just unfolded onstage. "Your paralysis. Wood shavings, in that blood you were just served. Now, you may be wondering, how did that possibly get in your drinks? With so many loyal vampires here, vampires like me, who have served you for decades, how did this possibly happen? It's quite simple."

On my left, Serena had already moved on from her death match, now approaching with a tablet held outward.

She was livestreaming this. Was it just to Eric's app or was it more?

Eric reached into his coat pocket and pulled out a small vial—the same type that I'd just witnessed. His thumbnail flicked off the rubber stopper and he downed the shot of blood. He closed his eyes and took a deep breath before setting the vial down on a table in front of a paralyzed Ancient.

"The common people are taking back control."

And with that, Eric *levitated* a good ten feet into the air.

"Whoa," Ian said behind me.

Eric floated, the movement causing his jacket to billow outward. He landed beside me on the stage, so gently that his shoes didn't even make a sound.

"I like that song you played," he said to me in a quiet voice before stepping up to the microphone.

"For centuries, the Ancients have maintained perpetual control over the entire vampire community. A ruling class that exists for no reason other than they got here first. A ruling class that decided how every single one of us lived, died, propagated. Did we murder humans to survive? We did until they decided against it. Did common vampires know the secret to turning humans? We did, until they hid that away. Did we know how to tap the hidden abilities within us?"

Eric held his arms out, levitating straight up again before landing back down with a bow.

"We did. Until they rendered us impotent.

"Why? Why would they do this? On the one hand, you could say it was simple population control. It prevents us from doing dangerous things, things that might expose us in eras of the telegraph, radio, television, internet, smartphones. But it also takes away our choice. It denies our very nature. It says that unless you are within their inner circle, you will struggle for sustenance, you will question your existence, you will live for your immediate blood needs because true independence is impossible.

"What I showed you right there—the ability to fly. You all have untapped power within your genetics as well. You all have the ability to turn a human. They come with a price and a limit, but *you* should have that choice.

"And more importantly, you should have the option to live the life you want." He turned and looked at Ian. "May I have the bottle I asked you to hold for me?"

Ian nodded, then stepped gingerly over the bloody trail of the exploded would-be assassin like it was no big deal. How did you describe this type of thing to a therapist?

One bottle of Eric's synthetic blood changed hands. Eric took it and held it up. In his other hand, he held up another small vial.

"There are three things that will change our world." He leaned over the edge of the stage, arm outstretched. The prisoner, who'd watched this whole thing in shock, stepped forward gingerly before taking the bottle. Eric nodded, and the disheveled man drank it like he hadn't fed in days.

Probably because he hadn't.

"That bottle of blood, manufactured to sustain us. This vial, previously hidden from the masses. And," he said, turning to look directly at the camera on Serena's tablet, "the phone you're watching this on."

# CHAPTER 39

**VAMPIRE POWER MYTH #12:** All of these silly vampire powers are fiction.

Absolutely, positively false.

Once Eric gave the same speech I'd heard about synthetic blood, he'd moved on to the fact that powers were very real. But, as the real world often demonstrated, they were much more complicated than what the movies showed. And also, some pop culture assumptions were just physically impossible. None of us would be transforming into mist anytime soon.

On the other hand? Flight. Glamour. Speed. Heightened senses of perception? Freakish strength, as evidenced by Serena pulling out superhero moves and stabbing would-be assassins with pieces of my guitar? All of those vampire power myths were true, and every vampire had some sort of ability written into their genetics. What an individual vampire actually got to do, that part sounded like a crapshoot, and only trial and error could reveal them. As Eric explained in a speech he must have rehearsed too many times, there was a twist to it all, something that grounded those myths in reality:

Those powers were indeed natural. But not always accessible.

It took a sip of blood, a special mixture sourced from various genetic backgrounds, its formula only known by the Ancients. Thankfully, Eric spared us the history lesson, and instead said that he'd hold a community forum in the coming days to discuss this blood's history, from its accidental discovery to its curation and storage. Which was good, because he'd been on the verge of turning an epic reveal into an educational lecture.

But he ended on a key point, one that I hadn't expected at all, though it made a lot of sense, about why these powers were so protected. Because, while the Ancients were concerned about powers exposing vampires and/or causing murderous chaos, there was also the fact that every sip of the special blood temporarily unfroze aging. Turns out tapping into inert genetic powers was quite draining on the vampire body, and drinking too much of the vial left a wave of exhaustion—much like what I saw in Serena shortly after we rescued Ian.

And while Eric's speech wore on, I noticed Ian holding one of those vials himself. I stepped over the shattered wood pieces that once made up Joan, then walked in a wide radius around the giant stain of splattered remains.

He held it up—one of *those* vials. Had I taken it from him and ingested the blood in one gulp, who knew what type of powers I might unlock? That temptation fluttered away as I focused on why we got through this madness, from my go-go dress to the exploding vampires:

*Possibilities.*

"This is what's going to do it," Ian said. "I feel like we should, I don't know, wrap this in a bunch of bubble wrap and put it in a cooler and put that in a box with even more bubble wrap."

"Wait," I said, squinting at the vial in confusion, "are you trying to get powers too?"

He shook his head no, then pointed back at Eric. "This blood's gonna save my mom."

I turned and watched, Eric in full community-organizer mode, talking with arms outstretched and a flowing cadence to his words. "So many of you have asked over the decades, 'Can I turn a human? Can I bring my brother, sister, spouse, friend into this world?'" He turned, then his fiery gaze landed straight on Ian. "'Can I save my ill mother?' The answer is yes.

"You can do it. One of the old myths is true—you can indeed turn a human by having them drink from you. How much, though? About half of your blood supply, over the course of several hours. Of course," Eric said, now connecting with me, "that would almost certainly kill you. The other option is this." He held up the same type of vial that Serena drank earlier, the same one in Ian's hand. "The blood in here can activate your innate power for a price. And it can also turn a human.

"It is in tight supply. An unstable formula that has been difficult to replicate for centuries. Now? We shall find out. More importantly—" he gestured outward "—you all will know.

"Including the Ancients. Now I want them to understand one thing." On cue, the ballroom's doors opened. On one side walked in more well-attired attendees, though they marched with confident steps not typical for people clearing glasses and setting napkins. On the other side, the staff rolled in carts with lit TV monitors on them, each of them showing a grid of faces watching the proceedings. "These are community leaders from around the world. People like me. People who watch over their regions, who assign fixers to situations. Well, that's what we're going to do. We're going to fix this new world *right now with the power of data, an app for every community.* And for those of you still in your seats," he said with a wry grin as he looked at the paralyzed Ancients, "you're welcome to stay and listen. And when you can move again, you're welcome to leave. Because our blood supply will be changed. Our access will be changed.

The only thing that kept you in power were your lies, and now, they are exposed. Your time is over. In the end, your power is false. Take away your rules and your institutions and," he said, his voice growing fierce, "you're just like everyone else."

The line was met with applause from the surrounding vampires, a noise so thunderous that the room shook like an encore for the world's biggest band. And during that, Serena tapped me on the shoulder, gestured Ian over, and started walking us out the side stage.

# CHAPTER 40

IN THE END, ERIC was right: the Ancients were just like the rest of us. The laziness and complacency that people absorbed as the years wore on, they faced that too. Granted, that came from centuries of controlling everything from a secret society that held fancy parties and indulged in drinking superpower fuel. But still, their status quo simply meant that this was another annual gathering, a drop in the ocean with formal attire.

Like giant arena rockers who mailed in their performance while playing recycled hits, they simply didn't see it coming when new bands emerged to pass them by. In this case, "pass them by" was literal, since most still sat immobilized. A few of the vampire staff kept watch on them, but without any vials to enhance their powers, they were woefully outnumbered. Though perhaps walking out of their own party, stripped of power and humiliated in a livestream across the globe, all of that probably made leaving the best choice for them.

"Well," I said to Serena as we hit the back hallway of the estate, "I really wasn't expecting all that."

"I'm shocked it went as smoothly as it did." She looked skyward as she walked in between Ian and myself. "We really thought someone would slip, especially with our people working in hospital and government positions. That's why we needed all that monitoring. It was a security measure, but now we can scale it down. Takes up too much of the bandwidth anyway."

I still didn't quite get it, but Ian burst excitedly into the conversation like he'd just beaten a video game. "Hey, can we talk about the obvious thing here?" He stopped midstride. "Your vampire kung-fu. Holy shit."

A rosy glow came to Serena's brown cheeks as she shrugged her shoulders. "It's aikido, not kung fu."

"Still. That lady looked like she wanted to murder us," I said. "Those are some badass powers you have."

"Nah. They're basic. Everyone has something different. I'll bet most are much more interesting. We'll find out soon enough."

"Cool, well, can't wait to see if I can, like, fly or something." I meant it as a joke. But Serena reacted with a serious nod, pulling up a spreadsheet on her tablet with a list of powers followed by all sorts of statistics.

"These are all the powers we've documented." Her finger dragged across the tablet, scrolling through words like *glamour* and *flight*. "Latent abilities written into your genetics that activate under the right formula. We don't quite have their ratios down yet. I know Eric gave a nice speech—" she rolled her eyes "—but these things take time. And then there's vial production. Way more complicated than bottling the daily-meal blood. Eventually, you'll access your innate power just by ordering a vial on the app. It'll age you, but individual choice is important."

"Wait, you're serious? You just request a vial on the app?"

"Well, you'll have to wait for delivery. And each person

would have caps on free requests. But yeah, that's what we envision."

A creeping anxiety bit at me, the idea of every vampire in the world suddenly having access to unchecked powers, leading to a grimace that caught Serena's eye.

"You look unhappy."

"Well…"

"I know it stinks having to wait, but the science behind it takes time."

"No, it's not that at all. That list," I said, pointing to the tablet. "That's not a good thing. Granting powers is way beyond feeding people."

We stood in silence in the middle of the hallway, vampires coming and going. The fact that they treated Serena like a coworker and not a revolutionary must have meant that everyone was in on this, and I smirked at the thought that this really was, in many ways, like a union. Just with food and powers instead of benefits and paid time off.

"I understand your concerns," she said, a quiet gravel to her voice.

"Oh good," I said, relief at the thought that some vampires who never bothered going to therapy might *not* gain the ability to be superpowerful.

"There's still much to learn about them. They've never been tracked and studied on such a scale. But the more people access their abilities, the better we can log their experiences on the app and we'll know much more about how long they can use them per vial, the rate it reactivates aging, and so on. That's the beauty of community—the data means we'll be able to correlate patterns…"

Serena went on, talking about algorithms to study duration and efficacy and all sorts of things that really *just didn't matter*. Because apparently Serena, Eric, and all the other community leaders overlooked one very simple fact—and problem.

Human or vampire, people were people.

"No, no, no, not *that*," I said. This prompted her brow to furrow, and she looked up, studying both Ian and me. "People deserve to eat. Not everyone deserves superpowers."

That furrow gradually shifted from a scrunched confusion, settling into a frown, like such a thought never even crossed her mind. "This is who we are. We should have access to use our natural abilities."

"But it's not natural," Ian said, chiming in with way more confidence than expected for a thirteen-year-old confronting a century-old vampire on morality. Or maybe it was the right amount of age gap. "It's like, um, when Olympic athletes use steroids. The vials are like drugs."

An Olympic cheating analogy wasn't on my checklist of topics for the night, but Ian hit it right. "Look, I don't have a bunch of college degrees. But as a musician, I mean, we just want people to hear our stuff, right? The internet gave musicians that exposure. And now bands can't make a living because it's all just *out there*. When everyone can take the songs they want in the fastest and easiest way possible, everyone wins except the people making the songs. Opening up to everyone means someone in the chain gets stomped on."

"Wait, wait, wait," Ian said, suddenly tapping on his phone. "We learned about this in class. This term…" Serena and I waited, all of us locked on his screen. "'Data equity.'" Ian held up his phone with a Wikipedia definition. "Like, when you write code to collect data, it's gonna be biased based on whoever wrote it."

Both Serena and I tilted our heads at that statement. Probably for different reasons.

"So, like, if you're rewriting the system for everyone to order a vial, that's because you think everyone deserves it," Ian said. He stood with slacked shoulders, a hand running through his still-slicked hair, as if that level of profundity came from him often.

"You know," I said, "I hate to say it. But this is the one area that the Ancients got right. There have to be rules. I mean, do you really think that vampires with sudden abilities to fly are going to remain hidden from human society?"

"There's gotta be a better way," Ian said.

"Eric always talks about community first. But this is really, really different from keeping people fed. These vials will pit everyone against each other." I thought about so many musicians, their songs and albums now available to anyone in the world with just a few clicks—heard, but not really listened to, music as background noise rather than a four-minute piece of art.

The tablet in Serena's hand timed out, the glowing screen dimming to black. She looked at us, and behind her eyes, I could sense gears turning.

"Listen to the human teenager," I said. "There's gotta be a better way than just opening the floodgates. You've been working on this plan for a really long time, right?" I asked. Serena gave a silent nod. "Hey, even people with seven degrees sometimes overlook stuff."

Her serious expression broke into her usual smirk. "What you've said," she finally said after taking a breath, "is quite pragmatic."

"What's that mean?" Ian asked.

"It's kind of like, you know, sensible," I replied.

"Oh," he said, head bobbing in acknowledgment, which prompted a small grin on Serena's face.

"We've waited decades to give the Ancients' secrets to the population." Her words came quietly, though it seemed that the tone came from an epiphany, not fatigue. "To take away their unfair rule."

"Yeah, but you're forgetting one really huge important thing."

"What's that?"

"Bad things are going to happen if you forget how real people think," I said, remembering what I told Eric back in the warehouse. "Because people are selfish assholes. Even if they are vampires." She laughed, but I was being totally serious. "You can't trust assholes with unchecked power. They're gonna find a way to do the dumbest things. Like how tech guys pay musicians point-zero-zero-zero-zero-zero-one cents for royalties, so musicians can't make money off their songs. So they stop recording music because they have to work elsewhere to eat. It's not like they can only survive selling swag off their website."

"I, uh…" She paused, her eyes dropping. "I don't know what 'swag' is. But I get it." The look in her eyes changed, a shift that echoed throughout her body as she eyed me up and down. "How did we not see this?"

"Ah, it's cool. You just got excited. Happens all the time. It's good intentions before shit goes downhill. Whatever you do—with the vials, with people's data, with your security measures—you have to let people know. Otherwise, it's really not that different from a bunch of Ancients making rules while partying in a country club."

"Mmm." Her lips pursed in a grim line as she nodded. "The world is changing so fast. I should probably get a philosophy degree to ground my morals. Otherwise it's like what Jeff Goldblum says in *Jurassic Park*."

"I've never seen it," I said, which prompted side-eyes from *both* Serena and Ian.

She turned to Ian, a small smile breaking the serious air of the moment. "We'll have to show her. It's a perfect movie," she said, before looking back at the hallway door leading to the ballroom. "There's a lot to discuss with the community leaders. You're right. There's a smarter way to do this. Maybe," she asked, her words slowing, "you'd like to help out? Since you won't have to worry about getting blood anymore?"

Several seconds passed in order to fully process what Serena offered. A job, a real purpose helping out vampires usher in a brave new world?

*Possibilities.* A world without day-to-day struggle.

I pondered such a thing, a completely impossible situation a mere hour ago, and now the offer for something monumentally shifting the direction of my life.

Except for one thing:

Of all the things I let myself daydream about while onstage with Serena, none of them involved career-type pursuits. Not now, anyway. I had better things to do.

Like find a band.

"Sorry," I said. We both turned at the sound of the far door opening, the first of the Ancients to apparently recover their mobility and leave in shame. "I'm far too underqualified. But..." I nodded at her. "I think all those degrees show that you're a quick learner."

"Me?"

"Yeah. Just, you know, read philosophy books before you go to bed. Plus you've seen *Jurassic Park* and I haven't. Eric's not the only leader here, you know?"

The suggestion caused Serena's entire posture to shift, as if she'd never considered just what her specific combination of knowledge, experience, and martial arts brought to the table. She sucked in a breath and started to reply when the door opened again, this time Eric dashing through. "There you are," he said, his hand outstretched. "The discussion is starting. Can you display data as I give my presentation?"

"Sure," she said before looking our way with a single raised eyebrow. "Actually, I'd like to bring something up as well. I think we need to look at transparent regulation for powers."

Eric's head angled at the statement but they quickly turned to a technical discussion that went way over my head, which I took as our cue to leave. I looked at Ian, who still held the vial in his hand like fragile cargo.

"Louise?"

We stopped and turned at Eric's voice.

"Would you like to see what your innate powers are?" He reached into his coat pocket and pulled out one more vial. "They wear off in ten, sometimes twenty minutes. Sometimes an hour, depending on your body chemistry. But it's nice to know."

"Dude," Ian whispered. "What if you could fly?"

Superstrength, like what Serena did, that might lead to more accidental holes in walls than anything useful. But flying? That *would* be cool.

I considered that point until something even better came along: what if I could finally get through the opening riff of "When Doves Cry" without messing up?

# CHAPTER 41

WE WAITED WHILE SERENA caught Eric up on her new perspective regarding vial distribution, though she used more polite terms than "people are assholes." He dashed back to reconvene with the other community leaders, though she insisted on sticking around for a few minutes as I contemplated the vial in my hand.

It shouldn't have been a big deal. I'd had some exposure to it before with my accidental drink, and all it did was give me some answers in the form of restored memories. But when I held the vial in my hand, my mind wasn't concerned with that night at the Iggy Pop show.

There was only one other night that I couldn't remember. And I wasn't sure if I wanted it back.

"Sometimes," she said, laughing, "people freak out when they discover they can jump really high or whatever. And some people get multiple powers. Like Eric. He gets to glamour *and* fly. Lucky bastard."

"What's the freakiest power you've seen?" Ian asked with eyes wide.

Serena's lips pursed, a genuine thoughtfulness at an absurd query. "You know," she said, holding up the list on her tablet, "it's all pretty standard stuff. A lot of myths have some basis in reality. I do hope someday someone transforms into a bat in front of me. I'd love to study whatever's happening there." She turned to me. "You ready?"

I wasn't, necessarily. That memory remained murky, a dual sting of regret and fury, all wrapped in an inscrutable blanket of melancholy.

But beyond vampires, beyond lifesaving vials, beyond the search for blood, one final confrontation awaited me, an unavoidable conversation that would finally cement the link between me and Ian by the way of his lineage.

Because if these family ties were going to be permanent, understanding my heritage would be a final step. And that meant remembering the night we found out my mom died.

I didn't say anything to Serena. Instead, I twisted the lid off the vial and took down the blood in one shot, like Marshall making a messy choice at the bar after a gig.

And I remembered, with a voice that whipped me directly into the past, a clarity of diction and tone with just a hint of an accent.

"Mixing vodka and blood?" Aunt Laura had asked that night, the autumn chill sneaking into the small house's ventilation.

"I've heard about it. I mean, as good a time as any to try, right?" I poured a splash into my mug of blood, then swirled it around. "I'll go easy. It's only a half shot."

Laura hadn't gone easy, though. She'd started as soon as the news arrived, apparently finding out with a phone call from a friend of a friend, a chain reaction of information that took several days past my mom's funeral before it finally got to us. And I'd come home from work at three in the morning to find her passed out in her favorite chair, a glass and bottle of whiskey sitting on the table. In between them sat a note that read:

*Wake me when you get home. I have to tell you something.*

"Maybe I should slow down," Aunt Laura said with a laugh, taking her glass and downing it before going back to her tea.

We sat, listening to a mix tape I'd jokingly labeled as "brooding." It seemed appropriate for today, and for the first ten minutes, we sat in silence, surrounded by the music coming from the three-foot-tall speakers. She sipped her tea, petting the mini schnauzer on her lap, while I drank my mug of blood faster than I probably should have. The sting of vodka hit my nose, followed by a burn down my throat, and by the time the opening synthesizers and marching percussion of Joy Division's "Atmosphere" came on, I asked Aunt Laura the burning question that lurked during our whole time together.

If not this moment, when?

"Aunt Laura," I managed to push out, the alcohol hitting my bloodstream way faster than expected. "My mom…"

Laura held up her tea. "To the homophobic bitch. Who was still my sister."

The bite in her words ignited all the times my parents cursed her existence, the person they marked as difficult, damaged, unnatural. And as those moments simmered in my brain, a guilt emerged, all the times I let those damning words exist without speaking up.

And yet, here Aunt Laura sat, saluting her passed sister in the only way she knew how.

"My mom," I started again, the vodka pulling the question down with a slight slur, "what was she like?"

"You know, don't you?" Aunt Laura blew out a wistful sigh, then scratched Howie's ears. "You grew up with her."

"No, I don't." I sat back in my chair, sinking into the recliner deep enough that the legs kicked out. "She was always just... Mom. In Mom mode. More like a boss than a person." My head started floating, the vodka circulating hard through my veins and unlocking my defenses step-by-step, urges to both scream and hide tugging at me.

But I didn't need to do either. Even with inebriation quickly sludging my brain, all I needed was Aunt Laura in front of me, teacup in hand and Howie in her lap.

That was enough to calm my nerves.

"Well, that's the thing," Laura said. "I don't think she knew either."

"She died at sixty-four. How could she not know?"

Laura bit down on her lip, then stared at the half-full teacup in her hand. "I don't think anyone told her she was allowed to." She paused long enough for Howie to look up, then get up and stretch before collapsing back down in her lap. "When I left, I knew I was different. And I refused to be stifled anymore. They wouldn't acknowledge that. So I made a choice. But to get to the point where it was all or nothing, I needed a push. Turned out, when I realized I liked looking at the pretty lady hawking a Coca-Cola bottle, I saw how I was different."

Music was the thing that pushed me through that moment. A connection to the fury of punk, the poetry of Lou Reed, the way that rhythm and melody could explode an emotion when words failed.

I'd needed that in my youth. Music gave it. And they tried to take it away.

"I feel sad for her, really," Laura said. "Wu Jin-Yi. Mary, the instant we got here. She was eighteen, I was sixteen. The most American names they could give us. Our parents wanted our story to be one about taking a new future. Problem was they didn't know how to give that. I left. And Mary met your dad, and they passed that on to you. And your brother. You just figured a way to escape." She smiled, stroking the ears of the mini schnauzer that resumed snoring. "She was whoever imprinted on her. Our parents. Her husband. China. America. Her greatest tragedy is that none of them ever let her be herself. If things had been different, if she was a lesbian like me or heard punk rock like you or something else happened in her life, she might have given herself permission. But she didn't. The barriers on her path were too tall for her, but no one ever told her to try. You want to know who your mom was?" Laura turned to me with clarity, despite the fact that I was probably nothing more than a human-shaped blur in her deteriorating vision.

"She was not you."

The goddamn vodka. At this point, blood tears started streaming down my cheeks and there was no garlic to blame.

"So," she said, "here's to you." Howie jumped off Laura's lap when she got out of her chair, and though her eyesight was faulty, the booze-and-feelings-induced sniffling gave me away. Her mug of tea clinked against my half-finished mug of alcoholic blood.

"Here's to you," she sang in her best Joan Baez voice, "Louise Chao."

The rest of the night was a sort of wake—not necessarily a celebration, not necessarily mourning, but just an acknowledgment of the life that my mom had led. After I'd finished my drink, I'd had another and another, stealing my memories. But thanks to my vial-induced recall, I clearly saw how things escalated until I finally collapsed in my dark room: dancing with Howie, hugging Aunt Laura to the point that my stupid blood tears stained her gray cardigan, and a very poor attempt at karaoke to the entire *The Message* album by Grandmaster Flash & The Furious Five.

I'd avoided that memory for so long, treasured its obscurity because I feared what it would tell me about my family. But the ironic thing was that the night I mourned the passing of my birth mother also revealed something far more significant:

Who my real family was.

"Louise?" Serena asked quietly as I returned to the present. My feet planted firmly on the floor in a stately mansion, not our small home on Moraga Street, go-go boots instead of Doc Martens. "Are you alright?"

"I'm fine," I said, breathing heavily after recalibrating to the here and now. "So, I guess I didn't levitate just now, huh?"

"You're doing the vampire-crying thing," Ian said. He scrambled in his pockets, presumably for a napkin or something, but only produced a half-torn sheet of notebook paper. I took it from him and dabbed the sides of my face, paper crinkling with each action.

"Photographic memory recall is a pretty boring superpower," I said through sniffles. "Like only good for the DMV test."

"Actually," Serena said, "I think memory recall would be the best power."

"You jumped like twenty feet in the air and took out an assassin vampire."

"Meh, there's always someone who's stronger. But memory... I'm envious of you." She tilted her head at an angle as she looked at me. "Think of all the things you could learn with that."

"You could debug code way faster with a photographic memory," Ian said.

"Good point," Serena said. "You see?"

Of course, these two would think that.

"We should go. We have to get to his mom." Around us, staff resumed coming and going, like a revolution didn't just take place in the ballroom and two vampires didn't just explode in public. They pushed carts and carried towels, and I wondered what would happen to this estate and others like it around the world. The Ancients no longer had the means to hold power, but these really cool buildings were probably still legally in their name.

Serena undoubtedly sorted that out ahead of time. She seemed the type.

"You know, we're going to have to break the rules again." I thumbed at Ian. "To tell his grandfather what's happening."

She looked around, her smirk returning. "Like I said, there aren't as many fixers as you'd think. So let's use rumors to keep his grandfather in line, alright?"

Before I left, one question remained, one thread left untied between all of the vampire revelations and changes. "How many are there?" I asked. "Fixers?"

"They're more of an idea than an actual job. Eric asks people for a favor to handle it when something gets really out of line." She squinted, head at an angle. "Did you want to help out?"

"No. I was just curious if someone might have been sent a few years ago. A rainy night on the highway by Oakland. A human in a car wreck."

"Mmm," Serena said, lips pursed and head shaking. "No, we wouldn't do anything like that. We'd be more discreet. Car accidents can bring collateral damage. Plus we usually leave humans alone unless it's really extreme. That sounds like it was just bad weather. It happens." Concern framed her for face. "What's this about?"

*Just bad weather.* A mistake. A function of bad luck and poor decisions. And nothing to do with vampires—myself or otherwise.

*It happens.*

"Maybe I'll tell you someday." I shot Ian a look. "We should go."

Serena's gloved finger pointed at the phone in my hand. Our gazes met, a new tint to them, as if we could see an unwritten future in our vampire eyes. "I'll give you my number. In case you need to talk."

# CHAPTER 42

I OPTED *NOT TO* get deeper into vampiric politics, and instead we strode out of the complex to find our ride home. But the grounds themselves proved confusing, and I went from path to path, the combination of outdoor lighting and overhead stars getting me more lost with each turn. Ian, however, insisted he knew which way to go.

He turned out to be right on his fifth try, finally returning us to the massive fountain where we'd originally split up. And while a car idled beyond that, I made Ian stop in midstride.

I didn't care too much about Eric's revolution antics. But one of its participants stood at the fountain, holding a long thin stick, smoke dancing off the end of it.

Madeline.

It took me several seconds to put together that as she stood, hand on hip and chin tilted up, the object in her hand was an old-timey ladies' cigarette holder. Like the kind in classic movies and photographs.

Vampires could…smoke? I'd never even thought of it.

Though I suppose if our bodies could keep cancer at bay, why not?

Madeline turned and caught my eye, then her head tilted as she looked at Ian.

Eric talked about community and connection, yet I got the feeling that if I didn't speak to this mystery woman now, the chance may never return. She didn't seem like the type to put down roots. The intense memory restoration answered so many questions about the night I got turned, but others burned, not the *how* but the *why* of the weeks after.

My memory could never resolve that.

I walked on the cobblestone path, my ankle wobbly from the go-go boots pacing on uneven stones. She dragged on the cigarette, then puffed it out, the smoke coiling up and dispersing before she moved to meet me, the thin stick still in her hand.

And unlike me, walking on cobblestones didn't seem to be a problem for her balance.

"Hey," I said, in something that sounded more like a challenge than a greeting. "I remember you."

"Wasn't she the lady singing earlier?" Ian asked, his teenage bluntness making the whisper into a very audible question.

"Yes, but it's not that," I said as we got closer. She paused midstride to take another drag, making me do the final ten feet or so. "You turned me."

We stood face-to-face now, though her height framed our conversation awkwardly. She looked me up and down, as if painting over the sight of my checkerboard dress with punk-rock attire and a flailing showman onstage behind me. "Iggy Pop," she said.

"That's right."

"Those punk years were so much fun. You've done well for yourself?"

Having never turned a human into a vampire, I had zero

context as to how these relationships went other than makers tended to disappear from people's lives. But wouldn't they care? Or at least be curious? I mean, I wanted to know more about the dog that hung out at Harold's Guitar Shack.

"Wait, that's all you've got to say? Asking me how I am?" I asked, an accusatory question that came out more befuddled. Questions like these plagued vampires all the time, and yet, such a throwaway answer created confusion more than anything else. "You chose to give me this life and then you just... disappear?"

"I gave you a gift. It was your choice to do whatever you wanted with it."

Serena had said that Madeline carried an air of the dramatic, but I couldn't tell if this was part of her shtick. "But..." I said, sucking in a breath, ready to ask the question I'd wondered for so many years, "why?"

"Why what?" she asked, a line of confusion over her face.

"Why me? Why at an Iggy Pop show?"

Madeline's deep green eyes looked at me, and though we connected, her face still read empty. "You love music?"

"I do," I said, nodding with my words. "Music is everything."

"Exactly. Music *is* everything. It is emotion and spirit and purity. And love." Serena really wasn't kidding about her dramatics. "Some vampires have physical gifts, and I pity them. How *boring* it would be to simply be human-but-faster, stronger. But my gift is unique—I sense feelings. And there is no better place to absorb those, to let them wash over you, than at a concert."

Live music. I knew exactly what she was talking about. It was everything I preached to Ian, every indescribable emotion shared among hundreds or thousands of strangers.

And to be able to absorb that among the audience? "Holy shit."

"That's right. That's perfectly right. Yes, it's exactly what you think. I save my vials for concerts, to heighten sensory elation into an emotional experience. Except that night, I saw you." My restored memory rushed back like a film playing in my mind's eye, except with full sensory recall: the heat of crushed bodies, the blinking of stage lights, the movement of the crowd. "You had the same response as everyone else, but also so much more. Like the hurt and pain of your life carved a hole that only the chaos and beauty of the music could fill. And though it had been decades since I had turned a human, I wanted to give that to you. So you might experience something more extraordinary than the pain of your everyday life."

Ian stood behind me, silent; this might have been too over-the-top for him to digest. But everything she said made complete sense to me.

"I understand. I mean, I get that. So much. Right?" I asked Ian. "That's why I took him to a show. And taught him guitar. But one thing still doesn't make sense."

She took in a long drag of her cigarette, holding it extra long as if to show me that such a thing was possible for vampires, then tilted her head at the moon and blew out a cyclone of unraveling smoke. "What's that, my dear?"

"Why turn me and then barely be there?" Those flashes of the early weeks, the panic and fear of the gradual aversion to the sun, the disgusting growing lust for protein and meat, the epiphany of blood, the horror of realizing my teeth sharpened—all of it completely unprepared for. "Those were hard weeks. Not just the transformation, but figuring out my new life. I could have used, like, at least a guidebook or something. To tell me what was safe and not safe. Which vampire myths were bullshit and which were real. I mean, the first time I passed by cooking garlic was not pretty."

Whatever connection we had, an empathy intrinsically built by our shared love of music, that disappeared in the moment, and in its place sat a blank stare. "I don't understand. What do you mean?"

"Just that," I said, searching for the right explanation. "Why don't makers stay and help us figure out this whole vampire thing?"

Several lines formed between Madeline's well-manicured eyebrows, the logic of my single sentence seemingly inscrutable to her. Her front teeth bit down on her lip, fang grazing flesh. "I still don't understand. That's how it's always been. Why would you want more?"

And that was that. Despite a deep connection to the way music could carry a person's spirit, despite being part of Eric's revolution, despite her flair for the dramatic, she couldn't wrap her mind around breaking vampire traditions.

"I see," I finally said.

"You seem to have turned out fine," she said, returning to her cigarette. "And you understood the basic rules of secrecy. So I didn't have to check in on you anymore." A smile formed across her perfect bone structure. "Be free, little bird. Live your life."

"Right, right." I looked at Ian, the vial in his hand, and my voice dropped. "Well, uh, we should go." I patted him on the shoulder and gestured forward. "We have family to take care of." In the distance, the walk down to our ride suddenly appeared much longer.

"Well, my dear," Madeline said, turning on her heel. "Perhaps I'll see you at a show sometime. Somewhere out there." Her figure swayed with each step, and she blew out smoke as if she didn't have a care in the world.

We got into the back seat of the idling SUV, the doors shutting with a *thunk* as we settled in behind the driver. The engine roared to life and we started moving, the car silent except for the crunch of gravel under the wheels. "Hey," I said, my hand on Ian's knee, "I don't want you to worry."

He turned to me, a weariness suddenly washing over him. "Worry about what?" he asked quietly.

"What Madeline said, about how vampires don't help each other when they get turned." I nodded as the car pulled away, and though we were in the dark, I knew he saw it and nodded right back. "You don't have to worry. We're going to be better than that."

**CHAPTER 43**

SUNDAY NIGHT HAD TURNED to Monday morning by the time we got home, which meant some restful corgi snuggles for me and a bag of fast food for Ian. And though I did my best to ground him through the insanity of what just happened, Ian seemed totally on board. All he cared about was getting to see Sonya safely.

Of course, he missed his flight. Which meant one very early, slightly uncomfortable phone call to EJ to explain we'd be here for one more day before driving down. That morning, I went to bed with Eric's app re-downloaded on my phone, but muted as I slept, a deep slumber free from any notifications. And when I woke at 4:00 p.m., I checked it, apparently now linked up with regionalized versions around the globe.

And the world *had* changed.

Blood manufacturing. Accessible distribution, even jobs for vampires who wanted one. More importantly, *truth*. And an acknowledgment that the Ancients' stranglehold on the vampire community collapsed through the power of simply *knowing* who we really were.

And yet, the world hadn't quite changed. Eric and Serena and others were leading some form of committee for transparency and equity. The old world swept away, and in its place, this revolution would also change into some form of vampire democracy, something with departments and officials and other things to keep things rolling and managing the fine balance of integrated-but-hidden within human society. And those vials? Some form of vampire DMV would probably authorize who got them and when.

However, none of that really mattered once we hit the road.

I wore layers upon layers, my proven armor against the sun for the long drive from San Francisco to San Diego. In the back seat sat three things critical to our trip: a cooler filled with Eric's bottles, Ian's guitar with the cracked case (which still needed a name), and a snoozing corgi curled up in the dog blanket hanging like a hammock between the front and back seats.

"I just realized, I don't know if we'll have a perfect blackout room for you," Ian said about an hour into the drive. By then, dusk had hit, though I still drove with my Daft Punk helmet on, shifting colors coming through the tinted visor. To my right, the radius of orange and pink gradually sank below the horizon, counting down the minutes until I could drive helmetless.

"It's okay," I said. "I've been through worse."

Worse than not having a perfectly pitch-black room for the day. Worse than not having just witnessed a vampire revolution complete with stake-through-the-heart explosions. Worse than even that dark period after Marshall died.

One specific time had been worse because it marked the first moment I truly felt alone.

The thing about being on your own was that, well, you were on your own, without any means of stability. I learned that the hard way, several years of running night jobs after I got turned. Work, it turned out, was reasonably easy to find, but getting on a schedule and maintaining that for a vampire with an irregular blood supply? That proved to be a problem.

Still, it made for a less-than-ideal start to my new-new life, the one that was supposed to be a step beyond "newly turned vampire in Los Angeles" to "somewhat experienced vampire in San Francisco."

And when I moved to San Francisco, one option lingered in the back of my mind, something I'd avoided ever since arriving.

But the strange thing was that my life hadn't turned for the better.

I needed a reset. Bartending six days a week, buying blood from a mix of street donors, avoiding outreach from Eric's community, generally just *not* having my shit together, it clearly failed as a road map for successful immortality.

The only silver lining was that I did discover cool local bands playing at my bar. But that never really made up for the lack of everything else, even a consistent place to sleep during the daytime.

I still had the sheet with Aunt Laura's address, the street name Moraga burned into my memory, as if the neat line that scratched it out tattooed the same thing on my brain. That purposeful crossing out was probably done to eliminate Aunt Laura from my parents' universe, a ritual exorcizing more powerful than simply tearing the page out. But it didn't remove her from the family.

It just passed her to me. When I was ready. And one quick lookup in the San Francisco phone book showed that of the seven Laura Wus listed in the city, one still lived on Moraga Street.

On a night off from bartending and with few fucks left to give, I walked. I walked so long that I considered if I should just lie down in the middle of Golden Gate Park and wait for the sun to incinerate me, to prove that my mother *had* been right all along. Because though I considered myself cooler, tougher, and far more real than my brother, I knew that he was simply better than me.

At least at whatever life demanded. *This* life, where people had responsibilities and educations and things like that, regardless of whether they lived off food or blood.

I waited for the red light to turn, traffic seemingly unending, and finally, I gave up, turning to go down the sidewalk, letting the rhythm of my own feet take me somewhere. And though I didn't plan it, I'd found myself on the corner of Moraga and 11th.

I stood close to Aunt Laura's house. I didn't intend to, but I was there. And I had nothing to lose.

I tracked the numbers from house to house, only needing to go a block and a half before I finding it.

The cool, thick air of San Francisco's night kicked at my disheveled hair and I stared at the door, a simple barrier of painted wood between me and this person who'd been a mystery all my life. I paused, a quick cross of my fingers and a breath, then reached up to rap my knuckles against the door.

Beyond the door, the rhythmic thumps of a bass drum stopped, soon followed by the sound of footsteps. "Who's there?" a voice asked.

Laura was my mom's sister, having adopted an American name when they moved to California as teenagers. I always found it strange that both my parents used American names for their work and bills and stuff, yet called each other by their given names in Cantonese. They'd explained that such a choice brought them closer to this culture. But for Laura, I wondered if it meant something different.

"Hi," I said, words suddenly catching in my throat. How did I answer such a question? My arrival required a whole lot of context that wasn't easy to sum up through a wooden door. "My name's Louise. Can we talk?"

Her muffled voice came through, followed by the sound of a sliding *bolt*. The door opened a crack, a short chain still holding it from swinging fully open. "Your name's what?"

"Louise. Louise Chao. I'm…" I'd been a vampire for just over a decade at that point, and despite all of the strange, impossible, and really gross things that I'd dealt with, nothing seemed more difficult than forming words for this moment. "I'm like you."

From the small crack in the doorway, I saw Aunt Laura blink. "You're into girls?"

Not quite accurate. Even before vampirism rendered my hormones benign, I was attracted to men. But on any level, those desires disappeared years ago. When sex was out of the question, all that remained was connection—and I clearly failed at any form of emotional intimacy, be it family or romantic. "That's not what I mean. I mean, I'm…" Laura's brow crinkled as I stumbled over myself and sought the big vocabulary word that framed my entire existence. "I'm cut off. From my family. Your sister is my mom."

Laura's gaze held steady through the few inches of open doorway, my pulse hammering as seconds ticked by.

The door slammed shut, a poof of air blowing dust into my eyes.

I stood, blinking as much for the debris irritating my eyes as the dumbfounded numbness that hit me.

Except before I could turn away, the sound of a jangling chain and sliding metal came through the wood. The door swung open, and there Laura stood, her face neutral, though smile lines creased her mouth and brow, and her long hair showed an even blend of black and white cascading beyond her shoulders.

"Mary is your mom?"

I gave a silent nod, and from the look in her eyes, I wondered how much saying that name tore at the calluses built up over the years.

With the door open, faint music came through, just loud enough to be heard over the neighborhood din of traffic and wind behind me. I tuned my ears in, a throaty female voice over an acoustic guitar. At my feet, a little white bundle of fur growled while looking up.

"What are you listening to?" I asked, because nothing else came to mind.

"Are you asking to be polite or are you asking because you want to know?"

Such straightforward talk caught me off guard, and it took a few seconds to calibrate to Laura's force of nature. "I want to know. Music is kind of my thing."

She eyed me up and down, her gaze lingering long enough that she probably saw pieces of her sister in my features. "Howie," she said to the small dog, "back up. We have a guest." Her right hand extended and I met it, her firm grip powering the shake. "This is my niece, Louise. Be nice to her." She let go and ushered me in, Howie sniffing my boots the entire time. "How are you?"

"Fine."

"You're probably not if you're here. Listen, Louise, here's one thing I want you to know about me. When I ask 'how are you,' I want you to give me the real answer. Not a polite one. So," she said, closing the door and locking it behind her, "how are you?"

"It's…" I said, kneeling down to let her mini schnauzer sniff me. "Well, it's a bit of a long story."

"It's okay. I stay up late," she said, a slight accent still coloring her words. "Unless you need to go?"

"No." Somehow, five seconds of sniffing changed Howie's opinion of me, and instead of growling, he ran back to his tuffet bed, grabbed a small plush bone, then dropped it at my feet. "I'm a bit of a night owl."

That moment leading up to Aunt Laura's door was indeed worse for me than what Ian feared, probably worse than any other moment in my life. But the moment I stepped inside Aunt Laura's door, it got better.

Things would get better for Ian too.

"Worse?" Ian asked, bringing me back to the long straight path of Highway 5.

"Yeah. You can stick me and Lola in a closet for the daytime. We can snuggle anywhere." I reached behind me, my fingers extending. Lola's collar jingled as she adjusted, too lazy to stand up in her hammock but stretching her neck out enough to sniff my fingertips and give them a quick lick. "How are you?" I asked, hoping for honesty over politeness. "I mean, given the fact that you saw two ancient vampires explode and a worker revolution unfold—and you played your first gig onstage. It's a lot. So, how are you?"

"You know," he said, staring out the window. "Everything has been terrible."

That wasn't a good start to a check-in.

"With my dad. With my mom. I'm just so used to things being the worst every time. But this weekend is different. At least I get a chance to take things back." Behind us, Lola adjusted and stretched, a quiet groan that filled the silence between us. Ian reached back to the dog, and she obliged with a gentle lick of his fingers. "So yeah, I'm okay. All things considered."

We arrived in San Diego close to two in the morning, with only a few bathroom/fast-food stops along the way. And though Ian swore up and down that he didn't do it, I was pretty sure he'd sneaked Lola a few fries.

I cut off the headlights as we rolled into the driveway, the quiet streets not unlike the last time I visited my parents' house in the middle of the night. Except instead of sneaking in through the back, Ian let us in the front door. History *did*

repeat itself in one way—we walked gingerly, keeping soft footsteps to avoid waking my sleeping brother. Lola began sniffing
the small entryway and as the usual tufts of corgi fur began
floating off her coat, I realized that at some point during our
stay, I'd owe it to Ian's family to vacuum their entire house.

Ian led us upstairs and down a hallway to a shut door. The
knob clicked as Ian turned it and entered, Lola's paws shuffling on the carpeted floor. Perhaps some vampires developed
night vision after taking a vial, but I certainly didn't have it,
and I scooped Lola up while my eyes adjusted. Dim silhou-
ettes mapped the room, the only light from the glowing orange numbers of an alarm clock.

"Mom," he said, edging up to the bed, a king-size mattress
though she slept on one side. "Mom, I'm home."

Sonya mumbled in her sleep, low words that failed to make it
to my ears, and I stayed at the edge of the room while mother
and son talked with each other. A click came from the bedside
table and a lamp snapped to life, a low light that cast shadows
across their faces.

"Mom. It's me."

"Ian? How'd… What time is it?"

"Mom, there's something you need to know," Ian said, and
though fatigue still tinted Sonya's face, she looked at me with
recognition.

"I remember you," she said softly. "Death in a hoodie."

"Hey," I said, my fingers waving while holding Lola.

"Why are you holding a dog?"

"She's a really good dog," Ian said. "Her name is Lola." He
took in a breath, then reached into his pocket. He pulled out
a small shoebox, and he opened it to show the vial sitting in
layers of bubble wrap.

"This," he said, "will make you better." He glanced back
at me before turning back to Sonya. "But it'll change things."

"Change things?" she asked weakly. "What do you mean?"

I set Lola on the floor, though she quickly followed at my feet. Ian gave me space to approach, and Lola, traitor that she was, hopped over to Ian before flopping on her back, a paw up to high-five.

"You'll become like me," I said, kneeling down. I opened my mouth, top lip pushing up to show my fangs for several seconds before taking her hand. "Like this."

Sonya managed a raised eyebrow above her smirk. "What are you, a vampire?"

Lucky guess.

"Actually, yeah. That's right." I looked at the closed bedroom door behind me. "And I'm your dad's older sister."

An hour passed as we slowly talked Sonya through the possibilities, and I noted that she had good timing because Eric's revolution meant that she could start her new life with bottled blood, not dealing with street sellers or catching rats in alleys.

Sonya took it all in stride, from the existence of vampires to the idea that she would have to sustain herself on blood to the fact that I'd gotten her son into punk rock. Even the idea that I was her aunt didn't seem to faze her at all. But maybe when facing the finality of cancer-induced death, accepting the impossible became quite easy.

"So they have bottled blood?"

"Yeah," Ian said. "They've got an app." I pulled out my phone and flashed the screen at her.

"This isn't just a fever dream?" she asked. "I've been on a *lot* of drugs."

"It's not," I said. "Otherwise, there wouldn't be corgi fur everywhere. I'll vacuum, I promise." On cue, Lola stretched on the floor and groaned. "You seem pretty okay with learning about the existence of vampires."

"Are you kidding?" Smile lines creased her face, her lips angling upward. "I was hoping for a miracle drug. But this works almost as well." She reached a hand over to Ian, who clasped his hands around it. "I can't leave this kid alone. Not until he learns to eat better."

"Hey, maybe you'll get the ability to fly too," I said. Ian nodded enthusiastically at the statement, obviously more enamored with flight than my supermemory ability.

The bed shifted under Sonya as she turned to look at the clock. "Four o'clock. The sun will be up soon."

"Do you want to see the sunrise?" I asked, thinking about all the times that film vampires had done that. "It's kind of a pain to see it. Both while you transition and after you turn."

"Nah. I said goodbye to that a few weeks ago. Let me do this before my body wastes away any more," she said. Her hand reached out to her son, fingers opening up and palm flat. "I'm ready."

## CHAPTER 44

**AS I UNDERSTOOD IT,** Sonya's first twenty-four hours or so would be a deep sleep before her body required extreme levels of protein and calories to power through its gradual transformation over the next two weeks. I texted a note to my boss at SFGH about a family emergency, then settled into Sonya's walk-in closet, sleeping bag in my hand. I rolled it out, protected from UV rays in a room of shoes and coats—things that would be used by Sonya again, but in a completely different context.

The sleeping bag unfurled, a kid-size one emblazoned with a San Diego Padres logo, and a knock came from behind me. The door swung open, and I expected to find Ian with extra bedding.

But instead, EJ stood in the doorway, dressed in pajamas and slippers with blankets stacked in his hand.

"I heard I should talk to you."

Beyond him lay the master bathroom, and from my angle, its window remained dark.

"Family, am I right?" I said with a weak laugh. Lola went ahead of me and flopped at the foot of the sleeping bag. I took the blankets from him and set them on the floor. An hour probably remained before the sun would creep out, and another hour after that before it would really reflect off the walls and mirrors of the house. "What did Ian tell you?"

"He said you're a vampire. And you saved my daughter."

"Well, technically I didn't save her. But in a way, yeah." I looked at EJ, his face a mixture of mourning fatigue, confusion, and disbelief. "It's a lot to take in, right?"

"I think the thing I'm really coming to terms with is that Sonya's going to live."

"Yeah. That part's pretty cool."

Behind me, the deep, even rhythm of Lola's sleep breaths came, and I considered the person in front of me. *"She was not you,"* Aunt Laura had said to me about our mom. Who was Stephen-turned-EJ? Sonya's dad, Ian's grandfather, my brother, the son of the same parents that repeatedly pushed me back into my place whenever I burst out of line. But those were all fragments, shards of the whole. In reality, I had no idea who he was.

This was the same question I had for Laura about my mom. And in the end, there was no answer—my mom's life didn't allow her to have her own identity.

But Stephen seemed to have lived a life. And though it fought against my familial instinct of avoiding questions, of snark and belligerence, of letting bitterness simply *exist* between myself and my brother, that wouldn't work anymore. We were in this for the long haul, a new path forged by our connection through Ian and Sonya.

I needed to say something to him. Might as well be now, especially since the next week or so with Sonya would get pretty wild.

"Well, it's early, so I'll—"

"No, wait," I said. He looked at me quizzically, head tilted and tired eyes squinting. "There's something we should talk about." I looked around for any sort of chair, but there weren't any in the closet, so instead I pointed to the edge of the bathtub in the master bathroom. "You should sit down. This might take a while. There are a few things about me you need to know." He sat with an old-man groan, and turned to the bits of changing sky coming in from the far window. I stayed safely in the shadows of the closet, and though I was tired, the prospect of stepping into the unknown pushed away any oncoming fatigue.

"Things our parents never really gave us the chance to say."

# CHAPTER 45

NINE DAYS HAD PASSED since Sonya took her vial, which was way more time than I wanted to be off from work. But the nice thing about having a long record in a job and shift that no one wants is that your boss can be sympathetic about family emergencies.

Still, I knew it would be time to go home soon, to start dreaming of the possibilities Eric talked about. And after the first week of Sonya's diet transitioning from high-protein tofu (even in a semiferal state, she still remained vegetarian for as long as she could), we gently transitioned to Eric's synthetic blood. Her own transformation seemed nothing like mine; while I had struggled through a half-mad state, the combination of a steady diet and family hand-holding made it more like a deliriously weird flu for her.

Also, for as much grief as I'd given him, Eric's app worked. West Coast only for now, but I had a six-pack of bottles delivered, to allow me an extended stay, along with some texts from Serena to check in on us. Technology was the best *and* the worst.

Really, the hardest part was the fact that Sonya was *not* dying anymore. But Eric texted that he'd be able to forge a medical cover story for us soon.

Vampires, after all, had to keep their community discreet.

Today, I'd woken up before Sonya—not surprising, given that her body's circadian rhythm was still adjusting to the day/night cycle. During this time, Ian had returned to his normal schedule, including human responsibilities of school. And EJ—whom I now comfortably called EJ, without any internal sneering about who Stephen Chao used to be—took on the caretaker role alongside me.

As for Lola, well, corgis made for excellent moral support. Ian would probably miss my dog more than me.

The front door opened, and I winced from my kitchen-table seat as the early evening's dying sun reflected off a passing car, a UV beam just enough to cause me to turn away. Lola the traitorous corgi left me and ran over to Ian, who walked in. "How's Mom?" he asked, pointing upstairs.

"*I'm* fine, thanks for asking," I said with a laugh. "Your grandfather is getting groceries. Your mom will probably wake up soon. Lola missed you."

His backpack slammed on the floor, a teenage carelessness that Lola ignored as she followed him into the kitchen. He opened the door and poked his head inside. "What are you doing? Writing lyrics?" he asked, his voice muffled by crunching into an apple.

"This?" I said, tapping the notebook in front of me.

"Yeah. New songs?"

"Not quite." I rotated the notebook into his view while he snacked, apple in one hand and box of crackers in the other. "You know, vampire life is really pretty boring. We're fairly normal other than working night shifts and drinking blood. But it's hard to learn that when you've just been turned."

"'Everything people assumed about vampires is wrong,'" he read aloud before skimming lower on the page. "'Vampire power myths: Number one—superspeed.' Are you gonna make a Wikipedia page or something?"

"No, this is for your mom. I gotta head back to the Bay Area in a day or so. And even though she's stable, this is still a new world for her. I'm giving her what I wished I had," I said, tapping the pages. "A guidebook to the weirdness of this life."

"Huh," he said, taking several more bites of apple before tossing the core into the garbage. "You know, we can always just FaceTime you with questions."

Kids and their tech. There was something to be said for having bound, physical paper in your hands. Eric had built an app that revolutionized the vampire world, and even he still had a leather-bound notebook.

"By the way," Ian said between chews. "I wanted to tell you something."

His cheeks rose, and despite trying to hide behind a tough exterior, his smile broke through, like he'd been waiting all day to let it spill out.

I, of course, played it cool. "Yeah?" I asked, meeting his gaze.

"I think," he started, his face beaming, "I finally figured out a name for my guitar."

# *Epilogue*

FIRST CAME THE STEAM. Then the bubbling, followed by a quick release of air pressure.

And soon came the sound of hot liquid dribbling.

Like blood.

Only so much better.

I waited for the last drop before picking up the small mug and taking in the aroma of freshly brewed espresso. So many smells of the human world dulled to my vampire senses, yet I'd never quite noticed the wonders of espresso before. In fact, it hadn't even been a consideration until Eric's mention, and now the rich brew tickled my nose before I mixed half of it into my first mug of blood for the day.

As I sipped, a cymbal crashed from the back room, followed by a very out-of-time version of "Left of the Dial" by The Replacements. Better than before, but Ian's use of practice pads over the last few months back at his San Diego home didn't quite nail the timing of a full drum kit. Shortly after, a woman's voice floated over the beat, along with very basic guitar strumming.

Serena. Whom Ian let in right as I was waking up. She was clearly the vampire equivalent of a "morning person."

Her voice soared despite the dissonant rhythm of out-of-time drumming and troubled chord changes. I'd tried teaching her guitar, but even though she knew pretty much every scientific discipline in the world, her fingers failed to cooperate with chord changes. Nothing quite worked in time, though the strength of her voice still pulled them forward. She sang Paul Westerberg's affecting lyrics, tales of a disaffected youth and feeling just out of place.

Of course, she hit those notes perfectly.

I'd introduced so many different artists and styles to Serena, from Bowie to Motown to new wave and so on, all on a quest to get her to acknowledge that modern music could blend contemporary sounds with, as she put it, "soul."

And out of the catalog of vocalists and artists, somehow only Paul Westerberg managed to connect with her, Serena devouring The Replacements and his solo catalog with the same methodical precision as she did with coding or European History or *Star Trek*.

My phone buzzed as I took another sip of my caffeinated blood, an icon appearing with Sonya's face. I set aside my Goth is Undead mug when a pixelated video of Ian's mom appeared.

Behind her, EJ sat, TV glowing with a white sheet of ice and hockey players skating around.

Some things never changed.

"Good morning," she said before her face scrunched up. "Good evening," she corrected herself with a laugh. And though her body hadn't recovered the weight it lost during her cancer treatments, her eyes came through bright and focused, filled with an ongoing curiosity that only came with second chances. "I'm still not used to that. Not the same without morning coffee."

"Did you try espresso in your breakfast yet? It's amazing."

"One of these days. Blood is still…" Her mouth twisted as she looked at the mug on the counter behind her. "It's still pretty gross. But hey, is Ian with you? I tried calling him."

I held up the phone and walked over to the hallway, the sound of drums and vocals getting louder, Sonya's wince at the crashing cymbal telling me that the noise came through clearly.

"He's a little busy now," I said, Lola following behind me. "Indulging in my drums while he can, before heading home in a few days."

On the phone's screen, Sonya made a face after sipping blood, all while Ian and Serena tumbled toward the end of the song. "Sometimes I can't believe what's happened to this family," Sonya said with a laugh so light it felt impossible to tell if she was joking or annoyed.

"I promise you'll get used to the blood thing. Think of them as smoothies. And you really should try the espresso thing, it's amazing and—"

"No, no, no," she said, shaking her head. "Not that. *That.*" Through the screen her finger pointed behind me, right when the drums came to a merciful close. "Your music is so *loud.* I hear it so much." Her mouth twisted, the mangled beat continuing. "Maybe he'll grow out of it."

Grow out of it? Months after he'd discovered how transformative, how life-changing a good song could be?

Not if I could help it.

"I'll tell him to call you back in a few. And try the espresso," I said, nudging Lola with my feet. I walked back to the kitchen, the dark evening draped over my small backyard. "Seriously. It's the best."

Sonya signed off, leaving me with an earnest—but inept— attempt at "Unsatisfied" in the background. They failed to launch, stopping several bars in, followed by Ian's loud *"fuck"* muffled by the sound-insulated walls. I looked down at Lola, who held up her paw for a high five.

And then I realized why: right next to Serena's purse on the kitchen table sat a fast-food bag, grease stains leaking through the bottom. Crumpled wrappers sat inside, but several fries remained. Lola's paw waved back and forth while her eyes tracked me, the whites nearly full circles.

"One fry. *One.* Only because we shouldn't waste," I said, wondering how Ian conned Serena into picking up food on her way. I reached in to grab the greasy potato when something in Serena's purse grabbed my eye.

A Blu-ray of *Jurassic Park*.

"Were you in on this too?" I asked Lola as she caught the fry. My back pocket buzzed again, and I pulled out my phone to see something different—not an update from the community app, not a follow-up call from a newly turned vampire, but a text.

From Pete, my old bandmate.

Hey, did you ever wind up practicing our songs a few months back? That guitarist just quit on us right before our show tomorrow. You got time to fill in?

Pete had texted the last time Ian had stayed with me, though that all got scrapped for a weekend involving revolution, Blondie, and an impromptu solo performance in front of a bunch of Ancients. Which was fun. But not as good as playing with a full band.

Maybe now was finally the right time. For many different things.

I considered my schedule with Ian. I'd planned on showing him my project for Berklee College of Music's online music production program, but I was pretty sure he'd swap that to help me prepare for a gig.

Yeah, I got time, I typed, hesitating before adding one last detail. I'll bring some guests to the show.

The message flew across the data network as I set my phone down on the counter. Behind it sat a framed photo of Marshall, guitar hanging off his shoulder and fingers up in vampire claws. "Pete and I are going to jam," I said to him. "I hope you find a way to listen." I held up my hands in claws and hissed at his image. I pictured him mirroring the gesture, as we'd done so many times, then kissed my fingers and tapped them against the photo.

★ ★ ★ ★ ★

# *ACKNOWLEDGMENTS*

I've always loved vampires. If you ask my high school friends, they'd say I was borderline obsessed. When I was a kid, vampire lore always drew me in, and when I was a teen, I discovered Anne Rice. That was also when I discovered the power of music. That angst is largely gone, though my love of vampires, indie rock, and all things goth remains. It also took decades for me to realize that these countercultures represented an internalized pushback to the cultural stereotypes I fought against: academic, quiet, and obedient. Decades of therapy have done me well!

Flash forward to October 2020, I noticed that vampire books were finally getting picked up by publishers again and I asked my agent Eric Smith "are vampires back?" He confirmed and I had a full pitch out to him in two weeks. The resulting story mashed up my lifelong obsessions of music and vampires with my lifelong struggles against my heritage. In short, this book sums up who I am.

A huge thank you to both Eric and my editor Margot Mallinson for signing off on the slightly bizarre idea of "a wholesome punk-rock vampire resolves her family trauma." Thank you also to Emily Ohanjanians, Kate Studer, and Dina Davis for seeing this through the final rounds of revision.

I wrote this in parallel with *Star Wars: Brotherhood*, which meant a lot of writing at odd hours with my sprint buddies Wendy Heard and Diana Urban. Kat Howard read an early draft while I was creating adventures in a galaxy far, far away and thankfully told me it was going on the right track.

Of course, if you're using vampires, they need consistent rules, and I discussed these details across emails, DMs, and texts with many friends, but with an extra shout-out to Sierra Godfrey, Kimberly Black, and Richard Donelly for answering some really obscure technical questions.

This book is dedicated to the musicians in my life, and characters are named after some of the really important ones. Laura Pickering was my piano teacher growing up and a woman who was like a surrogate grandmother to me. A man named Marshall at Studio Time in San Jose taught me guitar at age 13. I played in bands with Serena Joshi, Eric Bateman, and Eric Scharer (who also brought me on board to DJ an indie rock dance night in the early 2000s); so Laura and Marshall belong to the musicians that taught me as a kid, while Serena and Eric belong to the musicians I played with as an adult.

As for other names sneaked in here, there's a hodgepodge of vampire-related Easter Eggs for fans of *Being Human* (both US and UK versions), *Bunnicula*, *Adventure Time*, and, of course, Anne Rice. However, Lola the corgi is named for my beloved late corgi, and yes, we did sing her the Kinks song. And the band Grape Ape comes from Annalee Newitz's excellent novel *The Future of Another Timeline*.

Finally, it's not easy writing two books in parallel while dealing with a day job and parenting in a pandemic. So to my wife,

Mandy, who's also a fellow vampire/goth/music nerd, thank you for encouraging me to do these dream projects. And my daughter Amelia, who listens to David Bowie with us and loves Marceline the Vampire Queen—I hope someday this book helps you understand where I came from.

Because in the process of writing it, I certainly felt like I discovered that for myself.